Praise for The Next Step

"Koppel's humble shipping clerk delivers magic, heartache, laughter, tragedy and wonder to your doorstep at the speed of imagination. A spellbinding journey."

—Jonathan Freedman,
Recipient of the Pulitzer Prize for Journalism

"You do not need to leave your favorite reading chair to take *The Next Step*'s giant imaginative leap into the ecstasies of self-creation and a man's journey to squeeze new meaning out of life. When all seems to be lost, this book will sweep you off your feet."

—Tom Folsom,
The New York Times Bestselling author of *The Mad Ones*

"Leaping from the Bee Gees to the Baal Shem Tov, from Cecil B. DeMille to one Ploopy Goldberg, Koppel's kaleidoscopic novel takes on nothing less ambitious than the meaning of the universe."

—Ariel Sabar,
Author of *My Father's Paradise*,
Winner of The National Book Critics Circle Award

The Next Step

The Next Step

A Gobsmacking Odyssey of Reinvention

Robert Koppel

Book Country, LLC
375 Hudson Street, New York, NY 10014, USA

This is a work of fiction. Names, characters, places, and incidents either are the product of the authors' imaginations or are used fictitiously, and any resemblance to actual persons, living or dead, business establishments, events, or locales is entirely coincidental.

The Next Step

Copyright © 2012 by Robert Koppel

Cover design by Six Sisters Design, design by Christopher Beesley

All rights reserved.
No part of this book may be reproduced, scanned, or distributed in any printed or electronic form without permission. Please do not participate in or encourage piracy of copyrighted materials in violation of the authors' rights. Purchase only authorized editions.

ISBN 978-1-4630-0122-3

ISBN 978-1-4630-0123-0 (eBook)

Dedicated to Mara

"If it were just a story, critics would say how predictable."

FISHMAN CONSIDERED

Chapter One

Say what you will about Fishman but calling him Messiah seems out of the question. He didn't see himself as the deliverer or universal message bearer to the multitude. Not even working for the past year at FedEx or having revelatory dreams narrated by Steven Spielberg changed anything. Still, recent events made him wonder. Was the universe really trying to make contact? Was a higher power finally taking note of Fishman, threatening to reveal his true identity?

There are times in life when seemingly insignificant occurrences later prove to be harbingers of momentous shifts. It was just this sort of logic that started Fishman thinking. At first it was merely the stalled battery of his '92 Mercedes, later the intermittent power surges, which even years of automotive neglect could not explain. And then there was his computer's steadfast refusal to connect with the Internet, quickly followed by the sudden inexplicable cessation of his cell phone service. What was going on?

"Just coincidence?" he thought, "probably not."

At fifty-two, Fishman pretty much had the world by the balls. That is to say, he wanted for nothing. He lived a quiet, solitary life in an historic part of Chicago, known as Old Town. He resided with his wife of twenty-five years in a two-bedroom apartment in a renovated building that once served as a rectory to St. Michael's Church, which long ago had been sold by the Diocese to a real estate developer, a former fireman. Fishman paid his rent on time each month and marveled at his lot in life and good fortune.

His children, a girl and a boy, were now grown with families of their own. He regretted that they lived so far away, his daughter in New York and his son in Boston, but they spoke often and Fishman was content in the belief that they were raised well.

His wife Nadia, a beauty in her youth, was an artist. Fishman found her tall slim body, long red hair, now dyed, and soft blue green eyes as exciting as the first time he saw her. She had documented their life together in warm liquids. Oil paints, water colors, India ink and tempera; in journals and on furniture and walls interior and exterior, on clothing and floor boards. Even the ceiling. Her murals sometimes dealt with historical themes like the one over their bed where she painted Fishman as Adam and herself as Eve or the one of Shakespeare's Midsummer Night's Dream starring Fishman as a very regal Oberon and Nadia a nymphy Titania. Her many self-portraits were everywhere, each reflecting a colorful mood or temperament that Fishman knew well. There was also the painting of the teddy bear picnic in her son's room under which the family used to play Candy Land and Chutes and Ladders and read stories until fragrant young bodies, fresh from baths, folded into the arms of Morpheus.

Her first present to Fishman was a pen and ink of an old maple tree with two birds on its branches and the initials of lovers carved into its trunk. She placed it in an antique maple frame that she and Fishman had found together in the West Village when they were still living in New York.

Their home was her continuing gift to Fishman. He might awake to any variety of painting, drawing, sculpture, self-designed garment. Nadia was particularly fond of painting his shoes and jackets. Not once in twenty-five years, had Fishman ever risen to know for sure if the contents of his closet were as he had left them or if a ceiling, floor, hallway or wall would be as last seen. This was unusual because the virtue that Fishman prized most in the world was certainty. It was not a philosophy, though

Fishman could say quite a bit on that subject. It was more his psychology, from which Fishman derived his sense of well-being.

Is Fishman happy? Yes, he believes he is. There would be no hesitation on his part to point to the fact that he is happily married, in good health, with an active inner life that never ceases to transform and fulfill. But he is far from complacent and recent signs have led him to question some of the backbone assumptions of his life. There is also a certain unexplained residue of sadness that grows more perplexing. Fishman toys with the thought of starting his life over again. Perhaps he should have been a doctor or a lawyer as his parents had wanted. But he knows too much about himself and he is certain it would not have worked out. He reminds himself of a joke he had heard when he was still in his twenties about a psychiatrist interviewing a long-term mental patient at a release hearing.

"So what will you do when you get out?" The doctor asks.

"I was thinking, either a doctor or a lawyer . . . or maybe a teapot."

Fishman hadn't always worked at FedEx. As a young man he was intensely ambitious, with the temperament of a scholar and the energy of an athlete. He had a clear analytical mind and received his fair share of academic awards and prizes. By most measurements, success came easily to Fishman but about the past he cares to say little. And it is not because of the shame of having lost his millions, or operating for decades outside of his means nor is it because of the searing media accounts of his failures or the haunting stares in his children's eyes. It is just, he believes, that he is too old or perhaps too impatient for all of that. Despite everything that has happened, Fishman strives to become a better person. He continues to want to learn more about himself and his location in the universe. Occasionally, he'll catch himself working on humility and a self-ironic smile forms on his lips. Trying to tame his sense of pride by throwing a wet blanket on an excited ego is a lifelong feature of his personality that he knows all too well. He often thinks about the truth of music, pure, simple and to the point, and tries to live his life that way. No pretensions, criticisms of others or the arch, cold intellectualism of his youth. Fishman also knows that living like this helps the days picket by, allowing him to avoid getting bogged down with regrets.

Fishman is still surprised at his playfulness, his sense of fun and his profound love of fucking. At one time he was a serious student of philosophy, reading critical phenomenological arguments whose lengthy sentences extended without paragraph breaks for pages. He was easily seduced by the sexy agility and arabesques of quick minds and the blissful gymnastics of intellectual dialogue, which delighted in wrestling an idea down to the mat. Fishman discovered that the pleasures of the intellect are deep and affecting but his need for love and physical gratification was far more reaching. Fucking was both an escape and his calling. In bed he was intense and passionate, absorbed, voracious, always there. He had many lovers before he found the love of his life, Nadia, to whom he had always been faithful. He loved the feel of her soft pale skin, her long red hair, kissing the length of her body, breathing in her cunty aromas, making love. Although he devoted himself completely in the moment of celestial embrace, the utter absurdity and comedy of copulation never escaped him. Fishman saw fucking as a primal joke. Nature's gift of a promise-filled beginning of humor and laughter. An opportunity for pleasure given and reciprocated. And to the lucky, there was love. It had come to him one day at the zoo. There were two seals resting on a sun warmed rock before sliding back into the rocking vastness.

And his years as the famed Wall Street trader? Only rarely did Fishman speak about that. And it was not out of modesty or a fear that he might bore nor was it because of his aversion to talk about the past. In fact, the mere topic animated Fishman's conversation and sent sparks flying in his eyes. Most people have heard the stories or rumors or know the basic outline of the man's life. Of course, they wouldn't know the man as Fishman. The ups and downs and the ins and outs, the who is to blame, and the matters of fact.

Punctually at 6:15 a.m. Fishman arrives at the FedEx store. He is always the first one there. He works Monday through Friday to 4 p.m. and noon on Saturday. He prefers to enter through the same front door that the customers use rather than the employee entrance in the back. There is a buzzer to the right but Fishman always chooses his key. He disarms the security system, and then proceeds through the dimly lit store past a long reception counter. It stands in front of "the bull pen" that contains scales next to conveyor belts that process the day's flow of envelopes and packages. He unlocks a red metal door in back, waits for the lights to go on automatically and walks down a flight of stairs that leads to a room containing a wall of lockers. Fishman's locker is immediately recognizable. It is the only one with any sign of personality. It stands in relief like a solitary witness to life; a Kilroy was here in an otherwise drab interior. Its background is phosphorous blue with a painted six-foot smiling golden fish. Written on its body are the words "Overnight or overseas the FISH delivers."

It is a small claustrophobic room, in need of painting, neither really clean nor dirty, functional, with a small bathroom off to the side. There is a stove and a sticky microwave. A corner is filled by a small refrigerator, the kind that serves as a vault for decaying food abandoned in brown bags with names written in magic marker. There is also a kettle, a jar of instant coffee, Styrofoam cups and packages of raw sugar and the ever-present smell of lingering stale smoke.

Fishman reaches into his locker and removes his uniforms. He has two. Both are jump suits worn under a long black apron that ties behind the neck. There is a red one with the word freight in bold white letters on the right bicep. He chooses a purple number with FEDEX spelled out in orange caps across his chest.

Fishman proudly surveys himself in the bathroom mirror: glowing skin, handsome features, deep blue eyes, salt and pepper hair like a storm cloud around his head, and mischievous smile. He still believes he possesses a certain magnetism. He looks up and reads the sign over the sink to himself as he prepares for the day ahead. "Relax. It's FedEx."

It was an easy decision for Fishman to choose to work at FedEx. After all where else could messages be sent out so far and wide, circling the globe like paper carrier pigeons? There was the Post Office of course but somehow Fishman did not really feel, despite its representations to the contrary, that his mail was truly priority one. In fact, based on his many years of personal experience, he found the whole notion of priority mail rather misleading, like being sucked into a three-card Monte game where all that is ultimately delivered is a disappointing result. And then there was the occasional problem of workers going postal. Fishman did not fear bodily harm but he knew that there was work that he needed to do. At his age, he could not afford to be slowed down by a co-worker's psychotic episode that might result in a disabling wound or an unexpected hospital stay.

There was also UPS, a good company that dated back to 1907. Fishman remembered when it was still referred to as United Parcel Service. It operated in more than 200 countries and territories around the world and, as the world's largest package delivery company, had an admirable record of success with which there was little to find fault. But it was, let's face it, brown and possessed little of the energy and vitality of a FedEx. Just saying it out loud excited Fishman. Was there something in the similarity between sex and FedEx? Fed suggests providing life-sustaining nourishment. It was totally reliable. It carried pajamas, precious jewels, and just about anything else. FedEx had spunk. It was youthful and forward-thinking. It had ethics and values and believed in treating its people well. It also possessed a gravitas when it came to respecting the customer and the power of his message. It made one feel secure in the choice of the world's best, not largest, carrier. It delivered in more ways to more places worldwide. And you knew it was the right material at the right time. Its representations were pure, simple, to the point: "overnight or overseas, across borders or across towns, you can absolutely, positively count on FedEx." Its commercials told the truth and always had. With FedEx your package would get there.

As Fishman climbs the stairs, he smoothes any wrinkles in his pants with a brush of his right hand. A Kabuki dance of sorts begins to play in his head followed by a flood of memories. It is of a time, not that long ago, perhaps sometime in the 1980's. Fishman is sitting behind a glass desk in a large office on a top floor of a financial tower long before anyone had thought of using airplanes as weapons to bring down magnificent buildings. There are screens and monitors flashing data all around him. He is responding quickly but deftly, skillfully, artfully. Like a seasoned fighter pilot, he is in control. Lights on panels flicker, phones ring. He is connected to the world. Fishman takes in the full visual and emotional impact of what he is feeling. As he remembers it now, it was a reckless time when everything seemed possible at any cost. He looks down at his watch, suddenly out of the moment. It is 6:27 and he realizes his day and his mission are about to begin.

Fishman makes for an odd sight in his FedEx uniform. Not that it doesn't fit well or the mere sight of a purple jumpsuit beneath a black apron emblazoned with large orange letters doesn't take some time to get used to, nor is it the fact that the pants he wears were not meant for someone quite as tall. It is more the way he wears his clothes that is peculiar. For years, Fishman's wardrobe was the product of Saville Row. His room-sized closet was a library of suits by Gieves and Hawke and Huntsman, shirts from Turnbull and Asser, an odd waistcoat from Tommy Nutter and shoes only from John Lobb or Edward Green. Unfortunately, years of wearing clothes like that have influenced his bearing, the way he presents himself, the way he cinches his apron or pulls up a sagging collar. It is certainly not offensive nor does it appear affected, but at times does seem unnatural. Sadly comic.

There is a film noir quality to the way Fishman has chosen to make fundamental changes in his life. If on the one hand the measure of a man is his sense of personal identity and on the other are all the acts and deeds that make one's life his own, Fishman has transformed himself in astonishing ways. He has come to an essential realization. Let's call it his truth. He has found a way that allows him to rise above all the conventional limitations of individuality: a passport, a driver's license, a social security card, a diploma, a toe tag, god forbid. He is certain in his belief that he can affect real change in the world, where people can be seen for themselves, and he will do whatever it takes to do his part and get the word out. That is what has drawn him to FedEx. Like Fishman, FedEx cares about communities. It is a leader in charitable giving. A true corporate citizen committed to a better environment. Fishman sees all this as just the beginning of better things to come.

What was Fishman's great realization? It is important to note here the man's exceptional love for chocolate. Fishman was enamored of all the varieties: dark, milk and bittersweet. He had tasted many of the best makers: Maison du Chocolat, Teuscher, and Neuchatel. From his perspective it was no accident that the cocoa bean was considered the ultimate status symbol by the Mayan and Aztec cultures. It was a source of wisdom and power; an aphrodisiac, producing the same stimulating reaction as falling in love. Fishman slowly savored the delicious warmth of Vosges chocolate melting in his mouth, rolling it with his tongue, sweet as a kiss. Wrestling it against cheek and palette. And then in a flash Fishman knew.

The Next Step

  Years on Wall Street had taught Fishman many valuable lessons: the importance of being prepared, single-minded, always in attack mode, and instinctively performing with grace under fire. It was a state of mind that made him ready for come what may; always having an ace in the hole, a card up his sleeve. He knew when to act on impulse and when to override impulse with principal. Despite what had been written or said against him, Fishman knew in his heart that he had never mislead investors, cooked the books or benefited at the expense of shareholders. His crime was far more serious, even elemental. Fishman had offended the gods. He was guilty of multiple counts of hubris and Ate, insolence from excessive pride and reckless blindness. These are mistakes that many great men have made before. Fishman is committed to not making them again.

  Wall Street was his laboratory and his testing ground. Fishman believes without any doubt or hesitation that it was there that he learned everything that makes him who he is today. In the course of a career that stretched back a quarter of a century he had made many friends but also many enemies. He had never been one to suffer fools gladly and when he was younger had the unfortunate habit of easily offending and looking through people whose opinion he did not respect. The irony of all this is not lost on Fishman.

  At the FedEx store it is not uncommon for a customer's glance to travel over, past, and through him. Not acknowledging or saying his name, placing him on a landscape of personal indifference. If it were not for Fishman's ingenuity he could easily exist as a ghost, like a bus driver, cleaning person, or toll worker. His solution, although he would certainly not air this opinion, and surely not this way, is to cause human stirs and ripples. What Fishman wants to do, no, needs to do, is to deliver, to make each interaction, however small, matter. That is his discipline, not abstract or dry, rather pure, simple and to the point. Fishman chooses to fill the human soul.

Filling the human soul is a tricky business. It is not the elixir of choice for most people. The average person does not want an outing to FedEx to reside at the level of a therapeutic encounter or religious meeting. Most don't spontaneously seek out opportunities to communicate deeply when shipping packages. They don't care to gratuitously unburden their thoughts and feelings, excavate hidden motives and intentions. And that's where Fishman's genius comes in. He makes it all look so easy. You walk in and there is a shipping worry or anxiety and then you leave completely fulfilled, not wholly understanding what has happened. It resembles the role of religion. The Church. Enter heavy with troubles. Exit lightened and strengthened. Fishman just makes you feel good so you want to reach up to your highest nature. Even if you are a pessimist he can help you see a sunnier future. Fishman makes all this happen and you don't even realize that it is because he is there.

Not everyone at FedEx holds such a high opinion of Fishman. There is still an old guard of workers and managers who came up through the ranks or moved from the post office or companies like Trailway Express. They are locked into a system of traditional beliefs and attitudes. You know the type; they are of a pack 'em and stack 'em, grip 'em and ship 'em mentality. They lack the vision and expansiveness of someone like Fishman. They have no appreciation for his abstract grasp of delivering the message, traversing obstacles and borders, reaching out to more people in more ways, to more places worldwide. From their perspective, all that really matters are terms like ground, freight, packaging, distance, transportation. To them, Fishman is merely a threat, a thorn to their way of doing things, which some will stop at nothing to eliminate. But Fishman has spent most of his adult life swimming in shark-infested waters. He has learned many tricks and strategies, rarefied tactics, well thought out lines of attack and retreat. Before presiding over multi-million dollar deals where a dozen Mont Blanc fountain pens sat on antique desks waiting for signers to flourish them, there was the need to possess all the skills that he had mastered: personal charm, orchestration, meticulous research, securing reliable sources. Fishman brought all this talent and confidence to FedEx. Although, in general, working for someone who is intent on sabotage or subversion can prove problematic, Fishman refuses to let it intrude. From his point of view all that really matters is "absolutely, positively, whatever it takes."

Like Fishman, there are other FedEx workers who are inspired by higher ideals and callings. There is Frank Ingram, a FedEx Express courier in Holderness, New Hampshire who consistently puts the above-and-beyond philosophy into practice.

Last summer, on one of the hottest days of the year, the radiator of his van overheated. He returned to the station and loaded packages into his '84 Chrysler Le Baron, but it too broke down. Determined, he asked a customer if he could borrow the bike she rode to work. He then attached a FedEx crate to his back with twine and duct tape, placing the packages inside. In ninety-six degree heat, he pedaled fourteen miles up and down steep hills to complete his deliveries on time.

There is also Kaiisha Brown of Boulder, Colorado. It was a frigid January day with white out conditions. The elderly customer she had called who lived high in the mountains advised her not to attempt the drive but then added, "If you can make it, bring me three cans of kidney beans, some pork rinds, and a sixpack of Coors."

Kaiisha stopped by a grocery store and set out to reach the customer's home. Finding the roads impassable, she would still not allow for a delay of service. She ran 3.6 miles in the snow and then walked an additional two miles until she reached the house. On the same day, she delivered another shipment on her lunch break.

And then there are the couriers of legend: Buster Noir, Guy

Blanco, Katherine Cox, Roberto Salsa, names so revered at FedEx that they have erected a Cooperstown of sorts to honor these brave Titans of the shipping industry. Off the main hall at FedEx corporate headquarters, next to the Rotunda of Tracking and Pickup, is its International Hall of Fame and Museum. The collection began over a quarter of a century ago and represents all facets of couriering and delivery from its beginnings to the present. Its holdings includes packaging, envelopes, transit bills of fare, uniforms, processing equipment, artifacts, awards, artwork, textiles, stuffed pigeons, collectibles and assorted memorabilia. In addition, there is a dense archive of photographs, books, magazines, news clippings, films, and audio and videotapes. The collection is housed in a climate controlled environment, manned by a professional staff using state of the art museum practices.

Of all the exhibits at the museum the most popular still remains that of the company's founder, C.J. Tower. "CJ", or "The Boxer of Transport Brokerage" as he was dubbed in 1913, was an American original; the industry's first great courier, the most celebrated delivery man of his time. He lead all supply chain companies in shipping and handling in the categories of ground, freight, express, transit time, scheduling and pickup. For twenty-three consecutive seasons, even after he converted from surface to air, until his untimely death, "Boxer" set the standard. He had a vision and it is against him that all present day records are measured. FedEx is the house that C.J. Tower built.

Fishman is all too aware of the proud history of the company, its founder's legacy and the hall of fame talent of some of his co-workers and fellow couriers. These very facts, as well his personal mission, keep him going.

Fishman is concerned about the scary, high pressure times we live in. He tells himself that he must do something about it; terrorist threats, Anthrax scares, snarky world leaders, an attorney general who disrespects the first amendment. "What is our world coming to?" he wonders, "Where is our future?"

Chapter 2

Before he worked at FedEx, after all the exhaustive investigations and the trial, Fishman spends many months at a loss for what to do with himself. He reads magazines and newspapers, floats on large swathes of time on Internet web sites, chats and blogs, pores over Craig's List and is a faithful Googler. He is an explorer of strange, exotic destinations for occasional facts but mostly fictions. He is like a narcoleptic losing himself in the deep sleep of words and images. He also plays music, an ongoing Miles Davis melody of lugubrious funny valentines and sketches of Spain. Still drawn to philosophy, he buries his regrets and sorrows in old words hungry to discover fresh meaning. There are none.

Fishman wanders in a vast wilderness, mostly of his own making, against the backdrop of an impenetrable mountain of time. He watches hours turning into days; weeks and months pass by. He searches in vain for some footing, a ledge. There is not even the slightest toe-hold to be found. And then one day he has an encounter. Nadia asks Fishman to go to the store and pick up a few things. The never-ending need for more kitty litter and cat food, paper towels and strawberry yogurt. It is a short walk to Treasure Island where he shops. Just a few blocks from the cul-de-sac where he lives, up a tree lined street of sycamores, maples, and elms. There is a slightly surreal stage set assortment of homes: stately, modest, historic, some almost look do-it-yourself. The total effect is the whimsical architecture of a well-to-do eccentric. There is one in particular that never ceases to amuse him.

It is a large Victorian whose owner, a highly regarded university physicist, has chosen to paint it a blazing shade of orange. A kind of fuck you to a rational person's sensibility of what a house should look like. Fishman appreciates that. He enjoys the blurring of borders, the confusion of boundaries; like a good joke with an unexpected punch line.

He is returning home, breathing in the cool autumn air. Fishman decides to take a longer route through the Old Town Triangle when on the path ahead he notices a woman sitting on a bench, reading a newspaper. He recognizes her but does not know her name. Her age is indeterminate, probably in her early forties. He smiles at her, "Hello."

Craning her neck forward, she surveys Fishman from head to toe. She is small and thin, finch-like, with long grey-black hair, high cheekbones, and large dark eyes. Perhaps she is homeless or lives in a shelter or crashes occasionally in a relative's basement or laundry room. She has that air about her. Her clothes always look decades out of fashion, but stylish, worn, not dirty but in need of repair or alteration. Today she is wearing a gray coat and sweater over a yellowed white silk or satin blouse. The jacket has a peaked lapel and her dingy black skirt hangs almost to the pavement. Too many layers of fabric and a lost look in her eyes.

Fishman is taken with her. He has seen her countless times around the neighborhood, in Lincoln Park or sitting on the grass near the Children's Zoo. She has become a silent fixture of the landscape. As he passes her not another word is spoken but she has touched something inside of him.

But it is not just her. Fishman questions himself. How many people live these contained, Joseph Cornell, lives; unimaginable to others, built within their own interior walls? He finds the thought isolating but also freeing. He arrives at home feeling that something within him is changing. One of those moments better understood in retrospect, a turning point, a moment in time signaling a change of course.

Perhaps Fishman realizes that he needs to be decisive. That he isn't keeping his options open by doing nothing or maybe there is no great realization at all but it is just time to get off his ass.

That night he has a dream. The dream opens like a play. A curtain rises. There are footlights on an empty stage and then a narrator appears stage left. He is short with spectacles and a graying beard. He is wearing a black suit, white shirt open at the collar, and no tie. His speech is staccato, disjointed, faltering. He introduces himself.

"I am Stephen Spielberg, your narrator, here to tell you about the Adventures of Fishman, a play in many acts but so far no happy ending."

"Once upon a time, in a distant place called Queens, a little Fishman was born to two big Fishmen. There was the daddy Fishman, and the mommy Fishman and the little baby Fishman. For a while everyone was happy until one day," pointing to the middle of the stage, "Fishman spoiled everything!"

He declaims now in an accusing voice. "He had to contract a mind of his own."

Fishman is now center stage under the third degree lens of a spotlight. There is giggling and tittering and hissing from the audience. He is wearing his purple FedEx uniform that changes intermittently to prison stripes.

Still pointing, "He started to need things and learned to say 'no.'"

Fishman listens like a defendant at his own trial.

The spotlight moves across the stage focusing on three small children. They are no more than four or five. There are two girls and a boy.

"And he said, 'If you show me yours, I'll show you mine.'"

Fishman now stands up, testifying to the audience. "But we were kids."

There are audible boos and catcalls.

Spielberg continues, "You see, even then Fishman had an answer for everything. But let's go on. Because there is more to this story then first meets the eye."

"Fishman was good at school."

A motion picture, in black and white, now plays on a silver screen above Fishman, childhood images traveling in the dark, a world within a world with its own moral order. A confident boy of ten in front of an auditorium of students recites a poem. He concludes to thunderous applause.

> *"It matters not how straight the gate*
> *How charged with punishment the scroll*
> *I am the master of my fate*
> *The captain of my soul."*

"And he once saved someone's life."

The movie now changes to a grainy, washed out color film of the 1950's home variety. The picture is darting wildly across a beach in summer. There is the ocean and jetties, men in cabana suits and women in swim wear of a different era, children playing catch, building sand castles. A man with a crazed smile and a Jerry Colona moustache practically puts his nose on the lense of the camera. The frame is completely occupied with his surreal face. The camera then pans left and right until it settles on a teenage boy swimming to save a drowning younger child. It captures the rescue and the mother's grateful embrace.

Back to Spielberg. "Mind you, not Shindler's List, but still something to be learned here."

The movie has stopped and the spotlight is back on Fishman, again standing up from center stage, defending himself to the audience, "He was drowning, what else could you do?"

While he's drowning (he means dreaming) Fishman wonders if this is a Woody Allen, Jerry Seinfeld, Larry David, Jewish sort of moment. The endless need to justify existence, the tireless quest to secure meaning. Maybe it's merely a tragic response to the fear of annihilation, always in the background, or the collective guilt of survival. The talented struggle to flip tragedy into comedy. Entertainment is born. It's not an easy delivery.

Fishman knows (especially when he's dreaming) that it's important to believe that life matters. It does. Just ask CB. It does.

"But don't be disappointed. This is not just another story of a nervous, worried, or worrisome Jew. Always keep in mind this is Fishman."

"And then he went to high school, o.k., roll the camera."

A black and white, light-spotted newsreel starts playing. There is the sound of the rotation and crackle of old film. The announcer slowly begins in his "March of Time" voice, "Miracles are happening in Queens, New York."

We see a young Fishman holding a basketball with only seconds to go before the game ending buzzer. The crowd is erupting. He looks to pass, then shoot. He is indecisive for a moment before he sinks the game winner. For a very short while there is bedlam on screen and then the film is over. There is only white light.

Spielberg to the audience: "He was some athlete. The go-to guy on his high school basketball team. State champions. Fishman was All-American. Starred in college. MVP in the NBA."

Fishman stands in the relentless glare of the white light. "Lies. All lies, I missed that last shot. Lost the tournament."

Spielberg in a reassuring tone: "Fishman, it's ok. This is a dream, lies don't count. Dreams don't count. It depends on what really happens."

He continues. "Let me tell you a story. There was a time when more than anything in the world I wanted to be a weight lifter. It wasn't easy, I'm a small guy. Look at me. I'm 140 lbs. You don't have to be the Baal Shem Tov to know that I don't possess the body of a world class weight lifter, a filmmaker yes, a great lover, yes, but `a weight lifter, no."

"Fishman, are you listening?"

He nods affirmatively.

"It's like this. You don't need to be Indiana Jones to make Indiana Jones. You see what I mean?"

"Not really."

Spielberg tries to illustrate his point. He takes off his jacket and rolls up his shirt sleeves then pulls up his pant legs revealing his pale boney legs. "Look. I'm no Schwarzenegger, right?"

Fishman insists, "I don't want him in my dream."

"My point, Fishman, is I can hire Aryans a dime a dozen. I don't need to be a weight lifter to throw my weight around. I met a woman who looks like a finch who taught me that. Now it is your turn."

"But I don't want to be a weight lifter. This doesn't even make sense."

"Fishman, don't be a fool. It's a dream. It doesn't have to make sense. I'm no Cecil B. DeMille but I do know that, and it's time for you to get off your tuchus and do something with your life!"

There is overwhelming applause from the audience. The house lights go up. A standing ovation and the thunder of bravos. Spielberg is now yelling at Fishman, "Take a bow. Take a bow."

The stage set and scene now changes. Fishman is standing in front of a college class in a lecture hall that he remembers form his time at Columbia. There is stadium seating, wood paneled walls, state of the art for the turn of the nineteenth century. The air carries the aromas of chalk and vanishing time. Fishman is wearing a maroon crew neck over a blue work shirt and tan khakis.

"So, where were we?"

He points to a girl in the third or fourth row who for a moment resembles a Weimeranner, like a Wegman photograph come to life, before she transforms back to herself. She is small and thin with a pleasant smile and short-cropped light brown hair.

"We are at the part about your grandmother."

"Ok, then, let's go on," says Fishman.

In an animated voice: "My grandmother lived alone in a large white house in Jamaica. She bought it from the actress Fanny Brice, a childhood friend. It was a large and sunny house. When I was a child, my favorite place in the world. A peach tree, rare in New York, in the back; and an old barn converted into a garage. In the summer we would walk to the store and purchase bushels to hold the fruit. When we were done picking, we'd sit in the shade and eat tender fleshy peaches. She made me laugh with her stories, the warm juice dripping down our chins."

It's funny the little things you recall, especially in dreams. Like the change purse Fishman's grandmother kept under her dress or the monogrammed socks and handkerchiefs, the way she smelled of Chanel No.5 seasoned with goose liver. The tiny hairs embroidering her face.

"Any questions?"

A somewhat confused African-American student in the middle of the lecture hall stands to ask a question. Fishman knows him by name. He is Jason Bland, a promising young man with a great deal of charm, maybe even charisma. He has told Fishman about his abiding interest in story telling and his goal of becoming a journalist.

"What is the bigger story here?"

Fishman would like to answer that we are all mere microbes in relation to the vast size and scope of the cosmos, and recent discoveries from the Hubble have revealed that the universe has no up or down, but he doesn't answer Jason's question that way. Nor does he say that it's the fault lines between the cracks of a person's life that really matter, the silences between the spoken words, the half-forgotten dreams that determine who we are.

"There is an anatomy to my life" is his answer.

He also forgets to mention the power of transcendence and the trajectories and tranquilities, the projects that mean so much. He has not yet chosen to reinvent himself nor to adopt FedEx as his vehicle. He is still wrestling. Dreaming.

And then the scene changes again. The lecture hall is teeming with generation upon generation of Fishmen. The crazy family tree has shaken everyone out of its branches. There are his mother and father, grandmother blowing kisses and grandfather, uncles and aunts. Great grandparents and great uncles and aunts. Great-great and great-great- great. They are all there, sitting like judge and jury in black robes and gavels. Judging. Judging.

From the center of the auditorium a very old man rises. He is a brittle wizened figure, a Sophoclean character standing on the fabled third leg. Like an alien who has just landed on the planet Earth, he looks all around the room surveying the faces as if searching for a particular one. He begins to speak in a voice struggling with the difficulty of breathing.

"So, you are Fishman. Look at you, so young. I died twelve lifetimes longer than you have been alive. What do you think about that?"

All Fishman can muster is "I never knew there were so many of us. I am happy to meet you."

The elder Fishman raises his cane. His choking voice growing agitated. He knifes the air with his walking stick, as if cutting tough meat, emphasizing his words. "YOU are happy to meet ME. Well, I'm not so sure I am happy to meet you. I know all about you. Everything. What will become of you?"

The old man is in obvious discomfort, covering his eyes with his left hand, "and what is with these candles. Killing my eyes. And I am already dead!"

Fishman slowly turns the lights down until there is only darkness, wheezing, and the sound of the old man's voice beseeching.

"Fishman, make something of yourself. And if not now, when?"

Chapter 3

It was shortly after his dream that Fishman read about The Palefsky Chronicle. It was discovered two months after September Eleventh, in a manila envelope taped under a bench in Battery Park in lower Manhattan. A slate.com reporter by the name of Sandy Glass broke the story. The New York Times has called the Chronicle "one of the great works of cultural writing of the post nine-eleven world. Written as a personal statement of loss and longing, the document poses fundamental questions about the meaning of life and the role of story telling."

The Washington Post offered, "The Palefsky Chronicle simmers with feelings, quintessential in its seriousness and unimpeachable sophistication; an uncomfortable look at the haunting need for spiritual and emotional reawakening."

USA Today praised, "It is as serious as anything written by Camus or Sartre. A story of stunning precision and efficiency; more remarkable for its revelatory must-read portrayal of one man's response to a world in chaos."

The Weekly Standard called it "proof positive that the author, although anonymous, stands with the very best writers in the world today. Who is Palefsky? Who was Homer? Who wrote the Bible?"

Fishman needed to get his hands on his very own copy, but The Palefsky Chronicle was not easily available. Readers had quickly purchased the first printing and originals traded for many hundreds and, in some cases, thousands of dollars. The Chronicle was viewed as a cultural artifact from a time of collective national grief and suffering. Publishers were reluctant to print more copies, concerned about being accused of benefiting monetarily from a text of life as sacred as The Palefsky Chronicle. They were also unwilling to print them up for free and interfering with the market's natural consumption and digestive system. A bustling underground market of buyers and sellers of The Chronicle developed after Congress passed "The Anti-Palefsky Piracy Act" but Fishman exercising his highly toned instincts as a trader was able to obtain an original Palefsky of his very own.

The Palefsky Chronicle

Think of me as Palefsky, Max Palefsky, not the loser who goes around telling people he's me.

There was a time, less than a year ago, for what now feels like a miniscule second when it was unimportant to conjure Palefsky or to invoke the secret password or handshake; but all that was before the accident, before 9/11 and the constant and insinuating memory of Ploopy Goldberg. It's funny, isn't it, how it works that way? Where were you when it happened? Can you remember? New Yorkers always know exactly where they were when all the lights went out or President Kennedy getting his brains blown out all over his wife's pink suit. How about the World Trade Center . . . but what I'd really like to know is where were you and what were you doing at exactly the moment you knew? That's right, you knew! That it's all bullshit and none of it really matters!

You may be saying to yourself, "what a loser!" and you know what, you may be right; but then again, I wouldn't bet on it. Because there is an instant when it all hits you, like Ploopy Goldberg, that the whole thing is a con job and that the fix is really in. You know what I mean. It's not that complicated, but the tough part as Mrs. Bacon, my high school chemistry teacher, used to say is, "It's what you do with the information."

Even if it does only come down to choices in the end it is a hell of a sad irony. I mean, think about it, it is a person's life we're talking about. But shit, why go on!

Under a radiant sky, there is a white clapboard farmhouse on a phosphorous blue lake. A solitary boat is moored at its dock, a fragrant necklace of wild iris wanders along the shore.

Two children, a boy and a girl, neither more than seven or eight years old, play in a meadow under the watchful eyes of an elderly woman peering out of a kitchen window. In the doorway is the sweet succulent aroma of plums.

It makes no sense thinking about the past, dwelling on things that should have been or might have happened. All we really have is now, and ain't that the bitch! Of course, Hamlet had it right; but it's not the same when it's all down on paper or up on a stage. It's all too far removed from where I'm sitting, not in the audience. Each moment, electrified with doubt and second-guesses.

The Buddhists believe that there are five obstacles to enlightenment: desire, anger, inertia, worry and doubt. Jeez! I have all five in day-glo and a couple of others that work as a preventative for Christians, Muslims and Jews. But who gives a fuck! Look, there is this kid who thought he could fly. You know like Superman "faster than a speeding bullet, more powerful than a steaming locomotive, able to leap off tall buildings in a single bound" and all that other nonsense. But it didn't happen. Or did it?

You see, I know things that you don't. Call them secrets. And I sure as hell don't want to go down as a squealer or some opportunistic stool pigeon. I guess you could say I'm basically a rugged individualist, maybe even a cock-eyed optimist. Who knows, perhaps they are all right and I just have a few screws loose. I can't say for sure but I do want to find out.

There is something about walking down Central Park West on a rainy afternoon. Have you ever done it? Do you know what I mean? Just coming up Eighty-first Street. From Columbus with the park dead ahead front and center, like all of New York, a jigsaw puzzle of possibility where you put together the pieces and they all fit. The world's most beautiful women pass in a blur of colors and smells and the only true geniuses that you are ever likely to meet are hanging out on park benches just waiting to speak to you. They know time. Think about the conversations Einstein could have with them.

That reminds me, have you ever noticed that the less sex someone has the more it shows? You don't need to be a shrink to pick up on it. It's all about attitude and body language and I guess you could call it a certain generosity of spirit. It's too bad New Yorkers are not getting enough and if I were mayor I would sure to hell do something about it. But don't even get me started. It goes without saying that if I ever ran for office the only vote I would capture is the lunatic fringe and that's no joke! Not that I'm really nuts or couldn't do a better job than most of the professional hacks out there but let's just say I'm lacking the right temperament. Running a city isn't my thing. Jesus! I'm having problems just running me.

Remember the sound of a 16mm projector rotating after the last frame has passed through? White light, the size of a silver dollar, beamed in the dark, a poignant story or family picture like food dissolving from color to amorphous light in an instant and the slow inevitable coffee grind of turning metal and the flap of celluloid; the smell of vanishing time.

A play within a play has ended. The Chinese boxes and nesting dolls have nowhere else to go. The sequence is out of order. Pieces have gone missing. Unhappiness takes a long-term lease. Making noises in the walls like a rat in the night.

The first time I saw her she was standing in front of a Gothic tapestry, framed by stained glass, wearing silver slippers. There was a gold pendant dangling from her neck that I imagined to be Icarus. I watched as father and son flew over Crete, feeling the hot sun melt waxen wings. Later, I was told I had been mistaken. It was a thirteenth century Kufic coin designed to reawaken the religious loyalty and zeal of apostates and waverers.

There were seven sages of ancient Greece: Bias of Priene,

Chilo of Sparta, Cleobulus of Lindos, Periander of Corinth, Pittacus of Mitylene, Solon of Athens and Thales of Miletus but the least intellectually challenged was Socrates because of all the wise guys he admitted, "I alone know that I know nothing." I think about that a lot these days, especially when I get the urge to fly.

I know that I need to be careful because I'm beginning to think that I'm a crashlander. It's not something that comes naturally nor have I spent a lot of time honing it as a skill. But then again there was the accident and 9/11 and the persistence of Ploopy Goldberg. Icarus in Queens.

For a long time I didn't trust people who refused to dress well. They'll tell you once you start thinking that way you'll be hooked for life. But I don't buy it for a second; it's a big lie. And take it from me, and I'm no Dalai Lama, sometimes you just have to go with the flow, do you know what I'm saying?

Let me be honest, there are times I even seriously wonder about myself. It's not that I'm an idiot savant but my head is just chock-full with information, lots of facts and figures that I picked up along the way and uncovered from talking to the right people.

Take for instance the Bard of Memory, Samuel Rogers, 1763-1855, also known as the banker poet. He wrote The Pleasures of Memory. You might think it strange to remember something like that; I mean, after all, who really cares? OK, you can call me odd but it's these kinds of things and the accident that stick with me.

But still there is so much depressing news out there that I think I'm beginning to experience a loss of confidence. Have you ever felt that way? After all, with all the shit one has to take these days it's hard to find cover under wings of honesty or feathers of truth. It's funny how you keep thinking about the same things over and over again; like the image of planes crashing into skyscrapers or the soft balmy whisper of Amelia's voice.

Is there a more comforting phrase in the world than I love you?

Hey, but don't get the wrong idea. I'm no fucking romantic! Believe me when I say I know the importance of keeping my emotions in check. Of course, there was a time not too long ago when I was my own worst enemy. You wouldn't think so, but I was the kind of guy who could be a real pain in the ass. Take the time I found a worm in my salad at Stark's Salad Bar over on Seventy-sixth and First Avenue. As these things go, it wasn't even that big. Just a little white one, minding his own business under my radicchio. Do worms hibernate? I mean the little non-offender wasn't even moving but that didn't stop me from having a psychotic episode! I turned over the table, clearing out the restaurant and nearly sent old man Stark to his grave. When the medics carried him out on the stretcher he referred to me with one whisper: "Bulvon."

I really feel for guys like Stark, which, by the way, means strong in German. Old world businessmen who came up the hard way, real school of hard knocks. Not like the wimpy wipeass yuppy type who treats you as if you are as disposable as a condom. You know the type. Smug, narcissistic know-it-alls who shop at Prada and D&G and think they know something that you don't. If you walked into Barney's on any Saturday you could spit in any direction and there isn't a chance in the world that you would miss one of them.

I know, I've got to take deep breaths and think positive thoughts and remember the importance of practicing the power of now. I also have to accept this moment more fully and be at ease with myself and my fellow creatures. Maybe I should try yoga or Pilates or just plain meditate.

You see this is part of my problem: so many things to think about and do and so little time to make them happen. But I'm not complaining. It may not show but I think I'm really beginning to get a handle on things. It's just the persistent sight, sound, smell, and touch of everything that has happened and the memory of Amelia's pain.

There is a gentle breeze and the scent of jasmine. A lighthouse bell tolls in the distance. The old woman slowly removes her spectacles, wipes them carefully, returning them to her face, adjusting the posts to her right, then left ear, balancing them on the bridge of her nose until they feel just right. The small girl and boy run up to show off the treasure they have found. She claps her hands, and then pats the little boy on his head, her dress blowing in the wind.

It's hard for me to look ahead to the world of the future.

I was working for a long time in collaboration with the physicians in the Mt. Sinai psychiatry department, but we still could not come up with an answer. Go ahead, ask me why? That is my question. I guess I just can't shake my heavy reliance on the past. I'm still devoted to all the funny little things and memories that make me, me. It's one of the reasons I never applied to the CIA or MI5. You may think I have a self-centered view of the universe but the truth is you don't have to look any further than yourself. You know what I mean, and if you don't you are probably in worse shape than me.

What is a life anyway? What do you live and work for? Family, friends, a nice house, a car, dinners out and what have you? It is different for Palefsky. He has a mission and a purpose greater than himself, a vision. Let's call it an understanding. Not that I ever use the word but maybe it's just simple compassion. Who knows but don't worry I won't get religious on you.

Under a big tent in northern Alabama miracles are still happening. Desperate people, an army of drug addicts, hard drinkers and seasoned criminals are receiving faith at the Lord's altar. They sense his all-encompassing power. Praised be the Lord! They have come to hear a Swaggart anointed to preach the Word. "Jesusss we love and worship you!" All the music and pageantry of Rock&Roll without the sex and drugs. Twenty thousand supplicants feeling the Holy Spirit. "Rescue me. *Deliver me into your grace." "Oh, Lord", he thunders, "Heal those with cancer and those who are on crutches and those who would benefit from your merciful care." He urges them to purchase special cell phones to keep a line open to God on their way out. Who can believe it but all the phones go and an 800 number is given out.*

There are rituals and recitations and a defining personal moment when men and women speaking in tongues, like alien inhabited pods, find the Lord, "Praised be his name."

"But tell me something I don't know!" I used to have an uncle who said that all the time. And you know what, nobody ever could. I guess Marty really did know it all. Getting him to have an open mind was like the odds of converting a Fifth Avenue coop board to Hasidic Judaism. It couldn't happen. Not that I sympathize with any of those pretentious rich assholes who live there.

I guess I should make one thing clear; I didn't come out of the lumpen proletariat. The worker's plight and class struggle means squat to me. Not that I am a Republican either, mind you. But let's just say I've been around and know a few things.

I'm fighting against myself here, struggling to come up with some answers. I keep chipping away but sense there are some major shortcomings in my present regime. Do you know what it's like to constantly feel stressed with rising tensions? It's like those coal miners trapped after a cave-in with rising quiet black water printing a bar code on their bodies. Did you know there are a lot of perks living in Kuwait? Two air-conditioners per family and an all expense paid vacation. Free education but not free to be you and me. You see, that is why I am beginning to re-examine things, to make sure I'm on the right path. And why I need to be thought of as Palefsky.

What has happened to all those feelings of encouragement? Maybe it's more of a sense of direction that I'm lacking. I need to get back on the fast track. Recapture the momentum of going places and moving up.

Have you ever been to Holderness, New Hampshire, a Christmas postcard when the snow falls? Amelia grew up in a house on a lake. A large oak tree in her front yard. An old tire tied to a lazy branch that she and her brother Charlie used to swing on higher and farther. Where were you when you first knew?

I've stopped seeing friendly faces and based on documents that I have recently obtained I know there are people out to get me. Don't jump to conclusions! This is not a case of simple paranoia. I'm probably every bit as sane as you are. It's just that I have finally come to my senses. I've started to trust my intuition, not relying on the rational empirical side that gets you into so much trouble. If what I'm saying is getting a little hard to follow, have a little patience. I'm just getting started.

I wish I could write an African tone poem and resist the need to communicate in the Anglo-American vernacular but growing up in Queens has produced limitations. No other American to date has worked harder at trying to understand yours truly, and I don't see any immediate changes. One of life's chief distinctions is falling captive to a need to know. It can be a real shit kicker if you give it a chance. I'm sure you know where I'm coming from.

I made Amelia a garland of daisies to wear in her hair and a ring of blown dandelions to wear on her finger. We laughed at the monarch butterflies and soared with them on their long journey. We spoke of oceans and rivers and children's voices from far away. I watched her flying on gossamer wings by the harbor, beneath a white mountain, the laughter of crickets all around. In a drop of water, Amelia's reflection, and a blue-gray sky with a single cloud.

Welcome to the Excelsior. There is a burled walnut lobby with a marble floor and an attentive staff who makes every effort to ensure your pleasant stay. Roberto is cab side. His job is to greet you profusely while hoisting you out of the back seat, controlling your baggage, guiding you through a revolving door at an extraordinary speed. Before measuring you for his tip he will always say your hometown is his favorite place on earth and his mother was born just blocks from where you now live. Memories of summer vacations have formed all that he is today. He has handled kings and queens and will be relentless in his quest to please, for a price. Grandmothers, grandfathers and even first cousins, he will tell you are his favorites, but I would recommend not pursuing his attempts to engage. He will on occasion, under his breath offer a snide comment to an unsuspecting passerby. "Oh my God, talk about thighs" but then usually adds, "They'll never get better if you don't give them accurate feedback."

From fourteen floors above ground there are unimaginable things to be seen. The key is to close your eyes and let your mind go free. Planets revolve in primary colors: reds and blues and yellows and greens. There are of course the sounds of dogs barking, and angry men cursing about raw deals and poor location in the universe. On warm summer evenings there is also the smell of fresh cut grass, rare in the city and an occasional shooting star or two if you look real hard. There was also Habib manning a prime newsstand. A middle-aged Afghani, far from his wife and daughter, who gave away Hershey's and Mentos to "pretty ladies" and small children. Before he disappeared we spoke often. It is true he may have flown home; at times, I believe otherwise.

Do you think it is important to substantiate your personal identity through the ownership of tangible objects? Perhaps you truly enjoy tapping into aesthetic values as understood from the vocabulary of Twentieth Century modern art or maybe you really are nothing more than what you drive. Now that's really a scary thought. I'm not passing any judgments here. Don't get me wrong. I've been there. I know what you are going through or at least I have a sneaking suspicion that you are not all that different from me. Of course, I may be wrong but Ploopy Goldberg always relied on my judgment. Why would anyone want to be a Lexus anyway?

There is a Confucian Analect that states that The Master searches in vain for the man who seeks to build up his moral power as strong as his sexual desire. But why is that? Is the sex that much better in Beijing? I think not. I think basically people are ok. It's just that they get confused at times and don't know how to show it or their parents are too busy to point out the correct way. I've found talking to the right people at the right time can be very useful. And they don't need a degree or professional certificate. First rule is don't socialize with people who have nasty personal characteristics and are aloof. And rule two is never work for an employer who pays you a meager wage for doing everything for him but breathe. Believe me on these two points. I speak from experience and I'm pretty sure you don't want to be the last to know.

For a second there, I felt myself flying away, high on a gust of air headed straight for an ethereal rendezvous, a psychological Bermuda triangle, a Joseph Cornell boxed life; no exit. There is the stare of a Dan mask followed by a Marsden Hartley painting of the ocean before a storm with three hopeful white-capped blue-green waves rolling onto a deserted salmon beach; an ominous cloud, sliced at its very bottom like an onion, hangs threateningly in the dark green gray sky. A third image quickly comes to mind. It is the face of a vintage Longines aviator's watch, most probably from the twenties. It is a chronograph with all functions operated by the winding crown. It has a double-jointed case of 35mm diameter in eighteen karat gold. The dial is enameled with tachometric scale in blue and black and telemetric scale in red. It has a minute recorder and gold-plated Breuget hands.

I love watches, I always have. I'm not exactly sure why or

when and how it all started. What do you think? Does a good watch do anything for you? Would I feel the same if something other than time was clocked? Of course, my favorites are not always the obvious ones: Patek Phillipe, Audemars Piguet, Vacheron and Constantine, Blancpain and Breuguet nor do I particularly care for Cartier, or Gubelin. Give me a nice old Eberhard any day of the week and if it has added dials, functions and recorders, so much the better. I read somewhere that the Dalai Lama collected watches, the kind that are big and glitzy, rose gold or platinum with precious jewels and rare stones. I guess this is where you would have to say his monkness and I differ. Let me get it on the table for the record, I'll forgo sex for an aged Breitling! Amelia never completely understood my love of watches.

Psychologically speaking I've been beaten down, stabbed, shot at, blown up, nothing too heavy mind you. Ridiculed, of course not taken seriously, and ignored. Sometimes I feel my brain is in a holding cell with the other terrorists in Cuba. A voice reminiscent of a drill sergeant barks at me: "Is that a problem?" I guess not everybody in the world gets a shot at the brass ring, but still you can never stop asking yourself, "What is really important?"

In front of The Pillars of the Phillistines Café on Ninth Avenue and Forty-seventh Street psychic Delilah, a palm and Tarot card reader, is prospecting for customers. As I pass, she looks me in the eye and entreats, "Are you worried, troubled, sick; unhappy in love, business, marriage, luck or whatever?"

That pretty much covers it. Take that evil eye and fix on someone else.

I think the source of my problem has more to do with a doomsday scenario made plausible. You know, lack of command and control, the need for a sense of discipline and order, learning how to feel confident when under attack. Sure I'm unpredictable, mercurial, maybe even a little wacky, ok it's true; I really am a bumbling fool but I still need some general direction and the steps to be taken, no matter what the rationale. Face it. There has to be some benefit from all this for me! Let's just say I need to be engaged in a personal diplomatic offensive where there is some chance of securing better internal relations; where, finally, there'll be a way out and I'll be the one who is in charge.

A face, a touch, a memory: Pink and George, a Hank Williams favorite come to life; a cold, cold heart and rough years. A small notions shop near the North Carolina coast circa 1965. A strange sight in the South: a slight white woman, Pink, married to tall, muscular black man, George, who introduces his wife bragging, "She possessed every advantage and left everything to chance." I wonder to myself, like humming a song, "If the only world that doesn't disappoint is the one that is make believe."

A short drive out of town, away from the ocean past a trailer park of former circus performers and vaudevillians. They sing and dance, juggle and tell fortunes. My mother insists we stop. We walk by a troupe of tumblers, a fire-eater and a dog act. An old gypsy, perhaps merely as a sadistic joke, tells mother she will soon die: painfully, tragically without warning, and there is no catch. If she comes back, the deluxe reading could bear better news. She can't see it all yet.

A nervous laugh, an overturned table and "Did you ever!" Later, six miles down the highway our car is hit by a drunk driver nursing a bottle singing a country western tune. A child of five whispers to himself in an emergency room, "Mommy, what does reality mean?"

A cyclone hits a remote Pacific island. In an instant seven hundred inhabitants disappear like an unremembered wrong. The child, so long ago, is he really me? So much of that day is now forgotten. He waits in a gray green corridor, glass cutting sounds and the smell of blood and urine; tall men and fat women in white gowns rushing about. Soon after Amelia's acci-

dent I heard an interview with an ex-nurse who recently turned 88. She went white water rafting to celebrate and believes the secret to long life is being happy; just that simple. Palefsky's still going strong at 90; looking at him, I swear, you would think he was half his age.

On the evening of August 21, 1935, Max Palefsky was at the Palomar Ballroom watching Benny Goodman, as one reviewer observed, "transform himself from a mere commoner to the King of Swing." Earlier in the day, before his debut on the Make Believe Ballroom, the two joked about how when they first met Benny was still playing in his Rogers Park neighborhood in short pants for twelve dollars a week. Discouraged by the disappointing reception of his radio arrangements and the dismissal of the band from its brief New York engagement, Benny was prepared to give it all up and go back on his own; certain his career was a failure. But then came his playing of Henderson's arrangement of "The Sugar Foot Stomp" with Bunny Berrigan on the trumpet, Jess Stacey at the piano and Gene Krupa on drums and the explosion of success that Palefsky had predicted would follow. Looking around the Palomar Ballroom, his clarinet at the angle of a hand launched missile, Benny searched for Palefsky nowhere to be found.

He appears when you need him is the way he puts it and it's a mistake to think of him as an apparition, figment of the imagination or some kind of "It's a Wonderful Life" character. After all it's Palefsky we are talking about! You can bet your life on this: Palefsky is no Clarence earning his wings. Remember the movie, Field of Dreams; you know the one, "build it and they will come"; well that's kind of how it is with him. Never expected or predictable; although I will say this, Palefsky does have a knack of showing up just around the time when you really need him, or so you might think!

But you are probably wondering by now, where is all this going? And why spend so much time on all these seemingly un-

related details, obscure references and strange sounding names. I mean take it from me, Ploopy Goldberg! What kind of name is that? It doesn't even sound really Jewish, not that it matters; though I guess you would have to say Palefsky, on the other hand, has that issue covered. And what could possibly be the relevance of Icarus and the allusions to birds and butterflies, airplanes and crash landings? And who is Amelia, her brother Charlie, the old lady; and what kind of accident, and what does it all have to do with 9/11? And most importantly, I'm sure you're asking yourself, is there really a story here?

To tell you the truth, I'm not sure; but CB and I are trying hard to come up with answers.

***

If you haven't heard of Beano you haven't arrived yet. It could easily have been called The Breakers, La Caravelle, Marble House, Le Plus Meridian or some other tony sounding name. You see in a classic reversal of haute snobbery mixed with a sardonic wink, its members, who you will never discover, accorded this hidden emporium for the super wealthy a name that can easily be used in public without breaking the oath of secrecy and at the same time suggest to the outside world that they too are mere mortals with the same kinds of problems facing you and me.

But let me back up here for a second. You may feel you have a mental picture of what I'm talking about. Let me assure you, you don't. This is not your average extremely exclusive store. In this sense Bijan and Cartier may just as well be thought of as Costco, Sam's Club or Trader Joe's. What we are talking about here is the first real lifestyle store. Not one, of course, that bears any resemblance to yours or mine. But like many things that surround Beano it only provides the illusion of what we think we know to be real. Beano, the store, now that takes the cake.

First off, you have to change your thinking about what it means to be rich and what constitutes exclusive. You can't buy your way into this club. Even if you made a fortune in the Internet, a killing in real estate or own a large hedge fund, believe me when I tell you that there is no need to apply. You can't apply. The only way you get in is if they want you and not the other way around. And they never sink so low as to say don't call us we'll call you. It's just a known fact among the cognoscenti that this is the hardest ticket to get in town. Yes, they have rejected kings and princes, movie starlets and moguls. People have literally died to get in to Beano, not that it ever helped.

Think of a holographic, present day version of Studio 54; a 24/7 visual labyrinth that you can step into or out of at will; keeping in mind Beano is still so much more: your every fantasy, real or imagined on call whenever, wherever and however you want. Now, do you have that picture? OK, hold it because you are still only half way there. Add to this the most fascinating mix of people, also real and imagined, from the past and present and you will begin to get only an inkling of what it is like to be a part of Beano. It is your reality magnified or minimized at will, and again, sorry to repeat myself, so much more. You want to feel what it is like to win the Kentucky Derby, riding Man of War? It is your horse race; so go to it. Maybe you want to come in second, just because you have never done it before, and need to experience what it feels like not to be a winner; it is your crowd in the stands, placed and dressed or undressed, as you wish. They are there to cheer you on or kiss you off. And then of course there is the fun of competing imaginations. If you choose this option things can get really interesting not to mention at times, downright unsettling.

Imagine the possibility of crowding your life with ever more astonishing experiences and events. You can be a legend in your own mind and in the minds of others. Learn ancient Greek in an *instant and read Antigone in the original. A medieval joust, a trip to the moon. Sex like you never had or dreamed of before. Perhaps you favor the mundane, a huge disqualifier for membership, and are content to travel to the Balearic Isles in your custom designed yacht: a helm's chair made of Macassar ebony crafted by Jacques Emile Rulmann, a crew reminiscent of Busby Berkeley dancers and Fred Astaire as first mate; with chart plotters and thrusters, a full sized galley more appropriate for the kitchens of Cordon Bleu; all the amenities fit for someone like you.*

You're in your shower thinking about what it would have been like to attend the 1913 ball in the palace of the Romanovs, warm rivulets of water forming on your body; the surge and memory of sea spray at just the moment you decide to leave St. Petersburg. You know what you have to do: and so you sail into the history and mystery of Venice. Winged lions and the vision of Saint Mark and Tintoretto's Ecce Homo. You kneel at the pantheon of mythological heroes and Franciscan learning. Wherever you turn, colossal creatures more hospitable than menacing are there to greet your five senses. You pause before one that has no wings: a lion with a man standing on its head, atop a crocodile with the face of a dog. Wherever you go, the lions, miniscule and monumental, are never left behind. Images of Mars and Neptune and the wedding of Ariadne and Bacchus swim all around you. There is also Agony in the Garden, The Adoration of Shepherds and a vision of Paradise. But just then you are seized with the urge to destroy the Andrea Palladio.

You know what you are doing is wrong but you just can't stop yourself. No, that is wrong. You can but won't stop yourself. After all, you think, "life is too short and whose future is it anyway?"

The sky fills with a blue gray cloud of pigeons; the smell of gunpowder quickly turns to an aroma only slightly familiar: an uneven mixture of sea kelp, galbanum patchouli and geranium.

The Next Step 43

There is the sound of people running. A young child turns toward a photographer who captures his image, streaked with orange red light. He resembles the putto with dolphin in the Palazzo Vecchio in Florence and you remember it has been some time since you were there.

Out of the blue three photographs appear at the exact moment you detect the sound of a post horn playing the theme from Mahler's Third Symphony, which you remember vividly from a 1976 performance of the New York Philharmonic directed by Zubin Mehta.

The first, taken in 1921, is of a glowering Freud challenging the photographer with his archeological stare. Cigar in hand, his open jacket reveals a loopy gold chain dangling confidently from his vest. The stance and accoutrements, all signs of someone who is secure, firmly establishing his beachhead on terra incognita. A second picture, also of Freud, is taken later. He is stooped over and looks less sure. It is from the period when he was waiting for permission from German authorities to leave Austria. The third photograph speaks for itself. A Jewish boy forced to write Juden on the door of his family's home. His tormentors, young and old, laugh menacingly. But you urge yourself to think of more pleasant times because you know you can think or do whatever matters and one thing for sure will never happen: "and then you wake up and it's all been a dream."

But I am getting ahead of myself here and I need to hold on to the memory of the Schwinn Zephyr, the house in Long Beach, the rock that wasn't thrown and, of course, CB who I guess you might say is at the very beginning of this story. But first let me ask you a question, whose answer is seemingly obvious, but not necessarily so.

What is a story?

A narrative either true or false in prose or verse, designed to interest or amuse the teller, hearer or reader; a tale usually with, but at times without a clear plot; a narration of the events in the life of a person or the existence of a thing; a report or account of a matter, a statement or allegation; a literary device to ornament with pictured or colorful scenes as from history or legend.

A story is also a succession of events or impressions that are comic or dramatic, or both; an imaginary journey to the reflecting pool of cogito ergo sum or to the untapped fountain of I think therefore I am not.

A story is the abracadabra of our existence. You are your story and your story is you.

I am walking down a long wood paneled corridor reminiscent of Judd Hall, a transition space that I routinely passed through as a child attending the University of Chicago Laboratory Schools. It is the only place in the web and labyrinth of buildings and spaces where a code of silence was rigidly adhered to and enforced. I can still remember the soft squeak of children's sneakers on polished oak floorboards, the only allowable sound. We would file through Judd Hall daily on our way to gym. I used to think of it as the world's most official place. Wood and glass doors with the names of professors and administrators written in bold gold lettering. As we walked down the seemingly endless hall, the doors on either side might open randomly. Serious looking men in boxy jackets and grim ties and sexless women in dull gray, blue or brown dresses would appear for a moment, pay no attention to us, and then disappear back into one of their wood and glass rabbit holes.

But today is different; it is now. I enter the hall and I am aware that its name has been changed. I read the bronze plaque at its entrance and realize it is *Judge Hall*. The wood and glass doors on either side open and the hall begins to fill with judges dressed in the English style wearing powdered wigs and long black robes. The head judge, I presume, wears a somewhat more elaborate robe than his colleagues with gold striping on the *arms and a border of red at his neck. He walks over to me and sternly advises, "It is about time; you have kept us waiting."*

Everything suddenly changes and I am at the Mary Boone Gallery with New York's beautiful people. All the usual suspects you have read about or seen for the last quarter century are here; different faces and designer labels but you know the same crowd. Nothing really changes. They are still bitching about their help, the Mercedes, the cost of maintaining a place in the Hamptons and Gstaad, tuition at Dalton, and the bum rap dished out to Martha Stewart. And then it hits me: the exhibit is being held at the ASPCA. I look up and see a crimson banner with gold lettering that reads, Dogs as Art.

And there they are in cages designed by Molino, Eames, Prouve, Magistratti and Le Corbusier: Fighting dogs that were abused and neglected by their owners. One is a mottled brown black with three legs and large dark scars like keloids about its body. Its face still possesses infected red wounds around the mouth, inflicted by another dog's bite. It growls at first like a loud snore and then later breaks into a rabid bark. A delighted onlooker, a tall male dressed all in black with fine blond hair worn exactly as the Puritans did waves a limp hand at the dog whose name is Chico and tells him, "Easy, now, Chico is a good boy!"

And suddenly the scene changes again and I'm in the Temple of Dendur at the Met where an exhibit of Victorian gambling paraphernalia is being presented. My eyes move to an oversized red marble die with ivory inlaid dots. And now I am walking on a giant chessboard with two children: one, a chubby Maori boy who does not speak and a girl who reminds me of Tinkerbell and tells me in French that she is an Armenian. She pulls a diamond earring from her pocket, that I am informed is a fake, and places it on the top of the white king's cross. She asks me, if I like the Beegees and people who take chances, or do I prefer the ones who make themselves go slow. "I prefer Weber,

Schoenberg and Berg," I tell her and that I don't have deep pockets or know people in high places. "Je comprends," she whispers to herself and then hands me her journal.

On each page the hand written entry is the same: "one plus one is always two as long as the zero is on the right side of equal."

Is she a reality test in the form of a dream I wonder, or a shortsighted distortion right out of thin air? "When you fall off the cheval, you must place the foot back in the stirrup," she sketches a horse in the air.

I am certain now that this is a dream and just knowing that emboldens me, allowing me to think I can do whatever I want. Just as I am experiencing this moment of enlightenment, the three- legged dog leaps out of his Jean Prouve cage onto my chest; salivating wildly all over my clothes and then begins licking me in an uncontrollable way, rubbing its scarred head in a thrusting backward movement against my chin. It startles me when Chico begins to speak: "Easy, now, Max is a good boy!"

I am now falling down the all too familiar rabbit hole. Is it rotating or is it revolving? I can't be sure. I always get the two confused. It is long and dark. There are scents of cedar and aspen and hassenfeffer shit and the refrain of Papagino/Papagina from Mozart's Magic Flute mixed with the opening bars of Beethoven's Egmont Overture: a cascade of water turns into the Hoover Dam that I leap into like Harrison Ford in The Fugitive.

It is an exhilarating, orgasmic feeling, shooting the falls as fast as you have ever traveled and at the same time almost in slow motion; the wind and spray cleanses your spirit. You try to enjoy the ride but you also know this can be it! You feel you now know the greatest force on earth but remember at that exact moment an idiot actor who dated your cousin who farted for laughs in public; and carried a signed picture of Barry Manilow in his wallet.

There is a fat lady, sitting at a table drumming her fingers, challenging you to play to the strength of your character. "Think about what you are doing. Shoulders back. What is it that you really want to say?" she taunts. "If you don't know, stop. Realize that you need more time to find yourself so that you can lose the inhibitions that will allow you to move on." You ask yourself if she is being a bitch or is this merely a defensive maneuver on your part to shut her up.

You crash into a pool of water at the bottom of the falls and find yourself in the middle of a strange celebration with people dressed in formal attire. The heads of Peter, Paul and Mary float by singing, "It's the hammer of justice, it's the bell of freedom, it's the song about love between the brothers and sisters all over this land." You then spy another floating head that is circled by a thick gold chain. At first it can only be seen from behind but instinctively you feel that you should leave this one alone. You start to swim away but then realize you can't do it; it's your destiny to make its acquaintance: It is Puff Daddy who wants to be called P Diddy telling you the party can't start until you arrive.

And then I remind myself: "Humpty Dumpty sat on a wall. Humpty Dumpty had a great fall. All the king's horses and all the king's men couldn't put Humpty together again." And I know the eternal truth hidden in those few verses, weird but true, never before revealed until now. When everything has suddenly changed and nothing else really matters.

One of the lions you had seen in Venice reappears at The Ritz Carlton in Boston and then again at the 42nd Street library and later at the Art Institute in Chicago. When he is seen once more in an advertisement for a Dreyfus investment fund you don't know what to do so you just remain still. To be the king of the jungle, you tell yourself, you must do more than inhabit a castle in the sky even if you are a tenant of dreamland and a practitioner of magic.

Your sole purpose now is to convey crucial messages to aliens in live action and animation films, but despite this fact or maybe because of it, you force yourself to awake.

The telephone rings and I feel compelled to answer. I recognize the number of the caller: it is a Rabbi Mordecai Tannenbaum, a follower of the Satma Rebbi from the Bronx. The Satmas are a tight knit clan of ultra orthodox Jews: Chasids who follow a strict code of prayer and rituals. Mordecai, or Mordy as I call him, is of a short, stocky, no make that muscular build, kind of like a bonsai Sumo wrestler of the Hebrew persuasion or a super-sized Chasidic dwarf on steroid injections. He has a powdery white complexion and a scraggly red beard that looks like sagebrush blowing down an open highway and sausage-like fingers that resemble the jumbo non-kosher variety. He is a kind man with a big heart who only wears black suits with white shirts and a wide-brimmed hat, and possesses information that I am desperate to have.

He informs me that he is in a GAP, no an Old Navy, on Times Square, shopping for socks and underwear for his children and he might lose me soon because the reception is so bad. A moment later there is only silence and I wonder to myself if he was able to find out.

I've heard various people on several occasions say their sole purpose in life is to leave the world in a better state than they found it. I guess I would have to say, all things considered, that is pretty much my view. Of course, everything that we think or do tells a little story about us and what we believe to be true.

You can live in many places but you are always from only one place. You know what I mean. No matter where you go to or eventually end up you are forever from where you started, which is after all, right here. You can, of course fool the others, but you can't fool yourself. Well, you can, but as any good psychoanalyst will tell you, not for long. That was once my problem but not anymore. The facts of internal geography are just too real. Even

Beano can't erase that.

Say you're from Queens; maybe even Astoria and you grew up in a three-floor walk-up on the wrong side of the economic divide. You feel embarrassed to bring your friends over because of the dingy, plaster-torn conditions, but your father says, "Don't worry, we're not trying to keep up with the Joneses."

But the elderly German couple, the Schweinhundmillers who own and manage the building you live in, and who you are convinced are ex-Nazis go out of their way to make you feel not at home. Their retarded, forty year-old daughter Heidi, a six foot one inch genetic aberration weighing two hundred and fifty pounds runs down the street after you screaming she will make you into bratwurst and your mother into sauerkraut. Whenever she sees you alone in the building she tells you how much she hates you and that she is going to get you into trouble. She accuses you of tampering with mailboxes and destroying her father Jurgen's furniture, and tells you to confess to all the other crimes, about which only she knows.

Once in the laundry room she attacks you and sticks her cow's tongue deep into your ear. She warns you that if you ever tell, she will knife you in your sleep and that will be that.

Her mother Olga, a Wagnerian Holstein, stands at her front window watching your movements behind tattered lace curtains. She too finds you disgusting, the kind of little boy that she knows "what to handle." "In the old days we knew how to deal with your kind," she tells you, and you smile politely before you spit in her eye. Your father makes you apologize, she denies everything and you are punished. But ten years later you get the last laugh: she dies justly, stung by a bee.

If there is one lesson I have learned it is that everything we know or do is a matter of perspective and anything we accomplish is relative to molehills and mountains. Astronomers can view objects thirteen billion light years away just as the heavens looked when stars and galaxies first appeared. They can focus *their sights on quasars, shining objects, thought to be powered by massive black holes from the inception of the universe. They appear to the observer as luminous smears from the dawn of time, arcs of red and blue on the cosmic lens of space. Each of us inhabits our own glittering expanse of stars and sky; some so close to us as to be blinding to the eye and others so remote that they are forever beyond our field of vision unless or until we stretch our horizons; allowing ourselves to see what has always been there.*

A story is like a galaxy, a seemingly incoherent clusters of stars, some hidden from view, others swallowed into black holes or obscured by gas and dust; internal nebulae hiding or revealing dark matter of an unknown nature whose origin and gravity may be uncaptured by the telescope but never beyond the powers of imagination.

The Hayden Planetarium was one of the first museums of its kind in the Western Hemisphere. Its collection of astronomical instruments and rare books is among the finest in the world. When it was founded, its directors understood the need to exhibit artifacts from the history of astronomy and to establish a celestial theater without rival in America.

As a child, I spent many hours alone in the starry dark watching strange objects form over head; nearly perfect rings of hot blue stars, wheels within wheels spinning around a yellow nucleus of galaxies and comets from the farthest reaches of the solar system breaking apart. I would watch with special interest a system of comets called "sungrazers" so named because their orbits closely brushed the sun, arriving to their inevitable end in clusters on parallel paths. Their fragmentation, the result of gravity's strong pull, disintegrated their loosely piled chunks of dust and ice into luminous cascades of one comet falling into large families of smaller ones. Their gradual demise had a hypnotic effect, celestial fireworks in mysteriously orderly patterns, in natural life cycles and solar systems. It was my refuge from life on the wrong side of the divide.

But I fear that I am getting too synoptic here, offering a poorly compressed view of feelings and events where my associations and descriptions require something more on the order of grand sweep, dimension and cinematic spectacle—a Cecil B. DeMille extravaganza of vivid colors, raw emotion and personal pain.

I would have liked to tell this story differently.

Like perennials dying back into the ground only to reappear in the spring, my garden of remembrance resurrects forgotten secrets with weird, faintly known surprises that has to make me want to try even harder: a psychological last redoubt to the onslaught of singed memory and evaporating time with only occasional lucidity.

Max Palefsky. Ploopy Goldberg. Names and places long gone or hidden: like a mother dying in the night. Like a lover lost in an insane instant of towering twins falling apart under attack. And then there was CB with his bizarre rules; passwords and handshakes, and now I think you know why all this is getting so out of hand.

It was signed Max Palefsky and dated 11/13/2001.

Chapter 4

Fishman wonders what has happened to Palefsky and speculates where he could be? He finds the Chronicle disturbing, but the product of a master storyteller. Although in places deceptively incomplete and confounding, overall it is an eerily compelling excursion over the landscape of the collective psyche. Fishman believes the Chronicle's spare, cocky, elegiac, cynical, heartfelt language captures the underlying pain and uncertainty of the human condition. The text also reflects one person's mission to learn more about himself, to transform the world into a better place, a home. He is certain this hopeful, evanescent message is imbedded in its crystalline prose.

There are many thoughts, ideas and feelings in Palefsky that Fishman relates to deeply: Palefsky's sense of loss and self-doubt, his yearning for self-understanding, redemption; the importance of choices and how their antecedents and consequences affect the fictions and meanings in a life, and the need to come to the realization that in the final analysis we are all mortal. All of us, without exception, will die. And for the most part, our preoccupations, to use Palefsky's term, "are bullshit and don't really matter."

Fishman is struck by the sheer humanity of Palefsky in the same way he is moved by the unknowable woman on the park bench. He senses the shame and humiliation of people seeking reinvention, call it transformation. The longing to be renewed and recognized as human beings. Fishman also relates to Palefsky's brand of sarcasm, a blend of New York's upper West Side cured in a vat of three thousand years of persecution, like a perfectly seasoned kosher dilled pickle. He sometimes laughs and at other times cries at the writer's outrageous comments and observations, specters from the past and present and fear for his future; Fishman's future, anyone's future?

Fishman rereads the Chronicle telling himself to resist being Talmudic, not to light on a particular word or phrase, not to search for hidden intentions or meanings but he can't help himself. Replaying in his mind are the words "The tough part is what you do with the information."

He is now lost somewhere in Palefsky's narrative, he is not exactly sure where, maybe vacationing as a child in the Catskills or in southern Maine, in the Lake Sebago region, with his own children when they were young. *Presto chango!* He is "under a radiant sky near a white clapboard farmhouse on a phosphorous blue lake, a solitary boat moored to its dock, a fragrant necklace of wild iris grows along the shore. Two children, a boy and a girl, neither more than seven or eight years old play in a meadow under the watchful eyes of an elderly woman peering out of a kitchen window. There is the sweet succulent aroma of plums in the doorway."

Fishman is again back in his grandmother's arms; the fragrance of baking peaches heavy in the air; feeling her warm fleshy cheek against his forehead, the coolness of her cotton dress. In his mind he listens to her hilarious stories. The one about the man who went to the Rabbi, complaining about his lot in life, small house, not enough money. The Rabbi's advice totally crazy, right on the border of the three stooges meets Groucho Marx, but somehow she made a point, now forgotten. Fishman feels her soft kind voice, affectionate laughter.

Fishman also knows "It makes no sense thinking about the past, dwelling on things that should have been or might have happened. All we really have is now."

He understands the profound truth of Palefsky's words and how they apply to his own life. He wonders if certainty is the ultimate response to insecurity, if confidence is nothing more than a refusal to be afraid, and if life can really be "a jigsaw puzzle of possibility where you put together the pieces and they all fit."

Like Palefsky, Fishman yearns for a world where good triumphs over evil, where one doesn't have to be a squealer or some opportunistic stool pigeon and where the comically inept are appreciated for who they are, geniuses sitting on park benches brimming with expert opinions that would improve any cable news program. Of course he sees himself more in the Socratic mold: "I alone know that I know nothing." But he also knows you have to know a lot just to get there.

What appeals to him most in Palefsky, beyond the pickle barrel reality of complex psychological flavors and seasoning is its ultimate optimism; Palefsky believes in purpose and mission where "unimaginable things can be seen."

Fishman reads one line from the Chronicle over and over again. He finds it insightful, humorous, disengaging. "One of life's chief distinctions is falling captive to a need to know. It can be a real shit kicker if you give it a chance." Fishman would add that it's important to wear heavy boots and not to let anything stand in the way.

There is still so much he doesn't understand in Palefsky. Ploopy Goldberg. Amelia. Palefsky's love of watches. And then there is all the Beano stuff. Biting into a piece of warm dark chocolate Fishman imagines the possibility of "crowding" his life with ever more astonishing experiences and events.

Fishman is overwhelmed with both the manifest and latent meanings of the Chronicle but he is resigned without question to its ultimate truth and authenticity. He accepts Palefsky's pain and humiliation as his own. Fishman too has felt the slow tormenting twists of shame, like an Indian burn, on his road to spiritual reawakening.

He reads from the Chronicle: "Psychologically speaking I've been beaten down, stabbed, shot at, blown up, nothing too heavy mind you. Ridiculed, of course not taken seriously, and ignored. Sometimes I feel my brain is in a holding cell with the other terrorists in Cuba."

Fishman knows that feeling too. He remembers a time of intense pain. When he nearly lost everything, all his monetary preoccupations with houses, cars, boats, plane, the glittering symbols, landmarks, signposts of success. He asks himself, "How could I have let this happen?" Fishman knows the answer but at the same time is certain that "it is all bullshit and none of it *really* matters."

He reminds himself that the IRS investigation and securities fraud trial had found him innocent, but in his own mind he remained guilty. Nadia and the children had stood by him but so many wasted years of defending his name and reputation, fearing the imagined lacerations of colleagues and friends. Like Palefsky, Fishman has chosen not to dwell in the past, to make sense of his experience, even laugh about it, and most importantly, move on.

***

Fishman is on Lake Shore Drive. It is a late October afternoon. There are still a few sailboats, sticking up like pocket squares out on the lake. There is a rare clarity about the day, not a cloud anywhere. Everything in a place that seems right. The kind of light that motivates young children to ask why the sky is blue. Fishman can hear his daughter's gentle voice in his ear. He sees the way she looked at him when she thought he was the ultimate source of truth.

Fishman is behind the wheel of his Mercedes, a '92 190E. It is a rich shade of gray black with a gray leather interior, burled walnut dash and still possesses a new car aroma even after more than a decade. It is rarely serviced but then again has only put on some 30,000 miles. Fishman hardly ever goes on long drives, using it mostly for running down to the store or picking up Nadia from her work. Initially, when he bought it, Fishman would drive to the Exchange and park on the famed first level with all the other market hotshots.

A feeling of contentment is taking over Fishman when suddenly the car bucks and begins to make coughing sounds. There are a series of hesitations followed by power surges. Afraid of breaking down on the highway he gets off at the first exit. He is just south of Cermak Boulevard, just below Chinatown, midway between the meatpacking district and the housing projects. Fishman is in unfamiliar territory. He is a long way from Old Town. There are scores of abandoned buildings behind heavy padlocks and alleyways teeming with specter-like inhabitants. It is a great barrier reef of the homeless men and women who have created a gated community of their own, controlling the neighborhood, keeping the riffraff out.

Fishman drives for several blocks. He is lost and there are no familiar signposts to lead him back to civilization. He drives in a circle and then down an alleyway. Suddenly the Mercedes chokes a final time and dies. Red lights flash, an interior bell rings. Fishman is stranded on a fearful landscape, as desolate as the moon. He pops the hood, trying to evaluate the situation. Fishman has no idea what he is looking at. Everything seems normal, more or less in the right place. There is no steam rising or fluids leaking, belts and hoses show no signs of breaks. He reaches for the dipstick and touches a battery cable. His eyes stare at parts for which they know no name. He thinks to himself, "When it comes to fixing things, I'm a complete idiot."

In the distance he can see three black men heading in his direction as if on a train track. As they move closer he makes them out. The one on the left has a dark blue plaid woolen blanket slung over his shoulders and is clutching a bent golf club. The one to the far right is wearing a heavily soiled red ski jacket and hood. His leather gloves seem excessive protection against the October chill.

Fishman now feels a sudden shortness of breath; he is stunned by the enormity of the person in the middle. He dwarfs his two companions. He is as large and strongly built as an NBA center. He is dressed in a black leather trench coat with irregular duck tape patches, like an urban Darth Vader fallen on hard times. They stop in front of Fishman.

The one wearing the blanket asks, "Broke down?"

Fishman not able to move his eyes off the golf club.

"Just died on me."

There is rude laughter.

Making a circle in the air with his club, "You from around here?"

The man in the red ski jacket is silent. Nodding his head in agreement, content to allow his companion do the talking. The large one in the middle is impassive, assessing.

"One minute it was fine, the next . . ."

The man straightens out his blanket that has slid down his shoulder. He looks like some crazy chieftain. His tone is now stronger, more aggressive.

"You're fucked. This ain't no place to break down. Nasty shit happens."

Fishman now sensing the worst tries to find a solution. "What do you want?"

The big guy looks Fishman over, studying his face then opens the car's front door checking out the interior. He has a deep low voice, a basso profundo. "I thought Mercedes were good cars."

Suddenly he slams the door. "Shit. I know this dude!" He says it as if he is having an epiphany.

Fishman searching all his mental files all at once, everywhere, no answers.

"Motherfucker!"

Fishman still not making the connection, apprehensive.

"Board of Trade, right?"

Fishman shaking his head, yes.

"Man, I know you, read about you in the papers. The Feds did some bad shit to you. How's it going?"

He turns to his buddies. "This dude's ok, let's help him."

He now looks back at Fishman. "I'm Luther . . . Cool Breeze and," pointing to the one in the ski jacket, "Snoogy."

The three proceed to study the engine like heart surgeons. There is whispering, a considered diagnosis followed by a quick but unassailable solution.

"Start her up."

The engine turns over and the Mercedes sounds as good as new.

"Loose spark plug, thass all. Lucky for you we were out for a walk."

Fishman reaches into his pocket then catches himself. Instead he removes his watch and hands it to Luther. "Thanks."

Snoogy speaks for the first time. "Man. It's a Rolex. A real one."

Fishman thanks Luther and his friends again then drives away anxious to leave this bleak landscape. He turns a corner and sees a hand painted sign on an abandoned factory wall. There are large white letters on a black background.

Avoid Hell

Repent

Find Jesus Today

Fishman remembers back to his childhood and how he and his friends would alter Jesus Saves signs by adding the accompanying phrase, Moses Invests.

He says the phrase to himself repeatedly. "Jesus saves, Moses invests. Jesus saves, Moses invests."

Fishman begins to laugh uncontrollably perhaps as a way of

relieving his anxiety or maybe he is just struck by the humor of the expression and its sentiment. He is momentarily overtaken by the delirium of language: the syntax and grammar of a single phrase. And then the words change.

"Fishman considers, Palefsky redeems."

"Fishman considers, Palefsky redeems."

Chapter 5

That evening Fishman has a dream. Bud Abbott and Lou Costello are on stage doing their famous "Who's on first" comedy routine. Only it's not the usual sketch.

Abbott: "Well, let's see, who we have on the bags. Palefsky's on first."
Costello: "That's what I want to find out."
Abbott: "Palefsky's on first."
Costello: "You the manager?"
Abbott: "Yes."
Costello: "You the coach too?"
Abbott: "Yes."
Costello: "And you don't know the players' names?"
Abbott: "Well, I should."
Costello: "So, who's on first?"
Abbott: "Palefsky."
Costello: "I mean the fellow's name."
Abbott: "Palefsky."
Costello: "The guy on first."
Abbott: "Yes, Palefsky's on first!"
Costello: "And who's on second?"
Abbott: "Palefsky."
Costello: "That's his name?"
Abbott: "Yes."
Costello: "And on third?"
Abbott: "Palefsky."

Costello: "And in the outfield, let me guess?"

Abbott and Costello (together): "Palefsky, Palefsky, and Palefsky."

PAUSE

Costello: "Catching?"

Abbott: "Palefsky, also at shortstop!"

Costello: "Let me get this right, Palefsky is covering all the bags and the outfield too?"

Abbott: "Palefsky."

Costello: "When you pay off the team every month, he gets the money?"

Abbott: "Every dollar of it."

Costello: "All I'm trying to find out is the fellow's name."

Abbott: "Palefsky."

Costello: "The guy that gets . . ."

Abbott: "That's it."

Costello: "Who gets the money?"

Abbott: "He does. Every dollar. Sometimes his wife comes down and collects it."

Costello: "Whose wife?"

Abbott: "Palefsky's."

Costello: "He pitches too?"

Abbott: "No! Haven't you been listening?"

Costello: "He doesn't pitch?"

PAUSE

Abbott: "No, Fishman pitches. What's wrong with that?"

***

His dream continues. Fishman is now the leading character in a familiar FedEx commercial. It is the one where a man's career is made when he comes up with a simple plan, an effective course of action to solve an age-old delivery problem. Fishman is in a business meeting that is eager for a solution. His boss, a rum-

The Next Step 63

pled middle-age executive in a tie and short sleeve shirt; anxiously addresses his workers.

"Come on, I need an answer!"

Fishman, in a whisper, "If you are shipping internationally you gotta use FedEx."

His supervisor jumps up out of his seat. "Brilliant, Fishman. You are a real life saver!"

Later that evening over dinner Fishman tells Nadia. "So I told him, if you are shipping internationally, you gotta use FedEx."

Years later Fishman is speaking at the rostrum at a national convention. There is a banner of him in a FedEx uniform in the background. There are delegates waving Fishman placards chanting his name.

"So I told 'em, "If you are shipping internationally, you gotta use FedEx."

***

Earlier in the week Fishman read an article in the New York Times Magazine about FedEx. It was described as "one of the most admired companies in the world." The Times called FedEx "a blue ribbon company placing highest of all US companies in the six dimensions of corporate excellence: reputation, results-driven, customer service, emotional appeal, social responsibility and workplace environment."

What stuck in Fishman's mind most was its "absolutely, positively" attitude and its commitment to be best in class service. Fishman imagines himself in the role of the decorated FedEx workers who are profiled.

"A snowstorm had shut down Oswego, New York, but FedEx Express courier Fishman had an important delivery—visas for Gus and Irma Philbin traveling to Moldova to adopt a son. The weather prevented the documents from arriving on the expected day, and the couple was due to leave for Europe the next morning. Foreign adoption procedures made the situation dire: without the visas, the couple could not adopt the child. Frantic, they call FedEx for help. Fishman tracked the package down and despite the dangerous road conditions, on his way home drove out of his way to the couple's neighborhood to deliver the visas. The delivery allowed the couple to leave on time and bring home their new son. The happy parents expressed their thanks by naming their son 'Fish' and building him a chlorinated pool in their backyard."

***

"The Roadway Corporation had a critical shipment of wheels it needed to send via FedEx Freight. The wheel stems, which had to be installed before the wheels could be delivered, arrived late. FedEx Freight supervisor Fishman arrived to pick up the wheel shipment, but it wasn't ready. Not one to just sit in his truck and wait, Fishman assessed the situation and, because of his highly developed mechanical know-how, installed the stems, lubricated the wheels, balanced the tires and helped in every way to prepare the shipment to be moved on time."

***

"FedEx Express document handler Fishman came upon a highway accident. He called the police and then discovered from the frantic occupants of the vehicle that a baby had been ejected during impact and was missing. Fishman found the baby on the shoulder of the road with only minor cuts and bruises. He returned the baby to his mother while simultaneously offering aid to the other accident victims, treating their wounds and preventing them from going into shock. But that was not the end of it. Fishman looked over in the direction of the exit ramp and saw a small car drive off the shoulder, spin around, and slam into a tree. A moment later, its engine compartment ignited. A volunteer fire fighter, Fishman immediately ran down the highway and offered assistance to the two elderly passengers in the rear seat of the burning car. Fishman also forced open the front door to remove the unconscious driver and his wife and brother-in-law who had apparently been drinking and was completely incoherent. As Fishman was dragging the last victim away from the vehicle, the engine compartment, almost fully engulfed in smoke, burst into flames and the car exploded. Thanks to Fishman, who risked his life, all passengers survived. But there was still more. As he was driving away from the accident scene Fishman noticed something funny. He offered his help to a police deputy who jumped into his truck. The deputy instructed Fishman to drive past a convict who had just escaped from the local penitentiary. This allowed the deputy to pass the escaped prisoner unseen and then jump off the FedEx truck, block the prisoner's route and take the escapee back into custody.

For his heroic actions, Fishman was named the 2002 FedEx North American Highway Hero—the shipping industry's most prestigious award for heroism. 'This isn't something that you think about,' Fishman said of the rescue. 'It's something that you react to. You just see a bad situation like that, and you do what you think needs to be done. I was just one lucky dude, in the right place at the right time.'

When asked for his reaction by a local news reporter Fishman added, 'I started here part-time to earn extra Christmas money. I thank god every day for giving me the opportunity to work at FedEx. I love this company and would not work anywhere else.'"

***

As Fishman visualized himself in these heroic postures he

could not help but entertaining a compelling, inescapable thought: "FedEx, what a great place to work."

Chapter 6

The idea of having a calling is strange but not easily refused when you are asked to serve the highest power. And that is what has happened to Fishman. Amidst all his interest in FedEx and Palefsky, Fishman started to hear voices. These were not drug induced or the "you-must be-out-of-your-mind" variety but rather, specific statements delivered randomly by ATT wireless and Verizon.

Fishman's cell phone rings and he receives a recorded message, like the kind you get from Walgreens or Duane Reade when your order is ready, an innocuous, friendly voice; caring, solicitous. You know the type: "Your Zantac is ready. Please pick it up at your convenience."

Or "We are calling to inform you that your photographs are now developed and ready for pick up. Please come by or call for further assistance."

Or "And thy seed shall be as the dust of the earth; and thou shalt spread abroad to the west, and to the east, and to the north, and to the south: and in thee and in thy seed shall all the families of the earth be blessed, Genesis 28."

The first time Fishman received this sort of message he thought it was a joke. He had no strong religious convictions and possessed little interest in making contact with the Prime Mover. Fishman had spent years working with Norbert Cadell, arguably the most influential American psychotherapist of the twentieth century who had come to believe that religion was perpetuated by "irrational men who were out of their fucking minds."

Cadell was the founder of Rational Abstract Therapy or RAT and the author of more than seventy books including "The Case for a Rational Life: My Way or the Highway" and "Hillary: My First Great Heterosexual Love." Cadell believed God had little to do "with the price of spinach" and the fact that people believed in him just showed "how stupid they really are." He believed this observation applied to devout Moslems, Christians and Jews as well as to Hindus, Buddhists, Mormons, Sikhs, Pagans, followers of Shinto, practitioners of tribal beliefs, and other religions. Cadell harbored no resentment towards the religious and saw their pattern of observance as part of the sad fallibility of the human condition. "It is too damned bad that people need this kind of psychological crutch" he would say but always add, "Fuck it—it's not the end of the world." But he also insisted that it was important to confront irrationality in all its forms and manifestations.

When he was a teenager, Cadell, a Catholic and ever the practical joker, would enter the confessional assuming various guises. He would show up as a serial killer, transvestite, polygamist, even a politician. Once he confessed to the priest that he suffered from a penis that stayed hard for hours and hours at a stretch and could only find relief by watching television fourteen hours a day, eating Cheetos and compulsively masturbating. Cadell delighted in asking prelates, "Padre, what can God do for someone like me?"

Fishman had a different perspective. His is a more "live and let live" philosophy. He had no interest in confronting other people's irrationality. In fact, he found their fantasies and associations surrounding religion, however strange, interesting. Not that he disagreed entirely with Cadell's point of view either but he had a more generous appreciation for the wide range of human expressions and was more accepting.

Fishman was raised as an Orthodox Jew and that more than anything else explains his complete attraction to secularism. His

The Next Step

early education was spent in a religious grammar school that was segregated; boys on one side of the room and girls on the other. The day was also split in half: Hebrew studies in the morning and secular classes after lunch. His teachers were a Mel Brooks cast of characters that would have made Hollywood audiences howl.

Fishman's first grade teacher was Mrs. Carney, a tall no-nonsense woman who maintained discipline at the end of a ruler. She was the wife of a rabbi with an Irish last name, who suffered from chronic gastro-intestinal infections. She farted loudly whenever she sneezed or coughed. Because of her numerous allergies, this was quite often.

His fourth grade teacher was a Rabbi Poopko, a serious looking man in three-piece suits who wore rimless glasses but was otherwise unremarkable except that he taught Jewish history simultaneously impersonating the "Hunchback of Notre Dame." Stoop shouldered with his face contorted into a Picasso twist of mouth and nose, he skulked around the circumference of the classroom like Quasimodo, dragging a slow, heavy right foot across the hardwood floor for no apparent reason.

And then there was his sixth grade teacher, Mr. Myefsky. Mr. Myefsky brought a rare genius to his classroom. He was the kind of individual whose pedagogy and viewpoints fall outside the bounds of the politically correct world that we now live in. For the year that he taught Fishman, every day he wore the same lime green shirt, blue tie, gray pants, argyle socks and scuffed brown shoes. He had strong opinions, often on controversial, far reaching topics, frequently on issues that were outside his ken: strippers, nuns, homosexuals, dancing before marriage, and pet snakes. He also had an unusual physical disability, a constant dribble due to a severe case of Bell's palsy contracted when he was younger. It required him to speak with a constant handkerchief in his right hand. He was not a graceful man and his habit of chain smoking necessitated a comic juggling of props-cigarettes and hankies- punctuated by rivulets of runaway spittle.

There was also a more sympathetic teacher. Fishman's favorite was his advisor, Mrs. Elias. She was a short strong-willed woman, with long black hair and dark eyes. She had a warm laugh and spoke in a heavily accented voice. She confided in Fishman that she did not believe in God. How could she? Her husband and daughter were killed in the war, victims of Hitler's camps. Hannah Elias was her town's sole survivor. There were defined, black numbers, like a bar code, burnt into her arm. It reminded Fishman of the USDA stamp on raw meat. "How can you believe in a God like that?"

Long ago the synagogue also occupied an important role in Fishman's life. He was descended from Talmudic scholars. One of his earliest memories was of men and women calling on his grandfather for counsel. Often they were agitated, anguished, in need of words of wisdom or practical advice.

In the synagogue his family was highly respected, their name well-known. In Europe pilgrims traveled for miles to visit his great grandfather. He was called a Tzadik, a pious one, a saintly man, a Jewish version of St. Francis: kindhearted, generous, forgiving.

But Fishman knows that religion—all religion—can be a very ugly thing. That no matter what the orthodoxy, however high minded its doctrines concerning God, the universe and man; its morality for the individual and society, its regimens of rites, customs and ceremonies, its body of laws, its sacred literature and institutions. In the end it is still impossible to disentangle religion's avowed nobility from its putrid historical past and murderous fanatical present.

"There is no end to the heinous acts and intrigues of the true believer," Fishman concludes.

The twin towers explode. In their wake lay over three thou-

The Next Step

sand corpses. And men and women holding sacred texts pray joyfully.

"Thank God. Praised be his Name."

***

Fishman's cell phone rings. Because he has been receiving a series of weird messages he first checks his caller ID but oddly none appears. When he takes the call Fishman immediately recognizes the computer generated voice. Both the tone and its cadence are artificial:

"He shall build a house for my name, and I will establish the throne of his kingdom for ever. I will be his father, and he shall be my son. 2 Samuel 7"

Fishman is annoyed. "Who in God's name is wasting my time?"

But he is also intrigued. He wants to know what is behind all of this. Fishman's thoughts turn back to Palefsky and the Chronicle. He thinks about Palefsky's search for meaning in his life and the power of his story. He then reminds himself of a totally different kind of story. One that he remembers from his first days at Sunday school. A biblical story, a patriarchal story: the one about Abraham.

Over four thousand years ago a man named Terah lived in the ancient city of Ur in the land of Chaldea. Like the rest of the people, Terah was an idol worshipper. He was also an idol maker. He fashioned images out of clay and stone and then sold them to his people. His three sons, Abraham, Nahor and Haran were shepherds in the fertile pasturelands surrounding the Euphrates Valley and sometimes assisted Terah with the production of his statues.

With much time on his hands for thought, Abraham began to think it strange to kneel and pray to stone images; especially idols that he had just constructed with his very own hands. He asked himself, "What possible power or holiness can be contained in these idols that men make out of stone and clay?"

Abraham could find no answer to his question. And his question raised further questions that dared not be raised, because to doubt the deity of idols was considered a crime punishable by death. Abraham came up with an idea. One day when he was left alone in his father's yard, he smashed all the idols except for one. And into that one's hand he placed an axe.

When his father saw the destroyed statues he was furious.

"Why did you do this?" he demanded of his son.

"It wasn't I, Father," Abraham replied. "The idol with the axe in his hand did it."

"That is not true." Terah shouted. "You know these idols cannot move!"

"If this is true," said Abraham, "they have eyes but cannot see, ears but cannot hear, arms but cannot touch, and legs but cannot move; then surely they are good for nothing. And that is why I broke them."

"Idols should not be worshipped."

Fishman imagined himself axe in hand, Don Quixote-like wielding his weapon against the false gods. He could see and hear the wreckage of clay and stone. His body reeled from the power he generated in his arms and in his legs. He felt energized but the excitement did not derive as much from the destruction as it did from the authority to start a new. The inertia of all these months was dissipating. He heard Terah's question and Abraham's response.

"What then should be worshipped?"

"Worship the gods that made the sun and the moon and the stars; worship the gods that bring each season in season, and that give us rain, and that make the fields rich with pasture, and the sheep heavy with lambs."

Fishman could now see himself like Abraham of old compelled to leave the land of the idol worshippers. It was no longer safe to remain in the place where he had dwelled. Now there was only crossing over and moving on. Fishman was at the start of a long uncertain journey. He sensed a wild river in the distance and a ferry to a mythic realm and a destiny that had not yet been revealed to him.

Chapter 7

Often a great idea begins with fuzzy logic. The most important direction a life will take starts out as pure chance. Fishman, Palefsky, FedEx and God, now ask yourself, what are the chances?

It all began slowly but ended up like a perfect storm. For two years Fishman suffered an unrelenting paralysis, a self-inflicted lethargy of the soul brought on by shame and the fear of personal failure. But despite his feelings of humiliation and disgrace or because of them, Fishman ached for a mission in his life. And then he found The Palefsky Chronicle and read about FedEx in the Times. And, mirabile dictu, tectonic plates began to shift.

Fishman recognized that deep within his unconscious irreversible forces were at work. Slowly but surely he was undergoing the inevitable chemistry of reinvention. Palefsky was a catalyst, a means to stimulate change, an instrument to discover through someone else's story all that was lacking in his and all that his strived to be. Fishman was confident that was the meaning embedded in his dream about Abbot and Costello. Who was on first? Palefsky. Who was on second? Palefsky. He also played short stop and third base and most of the other positions. But who was pitching? Fishman and there was unquestionably no argument about that! Palefsky would catch but it was up to Fishman to throw.

Fishman would hurl his message near and far like a Cy Young winner, like a Roger Clemens, a Hall of Famer, up on the mound. Fishman was beginning to see his life again, for the first time, like the lines in the T.S. Eliot poem:

> *And the end of all our exploring*
> *will be to arrive where we started*
> *and know the place for the first time.*

And FedEx would be Fishman's vehicle— as crazy as that sounded.

"Am I insane?" he wondered to himself but then immediately rejected the thought.

There was no time to waste on self-limiting beliefs. What Fishman needed to do was generate a plan and take action. He was certain that the world only changed because of men and women who were up to the challenges of assuming great risk. There were just too many people who played it safe. Fishman knew the world was built by the daring and courageous, wildcatters, speculators; individuals who were not afraid to take chances and occasionally just flew by the flaming seats of their pants. Waxen wings became metal. Men had taken themselves to the moon. But still had trouble with daily life, the common cold of existence.

Fishman remembered going to the circus as a child, watching a man being shot out of a cannon. He recalled that was something he wanted to do when he grew up. Maybe even go over Niagara in a barrel. Breathless moments filled with risk with only the slimmest expectation of exceptional reward for daredevils and adventurers. Doing what few attempted and succeeding. His father had said find something you want to do and then do it better than anyone else.

Fishman would not allow himself to be prudent in this moment. He was too enthralled by the delirium of contemplating the lunacy of reckless behavior. After all, there was so much insanity already in the world that passed for normal. Fishman reminded himself of the craziness witnessed all of the time, everywhere. He suddenly had a funny thought: Twenty-four hours a day, seven days a week, somewhere in the world, right now, two fat bald men with moustaches are making love.

Fishman felt that there was a crucial message that needed to be delivered and he was the one to do it. And if it was going international, it had to be FedEx.

Like the ancient prophets, itinerants who descended from the hills of Judea to the market places and to the temple, Fishman viewed himself as a flawed but enlightened outsider who understood the real meaning of righteousness and truth and it fell upon him to destroy the false idols and get the word out.

The prophets were history's diviners. Wherever they could find an audience they spoke their minds, warning the people to reform their evil ways. The king looked after the laws of the land; the priests attended to the laws of the temple but the prophets taught the principles of mercy, morality, and justice.

It is a strange irony that someone like Fishman could be inspired to teach people in the ways of the Lord. Of course he was no bible thumping, charity hoarding, holy water splashing, gospel preaching phony, and he'd never be one. Let it be a matter of record: Fishman resisted hearing the voice of the Prophets and then one day he listened and changed his life forever. Listening is underrated.

Fishman's cell phone rings. He lets it go to voice mail. He doesn't want to be disturbed; especially by another one of those loony religious ads.

He is at home alone, reading the paper, engrossed in an article about the Madrid train bombings. He reads in horror about the attacks that killed over two hundred on four packed commuter trains. Reports of human flesh raining down on passengers, limbs severed from torsos and the unanswered phones of the dead still ringing. There are stories about the progress in the war in Iraq, a Taiwanese political leader who survived an assassination attack on the eve of a national election, more NATO troops to arrive in Kosovo with more to come, and Pakistan's intensified assault in its hunt for Al Qaeda and the elusive Osama. There is also an article about a fifteen year-old Palestinian suicide bomber and another one about the police in Washington D.C. closing down schools after an Internet threat referencing the Columbine massacre anniversary.

As Fishman's eyes move down the page he reads with considerable interest an exposé of a religious cult operating on Chicago's west side. It is told through the personal story of a successful Palatine businessman, Ross Irwin Le Hood, the owner and founder of Cheeky's Chicken with over one hundred fast food franchises in Saskatchewan, Alberta and the Midwest. The article is titled "Acts of Faith Wreak Havoc for Suburban Family."

The Le Hoods were described as the kind of people who are most susceptible to the ploys and practices used by the new cults, in particular groups like "The United Dravidians of Christ," of which they were members: men and women who are approaching middle age in search of spirituality or a just a quick way to make sense of their lives before it's too late.

At forty-two, Ross is an energetic 6'4 former Delta Force sergeant who was an all-state halfback in high school and still possesses clean shaven, strong-jawed, boyish good looks. He is originally from Munsey, Indiana. His wife Sharon, 40, a tall Sybil Shepard like blonde is his grade school sweetheart and a former Miss Munsey runner-up and homecoming queen. She is in public relations. They have two children, a son, Reed, 17, and a daughter, Dotty, 15.

For many years the Le Hoods were members of the United Methodist Church. They found the church's approach to religion expressed the spiritual beliefs of the majority of society and was well suited to their active, suburban life style. One might say, it went with their carpeting.

"We kind of liked the whole look and feel of the Methodists;

we were raised in it. They are our kind of people," explained Mr. Le Hood.

The Le Hoods enjoyed being part of the religious mainstream and showed little interest in participating in a different church or becoming involved in what they considered then to be divergent or exotic practices. Something akin to kinky sex. The very notion of the Le Hoods being attracted to the concept of personal resurrection through special acts of faith or falling under the charismatic sway of someone like Minister Pogo, to use Ross's words, was "just plain ludicrous."

He elaborates, "You have to understand we didn't care too much about things like God and religion. I mean, not in any kind of deep sense. We were mainstream. We thought that Jehovah's Witnesses, Christian Scientists and Mormons were freaks. What did we know? Who thinks about stuff like personal redemption? Well, we sure didn't. I guess that is why we got snookered and lost everything. It's like getting lost at Walmart."

Sharon Le Hood tries to explain. "It was just after 9/11 and the chicken business was going to shit. You could always count on chicken. Ross had overextended himself and we were facing, for the first time in our marriage, financial problems. It didn't help that I started drinking again and that Ross was having an affair with one of his bimbo secretaries. It was just around then that Reed came out and introduced us to his partner Pedro Alejandro, a vegetarian. If that wasn't enough, we discovered that Dotty was using Ex and pole-dancing when we thought she was at the library. It was a trying time and we were all searching for answers."

Mr. Le Hood began receiving religious cell phone messages. Initially he thought it was part of his Cingular wireless anytime bonus extra minute package or a favored customer upgrade.

"At first, I didn't mind a bit. I thought it was kind of inspirational. I'll never forget the first one. It was some of my favorite verses that I used to recite in Sunday school:

'Blessed are the poor in spirit: for theirs is the Kingdom of

Heaven.'

'Blessed are the meek: for they shall inherit the earth.'

'Blessed are they, which do hunger and thirst after righteousness, for they shall be filled.'"

But after awhile he did find them annoying. "You know, once they started they didn't stop and then they became more frequent. Towards the end there I was getting them three, four times a day. I'd be in a board meeting or in a line at the airport and the damn phone would ring. I swear this is a true story, once I was in the stall in the men's room trying to do my business, constipated, and my cell starts ringing. It was them! And you know what the message was? 'Ask, and it shall be given you; seek and ye shall find; knock, and it shall be opened to you. For everyone that asketh receiveth; and he that seeketh findeth; and to him that knocketh it shall be opened.' That really cracked me up. It worked too. The next time they called there was a call back number and I said, 'Tell me about yourselves, I'm all ears.'"

That's how it happened. Within six months the Le Hoods were stepping into the entryway of a rundown brownstone behind the United Center on the blighted West Side. They passed the "Captain of the Gate" offering up the secret handshake followed by the accompanying password. Their heads were shaven and they wore flowing purple robes topped by a hood and blindfold. They complied to each request and ritual with excited expectation, eager to join the ranks of the faithful. They were then led down a corridor that ended at a door, which opened into a candlelit chamber where the rest of the church's members had gathered. The Le Hoods took their vows amidst the aroma of incense burning in The Dravidian Sanctuary at the base of the holy altar.

Gladly, Ross Le Hood offered Minister Pogo all his worldly possessions for the simple promise of being part of the church's end time prophesy. In exchange, he would have self-realization and eternal life. What more could anyone want? It seemed like a no-brainer.

The Next Step

***

Fishman looks around his living room. Many objects titillate his eye. Nadia's paintings and a small sculpture of a horse, an African mask in the shape of a bird, and a small drawing his son had made when he was in kindergarten. It is a brown boat on a white background with three irregular masts, drawn in red. It sails on loops of cool water under a clear blue sky.

Fishman stands and then walks over to an open window. He likes the feel of the cool breeze against his warm face. He watches a black bird soaring, now lighting on the top of St. Michael's cross.

He thinks to himself: "Wherever you look there are ships in distress, S.O.S. signals hurtling through the air. All around us the world is crying out for help."

Fishman's cell phone rings.

Chapter 8

In the beginning Fishman created the heavens and the earth. The earth was without form and void, and darkness was upon the face of the deep; and the Spirit of Fishman was moving over the face of the waters. And Fishman said, "Let there be light," and there was light. And Fishman saw that the light was good; and He separated the light from the darkness. Fishman called the light day and the darkness He called night. And there was evening and there was morning, one day.

And Fishman said, "Let there be a firmament in the midst of the waters, and let it separate the waters from the waters." And Fishman made the firmament and separated the waters that were under the firmament from the waters that were above the firmament. And it was so. And Fishman called the firmament Heaven. And there was evening and there was morning, a second day.

And Fishman said, "Let the waters under the heavens be gathered together into one place, and let the dry land appear." And it was so. He called the dry land Earth, and the waters that were gathered together He called Seas. And Fishman saw that it was good. And Fishman said, "Let the earth put forth vegetation, plants yielding seed, and fruit trees bearing fruit in which is their seed, each according to its kind, upon the earth." And it was so. The earth brought forth vegetation, plants yielding seed according to their own kinds, and trees bearing fruit in which is their seed, each according to its kind.

And Fishman saw that it was good. And there was evening and there was morning, a third day.

And Fishman said, "Let there be lights in the firmament of the heavens to separate the day from the night; and let them be for signs and for seasons and for days and years, and let them be lights in the firmament of the heavens to give light upon the earth." And it was so. And Fishman made the two great lights, the greater light to rule the day, and the lesser light to rule the night; He made the stars also. And He set them in the firmament of the heavens to give light upon the earth, to rule over the day and over the night, and to separate the light from the darkness. And Fishman saw that it was good. And there was evening and there was morning, a fourth day.

And Fishman said, "Let the waters bring forth swarms of living creatures, and let birds fly above the earth across the firmament of the heavens." So He created the great sea monsters and every living creature that moves, with which the waters swarm, according to their kinds, and every winged bird according to its kind. And Fishman saw that it was good. And He blessed them, saying, "Be fruitful and multiply and fill the waters in the seas, and let birds multiply on the earth." And there was evening and there was morning, a fifth day.

And Fishman said, "Let the earth bring forth living creatures according to their kinds: cattle and creeping things and beasts of the earth according to their kinds." And it was so. And He made the beasts of the earth according to their kinds and the cattle according to their kinds, and everything that creeps upon the ground according to its kind. And Fishman saw that it was good.

Then Fishman said, "Let us make man in our image, after our likeness; and let them have dominion over the fish of the sea, and over the birds of the air, and over the cattle, and over all the earth, and over every creeping thing that creeps upon the earth." So Fishman created Himself in His own image, in the image of God He created Him; male and female He created them. And Fishman blessed them, and He said to them, "Be fruitful and multiply, and fill the earth and subdue it; and have dominion over the fish of the sea and over the birds of the air and over every living thing that moves upon the earth."

And He said, "Behold, I have given you every plant yielding seed that is upon the face of all the earth, and every tree with seed in its fruit; you shall have them for food. And to every beast of the earth, and to every bird of the air, and to everything that creeps on the earth, everything that has the breath of life, I have given every green plant for food." And it was so. And Fishman saw everything that He had made, and behold, it was very good. And there was evening and there was morning, a sixth day.

Thus the heavens and the earth were finished, and all the host of them. And on the seventh day Fishman finished his work, and He rested on the seventh day from all that He had done. So He blessed the seventh day and hallowed it, because on it Fishman rested.

***

Not a week goes by that Fishman doesn't marvel at his wondrous creation. From his perspective it is the genesis of all that is good and why he was chosen to fill the human soul. It is why he awakes energized early each morning six days a week, rain or shine to fulfill his FedEx calling. He knows only he, Fishman, understands how terribly messed up the world has become and it is upon him to set things right.

As Fishman climbs the stairs from his locker he smoothes out the wrinkles in his pants. In two minutes he will unlock the front door and his day at FedEx will begin. He knows that no one at FedEx could believe that the far range of business solutions and smooth level of customer service is all due to his behind-the-scenes, low-key, never micro-manage philosophy of leadership, no easy task since the acquisition of Kinko's. But that's another story.

Fishman just tries to keep it simple. "There's more to it than packages. It's about people," is the way he puts it.

Of course to those not in the know, Fishman looks exactly like a front of the house package handler, low man on the totem pole, a rank and file hourly wage earner. But needless to say, he would tell you, they just don't get it. Running the company is an enormous undertaking but pulling it off incognito, under the corporate radar, like a C.E.O. stealth bomber; now that takes genuine talent. To begin with there are over two-hundred thousand people who work at FedEx at everything from administrative support to aviation management to vehicle technicians to finance and accounting. And there are more than five thousand locations in one-hundred and twenty countries serving a billion customers each year. FedEx is digitally connected to the whole world. It has changed the rules of document outsourcing and nobody understands that better than Fishman.

Fishman lives to manage the power of messaging. He exults at the miracle of high-speed wireless access and the hundreds of millions of electronic transactions that "get to the right place, at the right time, every business day."

Fishman tells himself, **"In the beginning was the word and the word was with Fishman and the word was Fishman."**

Chapter 9

At first glance, Fishman's manner with customers seems a bit unnatural, out of the ordinary. He is formal yet, at the same time, strangely intimate. He tries to exhibit the best principles of customer service while simultaneously reconnecting with the primary source of energy in the universe. He has the ability to conceive of all human interactions in earlier and more fundamental forms.

Fishman can visualize on the protoplasmic level a Chicago mother's urgent desire to send her college-age daughter in Boston a needed pair of flannel pajamas. He perceives mother and daughter as complex semi-fluid substances; the physical basis of life itself, having the power of spontaneous motion and reproduction, the essential matter of all vegetable and animal cells. Each exchange is a microscopic dance of molecules and atoms; the cavorting of protons, electrons and neutrons. Sub-atomic horseplay.

Fishman believes that there needs to be more to customer service than merely understanding the customer. He goes beyond providing consistent, accurate and understandable information. Yes, he values his customer but that is not his point. It is not enough to just ask, listen, consider, and conclude. It is insufficient to simply provide a single point of contact to answer questions or to come up with timely responses or affect the accessibility of staff. Fishman knows that the most salient and obvious manifestation of existence is the miracle of automatic movement exhibited by living protoplasm. It is the one thing that unites us all and has motivated Fishman to offer the best customer service in the world.

Fishman delights in the fact that all wade in the same colloidal pool. Like primordial ooze, slick, grayish, semi-transparent, viscous. It is the physical and material basis of life. This was Fishman's great realization when sucking on a piece of Vosges chocolate. It came to him in a cocoa-intensified instant: we are stuck together as brothers and sisters, mothers and fathers, sons and daughters. All are united in a gooey matrix. Human life was conceived in the same ancestral pool of yeasty starter, unformed and void. In it we are caught up, slogging along, but within us is the capacity to assimilate and expand, building us in ever more inventive and complex ways. Fishman recognized that we create ourselves, radiating energy in the form of love and heat and electrical phenomena. He was certain that he found the true and undeniable secret of priority mail. It was at the very vortex of consciousness and technology. Teleporting his messages like a human fax machine "absolutely, positively wherever it takes", a portal through which protoplasm moves and reconstitutes itself at digital speeds; and it could be done over phone lines or the Internet, with or without a modem.

Fishman couldn't understand why no one else had thought of it; but then again no one else had created Fishman in just seven days.

***

Ever since the world began people were challenged by the idea of moving faster and further; traveling to a desired destination. The wagon, bicycle, airplane, rocket, even the Hyundai were all invented to speed up the time it takes to get from here to there. But inherent in transportation is a critical obstacle: physical distance, borders; boundaries to be crossed. For years science fiction writers have toyed with the notion of teleporting humans. They fantasize about making an object or person disintegrate in one place and reappear as a perfect instant replica somewhere else.

The Next Step 89

This they accomplish by scanning the original, extracting all his information then transmitting him, reproducing and arranging the atoms exactly in the same order and pattern, to another location.

Of course, Fishman recognized this had been achieved for real, with two dimensional objects, by the invention of the Fax machine.

(Fishman received a Fax earlier in the day from his State Farm insurance agent, Yossi Katz, informing him that he was late with his quarterly installment. He also suggested that now that Fishman would be traveling he should consider raising his coverage, fine tuning his comprehensive and collision deductibles).

But with humans the real challenge was to produce an exact replica, the person himself, rather than approximating a mere facsimile. From the viewpoint of science, genuine teleportation was an impossibility. It challenged a fundamental scientific theory, the Heisenberg Uncertainty Principle. Heisenberg stated with certainty that there is a problem transmitting particles larger than a photon. Even the Caltech physicists who came up with the theory of Entanglement based on a partially understood scientific effect known as Einstein-Podolsky-Rosen (EPR) couldn't make it work. Had they succeeded, it would have been a Nobel.

What these and other scientists discovered was an all too apparent shortcoming: transmitting sub-atomic particles isn't nearly as difficult as teleporting objects the size of George Foreman or Muhammad Ali. It seems so obvious.

It is amazing then that someone like Fishman, who could not even a hang a picture or change a flat should succeed so easily and elegantly in uncovering the secret of teleporting living things. And it came to him, so simply, in a flash. A sudden spark of insight, a burst of lightening. An explosion of inner light.

There are times in life when civilizations move forward for no obvious reason. Great inventions come into being by sudden happenstance. There is the pretzel and penicillin and a dish washer named Sanders who was to Southern fried chicken what

Ford had been to the car. And then there was Fishman.

The key to Fishman's genius did not lay in quantum mechanics or apprehending the subtle effects of facsimile transmission. His serendipity was the created intersection of imagination and accident. Fishman's solution was intuitive rather than scientific: unconscious, subjective, timeless. It was the full expression of the right hemisphere of the brain. Fishman's breakthrough was also a product of his dreams and his visions; déjà vu. There was also the power of coincidence, what some called synchronicity. It defied rational thought and Euclidian logic. It was the universe reaching out and revealing itself to Fishman, instigating its challenge: do something to make the world a better place.

The vaudeville flower pot encountering the top of his head.

***

Fishman stands at the FedEx counter waiting for the arrival of a new customer.

"Who will it be?" he asks himself.

"And what is next?"

Fishman knows each encounter is filled with endless potential. You never know who is coming in and where it is going to. It could be anything from wheel stems to passports to automobile batteries to an artificial heart. For Fishman part of the great excitement about working at FedEx is listening to what people wish for and then, like magic, helping make it come true.

The first customer of the day approaches. She is in her midthirties, short, a little overweight with a jolly, self-deprecating disposition. Maybe a too friendly manner belying her personal, day-to-day battle with insecurity and anxiety.

Fishman thinks to himself, "She could be on Prozac or Zoloft."

She is just trying too hard to keep it all together, not a single hair out of place. She has that familiar look of "I'm going to look happy even if it kills me." She has perky features: sparkling blue eyes, short blonde hair, a pug nose and wide, tight lips stretched into a studied smile. She is wearing black slacks and an open navy pea coat over a red floral blouse, a silken Tuileries of her very own. She is straight out of the catalogue pages of Banana Republic or J Crew, a devotee of the legion of the non-offending, conforming, safely dressed. She is holding a document envelope, nervously tapping it against the counter. She doesn't make eye contact with Fishman.

"Hi, I'm really in a rush, can you help me?"

Fishman's body language and demeanor says, "At your service, ready to go."

But he resists saying what is really on his mind: that he is a student of Jungian psychology, familiar with the phenomena of coincidence and synchronicity. Fishman knows intuitively that the two of them have not been brought together this morning by mere chance. He would also like to tell her that he believes their every moment together contains luminous opportunity. Protoplasmic entities are colliding at work or at play. And that everywhere the universe is radiating its meaning: we are all of the same source, interconnected, in the flaring haze.

But what Fishman tells her is quite different. "Nice shirt. Beautiful smile. Thank you for choosing FedEx today."

Fishman waits for her to acknowledge the compliment. He makes sure their eyes connect. He takes the envelope, hands her a receipt, and watches her reflection fade through the door. Momentarily lost in reverie, he carefully places the package on the conveyor belt behind him. It is the captured instant of eyes subtly locking and shared smiles that Fishman lives for. Something deeply human occurs suddenly, then vanishes like a lost memory or a half remembered story, a faded photo, the quick-silver passing of time. Pure Proust.

He is brought back by the demanding voice of a black man at the counter.

"Can I get some service? What's with you people?"

At the same time Fishman's boss, Sharath Mukitimukiti walks up from behind and informs him he would like to speak with him as soon as he is finished taking care of this customer. His tone is audible, patronizing, and unfriendly.

Mukitimukiti is in his early thirties and ambitious. He is five-six with dark hair, dark skin and dark eyes. He is lean and athletic and always impeccably dressed in cheap suits, bad ties and day-old white shirts with rings around the collar. He holds black belts in several martial arts: Judo, Tai Kwan Do, and Jujitsu, and he has his eyes set on becoming district manager before he reaches thirty-five. In the three-man operation, he makes sure that it is known that he runs the show. Often, he is in the back room practicing his fighting moves and positions. He is officious, self-absorbed. He finds Fishman to be a very odd sort of person. Not at all up to his standards and Fishman's charm is not working on him. Mukitimukiti doesn't appreciate Fishman's approach with the customers. He is of a get'em in and get'em out, fill 'em and bill'em philosophy, with no interest at all in protoplasmic possibilities. His favorite word is r-rrevenue. He does everything he knows to try to get more of it.

Fishman turns his neck and nods at Sharath's request and now focuses his attention solely on the disgruntled customer. He is an older man. It would certainly not be incorrect to refer to him as a gentleman. Maybe he is in his late sixties or early seventies. He is wearing a perfectly pressed brown suit, blue shirt, red and green striped tie. His shoes shine like freshly polished nails. He could be a retired school teacher or minister, the type that speaks convincingly in constructed sentences about fire and brimstone as if describing a resort you don't want to visit, or the importance of decimals.

Fishman visualizes him sermonizing on adultery and fornication with the sounds of tambourines and organ chords in the background. There is also a choir and bawdy shouts of "Amen."

Occasionally his words reach down to the souls of his feet and he dances for a moment or two before he returns to reprimanding the congregants. Fishman sees it as a top forty music video.

Fishman likes his face. It is a thoughtful, lived-through-a-lot-and here-to-talk-about-it sort of face. Penetrating eyes, strong wide nose and a mouth that is unafraid to say what's on his mind.

"Can I help you sir?" Fishman asks in his most polite tone.

"Can you help me? Obviously not or I wouldn't be here."

Fishman really working now to find the source of the problem, "Sir, what were you sending and where was it going?"

"I was sending my grandson his birthday present. It was supposed to arrive in Los Angeles. And you made sure it got shipped straight to hell. Who knows where it is?"

"Your name, sir?"

"Tibbins, Reverend Reginald A. Tibbins, Jr."

Fishman takes his tracking number and checks the computer. While he taps away on his keyboard he studies his customer's tense body language. He observes the stress in his forehead and the tightness of his jaw. The way his hands fidget with his keys. Fishman would like to but holds back from informing the reverend that it's his lucky day. He's got Fishman working on his problem and he will do absolutely, positively whatever it takes. Even teleporting himself like a human cannonball through inner space to make sure that his package is delivered to the right person at the right time at the right place.

But he doesn't reply this way.

Instead he just asks, "Mount Baptist Church, right?"

Impatient to find out what went wrong, Reverend Tibbins doesn't acknowledge Fishman's comment.

Still looking into his computer. Revelation.

"It's there. Delivered this morning. There were flash floods in L.A. Tuesday night."

"I didn't know that."

"How could you sir. The important thing is that . . ."

Fishman losing himself for an instant in the deep darkness of the reverend's eyes, waiting for him to fill in the blank.

"William."

"Yes, your grandson William has his present. A good, strong name. Kings and wise men."

"Thanks for your help. Sorry for coming on so strong."

"Glad we could help. Thanks for choosing FedEx."

A big smile breaks out on the Reverend Reginald A. Tibbins' face. "You are really something. What is your name?"

"Fishman."

"First name?"

"Just Fishman."

"I get it, like Picasso or Madonna." The Reverend breaks into laughter

"Yea, or Jesus or Moses, that kind of thing. Mind if I ask you a question?"

"Not at all, Fishman."

"You're a reverend and you advise people, right?"

"Yes, on occasion. Marriage, divorce, passing. Problems."

"Yes, that's what I mean. What do you think really makes a life worthwhile?"

"Now that's a good question. I have an answer."

Fishman listens intently.

"I know for sure it's not fornicating like all these young gang bangers but don't even get me started. And I'm not going to tell you money is the root of all evil or some other crap. It's the little things."

The reverend now holds his hands out, extending his fingers in front of Fishman.

"I get them manicured once a week. It's a small thing but when you talk at church it's important your hands look nice. God's hands. I get more pleasure from clean hands than driving a big Cadillac."

Fishman looks at his own hands, acknowledging his point.

The Next Step

He repeats the reverend's words as he leaves. "The little things."

While Fishman has been engaged in his Talmudic discourse, Sharath has been looking on disapprovingly. These long transactions take time and detract from making money, clogging up the revenue stream.

Sharath approaches Fishman. "Feeshman, vee nid to talk."

"Now? No one's here."

Sharath starts out matter of factly. "Do you tink dat you are too qualfyed?"

Fishman trying to be humorous. "Do you think it would be better if I were less qualified?"

Mukitimukiti, exhales audibly, scratches his head and starts over. "Vee hav a problem. Yu nid too be more aggressive. You nid to tink about rrrevenue. Yu spend too much time vit de custumers."

Fishman thinks to himself that if this were another time in another place, he would tell Mukitimukiti exactly where to get off. He can hear a much younger version of himself saying something like, "you greasy, money grubbing, revenue chasing, slime ball bouncing, thrift store dressing, self-important little twit."

He can visualize Sharath's stunned rage, an unhinged look in his eyes. He can also visualize the gleam of delight in his. He imagines a low blow response that he would then use to utterly eviscerate his adversary.

But Fishman does not stoop to this delicious strategy. Instead he says, "Sharath, I see your point from your perspective. Thank you for sharing your feedback with me."

This answer only makes Mukitimukiti more agitated.

"Feeshman, I don't think you understand. Eef tings don't change I'm going te hav to let yu go. It's not vorking out."

As Fishman listens intently a series of thoughts tumble around his brain like laundry in a dryer. The same phrase goes round and round: "not working out." He pictures a messenger on horseback arriving with a letter in hand, giving it to Beethoven. The letter reads:

> My dear Ludwig,
> The part of your Ninth Symphony that you refer to as the 'Ode to Joy" where a chorus suddenly breaks into song in your fourth movement; I must tell you with some regret, it's "not working out." I suggest toning it down.

He also imagines a committee of skeptics informing Jonas Salk after an oral presentation: "Dr. Salk, we are sorry to inform you that your proposed idea for a polio vaccine is 'not working out.'"

He can now hear the words announced at a sports stadium blared at ear piercing decibel levels "not working out."

Fishman can also picture the words in the shape of a knife sticking out from his chest. The words "not working out" floating on red billows dripping from his flesh.

But Fishman can also enjoy the irony and humor of the moment. He possesses the ability to rise above. A momentary gleam of madness is reflected in his eyes. Too subtle for Sharath to pick up on. He has made up his mind this very instant. He will make no change in his behavior; he will continue to work just like before, but harder; and all is going exactly as planned. Fishman knows there is no way to make everyone happy. And so he tells Mukitimukiti exactly what he wants to hear.

"Sharath, I'm *really* going to work at this job."

Of course Fishman would prefer to tell Mukitimukiti about the things that really make life worthwhile. The little things, like manicures, but he doesn't.

***

That evening Fishman arrives home late. Nadia is waiting for him at the door. She is wearing a Japanese robe made of cotton: grey and white petals on a black background, like stars twinkling in the night. She has a surprise for him. She has completed the painting that she has been working on for the last few months. It is a large canvas with two prominent male figures next to each other in a circus ring, amidst shadows of dark and light. One is seated and the other stands. The seated figure wears a leopard printed strong man's suit and is lifting a barbell. On one ball is a sparkling star and on the other is a sliver of a golden moon. He has a moustache and dark hair and heavy black boots. The standing figure is more genteel. He is wearing a white silk shirt, monogrammed CB, with black buttons, silk blue-grey pants, a scarf tied around his neck, a red cummerbund about his waist. He is clean shaven with blonde hair and black embroidered opera slippers, like velvet envelopes, on his feet. He holds a dark scalloped umbrella with a finial of half the moon above his head. To the left of the strongman are large, dark, square shaped weights. Each one has a year written on it in yellow. Next to the standing figure is a mysterious pile of gold and behind it a large brindled dog, like a mythological god, seated on a stool. It is dressed in a clown's collar and cone shaped hat, a fluffy red pom-pom on top.

Fishman stares at the painting then smiles at Nadia. "Are they me?"

"What do you think?" She's happy he likes it.

"Yeah. They *were* me alright, but not anymore."

"Were?"

"Before."

Fishman would like to think that he is not the same divided person pictured in the painting. He would also like to hear Nadia say, "Yes, I know."

Still, he enjoys looking at this rendering of himself. He understands that there are two strong sides to his personality: the muscleman who attacks any obstacle with sheer brawn and a more refined, even delicate nature that dissembles brute force with the subtle silkiness of a lyrical mind. He focuses for a moment on the collected weight of the passed years and the pile of gold still to be mined and lifted in the future.

And then there is the dog seated on a stool like a medieval gargoyle, impassively observing the occupations and preoccupations of man. A canine harlequin who seems to understand the frailties and frivolities of humankind. He is unmoved, almost disdainful of effort. Even holding the axis mundi of a celestial umbrella in the center ring doesn't faze his powerful stillness. Fishman studies the dog's mysterious almost comic features. He thinks to himself that it looks like it is half-dog and half-man. Suddenly he has a realization.

"I am the dog."

Fishman visualizes himself dressed as a clown, Fellini-like, propped up on a stool, observing the action in the center ring of the "Greatest Show on Earth." He can observe slapstick and pratfalls; a midget in a top hat on stilts, even the ever popular human cannonball. Fishman thinks to himself that he was once the two performers in the center of the ring, doing tricks, lifting weights, trying to control heaven and earth. But now he is firmly on the outer ring, behind the scenes; ready to act like a genie in a bottle, a magical incantation, a secret potion, a miraculous charm.

His heart beating quickly, Fishman turns to Nadia. He is ecstatic with his new discovery. He is shouting.

"I am the dog."

"I am the dog."

Nadia shines with delight. She hugs Fishman.

"Yes, I know."

Chapter 10

It is dawn. Still in bed, Fishman is awake. He enjoys an immense feeling of well-being. A soft light filters into the bedroom. Fishman studies the stained glass window in St. Michael's Church, across the alley. There is a red and blue robed Jesus flanked by green and grey disciples. His almost liquid form vibrates in the morning air.

Fishman thinks to himself that the image of Jesus is one of the most extraordinary creations in the whole of human history. Complete and convincing. Satisfying to both the mind and the eye. He reflects on the idea of the frail carpenter rabbi from Nazareth. It is an amusing thought. Fishman has known many rabbis but not one who could operate a clamp, cramp, vise, saw, drill, plane, or chisel.

He had an uncle who once tried to teach him the difference between a darby and a trowel as well as the finer distinctions of floats, ratchets, sacks and bolsters. But Fernando was only half-Jewish and definitely not rabbi material.

Fishman wondered why most Jews didn't appreciate the feel and craftsmanship of a well made staple gun nor protested strenuously to uphold the right to own one. It was just funny to think that Jesus knew the names of jigs, dovetails, screwdrivers, hammers and routers and no less, in Aramaic.

Fishman envisioned Jesus on a mountain, speaking to a great multitude, at the exact moment he spied his own image in the bureau mirror. He thought he detected a balding spot. Perhaps it was just the way he was sleeping. Playing with his long grey hair across his forehead, Fishman saw the mute speaking, the lame walking, the blind seeing and thousands giving praise to the glory of the lord.

Fishman feels in himself the clarity and confidence of what it feels like to be Christ. In his mind, he hears the prophecy from the Book of Isaiah: "For unto us a child is born, unto us a Son is given, and the government shall be upon His shoulder; and His name shall be called Wonderful, Counselor, the Mighty God, the Everlasting Father, the Prince of Peace."

Fishman watches a star traveling in the heavens resting above a shelter where a young child is born. He can see three wisemen presenting gifts of gold, frankincense and myrrh. He also feels a terrible storm, a great tempest at sea. There is a boat consumed by unrelenting waves. Fishman hears shouts in the distance, "Save us. We are perishing."

And a voice that rebukes wind and sea before a great calm is restored.

"Why are you fearful, O ye of little faith?"

***

Nadia is still sleeping. Fishman enjoys the warmth of her body beside his. He studies the hem of the blanket across her fair skin. He remembers making love to her. She is wearing a Dan mask that they had purchased at an auction house in Paris. The mask was jet black: a smooth oval face with a deeply cut groove below the chin. It's protruding lips parted under a short nose with drilled and incised nostrils. Large circular eyes keep watch beneath arched brows and a high rounded forehead. Nadia is sitting on top of Fishman. She is holding the primitive mask in her right hand covering, then revealing her face; balancing herself with her left hand, rising and falling in a tribal love dance, a ritualistic shifting of rhythms.

The Next Step

Fishman remembers another time he and Nadia made love. It was in Bergdorf Goodman, in a private fitting room in designer dresses. Nadia lifted her silk skirt, arching her back, watching Fishman entering her in a three-way mirror behind his back.

Fishman can see the first time they were together when Nadia was still living on Lexington Avenue over a Greek-owned drug store. She lived next to a former opera singer who suffered from an ear shattering tubercular cough. Fishman and Nadia sat on the floor listening to him sing a Wagnerian aria, "Dolce e calmo", a woman's part. They laughed wildly at the thought of the Valkyrie-riding tenor, hack coughing madly, cross-dressed in the horn-helmeted costume of a Germanic goddess. Fishman remembers what he wore that night. A plaid shirt and khaki trousers, a blue blazer and Frye boots. He remembers the way Nadia brought him into her bed, ran her fingers through his long hair, wrapped him in the warmth of her arms.

Fishman's thoughts suddenly return to Jesus. He is walking on water. Fishman knows that there are scholars who believe it was merely a trick. But he chooses to be a believer. He is sure that crossing the Galilee is not that different from teleporting a FedEx package. After all, it is only a matter of delivery, getting something or someone from here to there. Fishman thinks to himself that it is all pretty much the same sort of phenomenon. Prayer, miracles, instantaneous shipping. The challenge is to think outside the box. For too long miracles have been shrouded in a supernatural mystery. But if you really make an effort, you can understand them. It is obvious that they are just another part of life. Like the parting of the Red Sea or the tears of the Black Virgin or Lazarus rising from the dead.

Fishman is now about to take a shower. He studies his naked body in the full-length bathroom mirror. He still has the well-toned form of an athlete despite the fact that he rarely works out. He focuses on three large raised scars, like ruddy welts, keloids on his pale chest.

Fishman reminds himself of something he heard a radio minister say, "Those who search for signs will find them."

Chapter 11

Fishman can't help but believe that he lives in a time of miracles. Wherever he looks the world is flooded with signs. There are weeping icons and bleeding statues, crop circles and encounters with angels. There are reports of supernatural events from every country and culture imaginable, sacred apparitions witnessed by millions of human beings.

Fishman asks himself, "What in the world is going on?"

Years ago he read an article in Life Magazine, "Do You Believe in Miracles?" Fishman agreed with the author. There is a world-wide spiritual revival, and it is one of the great stories of our time.

Fishman wonders if UFOs are also a kind of miracle. The sheer volume of reports and sightings are just so numerous that the intention of the universe to reach out can not be mistaken.

Fishman has also read about the phenomenon of Crosses of Light. They began appearing in El Monte, California, in May 1988. They have since been seen in Canada, France, New Zealand and the Philippines. He reads about them on the Miracles Online website, a sort of digital "Popular Mechanic" for the spiritually inclined: "They appear fully-formed as holograms, usually in the frosted glass of bathroom windows. They radiate a golden, healing light and they have affected the lives of thousands who have come to witness them."

Fishman thinks about the image of Jesus he had witnessed, outside his window, across the alley in St. Michael's glowing in the light. He asks himself, "Was it a bona fide apparition?"

After all, Fishman could see his arms under the red robes vibrating, his staff jabbing up toward the sky then falling down. Perhaps he was waving to Fishman, sending him a sign. For a moment he can even recall Jesus saying, "Follow me, and I will make you a fisher of men."

On second thought, Fishman concludes it was more of a thought than an apparition and the voice that he heard came from within. But he also thinks he would have to give the matter greater consideration. When it comes to miracles, it's better to be certain. But on the other hand Fishman felt that whatever it was, he had experienced an encounter. There could be no doubt. The universe had chosen to connect with him.

***

Fishman knew that miracles presented themselves in many guises. A miracle could come in the form of a Jesus sighting, the birth of a white buffalo or the extraordinary milk-drinking Hindu statues, like the ones in Southhall Temple in London in 1995 where thousands had witnessed the miracle of the elephant-headed god Ganesh and Shiva, the destroyer, drinking gallons of milk by spoonfuls.

Although the cynics explained the inspired milk drinkers with theories of "mass hysteria" and "capillary absorption" the evidence was overwhelming. Something miraculous had happened.

The Daily Express wrote, "Most of the worshippers said they only showed up at the temple occasionally and were certainly not religious fanatics. But they were adamant that a new god, who was probably nursing on milk at this very moment, had been born to save the world from evil."

A religious leader at the temple offered his explanation. "All I know is that our Holy Book says that wherever evil prevails on earth then some great Soul will descend to remove the bondage of evil so that right shall reign. We believe this miracle, and those happening at other Hindu temples, may be a sign that a great Soul has descended, like Lord Krishna or Jesus Christ."

But when pressed about "why milk?" all he could say was, "We cannot be certain, but we do know it is high in protein, nutritious and good for you, even if you are a God, I think."

Fishman knew that the Hindu milk miracle was not an isolated event nor did it occur in a single place. From Calcutta to Canada, from Southhall to Singapore, millions of Hindus confirmed the experience.

A newspaper headline in New Delhi read: "India's Dairies Run Dry. All the Milk Gone to the Gods"

Even respected Western papers reported: "On Thursday, September 21, 1995, the news swept around the world of the extraordinary miracles of milk-drinking Hindu statues. Never before in history had a simultaneous milk-related miracle occurred on such a global scale. Television, radio and newspapers eagerly covered this unique phenomenon, and even skeptical journalists held their milk-filled spoons to the gods—and watched, humbled, as the milk disappeared."

There were other, more recent miracles too.

In September 2003, a Minnesota farmer, Wyle Guess, witnessed the image of Christ's face emerging from a stalk of wheat. It was at night and Mr. Guess saw a shaft of light illuminate his field. He watched astonished as the face of Jesus appeared from nowhere.

Mr. Guess who rarely attended church said: "Me and the boys had a few brewskeys. It was getting late. I was on my way back and it was just there. The big head of our saintly father. It didn't say a word or anything. I thought to myself 'Hallow be his Name'. About a week later he showed up again. This time I saw him on my TV while I was flipping channels. He said to me, 'Let the Lord show you the Way.'"

That same month the Iranian newspaper Akhbar reported that the image of Jesus was seen throughout Teheran on fences and in windows. Reuters quoted a local news service that stated the face appeared on the wall of a posh downtown Shiite Madrasa. Hundreds of people, Christians and Muslims alike, rushed to the building. The spontaneous healing of a paralyzed teenage girl was also reported.

Fishman had also heard of the many stories about angels. He had read somewhere that sixty-nine percent of Americans believed in them and thirty-two percent had reported a personal encounter. An angel could take part in a healing, provide practical advice, offer comfort and reassurance, or assuage a situation of anxiety or distress. Often they appeared to bring about a lifestyle change. An angel was like a special friend. There had been numerous TV shows, plays and movies about them.

One of the most famous encounters occurred to a Hewlett, Long Island schmatte executive. Arni Solomon was on his way home in his Lexus after cheating on his wife. After an evening of rough sex, Solomon, unexpectedly, experienced intense chest pains. With his last breath he phoned 911. The doctors informed Mrs. Solomon that her husband had suffered irreparable heart damage and there was nothing else they could do. The lawyers added that she would soon have the controlling interest in Kabala Fabrics. That evening a ten foot tall golden angel appeared at the side of Arni's bed. He swore he would change his ways, even promising not to take false deductions on his income tax. Soon after he made a miraculous recovery and formed The Mystic Travelers, a foundation dedicated to faith-based marital counseling.

Every night, Mrs. Solomon looks towards the heavens and says, "Thanks a lot."

Fishman had once read a story on the Internet told by the Evangelical Broadcasting Company of Holland. It takes place near a church in a Cairo slum where parishioners had experienced miraculous events. A five-ton block of stone fell from a construction site onto a woman out for a walk. It took forty men to remove the slab of rock before she was rushed to the local hospital. Aside from a few minor cuts and bruises, there were no serious injuries.

"It was God's healing power that saved me." She said.

Her doctors were incredulous. Dr. Mustafa Ibn Sadat, chief of medicine at Cairo's Mt. Sinai Hospital, exclaimed, "This poor wretched woman should be a paraplegic. Her vertebrae should be crushed. Her bones broken into bits and pieces. Her bodily functions shot. Science cannot explain it."

Fishman thought that all these stories and miraculous events, reports of entire villages being visited by "the man in white robes" added up to mounting evidence that such miracles were more numerous than one might suspect. And that they were simultaneously taking place around the world.

Fishman thought to himself "we are in the beginning stages of experiencing the true spirit and wonder of God."

Fishman knew you didn't have to be Christian to have a visitation by Jesus. He was also revealing to Muslims and Jews. He could appear to anyone at anytime, like a Freudian slip. Manifesting himself in meadows and forests; in suburbs, in the heart of the city, in the light and in the dark.

Fishman thought "Large numbers of people are experiencing the presence and power of the supernatural like me. The Soul of the Universe is sending forth signals in different guises to the poor and rich alike."

The evidence was irrefutable. Just the day before, Fishman saw a televised segment on Dateline about the miraculous aubergine. The Greensboro, South Carolina home of Salim and Hanana Khalidi has been visited by over three hundred people a day coming to pay homage to their sacred eggplant. Mrs. Khalidi foresaw the miracle in a vision before she bought the vegetable at her local Piggly Wiggly. On slicing it in half, she observed that the seeds formed the Muslim symbol "Ya-Allah", meaning God exists.

Mrs. Khalidi said, "I just felt so uplifted. It was wonderful. I felt so excited that I ran all the way to the mosque to see the Imam. He took it in his hands and studied it very carefully, squeezing it gently, smelling it for freshness. Then he confirmed that it was indeed a miracle."

After the eggplant has been on display for several months, it will be divided into small pieces and shared among the faithful.

And there were other examples.

There was the Senegalese miracle melon where the words "Praise be to God" were found written on its skin as it grew in the field. When it was opened an apparition of a smiling Mohamed appeared. The miracle was confirmed by the Islamic Institute of Dakar, the same religious body that verified the visitation of Allah last year seen on the scales of a fish.

There was also the miraculous potato that attracted thousands in northeast India and caused a week of looting and riots. These events were not restricted to former colonies.

In Manchester, England. Fiona Barker, thirty-two, a fish and chips worker in Manchester, England, while slicing a potato was amazed to discover a crucifix shape.

"It's simply a miracle," said Fiona's employer, who took the potato to his local church. "It's just such a perfect crucifix form. You can see it for yourself."

On the same day, a little green apple was cut open to reveal "Peace" in its pattern of seeds.

And the miracles were not limited to fruits and vegetables. Newspapers in Algiers published a photograph of a forest in Germany in which a verse from the Koran, "Be ye faithful or be ye sorry" could be clearly read in the shape of some trees.

And then there was one of the strangest miracles of them all, the miracle of The Rock 'n Roll Barbie. British Muslims hailed what was described as a miracle message from God written inside the head of a Barbie doll.

Osama Patel, fourteen, forbidden by his parents to play with dolls from the time he was a little boy, could not stop himself. Secretly, he played with a Rock 'n Roll Barbie late at night, hiding it in a trap door cut into the floor boards under his bed. Suspecting the worst, his father Yassir burst into his son's bedroom unannounced and caught him bathing his Barbie. Enraged he pulled madly at the blonde-haired blue-eyed figure, tearing off her limbs, decapitating her. Reaching into his pocket he pulled out a large folding knife. "Now I will teach you and your friend a lesson."

As he sliced the head in half, he found a message. On one side, burned into the raised plastic ripples of her skull were the words in Arabic "There is only one God," and the other read "Mohammed is the messenger."

Yassir believes he witnessed a miracle. "God wants Osama to play with dolls. Maybe it is a sign that one day he will have many, many virgins. These words are a message from God."

Word spread in the community and recently it has been observed that there is a greater tolerance for boys playing with dolls. Over one thousand people, some from as far away as Islamabad, have visited Osama and Yassir to see the Barbie.

They display her on a shelf in plastic Saran wrap to keep her free from fingerprints and unnecessary touching. A local shopkeeper said demand for Barbie has surged, but the nearby mosque was cautious. "We don't consider it an endorsement but it certainly is a miracle," a spokesman was quoted as saying.

***

Fishman knows apparitions are now being sighted more frequently than Elvis. They are part of the outstretched hand of the Universe, reaching out through its operatives and agents. Emissaries working on behalf of the best that people can be. Fishman is convinced that Jesus, Moses, Mohammad, Krishna, Mahavira, Lao-Tzu, Confucius, the Buddha are all right here, among us. If you just open your eyes, you are able to see. They appear and disappear. When you search for signs, you find them. Sometimes, if you are lucky, they find you.

And that is why Fishman loves to get up each morning and head over to FedEx. It is where he can manifest *his* love of mankind. There are visitations and the redemption of packages. And the miracle of customer service, the kind that guarantees peace of mind.

You expect more from FedEx and Fishman delivers. Teleporting parcels, documents and letters.

Chapter 12

Yisgadal, Viyiskadash, Shmay Rabah.
"Magnified and sanctified be God's great name, in the world that He has created, according to his will."

Fishman is now alone at FedEx. In his mind he hears the sing-song sound of the Kaddish recited at his mother's grave. The Kaddish is the ancient Jewish prayer said in praise of God at funerals in memory of the dead. Although called The Prayer *for* the Dead, the Kaddish actually celebrates life. At least that is what the Rabbis say. Fishman thinks that it's just so typically Jewish that the prayer for the dead has become a proclamation of God's sovereignty over all things, looking forward to a time when the Kingdom of Heaven will be established on earth.

"But it also makes perfect sense. We are all reborn in our suffering. It is through sadness, deprivation, and death that we are able to embrace life."

Fishman believes that is the true meaning of transformation: continually resurrecting ourselves, rising up out of our pain and sorrow. On second thought Fishman admits perhaps that is not a wholly Jewish concept. But for all of us, like Jesus, there can be life after the cross.

Outside the floor to ceiling windows, Fishman sees a large black and orange hand bill posted on a wooden fence across the street from FedEx. It announces slashed prices and big savings at Esther's Designer Dress Barn.

The sign reads "Final Days, Everything Must Go."

Fishman's thoughts gravitate to visions of *the* final days and the end of, not only Esther and her designer dresses, but of the entire world. He thinks about the second coming of Jesus, the war of Armageddon, the arrival of the Antichrist, the Tribulation and the Rapture. Fishman knows about many of the Endtime prophecies; of horrendous natural disasters, major social and political upheavals and predictions of sudden and violent occurrences that would terminate life on earth. He remembers that very special year 2000 when many people had predicted civil wars, major tornados and earthquakes. It was a year that some had determined was uniquely apocalyptical, a year in which cosmic forces were coming together to rain down God's ultimate judgment.

Fishman has spent a lot of time surfing the web, reading CB, gathering facts. He also has been a faithful student of fiction. He knows that the one thing that all these predictions have in common is that none of them seem to come true. Most recently there were predictions from a Russian prelate and scientist, Vladimir Oyveyakov of the Stroganoff Academy. Oyveyakov believes that the earth's axis will tilt about thirty degrees to the right sometime during the next two years. This will submerge Scandinavia and Britain under water in what he has termed The Lord's Cataclysmic Flood. Siberia will be spared and intervening aliens will lead the world into the fourth dimension at which time the second big bang is to be expected.

There was also Shlomo Rivkin of the International Zohar Learning Center who has predicted that any day now a great ball of fire will hit the earth unless Jewish women adopt head scarves and Jewish men grow peyas.

And then there was Shawn Paul Jeffrey Jr., the author of *Nostradamus Unplugged*. Mr. Jeffrey believes that unless the Jerusalem Temple is rebuilt, a meteor will hit the earth. It will cause tidal waves, earthquakes, hurricanes, and clouds of dust and sea salt. He also predicts political unrest, famine and years of solar eclipse. He is available for speaking engagements and guest appearances. He claims his calendar is filled for the next two years.

From Fishman's point of view, all this doomsday talk is ridiculous. He looks around the room, past the sorting area with its envelopes and packages, over the conveyor belts, beyond the chutes, and ramps and slides, across the little devices that operate as flawlessly as a finely running clock to prod or tip an individual package into its proper box or tray. Fishman looks up on the wall overhead until his eyes catch on the bold, colorful words that like a heartfelt religious verse say it all: Relax, It's FedEx. It could be a spiritual mantra like Allahu Akbar, or Shema Yisroel. The Lord's Prayer.

"Our Father, who art in heaven, Hallowed be Thy name. Thy kingdom come. Thy will be done, On earth as it is in heaven. Give us this day our daily bread. And forgive us our trespasses, as we forgive those who trespass against us. And lead us not into temptation, but deliver us from evil. For thine is the kingdom, and the power, and the glory, for ever and ever."

There is a gentle, no-demands-upon-you, transcendent ring to it. It is a call as magnetic as the pull to Mecca or Medina. You don't have to face East. The words are your very own magic carpet. Say them now slowly to yourself. "Relax, it's FedEx." "Relax, it's FedEx." Breathe. In. Out. In a wave-like motion. A comforting energy and feeling of wellbeing and calm expands in ever greater circles.

Fishman says to himself, "You must allow yourself to be transported to be delivered into a distant, miracle-filled realm."

Fishman places himself psychologically right on that vortex of consciousness and technology where everything is possible, a land of unending Abracadabra, transformation, and once upon a time.

***

There is a definite exhilaration accompanying arrival at a higher plane of awareness. Fishman does not underestimate the vast treasure he has found. Two phrases dance a pas de deux in his brain.

"Seek and ye shall find."

"Knock and it shall be opened."

But Fishman is all too aware of how easy it is to get lost in your own internal universe. For a moment he feels like the entire world is a figment of his imagination, a tangle of intuition lost in half-forgotten truth. Why is it he wonders that so often everything appears like distorted perception? But not at FedEx. FedEx is real. As they say in the company brochure, "we are reliable, responsive, relentless and remarkable." And that is exactly how Fishman sees himself. He will do whatever it takes to get the job done. No time to get ambushed from deep within. Fishman also knows that the information about a package is as important as the package itself, which is why he will deliver anything to anywhere at anytime.

The phone rings.

"FedEx. Agent Fishman. May I help you?"

At first there is only silence then the rising sound of an indistinct voice. It is gravelly. Fishman is certain it is an elderly woman.

"I have a terrible problem. I hope you can help me."

"Yes, ma'am, I'll do my best."

"My dogs. Franny and Al." Their names are said with a degree of sadness.

"Sorry, ma'am. We don't ship animals."

"I just have to get them to my daughter. She's leaving for Costa Rica tomorrow. I can pack them up for you."

Fishman hates to say it. "Have you tried the post office?"

"They can't do it. I was so sure I could send them by FedEx."

Fishman feels her disappointment.

The Next Step

He gives it a try. "What kind of dogs are Franny and Al?"

"They're big dogs. Very well-behaved. Wouldn't hurt a fly."

"The breed?"

"Wolfhounds. Irish Wolfhounds."

Fishman, always willing to go the extra mile, checks his rate sheet in the computer.

"Ma'am, can I assume they are each about one-hundred and forty pounds. Thirty-six inches high by forty-four inches long? This will have to be our little secret, OK?"

"Mr. Fishman, I don't understand."

"It's a new FedEx service and it is not yet being offered from this location. I would have to pick up the dogs personally and send them from our new global distribution hub."

"Will it take long?"

"Ma'am, will there be some one on the other end to accept Franny and Al?"

"Morgan. My daughter."

Fishman goes on to explain. "You see with this kind of service someone needs to be there at the time we ship them. It ensures a safe arrival. It's almost instantaneous. Don't even need a tracking number."

"Can you tell me how much it will cost?"

"Ma'am, all you need to do is give me your five-digit zip code from where you are sending it and the five-digit zip code where it is going to. Transportation charges depend on package weight, as well as the distance it is being shipped. Generally, other charges will apply if you choose additional services such as COD, or have other special needs. But since all this is our little secret, I'm just going to charge the standard rate. But please keep in mind this is our highest priority service, much faster than overnight."

***

It is a powerful feeling to know that you are the one that makes things happen and Fishman does not take his position lightly. But with so much need in the world he has to choose carefully. Fishman does not have the luxury to teleport just any dog. He needs to be selective. Irish Wolfhounds at first do not seem to be a logical choice but Fishman knows that they are an ancient breed, the tallest of the coursing hounds and remarkable in combining power and speed. He remembers from a National Geographic newsreel in grade school that they used to hunt wolves and elk and accompanied Irish nobles to war. It is also the breed that was held in such high esteem that its ownership was restricted to kings and poets.

But in truth Fishman tells himself, "I would have done the same even if they were lowly Chihuahuas."

He thinks for a second about the physics and aerodynamics of differently proportioned accelerating canines. Fishman constructs a scientific experiment in his mind. There are three dogs, all fully grown, consistent with the American Kennel Club breed specifications. There is a Boston bulldog, a Yorkie, and a standard poodle. Fishman watches them in his mind's eye traveling through space and time. He finds himself making subtle distinctions defining words such as distance, displacement, velocity and speed. He wonders if a dog flies as the wind blows. He sees the bulldog as a black-and-white blurred somersault, the Yorkie as a hair piece caught in a gale force storm, the poodle is a dog-shaped, strategic nuclear rocket.

Fishman reminds himself that speed is a scalar quantity that refers to how fast a dog is moving and velocity is a vector quantity that has to do with the rate at which the dog changes its position. It is an important difference. Fishman imagines the dogs moving rapidly—one step forward and one step back—always returning to the original starting position. While this might result in a frenzy of activity, it would result in a zero velocity. Because the dogs always return to the original position, the motion would never result in a change in position. Since velocity is defined as the rate at which the position changes, this motion results in zero velocity. If dogs in motion wish to maximize their velocity, then they must make every effort to maximize the amount that they are displaced from their original position. Every step must go into moving the dogs further from where they started. For certain, the dogs should never change directions and begin to return to where they started from. It was hard for Fishman to imagine a scenario where this would happen.

Fishman feels a sense of comfort knowing that Franny and Al are safely on their way to Costa Rica. He only wishes that the travel arrangements aboard ship with Morgan are half as comfortable as the first class accommodation he arranged. He also thinks about Mrs. Burnham, the old lady with the gravelly voice. He's glad that he was able to help her. There was something sad about her and now with her dogs gone, he imagines her even lonelier, at home by herself.

Fishman decides to cheer her up and give her a call. The phone rings a half a dozen times before it is picked up. There is no answer just the sound of slow steady breathing on the other end, waiting. Fishman imagines in the split second before speaking that the old woman fanaticizes the call is from a long lost lover or make-believe friend. He sees her as beautiful young woman with hazel eyes and fair skin. Her auburn hair is long. Fishman wants to have some piece of spectacularly good news for her: she has won a million dollars or an all expense paid vacation trip.

"Hello Mrs. Burnham?"

"Yes."

"This is Fishman. From FedEx. Franny and Al."

Now recognizing him. "Mr. Fishman. How are you?"

"Just checking to see how you liked our service and if there is anything else FedEx can do for you. Oh yes, I have some very good news for you. You won an all expense paid vacation trip for two."

The old woman is now animated. "I've never won anything before, not even a toaster. I've read about these scams."

"Don't worry, Mrs. Burnham. It's real. Your luck's changing. You can go anywhere in the world you want and you can relax because it's all on FedEx."

There was just one additional problem that Fishman needed to work on. But he was sure he could soon figure that out too. He imagined it was much easier to teleport currency than wolfhounds but there was the problem of doing it with someone else's money. But that was stealing. Unless, he thought, he could get a backer. Like a charitable organization or foundation to support him. Or a corporate sponsor. And then the answer came to him.

"Who else but FedEx."

It was just such a natural fit. In Fishman's mind there is no better corporate citizen than FedEx. He remembered from his own orientation the importance FedEx places on social responsibility, charitable giving and its commitment to the environment. After all, each year FedEx gives millions to the March of Dimes, The United Way and The American Red Cross. Fishman thinks a few hundred thousand should be no problem for a world class teleporting launch.

The idea of Fishman's own charity, like the National 4H, sends his adrenaline rushing. Names begin to swirl in his mind. "Fly by night and day", "The Unwinged Victory Foundation", "The International Association of Here Today Gone Today." There are also others. For a moment Fishman imagines his charity's headquarters as a high voltage nerve center, as large as a medium sized city. The glitzy illumination of Las Vegas in the shape of a human brain. Each region performing a distinct charitable function. There is a sign high above the frontal lobe whose letters radiate in psychedelic colors, like barium injected cerebral enzymes. The sign reads: Fish and Trips.

Fishman also imagines satellite offices, like municipal and

regional airports around the world. This is where all the grass roots work needs to be accomplished, building a world where people grow and work together as catalysts for positive change. If only Fishman had discovered teleporting earlier who knows what miracles might have been done?

Lives saved.

There could also be amusement parks: Fishman's World and Fishmanland and Fishman Studios and Nine Flags Great Fishman. There could also be Fishman's chain of seafood restaurant franchises. He could do for the salmon patty what Ray Crock and Dave Thomas had done for the burger. Fishman could also have a nationwide chain of cafés like Starbucks but instead of the wireless access or in addition to it, you would be able to travel to wherever and whenever you wanted. There would, of course, be certain restrictions.

And there could be a chain of motels like the old Hojo's. A comfortable room with a TV, warm shower, and teleport. It would be moderately priced and geared to the family traveler.

Suddenly Fishman realizes he is lost in the tropical rainforest of his own imagination. He is missing the point. It is not about a splashy name or setting up his own foundation.

He also reminds himself of the bureaucratic nightmare of getting all this done. There are lengthy reviews for requests for money. He will have to provide detailed descriptions of the scope of his charity, its organizational goals and the demographic breakdown of the population he is serving. He will need to supply contact names, mailing addresses, telephone numbers and qualifications. He will be asked for an overview of the proposed use of the money and why the funds are needed at all. There will be worksheets with expenses and revenues. Timetables and mathematical formulas for measuring success. And there will be more. Fishman will have to show IRS designations and nonprofit status, recent audits and annual reports. There will have to be a board of directors and a management team. And if requested, he will have to send presentation folders, videos, press clippings, and promotional material.

Fishman is slightly queasy at the thought of having to follow such guidelines. He knows that the decisions of charitable committees are lengthy; set up to ensure that evaluations have consistency and balance and, above all else, be uniform. The more he thinks about it, the more Fishman realizes that this is not for him and that he has to find another way.

Fishman thinks to himself, "What if I go right to James Early?"

Jim Early is the President and CEO of FedEx. He is a risk taker and always on the look out for the next wave of the future. Growing up in an alcoholic family in Boston's hardscrabble South End, Early seemed destined for a life on the streets. He was a scrappy kid who became a top-notch amateur boxer. A Golden Gloves winner, Early had an impressive 58 and 2 record. The twists and turns in Early's early life were truly remarkable. He was a gas station attendant, high school dropout, class valedictorian, professional dancer, Las Vegas blackjack dealer, and commodities trader.

It was in Chicago in the 1980's that Early made his first fortune, using it as a launch pad for taking over companies and funding start ups. At five feet four inches with a Peter Pan face and strawberry-gray hair, Early is a wiry and fast-moving opponent. He thinks of himself in Marine terms as "your most loyal friend, your most dreaded enemy." In the pork belly pit, Early honed and intensified his compulsion to be a winner. Standing shoulder to shoulder with guys twice his size, Early gave no ground. He recognized quickly that trading was a game of guts, brains and timing. An enterprise of top feeding and bottom feeding where survival of the fittest was the rule of the day. And the key to success was discipline.

Early knew that discipline meant many different things to

people. For him its main ingredient was having a single minded focus. Early observed the traders who came in at 8:30 A.M. and were gone by 2:00 P.M. He'd see them in their expensive cars driving down the expressway. But he knew to be really good you needed to focus one thousand percent on what you were doing, every second, and be consumed by it. The traders who didn't were lazy. They'd make money sometimes but eventually they'd get caught.

He'd say, "If you don't have the focus then the discipline can't follow because it's too easy to look away and rationalize."

Fishman had always wanted to meet Early. He was well liked by FedEx employees and known throughout the business world as a strategic leader. It was Early who came up with the concept "Operate independently, compete collectively." This idea held great appeal for Fishman. It was not a complicated business model. As the annual report noted, "just a flexible network of networks designed to focus on very distinct customer needs." According to this philosophy, operating independently, each member of the FedEx family of companies runs its own specialized business of services including express, ground, freight and expedited shipping, plus document management, international trade and supply chain solutions. Separate networks of service enable companies to focus on their core business, what they do best. Because, when it comes to shipping, one size does not fit all. Competing collectively, FedEx acts as the hub, allowing each network to operate independently but at the same time working together worldwide. This allows for each company to benefit from the FedEx brand, which strengthens the broad portfolio of corporate services and oversees future business development. Since taking over the company, Early's commitment to industry leadership and quality service made FedEx what it is today.

Fishman was sure Early would want to hear all about teleporting and anything else Fishman had to say.

***

Fishman reaches in his pocket for his cell phone and dials 1-800-GO-FedEx. After only a single ring a pleasant voice answers. It is a girl-of-your dreams sort of voice, full, intelligent, caring. It is also automated.

She (let's call her Marilyn, it's that kind of voice) says, "Welcome to FedEx. If you know the service you would like, please say it now."

Fishman would like to speak to James Early but that is not an option. Nevertheless he says, "James Early."

Marilyn says, "If you know the service you would like, please say it now. Schedule a pick-up, track a package, drop-off location, get rates, order supplies or ship international."

Fishman, now getting the hang of things, says, "Other services."

Immediately, Marilyn rejoins, "OK. You can say, billing, set up a new account, return a package, change a shipped package, claim or technical support."

Fishman growing a bit weary now says, "Customer service."

Marilyn on cue says, 'To repeat these services say repeat. To speak to a FedEx representative, say Rep."

Fishman finds these prods and prompts irritating like the way they make you board the trains in Disney World. It's all too orderly. It dismisses or tries to ignore the messy incoherence and chaos of the world. But despite this fact Fishman says, "Rep."

Not a second later a real voice appears. "This is Kylie. How can I help you?"

It is a perky, I-want-to-be-your-best-friend kind of voice. It is also athletic and suggests great physical endurance. For an instant, Fishman imagines Kylie with no clothes on undergoing martyrdom like St. Sebastian. Her lustrous white nubile body is shot with arrows protruding at odd angles. She has been tortured because she is so aggressively and relentlessly nice. Fishman would like to tell her about the real St. Sebastian, the patron saint of archers and athletes and soldiers. About his legendary energy and his enthusiasm for spreading and defending the faith. How he loved plague sufferers and was buried during the time of St. Ambrose along the Appian Way.

But instead he says," Kylie, could you please connect me to corporate offices?"

"I'm sorry sir I can't do that but if you would like I can connect you back to our main menu."

"Kyle, I work for FedEx. I need to speak to James Early."

There is silence followed by a possible solution. "I can let you talk to my supervisor. I need to transfer you to another location."

A second later a man's voice is on the line. "This is Rahim. How may I be so kind to help you."

It is not that Fishman, in principal, is against outsourcing and the exporting of jobs. In fact, he is all too familiar with the positive economic benefits of making such shifts. But at times like this he wants to throw his cell phone as hard as he possibly can against the ground. Fishman wants to watch it shatter like shards of glass. He wants to observe an electrical charge flare up like flint against rock then travel seamlessly to New Delhi or Jalalabad. He longs to witness Rahim's slow, silent, electrocution, but only after he is transferred, effortlessly, without another single word spoken, to the office of James Early.

Chapter 13

Eve Mulch stands tall in the inner sanctum of FedEx corporate headquarters in Memphis. She has been with Early since the cowboy days when she watched over the execution and clearing of his live hog and cattle futures trades. At five feet ten, the blue-eyed, raven-haired Mulch looks like she could be a WWF wrestler. She could fight as Diana the Huntress on special cards that feature "Women Who Wrestle Men."

Long ago, on the trading floor in Chicago, Eve learned how to handle aggressive and unwanted advances from brokers who taunted her about her big bosom and good looks. Now she brings all her talents to bear, making sure Early's schedule is full and smoothly running and not taken up by unnecessary intrusions. She is committed, reliable, ingenious and, above all else, loyal.

Eve's phone rings. She is told in the fatigued voice of a customer service operator that there is a Mr. Fishman, a FedEx package handler from Chicago, on the line. He insists on speaking to her. Eve explains to her (let's think of her as Dolores) that today is an impossible day. She simply has no time to speak with him.

Dolores continues, pleading with Eve. "You don't understand. This guy won't take no for an answer. He just keeps calling. I can't sleep at night. He says he needs to speak with Mr. Early."

After a moment's deliberation, Eve decides that she will deal with this lunatic herself. Of course, there was no way that she could have prepared for Fishman.

"Eve Mulch, Mr. Early's secretary." It is said in a strong business-like tone.

"Hi, Ms. Mulch, I'm Fishman from Chicago. I would like to make an appointment to see Jim Early."

Eve shoots back. Now in a stronger perfunctory tone. "Mr. Early is unavailable. What is it that you want, Mr. Fishman?"

Fishman pauses for a second. He is not about to tell Eve that he has unlocked the secret of teleporting humans and other living things. Nor is he willing to confide in her that his discovery will revolutionize the world of shipping, not to mention its profound implications for all of mankind. And though Fishman would have liked to tell Eve about the discord and disharmony that he observes all around and the vast untapped reservoir of human potential, he doesn't. He would also like to tell her about the antiquated notion of the importance of being special; that there is no longer a need for individuals to be apart. And that we are all aligned protoplasmicly. Our strength is in our unity. And most importantly he would like to say that he Fishman is committed to building a better world and that Jim Early is part of the vision. Fishman would also like to remind Eve, "No person is an island unto herself. Each of us can traverse inner boundaries and become as one."

But Fishman doesn't answer this way. He adopts a more personal tack. In his softest, most trying-to-create-a-human-bond voice, Fishman says, "Eve. May I call you Eve?"

There is no answer. Fishman listens to the audible exhaling of air. He continues, "I know something about you. You were born Eva Mulchokuzlowski. You moved from Milwaukee in 1986. You met Jim in the Last Roundup Bar and Grill, a dive that has long been closed but used to be *the* place for bad boys, bikers and urban cowboys. Sawdust and peanut shells on the floor. And you used to dance the two step. I'm told you were pretty good."

Disarmed, Eve's voice softens. "Are you a stalker, Mr. Fishman?"

Taken aback, practically shocked at the mere suggestion.

"Hardly. But I do believe in the value of research and information. If it is at all possible I would like to meet with Jim. I could see him at anytime, anywhere."

"Mr. Fishman, Mr. Early is a very busy man. We'll have to get back to you. Please don't call here again."

Fishman senses confusion in Eve's voice overridden by her fierce loyalty to her boss. He tries one last time.

"Eve, if you could just squeeze me in, I can be there in an instant."

"But you are in Chicago?"

"Believe me. Not a problem."

***

The entrance to James Early's office opens automatically, almost like a supermarket door. It is made of burled walnut; a thick, solid door emitting a strange hydraulic sound, announcing your arrival. The office itself is large and light with white metal and glass furniture and abstract paintings by Newman, De Kooning and Still. As Fishman's gaze wanders across the room his eyes light on a Pollack. It is similar, though smaller, to one he is familiar with, "Abstract Flight" at the Met. Fishman thinks to himself that the character of FedEx is captured in the art. There is the spirit of revolt and freedom, individuality and spontaneous improvisation. At FedEx everything is possible. But then Fishman is seized with a second thought. Perhaps he is over thinking things and should just relax, stop thinking so much, and just go with the flow, for a change. The mere thought of that puts a devilish smile on Fishman's face.

Early is at his desk finishing up a phone conversation. He waves Fishman over to a chair in front of him. His last words on the phone are, "Just tell him to relax, it's FedEx."

He is playing to Fishman as his audience. He winks and Fishman simultaneously smiles. James Early has the high glossed, tailored look of a retired general. The kind who occasionally runs for higher office of the White House kind. He is wearing a bold blue and white awning stripe shirt with a white collar and solid raspberry silk tie. He has a buttoned up though relaxed demeanor. He carefully studies Fishman who is wearing his FedEx uniform as if it were a Saville Row suit. He extends his hand warmly, holding tightly to his grip. His voice is gracious, boyish, in complete control.

"Mr. Fishman, nice to meet you. I hear you can be a real pain in the ass."

Fishman laughs, accepting Early's assessment as a compliment. "Well, Jim, I have that absolutely positively worked out to a science."

Early abruptly takes the conversation in a more professional direction, "I don't like beating around the bush. What exactly do you want? And what is it that you do in Chicago?"

"Jim, what I do is create good will and fill the human soul. And what I want is for you to join me, to help make the world a better place."

Early looks at Fishman like he is an alien just landed from Mars or possibly he is a mere runaway from a state mental hospital. He adopts a more solicitous, even therapeutic, non-offending tone.

"Mr. Fishman, is business slow in Chicago?"

Early picks up some sales reports and quickly reviews them.

"Which branch do you work at?"

Fishman answers matter-of-factly, "Brisk. And I can help you grow your business."

Early falls back naturally to a dollar and cents tone. "Mr. Fishman, do you have any idea of the scope of this company?"

"Yes, Jim. I think I do. The current annual revenues are twenty-five billion. The average daily volume is 5.4 million with shipments covering a service area of 215 countries including every address in the U.S.A. The company employs 245,000 peo-

The Next Step

ple. FedEx owns 643 aircraft-primarily Cessna 208B's but also a few A's, 103 Airbuses –both 300's and 310's, 132 Boeing 727's, 39 DC10's and 25, no 28 Fokker F-27's. They fly into and out of 378 airports on every continent. FedEx also owns or leases 71,950, give or take, motorized vehicles for express, ground freight and expedited delivery service. There are 1,265 FedEx pickup and delivery terminals, 6,873 shipping centers, 877 stations, 2,241 stores, and 41,892 drop boxes including 4,981 U.S. Postal Service Locations."

Early allows the numbers to wash over him like baptismal water. "What did you say you want again?"

Fishman is now the one who is doing the studying. He takes silent pleasure in observing his effect on Jim Early. He imagines to himself that Early must have first thought that Fishman was a complete nut but now doesn't know what to make of him.

But the important point, Fishman says to himself, is "I have his attention."

Like with most things in life, substance falls victim to the protocols of presentation. Fishman believes it is wise to take his time, to let Early arrive at conclusions on his own.

Fishman would like to tell Early about how thoughts are the glue of our belief structures and how the natural state is like the Zen mind. Everything is meaningful and meaningless all at the same time and no individual is separate from the one. We are all protoplasmic brothers. Everyone is part of the whole and no link in the chain is more essential than another.

But he doesn't. Fishman answers this way, "I would like your help and I would like to help you."

"What sort of help?"

"Well, at first I was going to just ask for money."

Early runs his well manicured hand across his chin. A look of skepticism takes over his face. "Of course."

Fishman knows Early doesn't understand. He starts again. "It's really not about money. That is only a very small part of it."

Early is still unmoved. "Fishman, in my experience . . ."

Fishman interrupts. He doesn't allow Early to complete his sentence. He takes a different tack. "Jim, if you could travel anywhere in the world where would it be?"

Early's eyes roll back in their sockets and he sees. "Venice. Never been there. Always wanted to go down the Grand Canal in a gondola."

Fishman now taking charge, calling the shots. "Ask Eve to join us."

Early checks his watch. "I have another appointment."

"Please. Jim. I promise you that this will be worth it. Tell her to clear your schedule and to come in."

Early uncharacteristically goes along for the ride. He raises no further objections. He is content to follow Fishman's lead. Figuring the joke will end shortly.

A second later Eve appears. As she approaches Early's desk Fishman is struck by the gold-winged lion that is dangling from a thin chain around her neck. He also takes in for the first time how beautiful she is. Dressed all in black, her phosphorous blue eyes sparkle. Eve has a quizzical but an I'm-up-for-anything look on her face. She defers to Early for direction.

Fishman breaks the momentary silence. "Tell her Jim."

"Fishman is taking us to Venice."

Chapter 14

The act of teleporting is like the City of Venice, a real thing on a fluid base.

Fishman, Eve and Early are in the middle of the Piazza San Marco. It is sunset. They walk towards the Basilica. Eve's eyes are wide open. She gestures to the golden dome. Fishman enjoys following her gaze moving from one smaller-scaled cupola to another. Early's attention is drawn to the loggia spanning the church's façade, surmounted by replicas of the four famous St. Mark's horses, the Triumphal Quadriga. All around them is a sea of marble, mosaics, alabaster, and porphyry. It is like walking on water, an undulating multi-colored, richly patterned ocean floor.

Eve announces that she wants to light a candle. She feels that she has experienced a miracle. She needs to say a prayer for her friends and family and for peace on earth. She hugs Fishman and for the first time really sees his face.

"I can't believe it. How do you do it?"

Fishman does not answer Eve's question. He would like to tell her that he knows something about miracles. He has studied them in there many guises and forms. He knows about crying Madonnas, angelic encounters and Jesus apparitions. But does he talk of them? No, he doesn't. Fishman is bursting with pride but he is trying hard to remain humble. His eyes delight at searching through the mosaic details, depicting scenes from the lives of St. Mark and Christ. He notices one that recreates the delivery of the evangelist's body, according to legend, hidden in a pork barrel, smuggled out of Alexandria and shipped to Venice.

In the Atrium the three marvel at the six cupolas illustrating stories from the Old Testament. Jim recognizes the Tower of Babel.

"The first Twin Tower."

Fishman is feeling that this little trip is having the desired effect. He thinks to himself that there is nothing like a perceived miracle to get someone thinking in a new way. He turns to the right and realizes that they are in the Baptistry. It is dominated by a Sansovino-inspired font.

Fishman turns to Early. "St. John is pouring water."

Just then Early catches sight of a mosaic of Salome dancing overhead. The glassy faced enchantress appears Madonna-like. She is wearing a star-studded, blood red dress with white fox tails, swaying under a platter, holding St. John the Baptist's head like a Sunday roast. Instinctively, he reaches for his own head, brushing back any loose hairs.

Fishman, Eve and Early walk onto the Loggia. The sky is a burnt blue-orange. They look out onto the Piazza. There is the Campinile, the Doge's palace and a view of the Canal in the distance. There are also visions of lions in all directions; colossal, miniature, docile and menacing. Some are winged, poised for takeoff, like the pendant around Eve's neck. There is another that is topped by a man, standing on a crocodile with the head of a dog.

Along the Grand Canal are boat moorings that look like peppermint sticks. Early is now excited. Riding in a gondola is something he has always wanted to do. They are waved into the boat by a young man dressed in the traditional black and white horizontally striped shirt and a woven straw hat with red silk trim on the crown and brim. He introduces himself as Roberto. In his early twenties he is tall, athletic with a thin mustache and gypsy hair. He has the personality of a favorite maitre d'. As they are boarding, a motorboat speeds by driven by two teenage boys who look like models for a Dolce and Gabana or Versace ad. They laugh out loud and yell "Ciao, turisti" as their wake jerks the boat, rocking it sharply from side to side.

Roberto yells at them, his right forearm raised in the familiar gesture. "A fongoola."

Eve points to his hat. "Very nice. I would like."

Roberto navigates expertly with his pole, occasionally jabbing at the water, then using it as an oar. He touches his hat as they thread through the canal.

"Baretero. Per l'estate, summer you say? Is red like the inside of gondola. And per l'inverno, how you say when it cold?"

Jim pipes in. "Winter."

Robert rolls his fingers around in a rapid clockwise motion at the side of his ear then he points to his head. "Ah yes, winter. Ah stuppeed!"

Fishman, Eve and Jim have a good laugh.

Fishman senses that his friends are sailing away into wonderland. They are surrounded by rococo palaces and Moorish mansions, gothic churches adorned with many of the greatest paintings and frescoes of the Renaissance. There are grand palazzi with pink and gold-tinted facades, tall arched windows, gothic cornices and Byzantine columns. There is also the constant lapping of water onto wood and stone. The green stained sides of ledges and buildings, their discoloring and bruising, the inevitable effects of time.

Early looks around and says to Fishman, "This has to be one of the seven wonders of the world, like the pyramids."

Eve interjects, "Or the Eiffel Tower."

Fishman laughs. "You mean the Seven Wonders of the *Ancient* World?"

Eve presses the point. "What about them?"

"Do you really want me to list them?"

Early and Eve in unison. "Yes."

"O.K. There was the Great Pyramid of Giza, the Hanging Gardens of Babylon, the Statue of Zeus at Olympia, the Temple of Artemis at Ephesus, the Mausoleum at Halicarnassus, the Colossus of Rhodes and the Lighthouse of Alexandria."

Eve is amazed. "How do you know so much?"

Early offers a possible explanation. "He's just a sponge for information."

Fishman continues. "There is also an eighth wonder. The three of us right here, now."

Suddenly, Roberto breaks into song amidst the sound of screaming gulls. It is not a familiar aria by Puccini or Verdi nor is it from the repertoire of Neapolitan love songs. His choice is surprising, almost ludicrous but somehow strangely satisfying. His voice travels far into the distance, beyond the vaporetti, past a funeral cortege draped in black and gold, piled high with flowers followed by a gondola of mourners. His words follow the tide down and along the canal.

> *"O Danny boy, the pipes, the pipes are calling*
> *From glen to glen and down the mountainside*
> *The summer's gone and all the roses falling*
> *'Tis you, 'tis you must go and I must bide."*

There is a dinner boat sparkling with Japanese lanterns and a fishing vessel tangled with nets. Fishman points to a wedding barge bound for San Marco and then to two waving children in a window of a refurbished palazzo near the Rialto.

Early looks up to Roberto who is lost in song. "It does my Irish soul good hearing an Italian sing a lullaby."

Fishman is enthralled by the wonder of the moment. He watches the flicker of lights like a gliding serpent in the water. He looks over to Eve and Early. Their eyes are dancing to the notes emerging from Roberto's lips, humming along, peaceful. Fishman imagines people all over the world joining together in hope and in healing. He sees them spreading a message for peace on earth. He is certain that Eve and Early share his vision. They see beyond race and religion, nationality and ethnic difference.

The three smile at each other and sing along.

> *"But come ye back when summer's in the meadow*
> *Or when the valley's hushed and white with snow*
> *'Tis I'll be here in sunshine or in shadow*
> *O Danny boy, O Danny boy, I love you so."*

***

The Hotel Enrico Dandolo, built in the Gothic style is a few steps from the Piazza San Marco along the Riva degli Schiavoni walk. Its rooms command sweeping views of the Plaza and the island of San Giorgio. Fishman, Eve and Early are sitting at a table on the rooftop terrace. They face the Church of Santa Maria della Salute. They can see as far as the Lido and Adriatic Sea and in the other direction there are the Dolomites. They are sipping Pinot Grigio and slowly chewing bread sticks. They are waiting for the dinner they have ordered: Gran misto di pesce al griglia, mixed grilled fish and a Venetian specialty, Garganelli con Melanzane, Pomodoro Fresco e Mozzarella, short pasta with eggplants, fresh tomato and mozzarella.

Early raises his glass. In the candlelight, the white wine has the color of ancient amber. "Here's to fate, I think I'd have to say that's why we are here tonight."

Eve now turns to Fishman. She enjoys looking at his face. Watching his eyes, the way they flash like a lighthouse.

"Fishman, do you believe in fate?"

Fishman would like to tell Eve that he has studied numerology, palmistry, astrology and horoscopes. And that he has also investigated panchang, vastu and dream analysis. He knows that she has no way of knowing that he has also been a student of fortune telling and the strange and unknown; that he has read about psychics and spiritualists, archaeological hotspots, UFO's and mystical experiences. But he doesn't speak of any of this.

Fishman simply answers, "Yes, Eve. I do."

"I'm glad because I know fate brought us all together."

She looks at Early acknowledging his toast.

Fishman seizes this opportunity. "I believe you are right. And you know what we could do if we really wanted?"

Fishman senses a myriad of possibilities are flying through both their minds all at once.

Eve and Early shout out together. "What?"

Fishman takes a deep breath. And then does not waste another second. He practically bellows. "We can change the world."

Eve and Early look into Fishman's face. A warm feeling washes over them.

Chapter 15

To transform the world is no mean feat. Since the dawn of time, it has been the preoccupation of passionate thinkers and doers. It has been the work of martyrs and mystics, intellectuals and charismatics from East and West. Even in the short span of Fishman's life he has witnessed men and women who profoundly changed the world for the better. They came from different backgrounds and beliefs, sharing a common purpose. Each was dedicated to serve humanity through perseverance and faith. There was Gandhi and Martin Luther King Jr., Mother Teresa and Albert Schweitzer. There was also Mandela and Desmond Tutu and the Dalai Lama. There was Abraham Heschel and J.Krishnamurti and C. S. Lewis.

Fishman knew there were many others. But these were the people who had first touched Fishman and inspired his patience. They were dedicated to creating a new and peaceful world based on principles of freedom and justice. They recognized that there was the need for unity among the world's races. That it is possible to create societies based upon cooperation, trust and a genuine concern for others. These men and women stirred Fishman to take stock of his own existence, moving him to want to make the world a better place. Fishman ached to affirm what really mattered and he believed that his discovery of teleporting and support from Jim Early could make his vision come true.

Fishman is dedicated to the promise of humanity's future. He is an optimist but years on Wall Street have taught him the necessity to adopt a pragmatic approach. Fishman is certain that we are on the threshold of an evolutionary leap and the power of kindness and understanding will illuminate the earth. He believes in his message that he hopes to deliver with the help of FedEx: the Five Principles. **Peace, Unity, Prosperity, Promise, and Youth. P.U.P.P.Y.**

"They are simple principles," he thinks to himself, "as irresistible as man's best friend."

But why are they not self-evident to everyone?

The first is Peace. All human beings need to commit themselves to a peaceful world, insuring our collective well-being. And the way this is done is to establish a positive purpose in life. There can be no peace in the world without individuals committing to a life of purpose for themselves and the entire planet.

The second is Unity. We are all members of the same human family. Mothers and fathers, brothers and sisters. We cannot allow national, religious, gender, orientation or ethnic differences to separate us.

The third principle is Prosperity. All members of the human family need to benefit together from social and economic development.

The fourth is Promise. The world community must hold out a positive vision of our collective future based on the imperative of building and strengthening the bonds that unite us.

The fifth principle is Youth. The world must make a special commitment to its most precious resource, its youth. It must make sure that no ethnic or racial or religious group is left out; no one takes second place.

Fishman asks himself, "How can our future be otherwise?"

***

Fishman is certain that disseminating his message will bring people together. Inevitably, governments and religions must accept a common fate. It is an exhilarating thought to be at the fore-

The Next Step

front of a world revolution. It is every bit as exciting as being Superman. Fishman feels that he is "faster than a moving bullet, more powerful than a steaming locomotive, able to leap from a tall building in a single bound."

Fishman cannot rely on world leaders or religious authorities to bring about changes. He knows that what the world craves is an exceptional person who can speak with a simple, straightforward voice. The person that he has in mind is humble, with a strong sense of self and a mission. He also possesses that rarest of human qualities, the ability to connect with the common man. He would be like . . . the absurd image of Johnny Appleseed flies into Fishman's head. Fishman can see himself in the wilderness planting seeds. He pictures vast orchards, still bearing fruit after hundreds of years. He visualizes a countryside of blossoming trees where no one is hungry.

Although he loves finely tailored clothes, Fishman sees himself sleeping outdoors, traveling barefoot, cultivating the landscape everywhere he walks. His shirt and pants are made of torn burlap sacks and his hat, a tin pot that is also used for cooking. Fishman spreads the word. He makes new friends and encourages kindness.

The insanity of this picture makes Fishman laugh.

Chapter 16

Back in Memphis there is agitation and disbelief.

A meeting of the Board is scheduled and Jim Early is about to offer a new vision. To the shock and dismay of some of his directors, Early has returned from Venice a changed man. Being teleported to the Basilica San Marco and experiencing life along the Grand Canal has made him a believer. He wants to join Fishman. He feels inspired that together they can transform the world and FedEx will be their vehicle. Early feels called upon or perhaps he believes he is a witness to communicate life's true purpose. He senses that for the first time he can see, like Fishman, into the future and warn the world of coming events. He knows that unless there are changes everything will continue to deteriorate. He can see pictures in his mind of Fellujah, Baghdad and Najaf.

He tells his Board about protoplasm and then blurts out, "There is no need for us to inhabit a world of false borders and boundaries always operating on the edge of chaos."

Early knows that life has a higher purpose and it is plain and simple: to make the world we live in better.

"Each of us is a child of God, inextricably tied to one another. But you don't have to believe in God. The answers are not in the sacred coffers of any religion or system of truth. But one thing is certain: life no longer can be lived apart. All of us are protoplasmicly attached to the same source. Our destiny is our common fate. FedEx can make the difference."

They look at him stunned, wondering whether he will ever return to his senses. Not unlike other missionaries who braved rough terrain to bring their message into a vast spiritual wilderness, Early is compelled by his challenge. He understands that through FedEx's global reach, he can bring PUPPY to distant lands. He also knows that any location that does not already have a FedEx is an area of the world that needs to be opened. Early embraces the pioneering activity that he has chosen. For an evangelist this is the work that needs to be done.

Eve jokingly tells Early, "You've got Fishman fever."

But the old guard, Oxley and Pittman, find nothing here to joke about. They don't care for spiritual conversions in their C.E.O. The world's condition is not their concern. Their mission, as they see it, is to reap ever greater, more aggressive, superior financial returns for shareowners. And the way to do that is through transportation, freight management and chain supply services.

There are six directors seated around the table with Early and Eve. There is Bruce Oxley, the Chief Financial Officer and Early's main rival; Lynette Hunt, an independent of Rensselaer Polytechnic Institute; August L. Dove, a family friend and long-time associate; J.R. Pittman of Pittman Family Consulting and Investments and Oxley's chief ally; George P. Hyde III, Chairman of Courvoisier, Daniels, Walker, Martini & Rossi; and Jesse Ventura, former Governor of Minnesota.

The boardroom is a fishbowl, with rounded floor to ceiling windows on three sides, suspended Olympus-like, thirty-three stories above the lives of most mortals. Bruce Oxley listening to Early speak is convinced that he has lost his mind. Oxley is a good old Southern boy in his mid-forties. He is tall and athletic. He graduated from Old Miss with a degree in accounting and has an MBA from Harvard. He crunches numbers for fun and has never met an off balance sheet ledger partnership that he doesn't like. He has been gunning for Early's position since first joining

FedEx.

Oxley chimes in, "Let me get this right, Jim. You want to change the mission of the company?"

Pittman is in his late fifties. He is overweight and bald and wears dark Brooks Brothers suits that always fit a couple of sizes too small. He runs his tongue across his lower lip. He shakes his head back and forth.

"I'm going to have to agree with Bruce. This is crazy."

Early starts again, "All I'm saying is FedEx stands for innovation. Our business model is known throughout the world. People expect a higher standard. We can do amazing things."

Lynette Hunt is the President of Rensselaer Poly. She is a strikingly beautiful African-American woman in her fifties who was a former high fashion model in New York and Paris in the sixties. She can usually be relied upon for her sensible approach. She is one of the world's leading experts on international commerce. She listens intently, asks questions and analyzes. She makes an effort to try to understand multiple points of view.

Her voice is calm, moderate in tone. "Jim, perhaps you can tell us why you want to make changes?"

Her question is seconded by Hyde, Dove, and Ventura.

George P. Hyde III or "Guy" is a recovering alcoholic who has found God. He is a descendent of Philadelphia's mainline but has been known throughout his life for his unconventional perspective. He likes to shock but he has positive instincts. He finds Oxley a "total bore."

Augie Dove is board dressing. He is a well-spoken gentleman in his mid-seventies who in truth is a little out of it. He is there to agree with anything Jim Early has to say. He can always be relied upon to break tie votes in the Chairman's favor.

Jesse Ventura will go to the mat with strongly held opinions. He has been on both sides of issues and is hard to pigeonhole. An ex-navy seal, he is relentless and ingenious when he is in a fight.

Early takes a different approach. "I know how this sounds.

Some of you think I'm crazy. But imagine if we could keep doing exactly what we are doing now, and take on a new mission."

Oxley interjects, "I'm afraid saving the world is not in our job description."

Early shoots back. "Look, let me answer Lynette's question. Now this is going to sound crazy!"

Pittman now comes back to life. "I knew it."

In a strong military sounding voice Ventura barks at him, "Let him speak."

Lynette follows up. "Jim, why now?"

"Ok here goes. I met this guy called Fishman."

Arthur dove emerges from reverie. "He's a fisherman?"

"His name is Fishman. No first name. Just Fishman. He works for us in Chicago. He's a package handler."

Guy trying to offer a little levity. "Sounds dirty."

"FedEx packages. He's a real character." Early continues. "He has a vision. He wants to transform the world and he's chosen FedEx."

Oxley is enraged. "Who is he? What do we know about Fishman?"

Lynette jumps into the fray. "What is his background?"

Early now adopts a let-me-relax-your-fears tone. "He was a Wall Street trader who was indicted for securities fraud, banned from the industry for life."

Pittman once again. "I knew it."

"And he was found *not* guilty."

Oxley seizing on this point. "The guy was a crook and you want us to give him control of our company?"

"Fishman is not a crook. And he doesn't want control. I said he was found innocent."

"But you also said he was banned from the securities industry for life. That does not sound so innocent to me."

"The government tried to ruin his life. They wanted to destroy him. He almost lost everything. His house, most of his money. He had to fight this thing for years. Look, I met him."

Eve, against board etiquette, (she is technically an observer) ventures an opinion. "I met him too. He's amazing."

Early reflects further. "I know this sounds insane."

Ventura makes a suggestion. "Can we meet him?"

Early looking around the board. "I think that's a good idea."

He focuses in on Oxley. "Bruce, would you like to meet him?"

Sarcastically. "Sure Jim. What do I have to lose?"

***

Early reaches into his pocket for his cell. He punches out Fishman's number and then leaves a voice message on his phone. Seconds later Fishman appears. He is wearing his red FedEx jumpsuit with no apron. He is standing behind Early. Sensing his presence, Jim looks over his right shoulder and with a warm smile welcomes him. He turns back to face the board and simply says, "Fishman."

As the members of the board continue to stare at him, Fishman greets each director from where he is standing, working his way around the table.

"Hi Bruce, it's nice to meet you."

"Nice trick. I'd like to know how you did that."

Moving counter clockwise. "Lynette. I remember when you did the Virginia Slims commercial. Was that '67, no '68."

"Yes. '68. I wore that tiny white patent leather mini."

Fishman smiles and then makes a deferential bow of his head. "Arthur."

He responds as if awakened from a deep sleep. "Do you like to fish?"

"No. Afraid not. Just my name."

Moving on. "And you must be George."

"Please call me Guy."

"A pleasure to meet you, Guy."

Flirting with Fishman. "I hope the pleasure will be all mine." He looks at Ventura.

"I'm Ventura. Nice to meet you, Fishman. We could use you in special ops." Ventura then turns to his right. "This is Pittman."

Fishman recognizing the name. "Yes. I know, Pittman Investments."

Pittman replies in a challenging tone. "I understand you worked on Wall Street, Mr. Fishman."

"Yes, I did J.R. but that was awhile back. A different lifetime."

"I understand things did not work out?"

"I made mistakes but I'm trying to correct them."

Oxley can not allow that opening to pass. "Yes. Tell us about your mistakes, Fishman."

Early senses the need to take back control of the meeting. "There will be time for that later but for now I wanted to give you a chance to get to know Fishman. I believe he has something planned."

Fishman turns to Bruce. He studies the skeptical lines on his face, his furled lip. It is a barely concealed grimace. He imagines Oxley thinks Fishman is a charlatan. He can also see that Oxley is trying to figure out his appearance as if it were a startling card trick. Fishman would like to tell Oxley and the others about the five principles and the enormous impact they can have on the world. He would also like to respond to their doubts. But he doesn't. He merely asks Oxley a simple question. "Bruce, if you could travel anywhere, where would it be?"

Oxley's answer is swift and in one word. "Jerusalem."

***

Even as they were about to launch there were loud complaints that carried through the air.

"I have a dentist appointment."
"I'm wearing the wrong shoes."
"I don't have my passport."
"I hate airplane food."

Chapter 17

The sky over Jerusalem is an open eye. It has observed great dramas and tiny miracles in the turbulent patterns of centuries of daily life. It has seen shepherds transformed into kings unifying a nation; ancient prophets preaching about retribution and redemption. It was witness to Jesus' last ministry and his crucifixion and it is here where Muhammad ascended into heaven. Jerusalem's air is thick with the aroma of almonds and tamarind. There is charcoal smoke and dolorous chanting and legends of messiahs rising from the dead. There is also the Mount of Olives and "The Way of Suffering" and the oldest cemetery in the world still in use.

Fishman and his entourage are standing before HaKotel haMa'aravi, the last remnant of Solomon's Temple. It is dawn, the sky is blue-gray and there is a warm, jasmine-scented breeze. Oxley and Pittman are standing next to one another. They mysteriously draw away from the group. They approach the Western Wall.

Early and Eve are observing Fishman's effect. Lynette, Guy, Augie and Ventura stand speechless.

Ventura, noticing Oxley and Pitman ahead, calls out. "Hey, Bruce, Pittman, wait up."

They look back at Ventura. Oxley notices for the first time something comic even endearing about Ventura. He feels he can be more open. "Pittman and I were going to say a prayer. Want to join us?"

"I'm not the praying type, boys, but sure what the heck, why not."

Fishman thinks to himself that he is standing only feet away from the ancient Wall in the midst of the Old City. He knows that for over two thousand years it has been the most sacred spot for the Jewish people. It is at the center of their consciousness. It is considered holy by virtue of its proximity to the Western Wall of the sanctum sanctorum, the Holy of Holies in the Temple from where the presence of God never departs.

Fishman's eyes study the enormous bricks, the color of camelhide, the variation of surface and shade, polished by human hands, touched in prayer down through the ages. There are stones along the "master course" of the Wall that weigh five-hundred and seventy tons and are forty-four feet long, ten feet high and twelve to sixteen feet deep. This is an amazing architectural feat when you consider that the largest stone in the Great Pyramid was eleven tons.

Three times a day, morning, afternoon and evening, observant Jews, wrapped in white and blue or white and black prayer shawls with phylacteries tied around their forehead and wrist, pray. On special occasions there is also the blowing of the shofar. The shofar is the ritual instrument of the ancient Hebrews. In biblical times it was a priestly instrument that was used in the Temple. It was made of either ibex or ram's horn. Its playing, closely connected to magical symbolism, was both powerful and liberating. According to legend, its blast destroyed the walls of Jericho.

Fishman remembers that the Temple Mount the Western Wall supports is also called Mount Moriah. It was here that Abraham bound his son, Isaac, prepared to sacrifice him, according to the dictates of the Lord. And also where Jacob dreamed of a ladder that reached all the way to heaven. Fishman imagines himself asleep, dreaming. He sees the ladder and the angels ascending and descending on it. He visualizes the many ways people try to reach God. He remembers the mosaic that he and Eve and Jim saw of the Tower of Babel at the Basilica San Marco.

"So many failed attempts at finding a stairway to heaven."

And then the words from John that he saw in Venice come back to him.

"I am the way, the truth, and the life: no man cometh unto the Father, but me."

Here in the Holy Land, Fishman feels certain that these words apply to him. He has been chosen to unite all of the world's people to live together in harmony. He says to himself, "I am the way."

And he knows this like he has never known anything before. This is the truth and of this he is certain.

Fishman tries not to lecture the group, still partially dazed by the teleporting experience, but he can't help himself.

"The Temple was built for all mankind. That was Solomon's genius. It was called the 'House of All Nations', the universal center of spirituality."

Lynette remembers something she had read as a child. "Have you ever heard of the mystical secret of the Wall?"

Guy, a recent "born again", speaks up. "Something about Jerusalem being sacked by many nations over thousands of years but the Wall never coming down?"

Lynette finishes her point. "Yes, through the centuries this stone wall, built brick by brick, has remained intact. It represents the indestructibility of God's bond to all men and women, past and present, around the world."

Fishman remembers that there is a Talmudic tradition that states that all prayers in the universe are drawn to the wall and from it travel along the ancient stones before ascending into heaven.

There is also another legend that Fishman wants to share. "When the Temple was constructed, the Western Wall was built by the poor and when it came under siege the Angels descended from heaven. They were crying but determined to save it. They spread their wings over it and said: 'This Wall, the work of the poor and humble, shall never be destroyed.'"

Still, Fishman thinks the idea of a wall is an unusual symbol. After all, the purpose of a wall is to separate. To keep out. To protect from intrusion. But in the case of the Western Wall it is viewed as a bridge, a means of connection. Even in its present state, it allows for a belief in a glorious past, the promise of restoration. It also resonates with what always unites people: frailty and spiritual resurrection.

Ventura, Oxley and Pittman return. They have that slightly odd converted look on their faces, like they know something special that others don't. It is immediately apparent to all.

Augie asks Ventura, "What did you do up there?"

"We said a prayer. I prayed for peace."

Augie confesses, "I'm not religious myself but this place does give you that feeling."

Eve and Early nod in agreement. Eve moves over to Fishman and slips her arm through his. She smiles at him and kisses him on his cheek.

The nine visitors are all standing bunched together with Fishman at the center. They have no real concept of Fishman's grand plan. They have no thoughts about transforming FedEx as a spiritual vehicle to reinvent the world. All they have now is a profound visceral feeling to follow him, to be with him, to learn from him, having him as their center, listening to him, interacting with him and working with one another.

Fishman can visualize the apostles of the early church. He can see himself surrounded by Peter, Andrew, James and John, all fishermen. Sometimes he is preaching to them on a mountain or beside a lake, in a meadow or in front of a fire. Many times it is at meals, speaking in parables. He can see his effect on them. He also imagines walking along a deserted road. The conversation is informal, intimate. His disciples are with him wherever he goes.

There is an eerie calm followed by a massive explosion.

A dark cloud of pigeons fly overhead. There is the stink of gunpowder and explosives, eyes tearing and burning nostrils. The group falls to the ground. There are horrific screams and blaring sirens, frantic running and shouts for help. An ambulance weaves its way through traffic.

Fishman looks over his shoulder and sees a twisted steel bench and a burning car with smoking skeletons. There are also charred pieces of arms and legs, a finger with a ring still on it, and the bodies of school children thrown about the street. There are wounded bystanders, dazed, dripping with blood.

Fishman instinctively runs towards the school bus. He sees a leg in a bed of tulips and next to it a woman's severed head. He can still feel the blast tingling in his arms and his legs. There is a young girl of ten or eleven who runs to him for protection. There is blood on her forehead but she is strangely still. The smoke in the air makes breathing difficult. Fishman holds her tightly. He can feel her warm wet blood against his cheek, her small fingers scratching at the back of his neck.

And then there is a second blast. Fishman sees a man dressed as an Orthodox Rabbi stab a pregnant women in her stomach and then in an instant he is engulfed in flames like a candle and disintegrates. There is a huge boom and then complete darkness.

There is a long continuing sounding of the shofar.

And then Fishman feels himself coming into the light. He is floating down a long corridor. He is greeted by his mother and father. There is a warm feeling of unconditional love. He can feel the liberation of the spirit from his flesh. He knows that he is part of God and he is God himself, like a drop of sea water and the sea itself.

Being separate is an illusion. It is the source of all the world's problems. Everything is connected. There is a matrix of souls and a web of light and a global link of human beings. What we do affects the whole world and everything fits together like a puzzle. The answer is so simple. It is love.

***

Fishman lies in a hospital bed, unconscious. The doctors don't know yet if he will live or die. He saved the little girl, Zipora, but he may have lost his vision and even his life doing it. He has a deep cut on his forehead where the shrapnel struck. A large bandage covers his eyes. He feels an unrelenting pain throughout his body. Each throb is like a second hand recording time. Fishman is burning with heat and suffers from cold sweats. He is nauseated and dizzy and feels a sharp drilling in the right side of his head. His teeth pulsate. His arms and legs ache. He wants to get lost somewhere, but he finds nowhere to go. He retreats deep into an internal cave, a catacomb, burying his pain in a subterranean chamber, a dark and secretive hiding place. He continues to dig as far as he can go, forming corridors and galleries underground. He hides himself in forma and cubicula, located outside the city, along great consular roads. It is here in his underworld network that Fishman finds refuge. He imagines a safe haven built by fossores in the faint light of their primitive lamps, using baskets and bags to carry the earth out.

He stays there for centuries engaged in furtive prayer and secret rites. He celebrates the anniversaries of martyrs and watches early Christians taking the Eucharist. He observes the treatment of corpses, in imitation of Christ, wrapped in a sheet or shroud and placed in loculi without any kind of coffin. He sees the crypt being sealed with a slab of marble and tiles fixed by mortar. On the tombstone the name is engraved. "Palefsky." Along with a symbol, a Star of David and a wish that he may find peace, wherever he is.

Fishman sees the faint flicker of an oil lamp and a small vase containing perfume, its aroma like clover, placed beside the tomb. Fishman's labyrinth is a restorative church, embellished with frescoes, mosaics and other internal handiwork. Every gallery he passes through, every symbol he sees, every inscription he reads reduces his pain and increases his faith in the power of his message.

Fishman's message to all mankind is embodied in PUPPY. It is the message of unconditional love. Embracing love celebrates the unity of existence. It recognizes the astonishing miracle of protoplasm, the substance that connects all life.

***

Suddenly Fishman regains awareness. He is conscious of a glaring shaft of light and a fly buzzing overhead. His eyes try to follow its sound and movement. It darts at right angles. Fishman watches the black hairy insect fly into a florescent bulb. Each time it hits it sounds like someone tapping on a lead pipe. The bug flies in a path that goes back and forth between the window and the artificial light. It rests for a moment on a wall or a table, creeping a few inches, and then is aloft, back in flight.

Fishman notices Eve sleeping in a chair, at the side of his bed, at the same time that he becomes aware that there is a feeding tube protruding from his mouth. He tries to speak to her with his eyes. The bandages have been removed. And then again the light turns to darkness.

Fishman is at the edge of a tangled forest next to a precipitous slope with the sound of a thunderous waterfall in the distance. He has been sent to immerse himself in sadness and suffering to experience the pain and barbarity that is here. He must wade through filth and bloody rivers and march through burning sand in time. He must also navigate uncharted waters, visit mythological sites in this world and in hell. For a time he is guided by Virgil and Dante and once he flies with Icarus high in the sky. Fishman travels the length of the earth from end to end. It is his mission to map the physical and moral geography of the universe. It is up to him to create a legend of his own.

Once again his eyes open. This time Eve sees that he is awake. Fishman stares at her soft, open smile, the glow of her warm pink lips. He would like to run his fingers across their silky surface. He begins to think about his hands and feet and heart.

Eve moves her hand across his forehead. "Welcome back."

Fishman makes a long plaintive sound like a muffled voice blown through a priestly instrument.

***

Weeks pass and Fishman is ready to leave the hospital. Eve has been with him the entire time. Fishman has an angry scar across his forehead but otherwise he is completely healed. He is anxious to get home but he needs to tell Eve his painful secret. He hopes that she will understand.

Fishman is not sure where to begin. He has entangled himself in a web of lies. Should he begin with Nadia and the children? Or Palefsky? Growing up in Queens? Or watching the suicide of Ploopy Goldberg?

Fishman feels that he needs more time.

***

Eve invites Fishman back to her home in Memphis but he insists that he must return to Chicago.

He wants to explain but he can't.

"I need to get back home."

"When will you call?"

"Tomorrow. I need to speak to you. But not now. I also have to talk to Jim."

Eve wants to be with Fishman. She tries to conceal her disappointment. "You know the others were unhappy with the return arrangements, especially Oxley and Ventura. They said it was much better leaving from Memphis. There were no I.D.'s or waiting on line."

Fishman would like to tell Eve everything but he doesn't. He tries to be humorous.

"Fishman Travel. Instant point to point service."

Fishman sees an airplane flying over a body of water. Suddenly it hooks a sharp left turn then crashes into the side of a skyscraper. There is a massive explosion with soaring flames. Fishman holds that image in his mind. His arms and legs tighten at the force of its impact. He feels it deep in the pit of his stomach. A profound sadness overtakes him. He looks at Eve.

"Come back with me."

Chapter 18

Fishman's life changed forever on September eleventh.

Nadia and the children were on Flight 175 from Boston when it crashed into the South Tower. Fishman's affairs were already in chaos because of the IRS case, but the impact of losing his entire family in one horrific instant hurled his world over the edge.

For months he could see nothing in his mind but packed jetliners crashing into the Twin Towers over and over again. Plumes of orange-white flames and billows of gray-black smoke. Charred human bodies and the agonized screams of loved ones in pain.

Fishman fought against himself trying to visualize the final moments of fiery suffering. Instead he strained to remember birthdays and celebrations. Like the time the family traveled to the Southwest to visit the pueblos of the ancient Anasazi Indians. They walked along mesas and plateaus, river bottoms and canyons. They wandered where the ancients raised towers and built hundred-room cities in cliffs and caves. They climbed kiva ladders and descended into ceremonial chambers and marveled at petroglyphs from a thousand years ago. There was one that his daughter Lara and his son James loved. It was the Kachina spirit Kokopelli, the wandering hunchbacked flute-player and magician who originated from the center of the earth. The Anasazi looked to him to bring rain and fertility. He would travel from village to village seducing women with the alluring strains of his enchanted instrument.

Fishman tried to imagine the Kachina Spirit providing his gifts to humanity. He tried to feel his invisible presence from wherever life came forth. Legend had it that Kokopelli carried seeds and babies and blankets in his hump. He also offered dreams and visions, fertility and love.

But Fishman was unable to welcome Kokopelli into his heart. There was no room for him there. Fishman was engulfed in darkness and ash. All he could see was black fire and burning smoke. And eventually Fishman collapsed. He was hospitalized at Mt. Sinai in New York.

Fishman thought to himself that if he were to be in a hospital anywhere, what better place than Mt. Sinai. Of course, there is so much mystery surrounding the mountain where God spoke to Moses. Fishman thought it strange to even think of Mt. Sinai in clinical terms. He knew that there was no archeological evidence of Moses' presence on the mountain but there were relics of the faithful assembled over thousands of years. There were also ancient chapels and structures honoring saints and the Virgin Mary and a hewn stone arch where long ago a monk heard confessions from truth-seeking pilgrims.

It takes many hours, following the course of Moses to climb to the highest peak but Fishman could not find a shorter, less strenuous route. He wondered if on the other side of the mountain there was a more scenic path but than decided that if this way was good enough for Moses then Fishman could certainly make do.

After all, Fishman knew along with God it is the figure of Moses, more than any other individual, who dominates the Torah. It is Moses who leads the Jews out of slavery, guides them for forty years in the wilderness, carries the law down from Mount Sinai and prepares them to enter the land of Israel. It is his vision and will that creates his people's future.

For the first time in Fishman's life, he had a bleak view of his own future. He could not see himself without Nadia and the children. He thought about killing himself but he knew he couldn't do that. He had seen someone else take his life many years earlier when he was a child. A small boy imitating Icarus in Queens. A sudden crazed act to see if humans could really fly.

Fishman wandered in a desert of sleepless nights and diminished appetite. He suffered from a profound loss of self-confidence and a depressed mood. He was weighted down with heavy fatigue and lack of interest. He also wrestled with guilt. Why did it not happen to him? Why wasn't he the one who died?

One of the doctors suggested that he write his thoughts down. Fishman joked about it. He said, "There already is a Book of Job."

But eventually he did get his thoughts on paper and was content with the results. It was a kind of statement he felt, a text of life, in some small sense, like job, that not only conveyed his pain and suffering but the sadness that existed throughout the world.

It took Fishman more than two years to emerge from his depression and his home. Only then could he return to work. Though this time he felt that he had chosen something meaningful, something like FedEx that would benefit all of mankind. But he still made believe or chose to believe that Nadia was still there with him. He still craved her comfort. He couldn't imagine not sleeping next to her warm body.

Even being chosen to save the world had not reduced Fishman's emotional reliance on her.

Until now.

***

Eve and Fishman are sitting on a bench along the lake front. It is early spring and despite a bright sun there is still a chill in the air. Lake Michigan looks like a gentle ocean on a summer's day. It is aquamarine with small lacey white-capped waves rolling onto shore. Fishman's right hand is playing with Eve's silky black hair. He moves across the outline of her face with his index finger.

Fishman takes a deep breath, speaks softly, affectionately. "Nadia used to like it here. We would take James and Lara and spend the whole day at the beach."

Suddenly another thought crosses his mind. "Why didn't you ever get married?"

"Who said that I didn't?" Eve's tone is playful.

Fishman now considers that there are many things that he doesn't know about Eve.

"Were you?" He is eager to learn more.

"Never met the right man. When I was younger I went for bad boys. I don't really go out a lot."

"Me neither. I've been obsessed with saving the world, jumping around from place to place."

Eve now getting into the spirit of the conversation. "Fishman, you can't allow a little thing like that affect your love life."

"Seriously, it takes up a lot of time and mental energy." He continues almost in a confessional tone of voice. "You wouldn't believe all the things that go on in my head."

Eve not exactly knowing what she is getting herself into replies, "Try me."

Her tone has the definite sound of I've-just-about-heard-it-all, nothing you can say is going to shock me.

"O.K., for example right now. I was thinking about psychokinesis."

Eve quickly responds, "Fishman, is it something that I bring out in you?"

Fishman would like to tell Eve that it is a phenomenon that has occurred and has been written about since ancient times. The movement of objects, the bending of metal and the foretelling of the outcome of future events. He would also like to tell her that current research now centers in the areas of meditation and altered states of consciousness. But does he tell her? No he doesn't.

Fishman just says, "Yes, you do."

The Next Step

He would also like to tell Eve that he believes psychokinesis helps to explain magical spells and curses, rituals to affect the weather, poltergeists and the evil eye. That it can occur spontaneously or deliberately which indicates that it is both a conscious and unconscious process. And most importantly Fishman would like to tell Eve that out of the blue, it is a talent that he just discovered.

Fishman turns to a stick that is on the ground in front of them.

"Eve do you think it is possible to make something move?"

"Is this a trick?"

Fishman suddenly shifts his tack. "Eve, forget that. I was thinking something stupid."

Eve is slightly confused. "What?"

"Do you wear reading glasses?"

Eve nods affirmatively.

"Have you ever noticed that you hear better when you put them on?"

Eve looks very thoughtful. "Let me think." In a tone that is certain. "Well I do. And so do most people."

Fishman's glasses fly out from his breast pocket and rest on Eve's face. They are oversized dark frames that make her look like a mad scientist.

Eve's amazed look suggests anything is possible.

"Can you hear me now? I love you."

***

There are many examples in the Bible of levitations and healings, luminosities and other magical phenomena attributed to holy persons. In the New Testament, Saint Paul and Silas were imprisoned in Ephesus. They prayed and sung hymns and their shackles fell off and the prison doors swung open.

With Eve in his life, Fishman feels his shackles loosening.

Loving just one person deeply is a far different kind of love than hoping to redeem the entire world's population but in no way does it curb Fishman's desire to be the Way. If anything, it strengthens it.

Fishman is certain that his newly discovered talent will allow him to be more convincing, to get people to pay attention to his PUPPY message. But he is also concerned that his unusual faculties not be seen as a freakish act, a sideshow trick, or a mere parapsychological phenomenon.

Fishman remembers a newsreel from when he was a teenager. There was a Soviet housewife who would concentrate, then flip coins from heads to tails, stop clocks, make knives and forks cling to her skin and with a blink of her eyes send toasters, even heavy furniture, flying across her living room.

Fishman is certain that his gifts were given to him for a purpose. Not for entertainment. He feels responsible to make the most of them.

***

The annual FedEx meeting is being held at the Leona Helmsley Convention Center in New York. It is located on the Hudson River in the heart of midtown Manhattan. It is a recently built, black steel and glass facility that includes 650,000 feet of meeting space and two city blocks of waterfront views.

James Early is standing at the rostrum beneath a orange and purple banner that reads, "At FedEx, Consider It Done", in the Ivan Boesky Ballroom in front of a full house of FedEx executives, managers, and employees. Early is surrounded by Eve, Oxley, Pittman, Augie, Lynette, Hyde, and Ventura. Jesse is particularly animated waving to the crowd, bopping up and down, dancing to the lyrics of "We Are the Champions" blasting on the sound system.

There is the raucous atmosphere of a political convention in the room, more Democratic than Republican, like an Elvis or Tom Jones concert during the sequined jumpsuit era. It is a carnival for the shipping and delivery faithful. Early thanks the host committee and then one by one the individuals responsible for everything that takes place within the hall. The organization people, hospitality, security, transportation and those in charge of the recruitment and training of an army of FedEx volunteers. Early then introduces the evening's featured speaker.

"It gives me great pleasure to introduce a man who requires no introduction. By now you have read about him in Newsweek and Time Magazine."

The room goes dark and a large split screen behind Early reveals Fishman on the covers of both magazines. In the Newsweek picture he is shown with a wide toothy smile over the caption. "FedEx finds Fishman."

In the Time Magazine cover Fishman is pictured in his FedEx jumpsuit carrying an Irish wolfhound above the headline, "Man of the Year."

There is a flash of magazine covers with Fishman's face on the screen: People, Maxim, Vanity Fair, GQ, Sports Illustrated (holding a football), US Weekly, National Geographic and Money ('Five Questions to Ask Fishman'). There are also pictures of him in the Times, the Wall Street Journal, USA Today and the New York Post.

Early continues. "He has appeared on Leno and Letterman and tomorrow night he will be interviewed right on this stage on Larry King Live. He has been on Hardball and Paula Zahn and can be found on the Fishman Homepage: www.puppy.org."

Now on the screen are the words from the official website. There is a pop-up window with the picture of children from all around the world hugging little dogs. It reads, "Yes, I'd like to accept PUPPY into my heart, click here."

Early is still speaking. "It was just a few short months ago that this package handler from Chicago had a vision. And what was it? He wanted to change the world. Can you imagine? And he was prepared to do "Absolutely, Positively whatever it takes." He has shown us there is a better way. With great pride, I mean without any pride, I give you, Fishman."

There is thunderous applause followed by boisterous shouts and loud music. There is also the release of orange, purple and white balloons and confetti. The spotlight is now on Fishman who seems overwhelmed by all the attention. He begins to address the audience.

"Thank you for this great welcome. As you know long before I decided to save the world. Long before I was shown how to save the world. I fell in love with FedEx. I ask you. Is this a great company or what?"

The audience in unison shouts his name over and over again.

"Fishman. Fishman. Fishman."

"Thank you. But it is you who I want to thank. You continue to amaze me with your 'whatever it takes' dedication, helping people discover a way to live together in peace, and brotherhood and sisterhood. You have been unfailing in delivering the right message at the right time to the right place. Unarmed truth and unconditional love is the Way. We are all united. We must teach the world to overcome violence and oppression without resorting to it. We have made a good start. Remember, 'United in protoplasm'."

The audience again shouts.

"United in protoplasm."

"United in protoplasm."

***

Just as Early had prophesied the previous evening, Fishman is onstage across the table from Larry King at the Helmsley Center in the Boesky Ballroom. Larry is wearing a shocking pink shirt

The Next Step

with red suspenders and a brightly colored, floral patterned tie. His producer starts counting down. "Five, four, three, two, one" then points to the star of the show who effortlessly speaks into the camera.

"Tonight's exclusive. A sensational revelation from the man who is trying to change the world. Now for the first time in public, Fishman breaks his silence that he has kept for the past three years. He is going to share a secret that could help others who've gone through the same ordeal. Fishman, an intense emotional hour next on Larry King Live."

The show then goes to commercial. Larry tries to reassure Fishman that there is nothing to worry about. Fishman is relaxed, ready to go.

"Just answer the questions. It's a piece of cake."

Larry's producer again points to him.

"Good evening, welcome to another edition of Larry King Live, our special guest tonight is –you've heard all about him- Fishman. He was a delivery person at FedEx but is known best to most Americans as the guy who wants to save the world. Fishman is coming forward tonight with a very difficult story to tell but he wants to tell it—why here, by the way?"

"You're the man, Larry."

"Let's go back now. What happened to make you think that you could change the world?"

"I had a vision. I was eating a piece of chocolate. Vosges. Have you ever tried it?"

"Is it dark? Don't think so. I'm a Hershey's man myself."

Fishman goes on. "It came to me."

"What came to you?"

"That the world was in trouble."

"Because?"

"Larry, are you kidding? All you have to do is look around."

"And you decided to go to work for FedEx. That doesn't

strike you like an odd solution?"

Fishman in a very certain tone. "Not at all."

Larry now probes for details. "Were you abused as a child?"

"No."

"Never molested?"

"No."

"No psychological abuse from your parents?"

"Absolutely not."

"Then why try to save the world and make a big deal about it?"

"Larry, let's back up. When you were born did your parents think something was wrong?"

"They may have. My father spoke in Yiddish. I didn't understand him so well."

"And this was painful?"

"Yes. Very."

"Why talk about it now?"

"Hey. Who's doing the interview? We'll be right back. With Fishman the FedEx delivery guy who wants to save the world."

The show is now back to commercial. They are off-air. Larry turns to Fishman.

"I heard you had a good sense of humor. When we come back I'm gonna ask you all about the stuff with your wife and kids getting killed. Tragic. And DOGGY."

"PUPPY."

"Right and your invitation to speak at the U.N."

Chapter 19

Fishman is standing at the rostrum of the General Assembly of the United Nations dressed in his purple and orange FedEx jumpsuit. He is about to speak to the delegates. Eve is seated in the front row. She gives Fishman the ok sign, then throws him a kiss. Fishman looks out into the great hall. He is covered in a halo of gold, reflected from the massive United Nations insignia, the world cooking on a barbecue grill surrounded by olive branches, throwing off an other worldly light from above the speaker's podium. Behind him, seated at an elevated marble desk are the Secretary General and the Presidents of the General Assembly and Security Council.

As he prepares to speak, Fishman perceives a shimmering abstract of human beings, a mosaic of radiant shapes and iridescent colors. Fishman studies the audience. Like a mad scientist he observes solids, liquids and gas. He sees mysterious proteins and connective tissue, biochemical functions converting energy to mechanical work. Fishman imagines enzymes adapting and biological transitions, molecular binding and the division of cells. Fishman sees protoplasm in all its potential. Its detailed structures and systems: nervous, muscular, circulatory, respiratory, digestive, urinary, and reproductive. He considers the response of skeletal muscles and synaptic transmissions, the transport of oxygen and the secretion of glands.

And then Fishman thinks about the human heart. In an average lifetime, it beats more than two and a half billion times. He says to himself, "It is a tireless worker from the instant it starts until the time it stops beating."

Fishman delivers his speech. "When I was about six I went to a Chinese restaurant with my parents in Astoria. That's in Queens. They ordered moo goo gai pan and I had my favorite, egg foo yung. A gypsy came up to our table and whispered something into my mother's ear. I didn't remember this incident but years later, at a birthday party, my mother, after having too much to drink, told it to me. The woman made a prophecy. Someday I would be a great leader. I would stand before millions of people. I prayed that I'd be an actor or maybe even a rock star. As a teenager I remember telling a teacher, 'Maybe I'm a modern day Hamlet. To be or not to be, ain't that a question?' I was a wiseguy even then but what I was really after was wisdom. But I never thought I'd be speaking to you today here at the U.N. I didn't choose to be with you. Believe me, when I tell you, that I *was* chosen. Perhaps it is because I have experienced a lot of pain in my life. Many of you know some of the details of my story. It is unexceptional for the most part except for the fact that I was tried for many years for crimes that I didn't commit. And then, like many other innocent people, experienced the irrational loss of loved ones. And then for reasons that I cannot explain I was given these miraculous gifts. But, why me? I have been troubled to find an answer to this question. And now I am sure there is none. Maybe it is just the universe's sense of humor. There is much of God to be found in a good joke. Why me? Why Moses or Jesus, Muhammad or Buddha? Why Christ Bob? Some questions have no answers. My grandfather used to say, "Gey freg Gut kashes:" Go ask God questions. There are answers that only He knows. My message is a simple one. I am committed to the unity and peace of all living beings and ask you to join me. I invite you to take part in the worldwide chorus of unconditional love. Together we are changing the world. It all started with a piece of chocolate, like a burning bush, in flames but not consumed. And then there was the

The Next Step

power of FedEx. The first shipping and delivery company to transform itself, reinventing simple messaging into a spiritual Internet for the entire world. Its broad reach and dedicated army of PUPPY lovers make things happen every day. Even now, at this very second, the power of protoplasm is being passed on!"

Fishman now pulls something out from under the lectern. It is a large poster of a spotty brown puppy. He holds it up with both hands for the delegates and observers to see and then allows it to fly up in the air, as if on its own, until it covers the United Nations insignia on the wall overhead.

Fishman is now yelling to the Assembly: "Love the Puppy. Love the Puppy."

He encourages the audience to join in. Both his hands are up in the air like Leonard Bernstein conducting a Mahler concert. With a strong inward movement of his arms, Fishman shouts even louder. "Love the Puppy."

Fishman beseeches. "Please join me."

And now Fishman starts barking. "Arf." "Arf." "Arf."

Three quarters of the General Assembly are barking under Fishman's able direction. "Arf." "Arf."

It is a simple doggy sound but right now in this place it resonates like "Ode to Joy."

"Arf." "Arf." "Arf."

Fishman surveys the room. He observes the Security Council's charter members taking hold of his message, chewing on it as if it were a Milkbone. The English and French ambassadors are locked in fierce competition. Who is making the purest sound? In truth, the Brit sounds more like a fox hound and the Frenchman, not unexpectedly, like a standard poodle. The American delegation makes a collective yelp reminiscent of a dog pound and the Russian and Chinese delegates improvise sounds that have never been heard before in the chamber. The Chinese ambassador's rendition in particular suggests he prefers to eat a dog more than to sound like one. It has to do with the way he licks his lips, showing his upper gums, and rubs his tummy.

But there is a hardcore group of nations that will have no part in these PUPPY antics. These are North Korea, Syria and Iran. There are others too. Some of the smaller African and South American countries are not sure what to do.

Fishman has an idea. He interrupts the boisterous shouts and laughter.

"May I have your attention, please?"

The room quiets down. The Nigerian and Venezuelan ministers stand up to leave the room.

"Please, everyone return to your seats."

He addresses them in particular. "Please Ambassador Ngomo and Señor Javiez de Quayar. Please be seated. I would like to say something to you. As I address this Assembly this morning, I am mindful of the great history of this organization dating back to 1945 when representatives of fifty countries met in San Francisco at the United Nations Conference on International Organization to draw up its charter. I am also all too aware of your sacred mission, to protect and preserve world peace. In that spirit our barks should not be heard as mindless or frivolous woofs, yaps, howls, growls, yowls, snarls, bays or shouts. We must always think of PUPPY as it was intended. Mankind's best friend."

Fishman looks around the room and sees that there are still unconvinced faces.

"Earlier I had mentioned that I had been given miraculous gifts. I have chosen to use these gifts sparingly. To enlist support. To spread the word. I have resisted requests from individuals, even world leaders to perform magic to satisfy selfish, personal or national interests. My gifts were given to me, to show you, your natural potential. You, each one of you in this room can change the world without the need or benefit of the *supernatural*.

"Now please bear with me. Do not be nervous or afraid. What I am about to do serves a purpose. In particular I am speaking to those of you in this Assembly who were opposed to or reluctant- perhaps you thought it was beneath you, lacking in dognity, just joking- to bark like a dog."

Suddenly robes, suits, head scarves, dresses, turbans, caftans, jackets, shirts, ties, underwear and trousers fly off the delegates' bodies and pileup in a colorful heap on the speaker's stage. The General Assembly looks like a convention of the world's leading nudists. There are presidents, prime ministers, secretaries of state, kings, queens and princes but in their current state all look, for lack of a better word, ordinary. There is finger pointing, some genuine admiration and hands covering smiling lips.

Fishman continues. "You see, we are all really puppies. Look around. When you are hungry, so am I. When you bleed, so will I. Made of protoplasm. We are the same."

There are amazed shouts, followed by applause and locker room laughter.

Fishman is not finished with his presentation. The garments fly up once more in a multi-colored swarm and transform into a wonder of symbols, emblems and signs. There are crosses, stars, crescents, mythological creatures, faces of heroes and prophets from around the world. Images of Life and death. Ancient, Semitic. Persian. There are symbols from alchemy, mystery schools and orders and esoteric tribes. And the last is of the Puppy before the clothes break apart and return to their owners.

Fishman thinks to himself the world's leaders finally get it.

***

Around the globe there are people delivering Fishman's message for unity and world peace. It has become a universal movement far greater than anything that he first imagined, way beyond his dreams for FedEx. Simultaneous rallies are held in London, Washington, Tokyo and New York. Word is spreading in the villages of Southeast Asia, the refugee camps in Angola, and the favellas of Brazil.

In a march in Germany between the cities of Bochum and Essen nursery school children carried colorful banners of Fishman holding a Doberman Pincher reading: "Puppy is our future." They walked for three and a half miles singing, "There was a man who had a dog and Bingo was his name-o."

In a separate demonstration, a rally is organized by clergy at the former Nazi concentration camp, Buchenwald. The ministers reaffirm a pledge made by the camp's few survivors. "We will struggle for world peace. This is the lesson that the Holocaust taught us."

The march is followed by the singing of popular folk songs:

> *"Mr. Bluebird on my shoulder,*
> *It's the truth, it's actual,*
> *Everything is satisfactual.*
> *Zippetty do dah, zippetty yeah.*
> *Wonderful feelings, wonderful day."*

In Pakistan tens of thousands of demonstrators from all across the country march in Karachi in support of PUPPY. Punjabis, Sindhis, Pashtuns, Baluchis, and Mohajirs walk arm in arm, placards held high, to celebrate the one-year anniversary of Shias and Sunnis United for Peace.

Sheik Sayyid Ali Achbar Ibn Satani is about to address the crowd. For more than half a century the sheik has been a guiding light and boundless source of knowledge and inspiration to his people. He has taught legions of jurists, clergymen, educators and public officials. He is a towering figure both literally and spiritually. At six feet eight inches, his presence is formidable. The sheik recently discovered Fishman's message in a Fatwa footnote. Before that his pious pursuits were restricted to prayer, purity, judgments, Hajj rituals and obligatory baths. Ibn Satani has a lighthearted although studious demeanor. He resides in a modest house and is fond of wearing inexpensive garments like the flowing black robes and turban that he has on today.

The Grand Ayatollah addresses the crowd. "Today we send a message to all peace loving countries around the globe. Our movement is alive and strong. We the defenders of peace are here to stay. I have a dream that one day all mankind will be united. Peaceful and free. This will be the day when all of God's children will be able to say with new meaning, 'One God, the source of protoplasm. We are all the same.' And if we are to be a great world, this must come true. So let its truth ring out from every Madrassah in Lahore, Muzaffarabad and Peshawar. From every back alley in Karachi, Rawalpindi and Quetta. Let its truth ring out from the great pyramids of Egypt to the nuclear reactors of Pyongyang. From the sugar cane fields of Cuba to the train stations of Madrid. Let truth ring out in Damascus, Beirut and New York. From the Negev desert in Israel to the seat of the Great Ayatollahs in Teheran. But not only that. Let its truth ring out from Fellujah and Baghdad. From Gaza, Ramallah and Jenin. From every insurgent's nest and defender's fortress let its truth be known. When we let the Truth be known, when we let the Truth be known from every village and hamlet, from every city and country, we will speed up that day when all of God's children, Shia and Sunni, Baluchi and Pashtun, Kashmiri and Palestinian, Christian and Jew will be able to join hands and sing out loud together, the Power of Protoplasm! The Power of Protoplasm! Thank God Almighty for the Power of Protoplasm."

Chapter 20

Fishman's message of peace spreads like wildfire.

Politicians and religious leaders as well as ordinary people are coming forward to support "the dog." But it is their actions, not their words, that speak the loudest.

In Israel, Prime Minister Chanah Bas Shalom has received a ringing endorsement from her Feminist Worker's Party. It solidly embraces her proposal to internationalize Jerusalem and create a holy land for the world's religions. The vote by party members is non-binding, but it sheds light on the plan's future as well as on the stability of Ms. Bas Shalom's government. The balloting was carried out on one of the most peaceful days in recent memory. Palestinians and former Israeli West Bank settlers celebrated together in their churches, synagogues and mosques.

Just weeks before interdenominational crews began construction on the Arafat-Sharon Interfaith Center, a 21st century residential and work complex designed to achieve, in the words of its brochure, "peak peace performance at an affordable price." The center boasts flexible office and conference room space where tenants can work effectively in peace and quiet. Each apartment has its own chapel for meditation and worship; a lounge for receptions, meetings and relaxation. There are peace displays and exhibits; in-house food service, kosher and pork-free upon request. There is also a one hundred and fifteen car parking garage, emergency health service and an ecumenical library staffed by professional librarians of all faiths and political persuasions. The Center also has its own sports teams that have joined the Ziono-Muslim Intramural Athletic League. Competition is fierce in track and field, soccer, archery, sling shooting, rock throwing and riflery.

In another development . . .

In a Ramallah news conference, prominent religious leaders, known here, as the Three Tenors, Constantinis Aristarhos, the Patriarch of Jerusalem, Rebbi Menashe Goldstein, the Chief Rabbi of Israel and Sheik Abdullah Al Sosari, the spiritual leader of Hamas, explained why just a few short hours earlier they feverishly danced the horah on the Temple Mount. They were joined by pilgrims from the El-Aksa Mosque, the Church of the Holy Sepulcher and a tour group of Lubavitcher from Brooklyn. According to the prelates, the three of them were miraculously brought together after observing a sky writer over Tel Aviv, drawing "the dog" in a fluffy white cumulus on a biblical sky of blue.

"The puppy's brilliant outline immediately suggested the possibility of inter-religious and political peace," said Al Sosari a former self-described freedom fighter.

Below its waggly tail were written two words in Latin, "Pax Puppiana", added Rabbi Goldstein, a classical scholar who wrote the popular best seller, "Latin for Dummies."

Once the "3T's" met, they discovered that they shared many common interests, above all the need to exist. And they had a similar molecular makeup. But there was more. Constantinis was a great joke teller and as luck would have it, no two people appreciated a funny story more than the Rebbi and the Sheik. In their youth both were cutups, fond of monkey business and horsing around. The Rebbi in particular was known as Menashe the Menace, a name he received for making underarm farts and other weird bodily sounds.

Constantinis told the story of the Patriarch and the Pope.

"The Patriarch of Jerusalem and the Pope are in a meeting in

Rome. The Patriarch notices a phone in the shape of an angel on a side table in the Pope's private chambers.

'What is that for?'

'It's my direct line to the Lord,' answers the Pope.

The Patriarch is skeptical. The Holy Father insists that the Patriarch try it out, and, indeed, he is connected to the Lord.

The Patriarch holds a lengthy discussion with Him. After hanging up he says, 'Thank you very much. This is great! But listen, I want to pay for my phone call.'

The Pope, of course refuses, but the Patriarch is adamant and finally, the pontiff gives in. He checks the counter on the phone and says: 'All right! The charges were 200,000 lira, a hundred and twenty dollars.'

The Patriarch gladly hands over the money.

A few months later, the Pope is in Jerusalem on an official visit. In the Patriarch's chambers he sees a phone identical to his and discovers it also is a direct line to the Lord. The Pope remembers he has an urgent matter that requires divine consultation and asks if he can use his friend's phone. The Patriarch gladly agrees, hands him the phone, and the Pope chats away. After hanging up, the Pope offers to pay for the call. This time, the Patriarch refuses to accept payment. After the Pope insists, the Patriarch relents and looks on the phone counter and says: 'One shekel, twenty-five cents.'

The Pope looks surprised: 'Why so cheap?'

The Patriarch smiles: 'Local call.'"

Constantinis belly laughs with his colleagues before reassuring them and the press with these words, "We in this holy land live in harmony. We are proud of the relationship between Moslems, Christians and Jews. How can civilized people representing the world's great traditions live otherwise?

"And now we pass on to the world the Puppy peace formula. Unity, justice, sustainable economies, universal access to education and compassion for living beings.

Think about it. If we have transformed the world here, *together* we can accomplish anything."

***

Back in Chicago Fishman has not given up his day job. It is his way of staying in touch with the people, like the holy men and women in the Bible who lead simple unadorned lives, dedicated to the service of others.

The FedEx store is Fishman's pulpit, his Mount of Olives and Sinai rolled up into one. It is here where all the real work gets done. Mukitimukiti is no longer critical of Fishman. He has come to value his personality. There is an appreciation of his people skills bordering on true respect. At times Mukitimukiti has even been overheard to tell customers, "I tink da man may be a genius." At other times he has said, "He is crazy, but he is our Feeshman."

But for the life of him, Mukitimukiti can't understand why Fishman has not applied to be a team leader or enrolled in the district manager training program.

He tells himself, "Strenj but dat's how it is vith people like Feeshman."

Even so, Mukitimukiti now solicits Fishman's advice. He is committed to finding out what makes him tick. He tries subtly to get inside his head.

Today for instance as Mukitimukiti orders the monthly cleaning supplies, he carefully checks out his choices with Fishman. "Feeshman, may I have a second?"

Mukitimukiti reads down a long list of products. Fishman appears to be engrossed in this subject as if it were a discussion of world peace with the Pope.

"I've ordered 3M lint rolla, Ajax Blich Cleansa, Simple Green commercial cleena, Goo Goo stain remova, Lift off ink, marker and graffiti killa, Lysol Disinfectant Spray, jumbo size and Rubbermaid all purpose, extra strength, heavy-duty, trigger-sprayer, advanced formula, country-scented, professional formula degreesa."

Fishman can't help but point out the obvious. "We're low on toilet paper."

Mukitimukiti defers to Fishman's judgment, showing his approval. "Tank yu Feeshman. I'll take care ov dat right away. I'll orda de Quilted Nordern. It is more expensive but feels much betta. Soft and gentle."

***

Business at FedEx has never been better. The line forms for blocks and people camp out over night just to get a chance to ship packages and speak with Fishman. Sometimes just seeing him behind the counter, one glimpse is enough.

And they just keep coming. They are hungry for answers and they know there is no one who can help them more than Fishman. They seek his advice about marriage and divorce, falling in love and raising their children. Fishman is asked to play the roles of Ann Landers and "Dear Abby", Jerry Springer and Doctors Phil, Laura and Ruth.

Once a retired stewardess came to the counter, placing a box at her feet and just began singing.

> *"You are my sunshine*
> *My only sunshine.*
> *You make me happy*
> *When skies are grey.*
> *You'll never know, dear,*
> *How much I love you.*

Please don't take my sunshine away."

A woman from Houston wanted to know Fishman's cure for bed wetting, a dentist from Louisville was determined to learn what needed to be filled in his life and a Tibetan landscaper asked, "If Jesus were alive would he be a Christian or a Jew?"

They grill Fishman for council about social services, educational testing, even erectile dysfunction. Is Cialus better than Viagra and why? And what do you do when you are bone hard for nearly four hours?

A customer from Nome, Alaska asked Fishman about the "male pump" and wondered if Fishman had ever thought about penis enlargement.

Fishman wants to be responsive but he feels the demands that are being made of him are increasingly burdensome. There are also e-mails and letters and telegrams. Fishman is told to work wonders and to perform miracles. There are elaborate pleas for teleporting junkets, just a weekend alone anywhere, without the children.

Fishman also receives urgent phone calls at all hours of the night, to cure the sick, even raise the dead. Fishman feels like he is being pulled apart, constantly being stalked. At these times he finds it more and more difficult to view things on the protoplasmic level. He finds himself forgetting about primal goo.

Fishman has made it known to the local TV and radio stations that he no longer does interviews and doesn't want reporters showing up at his door. He doesn't answer Oprah's calls. But still the hounding by sightseers and celebrity seekers is never ending. And so is the attempt by merchandisers and marketers to capitalize on the Fishman name. Fishman fan clubs are popping up all over the place. Street hawkers sell Fishman T-shirts and key chains and the official Puppy signet ring. There are also Fishman auctions on eBay, selling his used Levis, Converse and personal things. There is even the official Fishman Celebrity Website with special offers and autographs, birthday guestbook, holiday archive and schedules of upcoming events. There are also bonus mouse pads and screensavers and the unauthorized Fishman biography DVD. And there is more.

An entrepreneur out of Los Angeles has started a new company called Fishman Fan Media. For a small fee he provides pictures of Fishman with a favorite celebrity. There is Fishman and Britney, Brad, Kate, Christina, Oprah, the Williams sisters, and JLo.

There is also the Fishman signature fragrance, "Messiah." The ad copy reads, "As night falls over the world, the competition in the spirit world becomes more intense and the sensuality more intriguing. At this interlude the essence of rare patchouli is delicately captured. And spiritual memories are born. This is the time for 'Messiah'."

Fishman tries not to succumb to discouragement but it is hard with all the aggressive attention that he is getting. He wants to run away from all the predators eager to consume every ounce of him. He sees himself as a gazelle stalked by a lion. He imagines a ferocious creature hidden in high burnt grass in camouflaged coloring. He sees a commanding, fearless gaze, curved and elongated teeth, sharp claws, and broad shoulders suggesting incredible power. Suddenly the picture shifts and Fishman is the predator. But he feels vulnerable. He imagines snares and deadly ambushes, kills by rival lions and deadly poachers.

When all this began Fishman had imagined something different but even so he is still content. He believes that PUPPY has taken on a life of its own. Its message of unconditional love is taking root and growing all around the world.

But still Fishman grows sad when he reads about himself in the newspapers. He has been called the David Koresh of the canine crowd, the Pete Rose of unity and religion and the Elvis of world peace. Just last week, Dawn, a FedEx secretary from the Southside, told Fishman that next to Ashton Kutcher, he was the second most influential person in her life.

"You like really changed me," is the way she put it and then added, "Have you ever gotten punked?"

Another customer, a bar tender named Frank Savage from Winnetka, asked Fishman if he considered mud wrestling. He hadn't. But then imagined himself in a leopard patterned leotard flawlessly executing a chin lock, pile driver and Boston Crab.

Fishman tastes the dirt.

There are other disturbing events. It does not make Fishman feel good to know that Miramax is planning to make a movie about his formative years in Queens or that Geraldo is planning an exclusive which Fox News alone is bringing to light.

There are reports of a FedEx executive and a secret conversation, a possible conspiracy and an alleged cover-up.

There is also a series of programs called "Who Really Profits from Peace?" Hannity and Combs will get to the bottom of it.

Fishman thinks that the whole notion of *Fishmangate* is ridiculous. It is just another case of rumor and superstition posing as fact. Fishman laughs to himself, recognizing the many angles for covering the "Fishman Story."

There is the human interest angle, "Fishman Finds Success", the story of a failed stock trader, indicted for embezzlement, suffering the tragic loss of his wife and children in a horrific plane crash, but ultimately hailed a big success.

There is also the religious angle, "God Chooses Fishman", the story of a 21st century messiah who bites into a piece of chocolate and proceeds to save the world.

There is the fashion angle, "World Savior Fond of Simple Threads", the story of a former fashion plate, enamored of bespoken British clothing who yearns for only two things: peace between the nations and the opportunity to wear a purple FedEx jumpsuit with an orange apron.

And there is the sci-fi angle, "Religious Freak Invents Teleporting Puts Scientists to Shame", the implausible story of a mechanically inept fundamentalist who discovers the encoded mystery of teleporting in an alien's version of scripture.

Fishman is sure that there are many other ways to relate his story. But they too are all equally wrong.

***

Behind the old parish house, Fishman and Eve have started a garden. Today Fishman is planting a tree. It is a tiny spruce that is going in a large open area filled with sun. He carefully prepares the soil. It is critical to keep the earth moist, not to let the roots go dry. Fishman fingers the soft pliant needles. He knows over time the spruce will grow prickly and stiff, but if nourished and cared for it will survive. As he steps back from his work Fishman says to himself, "It could live for hundreds of years."

Chapter 21

Fishman and Eve are in Memphis visiting Jim Early. They have not seen him since last year at the FedEx convention.

These days the couple flies commercial airlines. It is not that Fishman is reluctant to teleport but he is adamant about using his gifts only when they are *really* called for. Although he is tempted after a particularly trying coach experience, he concludes it would take a lot more than free wine and a few extra inches to lure him to first class.

Jim meets Fishman and Eve at their hotel. Fishman now travels under an alias, Marty Shalibe, and he wears black glasses, a false mustache and whiskers. He calls it his Groucho get-up. The name change was proposed by the C.I.A. after an incident the previous summer that involved the closing down of Chicago O'Hare. Fishman groupies overran the American Airlines terminal totally jamming security procedures and backing up flights on the ground and in the air for hours causing nationwide disruption all too common to resigned travelers. It was a sad sight; mothers bringing forth sick and crippled children begging Fishman for a prayer or just the laying on of his hands. Elderly people beseeching him for more energy and power. The stressed and the tired demanding better health. A Baptist minister from Ashville, North Carolina asked Fishman to bless a gallon of Evian to transform it into holy water from the Lord's natural glacial spring.

As Marty Shalibe, Fishman travels undisturbed but looks a

little strange, a combination of L.A. and downtown Tehran. Today Fishman is wearing a dark suit with a lime green shirt, open at the neck revealing a thick gold chain. If Fishman discoed he would be all set. He imagines himself as a long lost uncle, converted to Orthodox Judaism, returning to visit his favorite nephew after just winning a 50th anniversary dancing contest in the sequel of the sequel to *Saturday Night Fever*.

Eve has learned to live with all the changes. She understands that choosing to save the world and live a normal life makes certain demands. But what they both yearn for is just a little peace and quiet. It's not so simple.

***

Jim is proud to show Eve and Fishman the new FedEx Peace and Fellowship Complex. It is a classical looking structure in the design of a temple, as large as the Parthenon, built around columns in the shape of a FedEx document envelope. The building overlooks a lake. In its waters is the radiating reflection of the sign that stands proudly on its roof, visible on clear days for miles: "Relax, it's FedEx."

The center is a combination all-purpose chapel and retreat. It is the prototype for all the FedEx spiritual centers that are being constructed around the world to spread the faith. It is also the world headquarters of the Fishman Corps or what has come to be known as Puppy Corps. Volunteers have been invited by one-hundred and thirty-four host countries to work on a range of issues to build better lives for individuals and whole communities.

Fishman is impressed. He smiles at Eve and then looks at Jim.

Early starts to laugh. He is staring at Fishman who is still dressed in his Groucho-disco guise. "I can't get used to you in that outfit."

Eve now looks at Fishman with fresh eyes. "I know. It's

really something."

Fishman for a moment imagines himself to be a spy, a double agent. He has been sent from a higher power to gather secrets and classified information.

Early interrupts his thought. "Fishman what do you call that look, hip-hop?"

"It's disco. Don't you know anything?"

"I guess not. I've always been a Brooks Brothers man myself."

Fishman turning more serious. "You've done an incredible job."

Early unwilling to take all the credit. "No, it's you who really did it. You had the vision. You're a lousy dresser but you do have vision."

"But you had the strength to see things through."

Fishman now looking all around. "Just look at this."

Eve now spots a group of people in the back of the Temple. They are pointing at the three of them. Eve has developed a sixth sense about being spotted. She knows that once Fishman is recognized all hell will break loose. News reporters and Fishman watchers will start arriving in droves.

Someone from the group screams, "It's Fishman."

Suddenly cries go up throughout the Temple.

"Fishman. Fishman."

"The man in the beard. It's Fishman."

"My child is dying. I need Fishman. Please."

For a moment Fishman is frozen in place. He has been through this many times before. Soon he will be confronted by the hungry mob asking him to provide only one thing: they will be loved and comforted, always, under every circumstance with no exception and all their suffering coming to an end.

And now Fishman is surrounded by a ring of supplicants who crave his unconditional love. He looks into the crowd unable to see individual faces. But he hears their cries.

"Help me."
"Save me."
"Fix me."
"Love me."
"Love me."
"Never stop. Love me."

***

That evening Fishman and Eve are alone in their hotel room. Fishman walks over to a sliding glass window through which he sees the city lights below, sparkling like a diamond choker. He turns to Eve.

"We're shut-ins. There's no place for us to go."

Eve laughs. "We could move."

Fishman considers the possibility but then can't imagine a place where he won't be recognized.

"To where, Antarctica?"

"I was thinking of somewhere warmer."

"Like the desert?"

"Yes, exactly. Where it's warm and they can use your talents."

"Where is that?"

Eve shouts out. "Las Vegas."

Fishman thinks to himself, "the city that has something for everyone."

And then adds, "But I'll have to change. I can get plastic surgery."

Eve is now rethinking her plan. "But I love your face."

"Don't worry, you'll get used to my new one."

Fishman can now see himself and Eve in the most exciting and entertaining city in the world. He feels its magnetic pull. He longs for bright neon and the Las Vegas strip. Where else, he thinks to himself, can you find dazzling lights, pyramids, erupting volcanoes, even Venice all in one place.

Fishman repeats the two words that most capture his state of mind.

"Salvation. Las Vegas."

***

Plastic surgery is easier said than done. Fishman finds it painful but is generally pleased with its results. His head is shaven and with a new nose and chin, Fishman is totally unrecognizable to the world and, in truth, even to himself. Fishman appears as a cross between Yul Bryner and the Dalai Lama, but as he looks in the mirror all he sees is Theo Kojak, the New York detective known for his tough talk, lollipops and shiny bald head. He imagines himself solving impossible crimes, looking straight into the camera saying, "Who loves ya', baby?"

In Las Vegas Fishman is determined to do things his way. Like Kojak he is prepared to follow his instincts regardless of what the bosses think. He sees himself outspoken and streetwise and not above stretching the literal interpretation of the law if it will help him crack one of life's mysteries: how to find peace of mind.

Eve and Fishman are settling into an apartment they rented less than a mile off the Strip. From their balcony they have a view of the Luxor Hotel and Casino. A ten-story replica of the Sphinx of Giza guards the entrance of the black pyramid hotel. At night the world's brightest beam of light atop the pyramid illuminates the desert sky. Inside is a true to life replica of the great Temple of Ramses II with colorful hieroglyphics and King Tut's Tomb. There are also authentic gaming tables for blackjack, baccarat and pai gow next to slot machines, a poker room, race and sports book, and a keno lounge.

Fishman works the casino dressed in the pleated linen garment of an ancient Egyptian. He is a hospitality worker. His job is to make sure the guests are happy and to mingle with the crowd. Thick kohl outlines his eyes and a fake gold and lapis lazuli serpent coils about his upper arm. Fishman imagines himself as Moses before the Exodus and the burning bush and the death of first borns and the Nile turning blood red.

As always, Fishman takes his work seriously. It is not exactly FedEx but he tries to make it the next best thing. He is still committed to making a difference, improving the world in any way that he can.

Fishman imagines an IMAX movie about hospitality workers. Over the opening credits is a statement delivered by the Pope.

"As hospitality workers, for every visitor with whom you interact, you are the embodiment of all that is positive in the world. Each of you epitomizes the values of humility, sincerity, service, and respect and most of all, treating another human being as if he or she is worthy of all these things."

Fishman is living out a fantasy in the land of mass produced homogenized fantasy. He is an underground savior in search of his cause. But he can again live something approaching a normal life. He has discovered a way to avoid the oppressive crush of endless needs, hurts and demands. Fishman is now certain that he will save the world on his terms.

"And what better place," he says to himself, "than right here."

In the rear of the Luxor casino in the shadows of the restrooms, a young couple is exchanging harsh words. They are in their early twenties. The woman is tall with dark hair, blue eyes and olive skin. He is Latino or middle eastern. They are both fashionably dressed in skin tight jeans and trendy tops. Hers has a blue Ganesh on a pink background. His is bright orange. She is wearing red Nikes with straps, and he is in Gucci boots as shiny as a showroom polished Ferrari. She pulls away from him. He grabs at her arm.

"Leave me alone. How could you do it? Everything."

"I said I'm sorry. It was for both of us."

He won't let her go. She tries to pull away even harder.

"You lost it all. We have nothing."

Fishman approaches them. They are both momentarily startled by the sight of a bald headed man wearing a pleated loincloth.

"Can I bring you something?"

The guy barks back. "No. Leave us alone."

"How about a drink, on the house?"

The guy goes off on Fishman. "Out of here, freak."

The girl tries to apologize. "He doesn't mean it."

Now turning back to her boyfriend. "Don't talk to him like that."

He yanks at her arm. Fishman against all common sense gets between the two of them.

"Please let her go."

Reflexively, the guy punches Fishman in the face.

"Ow, I didn't see that coming."

Fishman is down nursing his lip, feeling for blood.

At the sight of Fishman hitting the floor the couple now seems to be brought back to their senses. The guy turns to Fishman.

"Jesuz. I'm sorry."

"Are you ok? I don't know what got into Frank."

Fishman matter of factly. "I'll live. What's your name?"

"Angie. And you are?"

"Think of me as Akhenaten, the heretic king. Father of monotheism. According to Freud, Moses."

"I mean really?"

"Akhenaten. Moses. Take your pick"

Fishman sees something familiar in Frank's hand. "What's that?"

"Just something I picked up. It's called the Palefsky Chronicle. Have you read it?"

"Yes, I have."

Fishman would like to tell Frank and Angie all about the Palefsky Chronicle and how writing it changed his life. He would also like to tell them about growing up in Queens and the Excelsior's revolving planets and about what happened to Ploopy Goldberg. But he doesn't. He merely says. "Some imagination."

Frank takes on a more serious look. "I think it's all true."

"True?"

"You can feel the guy's pain. Amelia is killed in a plane crash and Palefsky's whole world turns upside down. Angie and I know what that's like."

Frank now trying to make up to Fishman, looking at his swollen lip. "I'm really sorry about that. Wish I could make it up to you."

Fishman in a definite tone. "You can."

"Huh?"

"I get off in ten minutes. Let me buy you dinner."

Angie now chimes in. "We couldn't possibly accept after . . ."

"After Frank nearly tore off my head?"

She smiles. "Well yes."

"I insist."

***

Fishman is now back in his street clothes. He takes Frank and Angie to the Wheel of Fortune Café. The restaurant resembles the interior of a pinball machine with a virtual wheel that revolves on the ceiling twenty-four hours a day. Each booth has a number corresponding to the twenty-seven pie slices of equal size that turn in an unending illumination of light, like a spinning visitation, from above. For a small wager, or even the price of the check, you can play and eat a sandwich to your heart's content.

Fishman looks around the restaurant. He is seated opposite Frank and Angie on a banquette of red and yellow vinyl. He studies their young faces. Fishman knows what it is like to be lost in a net of suffering and sadness. He senses pain and wants to help Frank and Angie find their way back.

Frank is impressed by the "wheel." He is still in play mode even though he has lost everything.

"Some place!"

Fishman almost chastising. "Frank, look around, it's for losers. You and Angie need to get out of here. I can help but it is up to you."

Angie starts to cry. Frank puts his arm around her. He tries to comfort her. "Angie. Please."

"We have nothing. We lost everything."

Fishman takes Angie's hand. "Your child?"

She searches his eyes. "Jed. He was my baby. Last summer. Hit by a car."

Frank reaches into his pocket, pulls out a brown cowhide wallet from which he removes the dog-eared school photograph of a five or six year-old. "Hit and run. They never got the driver."

Frank tries to fight back the emotion. "I told him not to ride in the street."

Fishman in his most sincere voice. "I lost my children too. It's not an accident that we met."

Angie is lost in the kindness of Fishman's face. She no longer sees the man half-clad as an Egyptian. "Who are you?"

"I told you earlier. Moses." He laughs.

"Who are you really?"

"It's a long story."

"How long?"

"Longer than a chronicle."

Angie not relenting. "Please, tell me."

Uncharacteristically Fishman does not think before he answers. "Can you keep a secret?"

Angie answers quickly. "Yes."

"Frank?"

Frank only half believing his response. "OK."

Fishman is not satisfied with his reply. "Frank, you'll have to do better than that."

Angie nudges Frank.

"OK. OK."

There's the long pause of someone diving, holding his breath for an extended time before resurfacing.

"I'm Palefsky."

Frank suddenly animated. "No shit. You're Palefsky?"

"Shh, not so loud. In a way. Not exactly."

Angie looks totally lost. "You're confusing us. You're Moses, you're an Egyptian. You're Palefsky?"

Fishman continues. "There is no Palefsky really. He is made up."

Frank almost incensed. "I could have sworn he was real."

"Frank, it is real. Very real. Too real"

"But you just said . . ."

"I said I'm Palefsky. I wrote the Chronicle. It's a text . . . I was sick. My heart was broken. Like yours. I lost my wife. My children. I wanted to die. I was dead. Then I found a way back. I imagined a person whose sole mission in life was to help others, to make things better, to save the world. I called him Palefsky."

"But Palefsky doesn't save the world. He can barely save himself."

"That's right and that's why God created Fishman."

Angie is beginning to think that maybe there is something the matter with the former Egyptian. Is he deranged? After all, what does she know about him?

Fishman sees Angie elbowing Frank below the table. He tries

to reassure her.

"I told you. It is a long story."

For a second Angie entertains the notion that this has all the makings of an elaborate con job or work of fiction.

"I'm listening."

Fishman begins slowly. "Ok, let's start with Palefsky. The real Palefsky.

"You just said you made Palefsky up."

"I said there was no real Palefsky, in the Chronicle. But there was a *real* Max Palefsky. He was born on May 16, 1902 in Vienna. His father Leopold was a poor merchant descended from five generations of rabbis and scholars. When Palefsky was eleven, he and his three sisters followed their father to Chicago. He attended public school and graduated from City College at nineteen. He loved to argue and was a man of the most intense passion. But you never heard of him, right?"

Angie and Frank shake their heads. Frank now only half understanding. "So he is real?"

"At twenty-seven Palefsky was one of the wealthiest men on Wall Street. A brilliant commodities trader and dealmaker. He had an incredible mind and the ability to get things done. He was small. Just five feet two but he had a king-size heart and though he was childless, he had a special love for children, and they for him. I'm told his concern for other human beings had to be observed to be believed."

Frank wants to get all of the facts at once. "How did you hear about him?"

Fishman takes his time. "I'll get to that. At the peak of his career Palefsky quit his business and devoted himself to more important things. A lifetime dedicated to helping others. He built schools and hospitals, playgrounds. He provided money to fight discrimination and pass fair labor laws. During the Holocaust he saved thousands of lives. And always anonymously. His sole intention was to leave the world in a better state than he found it."

Angie listens intently. Frank asks a question, "Did you know him?"

"I knew *about* him. Remember I told you that I was sick?"

Angie speaks in a comforting voice, "You were depressed after you wife and children died."

"Yes, Angie. I didn't think I would be able to go on."

"I feel that way sometimes too. So does Frank. I think that's why we came here. It makes you feel numb. You forget and then feel guilty because I want to remember. I love Jed."

Tears well up in Angie's eyes. Frank puts his arm around her. Fishman reaches across the table, holds her hand.

"That's how I feel about Nadia, James and Lara. Most people live their lives that way. I tried to, but it didn't work. That's why I created Fishman. But I'm getting ahead of myself."

Angie suddenly has an urge to know. "Why are you telling all this to *us*?"

"Angie, I think you know."

Frank searches Angie's face for an answer. She shrugs her shoulders.

Fishman returns to his earlier point. "I felt like Moses on Mount Sinai. You know where he receives the Ten Commandments."

Fishman laughs. He realizes that he is lost in a private joke and then continues.

"Mt. Sinai Hospital. In New York. I was there for the depression."

Frank remembering a detail. "Oh yeah. There was something about that in the Chronicle."

"Good memory. My doctor told me the story about the man, during the war, who had saved his father's life. He was the same person whose name was on the hospital wing."

"Palefsky?"

"Yes. That's when I decided to make the change. At least, I thought to myself, 'Think of me as Palefsky, Max Palefsky. Not the loser who goes around telling people he's me.'"

Angie isn't sure she really gets it. "Did that help?"

"Changing my name?"

"Thinking of yourself as Palefsky?"

"It helped me to remember. Like you and Jed. I started to think about things that were half buried or completely forgotten. Like Ploopy Goldberg."

Angie returns to her earlier question. "But why tell all this to *us*?"

"Ploopy was four when he died. He thought he could fly. Little Icarus in short pants."

"Your friend?"

"My brother. I was watching him."

Tears form in Fishman's eyes. He wipes away a tear that has run down his right cheek.

"Ploopy loved to watch the birds fly. I was only gone for a minute but it was long enough. He fell from our bedroom window."

Angie squeezes Fishman's hand. "And you blame yourself?"

Fishman lifts his head up and looks straight into Angie's eyes. He smiles at her. "We have to stop doing that. It's not our fault."

***

In a few short hours Fishman has managed to transport Angie, Frank and himself from the Nile Valley to the Via Appia of ancient Rome. They are standing between the Coliseum and the Forum. They walk by opulent fountains, bas reliefs and roaming slightly bored centurions. Outside of Caesar's Palace you can observe everyday life on the Strip. There are wedding chapels, gift stores, gentlemen's clubs and ever more casinos. It is a fantasyland, devoid of the everyday landmarks of supermarkets, post offices, bakeries, video rental stores.

As they approach the Palace's entrance Fishman stops and looks at the young couple. "Here is the plan. You won't have to sleep in your car. We are going in here because your luck is about to change."

Angie and Frank look at Fishman dubiously. Frank volunteers, "We've already done this once tonight."

"Angie, trust me on this. It's practically a sure thing."

Fishman hands Angie a hundred dollar chip. "What is your favorite number?"

Frank answers for his wife, "Three, right?"

"You know it is."

Fishman takes charge. "Ok. I want you to play Angie's number. We will just do this once and then meet in the morning. When you've won, you'll have enough to stay here tonight."

They both look around. They are eager to go along with Fishman's plan but don't think they have a prayer. Angie and Frank approach the roulette table and place their bet. Fishman stands in the background. Angie and Frank watch the pallid sphere rotating like the Earth. It circles the revolving wheel, whirling; turning, spinning reality into dreams, spiraling also the other way around. And then the ball starts to drop, it stutters, dives then plunges, hopping out of an undesired hole, inevitably coming to a complete stop on three, exactly as Fishman predicted.

He remembers the Planetarium. Planets set like pearls in peaceful space.

Angie screams, hugging Frank. "We did it."

"We did it."

Chapter 22

Something strange happens to your sense of reality when you are exposed to desert heat. Moisture disappears from the skin. Within minutes you begin to see things you have never seen before.

Angie and Frank are now with Eve and Fishman. They have been driving for eight hours to become part of *Burning Man*.

Fishman pulls off the highway and exits at the entrance of Black Rock Desert, hundreds of square miles of nothing, a remote wilderness. Civilization is far, far away. It is as if they are touching down on another planet.

Fishman tells Angie and Frank, only half joking, that he's taking them to a place where "you may die but you'll never feel so alive."

The temperature is in excess of 110 degrees.

Frank wants more facts. "What is it?"

Fishman tries to reassure him. "*Burning Man* . . . it's like trying to explain color to someone who is blind. Do you remember Beano? From Palefsky? It's something like that."

Fishman tries a different tack. "Frank, we're all here to participate."

They pull onto the Playa and park. It is an ancient lake bed, a desolate landscape of mirages and magic. A vast sweep of natural emptiness, an ocean that you can walk on. It is one of the largest, flatest places on earth, over twenty-five miles long and fifteen miles wide. It is so barren that surface curvature is evident.

Fishman hands everyone a bag, keeping one for himself.

"Don't open them till I tell you to. It's my little surprise."

He also hands out glasses to protect their eyes from the dust.

"We need to wear these."

They can already feel the dust on their tongues. It has a slick silty taste.

And then suddenly, out of a dream, a vast misty apparition in the form of a makeshift city appears. A play within a play, concentric circles of nesting dolls and Chinese boxes reveal themselves for the first time.

Frank and Angie experience a haze of images. A shelter made in the form of an egg, a car that looks like a giant centipede, A pink space ship from a far-off galaxy, Marie Antoinette walking on stilts and a woman who looks like someone's grandmother wearing only a pearl necklace and straw hat.

Angie turns to Frank and Fishman in disbelief, then grabs Eve's arm. "It's like the circus, only better."

Frank looks like he is in shock. "I've never seen anything like this. It's a dream."

As he says that they pass a ten-foot tall geranium.

Burning Man is parts Satyricon, Cirque du Soleil, la vie Boheme, Apocalypse Now and Day of the Dead. It has more Daliesque slices than a whirling Mad Max wheel of fortune, spinning on and off its axis.

On the tabula rasa of the Playa everything is possible. Inventions are limitless with no contradictions. There are hot springs releasing mystical steam and prophets with full-body tattoos and nose rings.There are fairies, nymphs and pixies. A dog and a cat carry human mannequins. Everywhere there is music and magic in the air.

In front of Bianca's Smut Shack, Fishman says, "OK, let's open our packages.Frank you first."

Frank tears at his bag and starts to laugh.

Angie doesn't get the joke. "What's so funny?"

"It's a Maverick costume with short pants. The gambler. I

guess someone's making a comment on my poker playing."

Frank makes a mock glower at Fishman. "Glad you like it."

Fishman then points to Angie's bag. "Open yours."

"Mr. Potato Head!" She shouts. "I love it!"

Eve doesn't wait for Fishman's cue. She opens her bag and annouces its content.

"Wonder Woman."

"Yes, you are." And Fishman then asks, "Guess what mine is?"

In unison Frank, Angie and Eve answer correctly. "Akhenaten. Moses."

They all have a good laugh.

They change in The Body Politic, the communal bath house, and walk further along the Playa. They pass a large hand-painted circus sign of a giant crimson bird that reads "Man-eating Chicken" and as they turn the corner they see a man seated at a table eating chicken.

Whichever way they look they see people in costume, many in dust masks and goggles. There are elves and gremlins, men and women in striped and patterned bathrobes, sheiks in turbans, belly dancers, tribal elders in war paint and feathers, and a girl dressed as a flaming phoenix, rising from the ashes over and over again. To the left and right there are giant structures and installations. There are floating worlds of paint and fabric. Clipper ships with their crews of half dressed and nude singers and dancers. Musicians painted in silver and gold whose tempos match the rhythms of the wind. There are also schools of human fish, swimming on land in dazzling aquatic colors. There is a Temple of Joy and a Temple of Tears and a twenty foot Aeolian harp. A picket fence made of flourescent tubes and The Great Hamster Wheel of Doom. In it painted figures run around a continuous treadmill. One holds up a sign "Pinwheel of Broken Dreams," another warns "No Time to Stop Now."

There is also an exhibit laid out as a boardgame called "The

Seven Ages of Man." Frank and Angie, Fishman and Eve follow its path. It begins with the cradle where you have the option to return symbolically to the womb and be reborn. You are encouraged to go at your own pace. There are tunnels and passageways, paths leading nowhere and occasional blind alleys. There are chutes and trap doors that require decisions with consequences for bad choices. The game ends at Enlightenment but few make it to the end.

There is also the Mausoleum of Distorted Memory where you can revise your past and the Optometry of Perfect Vision where you can see far into your future.

Fishman is sitting off to the side mesmerized by the unending human parade. He is waiting for Frank, Angie, and Eve. They are still working their way through the "Seven Ages." Fishman watches the sun going down. He sees its colorful descent as just another element of this amazing theater. He thinks to himself that it is in just this sort of natural surroundings that great ideas and religions are born, baking in an open air kiln of constant heat and occassional dust storms.

In the distance Fishman sees the fifty foot Burning Man not yet ignited on his ziggurat-like pedestal. He imagines if it could speak it would say to him, "For you, I love, pray, work, sing, dance, create, seek enlightenment and die. Welcome home. I will burn for you."

***

The night offers relief from the day's heat. Fishman, Eve, Angie, and Frank are sitting around a small campfire, one of many that encircle the Burning Man. It is a moonless night but the group overhears someone nearby saying, "Mars moved to its closest point to Earth in sixty thousand years." They look up and see, through the clouds, a winking red eye.

A woman in her early thirties, dressed in a long flowing gown of floral silk, her face painted in shades of blue, purple and red joins the campfire. Eve welcomes her.

"Hi, I'm Eve. This is Angie, Frank, Fishman. I mean Moses."

"Oh, like the peace guy they are looking for?

"I'm Rita, the Benevolent Mother. Is this your first burn?"

Fishman speaks up. "Eve and I have been here before. First time for Angie and Frank. What brings you here?"

"This is my sixth burn. A friend told me about it after my son Charlie died. He drowned in Crystal Lake."

Angie joins in. "Frank and I . . . our son Jed was killed by a drunk driver."

"I came here and I was reborn. I have a son Max who is five. He is a wild child and a daughter who is three. Dawn."

A tall dark man wearing a swan dress who looks like Björk arrives. His feathers puff up from the heat of the fire. Rita turns to him. "This is my man Nick. He's an artist."

Nick waves to everyone then shakes Frank and Fishman's hand.

"Rita, we've got to go."

"Wait." Rita turns to Angie.

"You know what I learned here? Grief doesn't equal love. I found out I wasn't betraying Charlie when I laugh. I just made him the source of my joy."

Rita and Nick walk off. Angie hugs Frank and then Fishman and Eve join in.

Fishman loves the warmth generated by their bodies holding on to each other. He imagines like him, Eve, Angie and Frank feel connected. They are all part of the One, part of the only thing that ever really matters, unconditional love.

Fishman looks into the distance and sees rings of fire extending as far as his eyes can see. It reminds him of when he was a child in the Hayden Planetarium in New York, spending many hours alone in the starry dark watching strange objects form over head, nearly perfect rings of hot blue stars, wheels within wheels spinning around a yellow nucleus of galaxies and comets from the farthest reaches of the solar system. He reminds himself of the system of comets called "sungrazers" so named because their orbit closely brushes the sun, arriving to their inevitable end in clusters on parallel paths. Their fragmentation the result of gravity's strong pull disintegrating their loosely piled chunks of dust and ice into luminous cascades of one comet falling into large families of smaller ones. Their gradual demise has a hypnotic effect, celestial fireworks in mysteriously orderly patterns, in natural life cycles and solar systems.

But as he reconstructs them now in his mind there is no fragmentation. There is only connection and energy, spontaneous and unpredictable.

***

Fishman looks above the rings and discovers the looming figure of the Man in all its surreal splendor. Around him illuminated by campfire are the performers of secret rites and rituals and the pervasive alkali dust from a blowing wind. There are kaleidoscopic colors, pageants and processions, prophets and poets, men and women dressed as Russian icons. You are hypnotized and entertained, touched by boundless energy and spontaneous celebration. There are also singers and dancers, tumblers and drummers, fire performers and thieves in the dark whose ecstatic rhythms steal your breath away.

Fishman points up to the sky and makes sure Eve, Angie and Frank again see Mars' blinking red eye glowing like a sign.

And now there is a belly dancer pulling people out, encouraging them to dance in front of the Man. A male dressed in an eighteenth century ball gown shouts out something from the crowd. People from all directions approach the figure with poems and hair lockets, hand written notes and personal mementos.

Fishman hands Frank and Angie a small folded piece of paper. They look at each other, then Angie writes, "We love you Jed." Angie kisses it, so does Frank.

Fishman wiping away tears just writes down three words: "Nadia James Lara" on the other side of it are the letters CB.

They approach the structure with the others who have lost or wish to honor loved ones. And then the music abruptly ends. Fishman, Eve, Angie, and Frank are wrapped under a single blanket. There is silence. A speaker addresses the crowd through a bullhorn. He's older, lean and muscular, part aged hippy, part auto mechanic. He has a long salt and pepper pony tail and a pleasant voice.

"When all this started no one imagined that Burning Man would be a yearly ritual. I'm going to start with the first question I always get, and that's about how this began. The story is that one day in June . . . of course you've all heard the story about my girlfriend, and that's gonna be written on my tombstone, no doubt . . . and it's true. I had heartbreak. Then I moved on to a mid-life crisis. There was always something. I got tired of it. If you've ever had a heartbreak you know it's the anniversaries that'll kill you. You know, you walk into a bar and they're playing your song. It's another crisis. She's gone but hey, enjoy the memory. It was good. It's a big world. And each one of us has a place in it."

There is laughter around the campfires.

"We'd go down to Baker Beach, and an old friend of mine had a little solstice celebration she did. It was nominally pagan, although with a certain San Francisco twist. I remember she had a little boom box that was an electronic shaman drum. It was the most soulless instrument I've ever heard. And it was making these mechanical thuds around the fire. They dressed a couple mannequins in polyester, piled them on a couch and threw it into the fire."

There are cheers and applause.

"I felt better. I thought 'This is my kind of solstice celebration.' And I'd taken my girlfriend down there, and her son was doing something only a fourteen year-old would invent. He was saturating the sand with gasoline, and then taking a burning stick and writing in fire. So I knelt with my lover and we wrote in the sand . . . yeah, you get the picture . . ."

There is an audible sound of awwww!

"And it was supremely romantic. And so two years later, having thought of this morning and night for a couple of years I woke up and it was the solstice, and I thought 'I'm tired of all this.' So I called up a friend and I said 'Hey, Let's burn a man.' And he asked me to repeat that statement. So we went over and we made this man out of scrap lumber in a basement in Noe Valley, and it looked big to us, it was two feet taller than we were. And then we hauled it, we called a couple of friends, and there was about twelve of us, and we hauled it down to the beach and we soaked it with gasoline, because we didn't know any better. And gasoline's very volatile, and when it flamed up, it was like a second sun brought down to earth. It just transfixed us. And that's where the story begins."

He points to the fifty-foot high man and says, "And this is where we are now. It gets bigger every year. More people pour their energy into it. It's a big fucking coming together, which is what it's all about."

There is loud applause followed by a troupe of dancers, carrying torches, emerging from the night. Their bodies are painted in all the colors of the rainbow. They are only wearing elaborate headdresses and glowing in the dark. As the music builds the Man's legs catch fire. There are shouts and chants, prayers and reaching out. There is impromptu singing and dancing and people making love. There is also the occasional dust devil spinning around the fire. The fire reaches above his shoulders to his face. You can hear Him, inflamed, calling out into the desert night.

"Burn me. Open your arms and hearts. Be reborn with your

gifts and drumbeats. Offer me your heartbreak and regrets. I am here to consume your sadness and sorrow. I welcome your tortured screams and painful shouts. In me find a new beginning. Reinvent your human nature. Burn me. Burn your sorrow."

Fishman smiles at Eve, Angie, and Frank against an arc of fire-lit faces. Together, arms entwined, they experience the power of the burn. There is no escape from its omnipresent flame.

In the night air Angie and Frank hear a song played on a bagpipe just as the silhouette of the large man disappears.

Chapter 23

It is mid-afternoon and Fishman and Eve are sitting with Angie and Frank at Birdland, a small restaurant in Las Vegas' McCarran Airport around a yellow Formica table with a pair of red dice drawn in its center. Everyone is sipping coffee and Angie orders a slice of pie. She holds up a forkful to Fishman and Eve and asks them, "Want some?"

They decline. Angie undeterred, takes a bite. She lets the fruit slowly dissolve on her tongue, sucking in all its sweetness, licking her lips.

"Peach, my favorite. They don't ever seem to make it just the way I like it back in Holderness." She then quickly adds, "New Hampshire is a great place. You'll have to visit us."

Fishman jumps in. "Near Squam Lake? I was once there with my family. As a boy, on vacation."

There is a short pause and then he resumes. "You know I was just thinking. We know almost nothing about you. What do you do out there?"

Frank asks, "You mean for work?"

Angie can't help herself from interrupting. "It's a great story. You want to hear how we met?"

Frank throws Angie the look of someone who has heard this story way too many times.

Angie continues. "It was at work. Well, it was and it wasn't."

Frank is softening. "Ok, get it over with."

"Frank and I worked for the same company but we'd never

met. I mean I knew there was this cute guy that the other girls talked about but we didn't speak."

Frank adds some details. "I saw Angie and wanted to but . . . you know how it is."

Angie picks up the story. "I was on I-95 in a snowstorm and hit a patch of ice. The car swerved to the left, then right then spun all the way around and slammed into a tree. Miraculously I was ok. But then the engine ignited and burst into flame and my doors jammed and my foot was stuck down on the gas petal. I couldn't free myself or find a way out."

"Enter my hero."

Frank continues. "I'm driving to work and I see this car go into a spin. It looks real bad from where I'm sitting. When I get to her she's screaming. Then I see the fire and know there's no time to think. I just have to get her out."

"Frank tried to force the door open but it wouldn't budge. He picked up this huge rock from the side of the road and broke the rear window. He reached in and pulled me out. He saved my life."

Fishman's face takes on an astonished look. He turns to Eve and says in a half- whisper, "He's Frank Ingram."

Fishman looks at Frank. His voice is now louder. "You are Frank Ingram. Am I right?"

Fishman yells over to the waitress who is awakened from her rote filling of sugar bowls by Fishman's loud voice. "He's Frank Ingram."

"Tell me Frank. Am I right?"

The whole restaurant can now hear Fishman.

Frank nods his head. "Yeah. That's me."

Eve is still non-plussed.

Angie too wonders what's up.

"Eve don't you get it? 'Worker of the Year.' FedEx."

Frank misreads Fishman's agitated behavior. "You've got something against them?"

Fishman laughs to himself and decides to have a little fun

with Frank.

"Frank what could I possibly have against FedEx. In fact, I know a little bit about the company. In your professional opinion do you think it is better than the U.S. Postal Service? Please don't answer. Frank, Eve and I worked for FedEx."

"Doing what?"

"You name it."

"Transit?"

"Yes."

"Freight?"

"Yes."

"Packaging?"

"Yes."

"International?"

"Yes."

"How could you possibly do all those things?"

"Frank, I ran the company. Well sort of. Let's just say I did absolutely, positively whatever it takes."

Angie now enters the conversation. "Something's been bothering me. The whole Fishman thing. A few nights ago you said, 'And that's why God created Fishman.' What did you mean?"

Fishman takes a long breath. "Angie, do you remember that I said it was a long story? It is. Have you heard of Fishman?"

"Sure. Everyone has."

Frank interrupts. "Angie and I once heard him speak in Boston and then at the FedEx convention. We saw him on TV when he was at the U.N."

"Frank, Palefsky and Fishman are the same person."

"You've got to be shittin'. You're Fishman?"

Fishman continues to talk about himself in the third person. "Fishman had a realization. A visionary without will and ability is just a dreamer. He developed a plan and came up with a vehicle, FedEx. Fishman was determined to save the world."

Angie studies his face. "But you don't look anything like

Fishman."

Eve tries to clear things up. "The wonder of plastic surgery."

Fishman reflexively points out some of the finer points. "It's a miracle what they can do today. Eyes. Lips. Nose."

Fishman makes a combing motion with his palm across his head. "Even bad hair can be fixed."

Angie works at putting all this together. "And that's why no one has heard from Fishman for the past few years?"

"That's right. I felt I had accomplished my work."

Fishman grows more enthusiastic. "Look at FedEx. It is changing lives all around the world. People recognize that all of us are connected. We really are the same."

"The power of protoplasm."

"Exactly. Peace is breaking out all over the world. But my work is still not finished. It will never be through. You and Frank have shown me that."

"But why did Fishman . . . I mean, why did you go away."

"I was afraid. I felt I was being consumed, swallowed up. But what I didn't see until now is that you can't run away. Changing your name or identity is no solution. There is so much hurt that never stops. But facing up to it gives strength. That's what you taught me. That no matter how much pain, love is always the answer."

***

Fishman and Eve wave goodbye to Frank and Angie as they board their plane. Angie looks over her shoulder one last time and mouths, "Thank you" before she disappears. Fishman thinks back to the first time they met at the Luxor Casino and how their lives serendipitously became entwined. He puts his arm around Eve.

"It's time to go back."

"Home?"

"I'm tired of running away from myself. Tired of looking

like Kojak. Much as I feel at home in ancient Egypt."

"It's fine with me because I'm sick of Las Vegas. I'm not ready for retirement living. Let's move back to life."

Chapter 24

Fishman tells Eve, "This will be the last teleport. I'm going to give it up. But there is something that I want you to see and there is something that I must do."

Fishman and Eve are on the corner of Columbus and 81st in New York. It is early evening, the sky is just turning dark. The city is becoming a pulsating galaxy of light and energy. If sex is a city, New York is it.

They walk about a hundred feet east in the direction of Central Park until they're in front of the entrance of the Excelsior Hotel. There are two men in uniform standing next to the highly polished brass revolving door.

"That's Roberto. The tall one in the blue military jacket with the gold epaulettes. The one in red is Victor."

Fishman walks over to Roberto. "Excuse me, could you help us out."

"Your luggage?"

"I had a cousin who used to live here. Maybe you remember him?"

Roberto has heard just about everything and has little time for inquiries like this.

"I'm afraid I couldn't help you out. I'm new here."

"His name was Goldberg. Paul Goldberg."

"Mr. Goldberg. The Wall Street trader? Yeah, I knew him. Great guy. Did you say you were his cousin?"

"Yes. We're from the Midwest."

"My favorite part of the country. What city?"

Fishman plays to Roberto's strength. No matter what city he is from it will be Roberto's favorite and he will surely mention that his grandmother resides there too.

"Chicago. Ever heard of Old Town?"

"What a coincidence. My grandmother is from there. I bet her house is within blocks of where you live."

"It's possible. Is anyone in 14A?"

"Mr. Goldberg's suite. You'll have to check at the front desk. Wait, let me help you. I liked Mr. Goldberg. Great tipper."

Roberto escorts Fishman and Eve to the front desk. A young Hispanic woman, Rosa helps them. Fishman remembers Rosa from when she first started to work at the Excelsior. He also reminds himself of the name of the German woman Elsa who used to manage the desk. There was also Peter and Marissa. Fishman looks around at the hotel's burnished walnut interior. His eyes move from the polished wood to the marble floors to the shimmering chandeliers above. He recalls the many days and nights and years that he resided in the hotel when he lived in New York.

The sound of Rosa's voice brings him out of his reverie.

"Your name, sir?"

"Mr. and Mrs. Paul Goldberg, like my cousin. Did you know him?"

"Yes sir, everyone here knows Mr. Goldberg."

"Really?"

"If you go around the neighborhood you'll see. Mention his name. Anywhere. In the dry cleaners, at the flower shop, at the bakery, even at the hardware store. There is an Italian restaurant, Assagio, where he used to eat all his meals. Ask for Claudio. They were friends. He'll be able to tell you a lot. Mr. Goldberg used to bring me chocolate bars and one New Year's eve he brought dinner and champagne for everyone who was working here. What happened to him?"

The Next Step 219

"You mean?"

"Yes. How is he doing now? Is he out of the hospital?"

"He's fine. He remarried, to a very nice woman. I'll tell him you asked about him."

"He had us all so worried we thought he was really going to do it. Chico talked him out of it."

"Does he still work here?"

"Chico. He'll never quit. He gets on at nine thirty."

Fishman thinks about Chico. He lingers on his image for a long time before he speaks.

"Would you please ask him to come up to my room. I need to speak to him."

***

There is a knock on the door of suite 14A. Fishman looks through the peephole and spies a man in his mid-fifties dressed in a grey workman's uniform. He is short, medium built and balding with kind eyes and strong sun-tanned arms. Fishman watches him slick back his hair and tuck in his shirt. He wipes his lips with the back of his hand.

As the door opens Fishman fights to hold back the emotion.

"You asked to see me, señor?"

"Yes. Are you Chico?"

"Sí, señor. How can I help you?"

"Please come in. What would you like to drink?"

"Just some water, if you have."

Fishman tries to remember back to that evening, when lucite planets were revolving red, and open windows challenged pilots, eager to launch barefoot into the dark.

"You saved my cousin's life. I wanted to thank you."

"Señor Goldberg. How is he? I pray to Santa María for him. It was in this room."

He points beyond a sofa and wing chair. "That window."

Outside the window is Theodore Roosevelt Park adjacent to the Museum of Natural History and the Hayden Planetarium. There are sweeping views of the upper West Side and to the east, Central Park. Fishman recalls waking up in the morning listening to the sounds of 81st Street, the simple music of life buzzing, like an urban rainforest. City buses and people hailing cabs, dog walkers calling their pets, homeless men and women waking up from sleeping on benches, car alarms, boom boxes, breaks squeaking from pulling up short, the rush of water washing pavement, shouts over parking spots. Doormen greeting residents. Supers barking orders. Delivery men honking their horns. In the spring and summer there were also birds chirping. And always the dense layering of human accents and dialects fighting to make their will known.

Fishman walks over to the window and opens it partway. There is a warm breeze and the aroma of chocolate.

Chico sips on his water then breathes deeply, taking in the night air. Fishman turns toward Chico. "What happened that night?"

"I was right here. Just where you are standing. I talked to him. We all knew his sadness. Thank god he listened. "

Chico walks up to the window. His eyes, out of habit, inspect the heating and air-conditioning unit. He examines the sill, running his hand across its high gloss finish. He stares at the blurs of blue and red from the park below.

"It was an unbelievable time. All the way up here you could smell the Towers burning. Down there, people stood in the park holding candles, saying prayers, singing songs. You couldn't breathe because of all the black smoke."

Chico has taken Fishman back to thoughts and memories that he hasn't had since the time of the attack.

"I remember sometimes late at night when it was very quiet I could hear Maya Angelou's voice. You could hear her narrate the story of the Big Bang and the origins of the universe. I would get up and look at the Hayden Sphere. I'd see Neptune and Mercury, even Pluto revolving in the night. Always a different color. Look, right there. See how small it is compared to the others?"

Fishman points with his finger.

"The little blue one is where we live, Earth."

Chico watches Fishman's face. He studies his eyes then yells out.

"Dios mío, Mr. Goldberg."

"Chico. Do you remember what I told you to call me that night."

"Sí. Paul."

They hug. Fishman laughs.

"I said no need for formality at a time like this."

Chico continues to study Fishman's face. "I'll never forget the eyes. There is a little black dot but . . ."

"Plastic surgery. Different nose and chin. It's a long story, Chico."

Fishman allows himself to feel a warm rush of emotion. He remembers sitting, his legs straddled half in and out, on the window sill. He can see the glare of street lights and the haze of color from the sphere below.

"Chico, I am so grateful. You saved my life. If it were not for . . ."

Suddenly Chico has an idea. "I want you to meet somebody."

Chico writes down an address on a piece of paper. "Go there tomorrow morning. Apartment 4B."

***

137 East 115th is a five story walk-up on a rundown block. There are kids playing out on the stoop. A teenager with pencil thin beard and mustache, wearing a black sweat suit approaches Fishman and Eve as they are getting out of their cab.

"Who are you looking for?"

"Dominguez."

"They're on the fourth floor in the back. Chico is my uncle. He asked me to look out for you, Mr. Goldberg."

"Paul. This is Eve."

"They call me Chucky. I'm a Chico too."

Fishman and Eve climb up to 4B. It is an old but clean building with wafting aromas of plantains and yucca, chiles rellenos and chicken and rice. The floor leading up to Chico's door is white tile with black inlays in a celestial design only partially intact. To the right of the door is a mezuzah covered over with generations of thick dark paint.

In an instant before Chico opens the door Fishman imagines his grandfather living here. He can visualize him returning from the synagogue or after a long day's work. He watches him pulling his heavy body, resting at each landing, sighing in a way that only older Jews sigh. He sees the door opening. His grandmother is wearing an embroidered apron, the one her sister Ida made for her. Two Dutch girls separated by a multi-colored rose, all done in tiny cross-stitches. There are four children playing in the living room, Fishman's father, his younger brother and two sisters, now all dead. His aunt Rose is reading a story to a three year old, Uncle Joe. It is a fairy tale about survival, in a magic kingdom, in a distant place, a long time ago. Caruso is singing "Vesti la Giubba" from "Pagliacci" on a grainy seventy-eight and the blue-orange flicker of Sabbath candles burning eternal against the darkness of the night.

Eve knocks twice and the door opens.

Chico greets Fishman and Eve warmly, directing them into his small kitchen. He motions them to sit down at a pink wooden table by extending his large open palm.

Chico holds up a yellow and red coffee can.

"Café? I hope you like Bustelo. World's best coffee."

Chico brings over the can. It has a pleasing graphic. A smiling woman lifting a steaming cup to her lips. He reads from the can theatrically.

"Siempre Fresco. Puro y aromático como ninguno."

Eve translates almost immediately. "Always fresh. Pure and flavorful."

Chico looks at Fishman approvingly.

"Very good, Paul. You chose well."

Chico prepares the coffee the old-fashioned way. He boils it in a pot then strains it. He is meticulous about filtering out the fine grains. He pours each cup as if it were holy water from a miraculous spring.

"I'm glad you could come. There is someone I want you to meet."

After they finish their coffee Chico brings them into the living room. The room is as Fishman had imagined it. There is a little boy drawing in a coloring book on the hardwood floor exactly where, in his mind, Fishman had visualized his father. He is coloring a silvery spaceship against a universe of blue and red. He pulls his crayons beyond the heavy black lines, refusing to be bound by its borders. He also draws an occasional star and moon by hand.

"This is my grandson Paulino. Niño, say hello."

The boy continues to draw. He doesn't look up. "Want to draw with me?"

Fishman observes his small hand moving across the coarse gray paper. "What are you making."

"A spaceship. To fly to the moon. Want to come?" The boy laughs. "Really, come to the moon with me."

He now points to the moon that he has drawn above the rocket. "We can land right over here."

Chico pats his grandson on his behind. "What an imagination!"

Eve points out the obvious. "You two have the same name."

"He's named after Mr. Goldberg. That's why I wanted them to meet. After what happened to Paul I felt I had saved a life. It was the first time I ever did something like that. Mr. Goldberg is a good man and he was always helping others I wanted my grandson to have his name."

Chico now starts to tickle Paulino. "Isn't that right, Plupe?"

Fishman's ears prick up. "What did you call him?"

"Plupe. It's his nickname."

"I had a brother by that name. Ploopy Goldberg. The little boy who wanted to fly."

***

Fishman tells Plupe to make a wish.

Soon the two of them are captives of high-intensity white light randomly twinkling in the night sky. They move across an arc of stars, along the surface of the moon and among the farthest planet visible to the naked eye.

Fishman's mind wanders. He thinks about the laws of physics and chemistry. Fundamental forces, electromagnetism and gravity. He visualizes the structure of atoms and the composition of elements. He hears the Big Bang and feels infinite space. He sees the design of molecules, the smallest units determining the chemical properties of matter. He observes bonds everywhere: ionic, covalent and metallic. There is also the production of compounds. Fishman is still amazed that the world is alive with iron, copper, zinc and aluminum. And, of course, human organisms.

Fishman and Plupe experience the recreation of the universe. They soar into the Orion Nebula deep in intergalactic space. They feel the extreme pull and release of gravity, the warping of time and the shaping of light. They are drawn into a spiral galaxy composed of three parts: a thin disk composed of stars, gas and dust; a central bulge made up of old stars; and a spherical halo of the oldest stars and massive star clusters.

Fishman and Plupe travel along the elegant pattern of the disc star. It moves in a nearly circular orbit like a puppy awakening to chase its tail and then it dissolves into the stars of the bulge and the halo, moving in orbits at all angles.

As he abandons himself in the vast celestial darkness he watches Plupe's face. He is reminded of another child who also sat in the blackness of this space. A lost and grieving child. Fishman remembers back to his parent's home on Highland Avenue. He remembers actions, responses, moods, thoughts, desires, hopes, most of them seemingly irrelevant to one another. He sees patterns and constellations once taken for granted, now no longer known. He sees a rock shattering a window like a meteor landing from space. His grandfather on a country road falling from a moving car. An aunt, daydreaming, hit by a bus.

Fishman turns to the child. "We are lost in space."

Plupe smiles. Fishman imagines a different child sitting next to him although sharing a similar name. He sees his brother traveling across time into the night. Two children sitting side by side at peace with each other in a peaceful place. Fishman takes in the warmth of Plupe's smile. He looks at his small hands and gentle eyes. The excitement of one's first trip to the moon!

After reaching the farthest outposts of the universe, Fishman and Plupe head back to Earth. They take a shortcut through a black hole, headlong in free fall, until unexpectedly there is light.

Chapter 25

In Chicago Fishman is now known as Goldberg. It was a little confusing at first, but everyone who matters has grown used to it. Without any fanfare, he quietly works at FedEx. The one on the corner of Broadway and Devon. The customers he serves are mostly from India and Pakistan. There are also people of Arab descent and Hasidic Jews.

He still exercises his genius when helping customers. He feels blessed to have been selected the one who brought peace to the world, the one chosen for a while to possess magical gifts. He no longer teleports or moves things in a flash. He refrains from all manner of show and excess.

Say what you want about Goldberg but calling him Messiah does not seem out of the question. Not that he saw himself as the deliverer, or universal message bearer to the multitude. Not even working at FedEx or having revelatory dreams narrated by Steven Spielberg changes anything. But still, recent events made him wonder. Did the universe really try to make contact? Did a higher power finally take note, offering to reveal his true identity?

There are times in life when seemingly insignificant occurrences prove later to be harbingers of momentous shifts and it was just this sort of logic that started Goldberg thinking. At first it was merely the stalled battery of his '92 Mercedes, later the intermittent power surges that even years of automotive neglect could not explain, and then there was his computer's complete refusal to connect with the Internet, quickly followed by the sudden inexplicable cessation of his cell phone service.

"Just coincidence?" he thought, "definitely not."

At fifty-seven, Goldberg pretty much has the world by the balls. That is to say, he wants for nothing. He lives a quiet life in an historic part of Chicago, known as Old Town. He resides with his wife Eve in a two bedroom apartment in a renovated building that once served as a rectory to St. Michael's Church, which long ago had been sold by the Diocese to a former fireman turned real estate developer. Goldberg pays his rent each month on time and marvels at his lot in life and good fortune.

His children, a girl and a boy, sadly, are now gone. At times he is still heartbroken that they live so far away.

His first wife Nadia, now deceased, was a beauty in her youth, and an artist. Goldberg found her tall slim body, long red hair and soft blue- green eyes as exciting after twenty-five years as the first time he saw her. They were two seals on a sun-warmed rock. She had documented their life together in warm liquids: oil paints, watercolors, India ink and tempera: in journals and on furniture and walls, on clothing and floor boards. Her murals sometimes dealt with historical themes like the one over their bed where she painted Goldberg as Adam and herself as Eve or the one of Shakespeare's Midsummer Night's Dream where Goldberg appeared as a very regal Oberon and Nadia a nymphy Titania. Her many self-portraits were everywhere, each reflecting a colorful mood or temperament that Goldberg knew well. There was also the painting of the teddy bear picnic in their son's room under which the family used to play Candy Land and Chutes and Ladders and read stories until fragrant young bodies, fresh from baths, folded into the arms of Morpheus.

Her first present to Goldberg was a pen and ink of an old maple tree with two birds on its branches with the initials of lovers carved into its trunk. She placed it in an antique maple frame that she and Goldberg had found together in the West Village when they were still living in New York.

Their home was her continuing gift to Goldberg. He might awake to any variety of painting, drawing, sculpture, self-assigned garment—Nadia was most fond of painting his shoes and jackets. Goldberg, not once in twenty-five years, ever awoke to know for sure if the contents of his closet were as he left them or if a ceiling, floor, hallway or wall would be as he last saw it. This was unusual because the virtue that Goldberg prized most in the world was certainty. It was not a philosophy, though Goldberg could say quite a bit on that subject; it was more his psychology, from which Goldberg derived his sense of well-being.

Is Goldberg happy? Yes, he believes he is. There would be no hesitation on his part to point to the fact that he is happily married, in good health with an active inner life that never ceases to transform and fulfill.

But he is more than happy. Goldberg is grateful. He is grateful for the power of memory and imagination. He sees his children playing at the beach. He is singing with them and Nadia around a campfire and on trips in their car.

> "She'll be coming round the mountain when she comes
> She'll be coming round the mountain when she comes
> She'll be coming round the mountain, she'll be coming round the mountain
> She'll be coming round the mountain when she comes."

The songs are always subject to strange voices and dialects, original verses and interpretation. Many are of CB's own creation. A favorite is Skinnamarink.

> "Skinnamarinky dinky dink, Skinnamarinky doo, I

> love you;
> Skinnamarinky, dinky dink, Skinnamarinky doo, I
> love you.
> I love you in the morning and in the afternoon.
> I love you in the evening underneath the moon.
> Skinnamarinky dinky dink, Skinnamarinky doo, I
> love you."

At times they had a trip mascot for good luck. Like the year they chose Junior Birdman, singing its verses over and over again through the Smokey Mountains and along the New England seashore.

> *"Up in the air junior birdmen*
> *Up in the air upside down*
> *Up in the air junior birdmen*
> *Keep your noses off the ground."*

There is so much Goldberg is thankful for. There is the richness of existence and the phrases "anything is possible" and "make a wish."

Goldberg remembers aching to come home with only one thought burning in his mind. "I just want to be with my family."

There is also the memory of a Willie Nelson song.

> *"There's a somebody I'm longing to see*
> *I hope that she turns out to be*
> *Someone who'll watch over me*
> *I'm a little lamb who's lost in a wood*
> *I know I could always be good*
> *To one who'll watch over me*
>
> *Although she may not the girl some men think of*
> *As handsome to my heart*

The Next Step 231

She carries the key

Won't you tell her please to put on some speed
Follow my lead, oh how I need
Someone to watch over me
Someone to watch over me."

Goldberg believes in a world where one person can still make a difference, restore order and set things right. Where there are miracles, turns of phrases and twists of fate.

Goldberg hadn't always worked at FedEx. As a young man he was intensely ambitious, with the temperament of a scholar and the energy of an athlete. He had a clear analytical mind and received his fair share of academic awards and prizes. By most measurements, success came easily to Goldberg but about the past he cares to say little. And it is not because of the shame of having lost millions, or operating for decades outside of his means nor is it because of the searing media accounts of his failures or the haunting stares in his children's eyes. It is just, he believes, that he is too old or perhaps too impatient for all of that. Despite everything that has happened, Goldberg strives to become a better person. He continues to want to learn more about himself and his location in the world. Occasionally, he'll catch himself working at humility and a self-ironic smile forms on his lips. It is a life-long feature of his personality that he knows all too well: trying to tame his sense of pride, throwing a wet blanket on an excited ego. He often thinks about the truth of music: pure, simple and to the point, trying to live his life that way. No pretensions, criticisms of others or the arch, cold intellectualism of his youth. Goldberg also knows that living like this helps the days picket by, allowing him to avoid getting bogged down with regrets.

Goldberg is still surprised at his playfulness, his sense of fun and his profound love of fucking. At one time he was a serious student of philosophy reading critical phenomenological arguments whose lengthy sentences extended without paragraph breaks for pages. He was easily seduced by the sexy agility and arabesques of quick minds and the blissful gymnastics of thoughtful dialogue. Goldberg discovered that the pleasures of the intellect are deep and affecting but his need for love and physical pleasure was far more reaching. Fucking was both an escape and his calling. In bed he was intense and passionate, absorbed, voracious, always there. He had many lovers before he found the love of his life, Nadia, to whom he had always been faithful. He loved the feel of her soft pale skin, her long red hair, kissing the length of her body, breathing in her cunty aromas, making love. Although he devoted himself completely in the moment of celestial embrace the utter absurdity and comedy of copulation never escaped him. Goldberg saw fucking as a primal joke. Nature's gift of a promise-filled beginning of humor and laughter. An opportunity for pleasure given and reciprocated. And for the lucky, there was love. Something he has discovered anew with Eve.

And his years as the famed Wall Street trader? Only rarely did Goldberg speak about that. And it was not out of modesty or fear that he might bore nor was it because of his aversion to talk about the past. In fact, the mere topic animated Goldberg's conversation and sent sparks flying in his eyes. Most people had heard the stories or rumors or knew the basic outline of the man's life. The ups and downs and the ins and outs; the who is to blame, and the matters of fact.

Punctually at 6:15 a.m. Goldberg arrives at the FedEx store. He is always the first one there. He works Monday through Friday until 4 p.m., noon on Saturday. He prefers to enter through the same front door that the customers use rather than the employee entrance out back. There is a buzzer to the right but Goldberg always chooses his key. He disarms the security system, and then proceeds through the dimly-lit store past a long reception counter.

The Next Step

It stands in front of "the bull pen" that contains scales next to conveyor belts that process the day's flow of parcels and packages. He unlocks a red metal door in back, waits for the lights to go on automatically and walks down a flight of stairs leading to a room containing a wall of lockers. Goldberg's locker is immediately recognizable. It is the only one with any sign of personality. It stands in relief like a solitary witness of life, a Kilroy was here, in an otherwise drab interior. Its background is phosphorous blue with a painted six-foot smiling gold fish. Written on its body are the words "overnight or overseas Goldy delivers."

It is a small claustrophobic room, in need of painting, neither really clean nor dirty, functional, with a small bathroom off to the side. There is a stove, a microwave oven and a small refrigerator in a corner; the kind that serves as a vault for decaying food abandoned in brown bags with names written in magic marker. There is also a kettle, a jar of instant coffee, Styrofoam cups and packages of raw sugar and the ever present smell of stale smoke lingering in the corners.

Goldberg reaches into his locker and removes his uniforms. He has two; both are jumpsuits worn under a long black apron that ties behind the neck. There is a red one with the word "freight" in bold white letters on the right bicep and the one he chooses: a purple number with FEDEX spelled out in orange caps across his chest.

Goldberg proudly surveys himself in the bathroom mirror: glowing skin, handsome features, deep blue eyes, salt and pepper hair, like a storm cloud around his head, and mischievous smile. He still believes he possesses a certain magnetism. He looks up and reads the sign over the sink to himself as he prepares for the day ahead. "Relax. It's FedEx."

It was an easy decision for Goldberg to choose to work at FedEx. After all, he thought, where else can your messages be sent out so far and wide. There was the Post Office of course but somehow Goldberg did not really feel, despite its representations to the contrary, that his mail was truly priority one. In fact, based on his many years of personal experience, he found the whole notion of priority mail rather misleading, like being sucked into a three-card Monte game where all that is ultimately delivered is a disappointing result. And then there was the occasional problem of workers going postal. Goldberg did not fear bodily harm but he knew that there was work that he needed to get done. At his age, he could not afford to be slowed down by a co-worker's psychotic episode that might result in a disabling wound or an unexpected hospital stay.

There was also UPS, a good company that dated back to 1907. Goldberg remembered it when it was still referred to as United Parcel Service. It operated in more than 200 countries and territories around the world and, as the world's largest package delivery company, had an admirable record of success with which there was little to find fault. But it was, let's face it, brown and possessed little of the energy and vitality of a FedEx. Just saying it out loud excited Goldberg. FedEx had spunk. It was youthful and forward thinking. It had ethics and values and believed in treating its people well. It also possessed a gravitas when it came to respecting the customer and the power of his message. It made one feel secure in the choice of the world's best, not largest, carrier. It delivered in more ways to more places worldwide. And you knew it was the right material at the right time. Its representations were pure, simple, to the point: "overnight or overseas, across borders or across towns, you can absolutely, positively count on FedEx." Its commercials told the truth and always had, With FedEx your package would get there.

As Goldberg climbs the stairs, he straightens any wrinkles in his pants with a brush of his right hand. A Kabuki dance of sorts begins to play in his head followed by a flood of memory. It is of a time, not that long ago, perhaps sometime in the 1980's, Goldberg is sitting behind a glass desk in a large office on a top floor of a financial tower; long before anyone had the thought of using airplanes as weapons to bring down magnificent buildings. All around him are screens and monitors flashing data. He is responding quickly but deftly, skillfully, artfully. He is in control like a seasoned fighter pilot. Lights on panels flicker, phones ring. Goldberg takes in the full visual and emotional impact of what he is feeling. As he remembers it now, it was a reckless time when everything seemed possible at any cost. He looks down at his watch, suddenly out of the moment. It is 6:27 and he realizes his day and his mission are about to begin.

Goldberg makes for an odd sight in his FedEx uniform. Not that it doesn't fit well or the mere sight of a purple jump suit beneath a black apron emblazoned with large orange letters doesn't take some time to get used to nor is it the fact that the pants he wears were not meant for someone quite as tall. It is more the way he wears his clothes that is peculiar. For years Goldberg's wardrobe was the product of Saville Row. Suits by Gieves and Hawke and Huntsman, shirts from Turnbull and Asser, an odd waistcoat from Tommy Nutter and his shoes only from John Lobb or Edward Green. Unfortunately, years of wearing clothes like that have influenced his bearing, the way he presents himself, the way he cinches his apron or pulls up a sagging collar. It is certainly not offensive nor does it appear affected, but at times does seem unnatural, sadly comic.

There is a film noir quality to the way Goldberg has chosen to make fundamental changes in his life. If on the one hand the measure of a man is his sense of personal identity and on the other are all the acts and deeds that makes one's life his own, Goldberg has transformed himself in astonishing ways. He has come to an essential realization. Let's call it, his truth. He has found a way that allows him to rise above all the conventional limitations of individuality. A passport, a driver's license, a social security card, a diploma, a toe tag, god forbid. He is certain in his belief that he can affect real change in the world, where people can be seen for themselves, and he will do whatever it takes to do his part and get the word out. That is what has drawn him to FedEx. Like Goldberg, FedEx cares about communities. It is a leader in charitable giving. It is a true corporate citizen, committed to a better environment. Goldberg sees all this as just the beginning of better things to come.

What was Goldberg's great realization? It is important to note here the man's exceptional love for chocolate. Goldberg was enamored of all the varieties. Dark, milk and bittersweet. He had tasted many of the best makers. Maison du Chocolat, Teuscher, and Neuchatel. From his perspective it was no accident that the cocoa bean was considered the ultimate status symbol by the Mayan and Aztec cultures. It was a source of wisdom and power; an aphrodisiac, producing the same stimulating reaction as falling in love. Goldberg slowly savored the delicious warmth of Vosges chocolate melting in his mouth, rolling it with his tongue, sweet as a kiss, wrestling it against cheek and palette. And then in a flash Goldberg knew.

Years on Wall Street had taught Goldberg many valuable lessons. The importance of being prepared, single-minded, always in attack mode, and always performing with grace under fire. It was a state of mind that made him ready for come what may; always having an ace in the hole, a card up his sleeve. He knew when to act on impulse and when to override impulse with principal. Despite what had been written or said against him Goldberg knew in his heart that he had never mislead investors, cooked the books or benefited at the expense of share holders. His crime was far more serious, elemental. Goldberg had offended the gods. He was guilty of multiple counts: hubris and Ate, insolence from excessive pride and reckless blindness. These are mistakes that many great men have made before; Goldberg is committed to not making them again. He prays the gods are finally appeased.

Wall Street was Goldberg's laboratory and testing ground. He will tell you without any doubt or hesitation that it was there that he learned everything that makes him who he is today. In the course of a career that stretched back a quarter of a century he had made many friends but also enemies. He has never been one for suffering fools and when he was younger had the unfortunate habit of easily offending and looking through people whose opinion he did not respect. The irony of all this is not lost on Goldberg.

At the FedEx store it is not uncommon for a customer's glance to travel over, past and through him, not to know or say his name, placing him on a landscape of personal indifference. If it were not for Goldberg's ingenuity he could easily exist as a ghost, like a bus driver, cleaning person or toll worker. His solution, although he would certainly not air this opinion, and surely not this way, is to cause human stirs and ripples. What Goldberg wants to do, no needs to do, is to deliver; to make each interaction, however small, matter. That is his discipline, not abstract or dry, rather pure, simple and to the point. Goldberg chooses to fill the human soul.

Filling the human soul is a tricky business. It is not the elixir of choice for most people. Your average person does not want an outing to FedEx to reside at the level of a therapeutic encounter or religious meeting. People don't spontaneously seek out opportunities to communicate deeply when shipping packages. They don't care to gratuitously unburden their thoughts, and feelings, excavate hidden motives and intentions.

And that's where you would have to say Goldberg's genius comes in. He makes it all look so easy. You walk in and there is a shipping worry or anxiety and then you leave completely fulfilled, not wholly understanding what has happened. He just makes you feel good so you want to reach up to your highest nature. Even if you are a pessimist he can help you see a sunnier future. Goldberg makes all this happen and you don't even realize that it is because he is there.

***

Goldberg can breathe deeply and sleeps well at night knowing that he has saved the world. But still, at times, his life feels to him like a cubistic screwball comedy. He feels things just repeat and repeat.

It's on days like today, tragic anniversaries that Goldberg still worries about his urge to fly. He remembers something that he has heard recently on the radio that he keeps thinking about. A Lutheran minister from Grand Rapids, Michigan had these words of advice. "The key to a good life is a wife that loves you, children who honor you and a faith that sustains you."

Goldberg feels that he has all his bases covered. There is Eve's love, his godson Plupe's honor and his complete faith in the power of protoplasm. But somehow, and he is not sure why, in this very moment, all this still does not seem like it is enough.

Goldberg decides to make a trip, a little fantasy he has been planning in the deepest recesses of his mind. He has always wanted to see the view from the observation deck of the Sears Tower, one-hundred and ten stories above ground. He pictures soaring like a bird up in the sky.

As he gets off the elevator there is an exhibit that details little known facts about the Tower. There are over sixteen thousand bronze-tinted windows with six roof-mounted robotic machines that clean each and every window. The elevator travels at one-thousand feet per minute making it the fastest in the world. The Sears Tower was designed for more than twelve thousand occupants and twenty-five thousand people enter the building each day.

Goldberg steps out onto the observation deck. He is told that he can see for fifty miles in every direction. In the distance lie

Indiana, Wisconsin, and Michigan. It is clear and sunny. He thinks to himself, "It is a perfect day to fly."

As Goldberg looks towards the horizon he is overtaken by a storm of thoughts and memories. He sees Nadia and Lara and James and feels more than anything he wants to be with them.

He thinks about Palefsky and Fishman and sees himself again in the starry dark watching strange objects from overhead; nearly perfect rings of hot blue stars, wheels within wheels spinning around a yellow nucleus of galaxies and comets from the farthest reaches of the solar system breaking apart.

Out of the blue three photographs come to mind at the exact moment Goldberg detects the sound of a post horn playing the theme from Mahler's Third Symphony, which he remembers vividly from a 1976 performance of the New York Philharmonic directed by Zubin Mehta.

The first, taken in 1921, is a glowering Freud challenging the photographer with his archeological stare. Cigar in hand, his open jacket reveals a loopy gold chain dangling confidently from his vest. The stance and accoutrements, all signs of someone who is secure, firmly establishing his beachhead on terra incognita. A second picture, also of Freud is taken later. He is stooped over and looks less sure. It is from the period when he was waiting for permission from German authorities to leave Austria. The third photograph speaks for itself. A Jewish boy forced to write Juden on the door of his family's home. His tormentors, young and old, laugh menacingly.

A child of five whispers to himself in an emergency room, "Mommy, what does reality mean?"

Goldberg is back again in his grandmother's arms, the fragrance of baking peaches heavy in the air. Feeling her warm fleshy cheek against his forehead, the coolness of her cotton dress. In his mind he listens to her hilarious stories. The one about the man who went to the Rabbi, complaining about his lot in life, small house, not enough money. The Rabbi's advice totally crazy, right on the border of the Three Stooges meets Groucho Marx, but somehow she made a point, now forgotten. Goldberg feels her soft kind voice, affectionate laughter.

He thinks about Benny Goodman and the Make Believe Ballroom.

And now there is the memory of a tremendous blast and saving a little girl, Ziporah. Her name means little bird in Hebrew.

Goldberg is at the edge of a tangled forest, next to a precipitous slope with the sound of a thunderous waterfall in the distance. He has been sent to immerse himself in sadness and suffering to experience the pain and barbarity that is here. He must wade through filth and bloody rivers and march through burning sand in time. He must also navigate uncharted waters, visit mythological sites in this world and in hell. For a time he is guided by Virgil and Dante and once he flies with Icarus high in the sky.

Goldberg retreats deep into an internal cave, a catacomb, burying his pain in a subterranean chamber, a dark and secretive hiding place. He continues to dig as far as he can go, forming corridors and galleries underground. He hides himself in forma and cubicula, located outside the city, along great consular roads.

There is the stare of a Dan mask followed by a Marsden Hartley painting of the ocean before a storm. Three white capped blue-green waves roll onto a deserted salmon beach. An ominous cloud, sliced at its very bottom like an onion, hangs threateningly in the dark green-gray sky. A third image quickly comes to mind. It is the face of a vintage Longines aviator's watch, most probably from the twenties. It is a chronograph with all functions operated by the winding crown. It has a double-jointed eighteen karat gold case 35mm in diameter. Its dial is enameled with tachometric scale in blue and black and telemetric scale in red. It has a minute recorder and gold-plated Breuget hands.

Goldberg checks his watch. Soon it will be time. He thinks about Chico and Plupe. The Excelsior. He reminds himself that even from fourteen floors above ground there are unimaginable things to be seen. The key is to close your eyes and let your mind go free. Planets revolve in primary colors: reds and blues and yellows and greens. And there are the sounds of dogs barking, and angry men cursing about raw deals and poor location in the universe.

And now Goldberg sees a fire raging. He is blinded by plumes of orange-white flames and billows of gray-black smoke. Charred human bodies and the agonized screams of loved ones in pain. Wherever he looks. Nadia and Lara and James.

Goldberg can feel the cool air blowing just above the railing. He breathes it in like a dog riding in a car.

He sees a little boy drawing.

"What are you making?" he asks.

"A spaceship. To fly to the moon. Want to come?" The little boy laughs. "Really, come with me."

He imagines experiencing recreation. Soaring into the Orion Nebula deep in intergalactic space. Goldberg feels the extreme pull and release of gravity, the warping of time and the shaping of light. The human cannonball. Defying. Certain death.

"Hey, it's all make believe. A trick. Entertainment."

And then Goldberg reminds himself of his love for Eve and life and the memory of a little boy named Icarus and a fifty-foot man. He hears him calling in the distance. "Burn me. Open your arms and hearts. Be reborn with your gifts and drumbeats. Offer me your heartbreak and regrets. I am here to consume your sadness and sorrow. I welcome your tortured screams and painful shouts. In me find a new beginning. Reinvent your human nature. Burn me."

Goldberg smiles. He thinks of CB and remembers that there was a time, not so long ago when nothing quenched his thirst like the thought of flight. Now, he feels more grounded. Earthbound. In his mind he visualizes only one thing. He is at the counter at FedEx. Goldberg thinks to himself, "Next?"

WEINTRAUB EXPOSED

Chapter 26

It all began innocently enough with a Lebanese curse and ended in a spectacular explosion in a Bulgarian craft stall along the parade route of the Festival of the Roses. Although there are witnesses who will say otherwise, Weintraub is not to blame. Not that he is entirely innocent either, but let's just say his attention was elsewhere when the shit finally hit the fan.

A day earlier he had received a letter from a New York literary agent who had rejected his latest novel. What follows is an excerpt, and some may say, one of the reasons that propelled Weintraub into his downward spiral.

> *Dear Mr. Weintraub,*
>
> *Thank you for giving us a look at **DOPE SLAP** and we very much appreciate the detailed illustrations. I apologize for the delay in my response.*
>
> *This novel is indeed exceptional. The prose is clear and often poetic; there is genuine beauty to your phrasing. Weingarten is an engaging character, complicated and sympathetic enough to capture and keep our interest. There are many levels from which a reader can approach the text, but the underlying, insistent whisper of the human search for meaning is never lost in the complexities . . .*
>
> *Unfortunately, I am afraid I have to pass on your manuscript. As strong as **DOPE SLAP** is, I don't believe there is room in the market for another post-9/11 reflection.*

There is such a plethora of 9/11-inspired fiction, memoirs, and non-fiction accounts that publishing houses are wary to take on 9/11 themed projects at this time. Another agency may feel differently about their chances and be better suited to represent your work to publishers.

*Again, I am sorry for the delay and am grateful to have had the opportunity to read **DOPE SLAP**. I wish you the best of luck with this project.*

Best regards,
Samantha Twitty

It was the final straw. Months of hard work and sacrifice for what? Living like a shut-in. No money left to buy even the simplest things. Was it really possible, 9/11 had already become a cliché? What about Madrid and Beslan? Next thing Stephen Hawking would be rethinking black holes. Where was the stability Weintraub had grown to appreciate in his life? Wherever he looked there were pseudo- intellectual acrobats, truth defying jugglers and nihilistic jerks; partisan spinners and side-show freaks. Hell, they were running the country.

Weintraub reminded himself of the advice that Conrad Hilton once gave to a TV reporter, "The shower curtain should always be in the shower." It was a tidy way to think of his universe.

Weintraub had grown up in Brooklyn, in an era when teenage boys delivered afternoon papers on Schwinn Zephyrs, a time span caught in the glassy net of a shuttering lens. His mother drove a battleship gray Buick, chain smoking Camels, her fur trimmed sweater reaching across the dash like an agitated Pomeranian. It was a time as simple as marginalia and metaphysics, Derrida and Nietzsche.

Still, for the most part, Weintraub remains a cock-eyed optimist, although there are many others who will tell you that even though he went to M.I.T. he is as crazy as a looney bird. Weintraub has a recurring image of himself parachuting in free fall or landing somewhere new wearing a rocket pack. Weintraub hears strangers speaking in foreign tongues, twangs and drawls and Boston accents. He remembers long days at Coney Island laughing at the shtick of Sam Brownbag and the tall tales of The Celestial Zamboni. He tastes the Wonder Wheel spinning in lifesaver candy colors—greens and reds and lemon yellows—against a blue-black summer sky. The Cyclone and the Mermaid Parade. The ocean slapping salty wet against his lips and teeth.

"If you lift up your hand and just think back," he says to himself, "you can feel the memories rushing through your fingers."

And he remembers something he had read. A Basie band saxophonist describing the jazz blown through his horn. Weintraub hears a flood of images from his past.

"His music osmosed to us and we just osmosed it back."

Weintraub delights in the pleasures of a feral imagination. He searches for routes, streets, passages; back alleyways that will lead him home. He yearns for redemption along the third base line or up in the left field bleachers at Ebbets Field. For today Weintraub will forsake quantum mechanics, unified field and string theory. He will divorce himself from all thoughts of cosmology: space, time, gravity, even geometry and other notions of the universe.

A young boy who has traveled by foot and subway beyond dirt hills and public meadows, across the wide lawns of Prospect Park onto Flatbush Avenue climbs with his comrades to distant reaches. There is a din of muffled voices and Vin Scully and the cool, stale aroma of beer mixed with urine. He lifts his nose into it, breathing it in deeply like a happy dog along an open highway. He follows his instinct, moving higher on dark ramps and gateways until there is an instant of total eclipse and then suddenly like a scene from revelation there is the blindness of pure light followed by a diamond of the greenest grass on the face of the earth. Here there are no men with graying hair suffering from weariness or life's anguish, only cherubs in the corners of paintings who share one purpose: to save the day. Roy Campanella, Don Drysdale, Sandy Koufax, Pee Wee Reese, Jackie Robinson, Duke Snider and Don Sutton. It seems like another century. It was another century.

Weintraub knows that a riddle posed is not a riddle answered.

He asks himself, "Am I out of my mind or is this not a dream?"

He imagines himself wearing a T-shirt that reads, "I'm having a wonderful life", written in invisible ink. He is now standing on a boardwalk eating a hotdog listening to kids laughing. There are colorful striped umbrellas, one with a seagull on top, growing out of the hot sand. More mermaids on the horizon. Living in the past. Lost in time.

At 52, Weintraub is something of a mystery, a wascally wabbit, saturnine and natty. Mercurial and moody. Some have even thought him a Martian. As a child he favored costumes. His third grade teacher once asked him, "Hey, what's with all the masks?"

Weintraub didn't answer.

"How many stories do you have?"

Weintraub replied, "As many as you want."

He could spin out a yarn on almost any subject. There was the one about the one- armed accordionist who only played bad music, the twin Buddhas of Long Island City, the giant hamster of Midland, Texas or the real story behind Irving Berlin composing "I Love a Piano." There was also his award winning serialized memoir that appeared in The New York Review of Books, "This is the Shiznik" and The Fishman Quartet written in three volumes.

At 6'1 Weintraub is proud of his looks: glowing skin, handsome features, deep blue eyes, salt and pepper hair like a storm

The Next Step

cloud around his head, and mischievous smile. He still believes he possesses certain magnetism. But why you may ask is Weintraub now hiking for answers? I can assure you it is more than just wanting to get in touch with the sensation of not needing to drive a new Lexus or dying the richest Jew buried in the cemetery. Weintraub is spitting mad and one way or another he'll find a way and get even. Of course he doesn't have lumps on his prostrate or cancer nor does he carry around a colostomy bag or breathe through a respirator. As far as health goes you'd have to say that Weintraub has the body of a man half his age. No high blood pressure or raised cholesterol and as far as his sex urge... it is constant, unending.

Why all the dissatisfaction?

Weintraub looks at a photograph of Leni Riefenstahl on Athuruga Island dated March 13, 2003. She is 101 years old, dressed in a blue-green silk robe and swim suit, as if walking on water, white combed sand beneath a wide blue-gray sky. Her deep red lips smile brightly. Her eyes covered by large tortoise-shell frames. Her blond hair perfectly etched, not a strand out of place. She smiles warmly, ingratiatingly at the camera.

Weintraub looks at other pictures of her, one where she is embracing Mick Jagger and another kneeling on the ground, petting a leopard in the Las Vegas mansion of her friends Siegfried and Roy.

Weintraub is not the kind of person you'd describe as a Brooks man, breastman, boat person or Harley guy. He is no friend of German slave labor corporations, political pundits, multi-national predators, hymn singing do-gooders and ass kissers. Let's just say, his old wounds that were sleeping like a beetle on a leaf are acting up. One thing Weintraub knows for sure: there is an urgent need for change. Now it's just a matter of what needs to be done, in what order, and how?

Chapter 27

A shocking pink tractor trailer pulls up in front of a three story red brick building, missing its front door, in an affluent Chicago neighborhood. Emblazoned on its side panel are the words "Samson Moving and Storage, our strength is your satisfaction." Suddenly, unexpectedly, Weintraub is reminded of an incident that occurred to him just the other day under a painting of a strongman in a leopard printed leotard at the exact instant he thinks about swamis, Stumpy Jones and cosmetic dentistry.

"His favorite musician was Miles Davis. He imagines what it felt like to be his tongue."

And then there is Marlene Dietrich. On stage. It is a chilly melody sung sang-froid. Weintraub winks at her in a dream.

Weintraub is sipping coffee at a local café. He thinks to himself, "If I could name a vegetable after me what would it be?" And then he sees himself as the recipient of a MacArthur Genius Award followed by the thought: "Ordinary life is pretty complex stuff."

He now imagines an amputee feeling a phantom limb. He can see Pepito the one-armed midget accordionist playing the Pennsylvania Polka. He is wearing a white shirt with a disco collar with ruffled black and white sequined arms. One arm. Pepito trills his words like a Mexican Warbler. The image of the strongman lifting barbells against a background of saffron-black keeps popping into Weintraub's mind.

*"Strike up the music
The band has begun
The Pennsylvania Polka
Pick out your partner
And join in the fun
The Pennsylvania Polka
It started in Scranton
It's now number one
It's fun to entertain ya
Everybody has a mania
To do the polka from Pennsylvania"*

After he finishes, Pepito looks at Weintraub challengingly.

"I'm good at what I do, let's see you do it."

Weintraub thinks to himself, "I probably should get back to work but I just can't let go."

The image of the weightlifter fades into the ether.

And then he remembers another conversation he overheard earlier. A fat guy from the suburbs who drove up in a Cadillac wearing a gold chain and pointy blue crocodile shoes.

"And that's it"

"And that's all I can tell you."

"And my dad done it in Illinois in 1972."

"I was the youngest butcher."

"I worked the veal."

"I sliced it right down the middle."

Weintraub sips his coffee slowly. He winds the bitter coffee grinds along his cheek and under his tongue. He thinks about the delicious tastes and aromas of sex. And then he remembers the words he heard earlier in the day on the radio. "I'm a first time caller but a long time listener and I had to call to tell it like it is."

Out of the blue, Weintraub can hear the voices of Cousin Brucey, Scott Muni and Murray the K, radio disk jockeys who spoke to him when he was a boy. In many ways he still is. And he still listens. He sees the Beatles arriving at La Guardia for their first U.S. tour, the Twin Towers evanescing into the mid-day sky. A mother searching under a sheet to see if her child has died. A country western singer promising, "Jesus Christ is alive let the music please him."

Weintraub looks up. In front of him is a homeless man in his thirties. Weintraub thinks he is of Philippine origin or maybe the child of a South-east Asian woman and an African-American ex-GI. He stands quietly in front of Weintraub, like he knows him, admiring with a glance Weintraub's custom made, soft leather, heavily perforated, Italian, wing-tip shoes. He is short but stocky with one incredibly distinguishing feature. To the right of his thin lips above an ordinary chin beneath an unremarkable nose and completely average looking black eyes is a raised mole the likes of which would garner the interest of Guinness and in his day Ripley. Believe it or not. It stands off the face like one of those red clay marvels in Bryce Canyon or Sedona except this one is the color of a California raisin but its dimensions more closely resemble a very juicy Concord grape. And miraculously in its center are three black and gray hairs, as long as an FM antenna, blowing carefree in the summer breeze.

He speaks in a halting, almost robotic, child-like way.

"Barry Manilow?"

Weintraub answers matter-of-factly. "Haven't heard that before."

"You look like him. My name is Ted. I don't mean to offend. How are you?"

***

The time is here and now. Weintraub surveys the calendar of events of the upcoming Chicago Humanities Festival. Another year passes and he is not invited to speak. 25 presenters at 23 venues with some 55,000 tickets expected to be sold or distributed free. Weintraub is not even nominated for the children's program. Sure it hurts. But what can he do?

Weintraub reads the full schedule and the critics' picks. He sees the list of speakers: the actress Joan Allen, Germaine Greer, Joyce Carol Oates, Bernardo Bertolucci, Maxine Hong Kingston, Justin Timberlake, Christ Bob, Ice-T and many others. Two of the panels spark Weintraub's interest: The Shaggin Bone: Misconceptions of the Phallus in Life and Literature and Karaoke against Racism: Singing Your Way to a Better World. The brochure indicates that panelists in both groups are led by been-there, done-that guys who can give the skinny on almost any topic. Are they hooked on books? You betcha, but why has the world stopped wanting to hear from Weintraub?
Now that is the question.

***

There was a time, not so long ago, that those in the know knocked frequently on Weintraub's door. He was recognized on every continent. Yes even on Antarctica, for his spell-binding intellect, razor sharp witticisms and gifted mind. Weintraub was revered as the cognoscente of the cognoscenti, the literatus of the literati, the man. After all, he was a frequent guest of and advisor to the world's crème de la crème. Pablo Casals, Coco Chanel, Winston Churchill, Charles De Gaulle, Helen Keller and Mao Zedong. Even Vladimir Nabokov's technical brilliance and mastery of form owed a great debt to Weintraub. He taught him how to see that the comic and cosmic aspects of daily life were one and the same unpredictable butterfly. Just another story. Weintraub helped Nabokov refine his vast powers of imagination, his sense of flippancy and love of parody. Like Nabokov who was "a perfectly normal trilingual child," Weintraub grew up in a house-

The Next Step

hold of English, Yiddish and French speakers who perplexed, Fadreyed, and soufflèd him into a little genius.

Weintraub had met Nabokov when he was thirteen, his first year at Harvard. What had attracted Nabokov's attention was Weintraub's love of Nymphets, a little known species of erotic butterflies often used as a metaphor for the eternal quest for innocence. The two found great comfort in one another. Not only did they share a great love of lepidoptery but each in his own way found some special meaning in theories of matter and antimatter, the works of John Milton, Andrew Marvell, Lord Byron and T. S. Eliot, and theological speculations about prelapsarianism, that he could offer (with a wisecrack or ribbing) to the other. The fact that each was fluent in French and Russian didn't hurt either. A little known fact about Nabokov, he was an enthusiastic Yiddish speaker.

They also loved telling each other jokes. Throughout his life Nabokov insisted all writers worth anything were humorists. This was a favorite that he told Weintraub on an entomological expedition to Walden Pond in search of the perfect Philistine moth.

"An old Jew marries a much younger non-Jewish woman with whom he is very much in love. However, no matter what he tries with her sexually, the woman never achieves orgasm. Since a Jewish wife is entitled to sexual pleasure, the man decides to seek counsel from the rabbi. The rabbi listens to his story, strokes his beard, consults the holy books, and makes the following recommendation.

'Hire a strapping young man and while the two of you are making love, have him wave a towel over you. That will help your wife fantasize and should bring on her orgasm.'

The old man goes home and follows the rabbi's advice. He hires a handsome young man who waves a towel over the old Jew and his wife as they make love. But it doesn't help. She is still unsatisfied. No orgasm. Perplexed, he goes back to the rabbi.

'Okay,' says the rabbi, 'let's try it reversed. Have the young man make love to your wife and you wave the towel over them.'

Once again, the old Jew follows the rabbi's advice. The young man gets into bed with the wife and the husband waves the towel. The young man makes love with great enthusiasm and the wife soon has an enormous, room-shaking, ear-shattering, full blown orgasm. The husband smiles. Holding up his right index finger he stares at the young man and says to him triumphantly, 'You see, now that's the way to wave a towel!'"

Weintraub had a joke of his own that he told Nabokov and pretty much cemented their fifteen-year friendship. The joke, which may have been printed elsewhere, without question, originates with Weintraub.

Three men arrive in New York from Europe, and decide to meet again in 20 years to see how they all made out in America. 20 years pass . . .

The first man asks the second, "So, how'd you do?"

"Vell, ven I came to this country I had no idea vhat to do vit myself to make a livink. So I looked at my last name. Goldstein. So I vent into da gold business. And boy, did I make a fortune!"

He turns to the next man and asks, "And how 'bout you?"

"Vell, like you I had no idea vhat I vas going to do to make a livink, so I too, looked to my last name. Silverberg. I vent into silver. And boy, did I make a killing!"

They both turn to the last man and say, "And you? Vat happened to you?"

"Vell, I too had no idea either how I vas to make a living here in America, so I looked at my last name. Taylor. I said, das no good. I vill never make money as a tailor! Never in a million years! So I went to shul and prayed. I said 'God, if you make me a wealthy man, I promise. . . . I will make you my partner.'"

Goldstein and Silverberg now look at the man.

"So, vat happened?"

The man replied, "Vas the matter? You never heard of Lord

and Taylor?"

Together, Weintraub and Nabokov, donning space helmets, searched for butterflies, hidden meanings and buried truth. They often snagged imaginary flights of fancy in their common net, wandering together in dreamlike confusion avoiding the annoyance of time and place, unencumbered by pesky facts. Interestingly, they had a common birthday. Both were born on April the 23rd, the same one shared by Shakespeare. Nabokov was often troubled with a burning weltschmerz. He found little relief in losing himself in research, even when consuming large amounts of Zantac, although his conversations with Weintraub helped.

"Weiny," he would say, "How can I talk about the novel when I don't know what a novel is? There are no novels, no writers, only individual books."

"But Vlad, there will always be stories, right? Words and colors, images to convey feelings?"

"Seeing things as if they were new is funny in itself. The unusual is funny in itself. A man slips and falls down. It is the contrary of gravity in both senses. That is a great pun, by the way. And if you haven't noticed, I am a very funny man."

"Ok, here is one for you. The first riddle my father ever asked me. What hangs on the wall, is green and wet. . . .And it whistles?"

"I give up Weiny, what is the answer, the novel?"
"No Vlad, it's not the novel. It's a herring!"
"A herring. A herring doesn't hang on the wall."
"So hang it there!"
"But Weiny, a herring isn't green."
"Paint it!"
"But a herring isn't wet."
"If it's just painted it's still wet."
"Come on Weiny, everyone knows a herring doesn't whistle!"

"Well Vlad you are right. I just put that in to make it hard."

***

At 16, Weintraub completely modeled himself after Nabokov. In addition to studying the mating habits of the hawk moth that could fly at speeds of up two to three hundred miles per hour—this fact was discovered by combat pilots who observed the little creatures outdistancing their planes making them feel as if they were standing still or flying backwards—he also learned to box and play tennis, often mistaking an overhead slam for a simple upper-cut.

Weintraub became an expert chess player and Scrabble whiz and, like Nabokov, loved a vigorous verbal joust. He would introduce himself to classmates, his voice parodying the manners of a skilled 19th century actor: "My name, if you must know, is Vynetrowbe. But only a Russian can say it with its true inflections." And then he would always add (slowly and purposefully): "The life of a Russian emigré in an American university is a difficult one."

Weintraub would memorize conversations he had with Nabokov or parrot verbatim long passages of his friend's writing, pawning it off as his own. He would entertain his professors in study hall or at the university club, sharing the refreshment of a good cigar and donnish sarcasm.

"Poking fun at suburban genteelness or inventing a half dozen grotesque motels does not mean sneering at America. Let us not make a mockery out of a mock-up."

And then after several long drags without expelling a puff, Weintraub would continue: "Many accepted authors simply do not exist for me. Brecht, Faulkner, Camus, mean absolutely nothing. I must fight a suspicion of conspiracy against my brain when I blandly see accepted as 'great literature' by critics and fellow authors Lady Chatterley's copulations or the pretentious nonsense of Mr. Ezra Pound, that total fake."

And then Weintraub would wait at least five more seconds before exhaling with the incendiary rage of an offended dragon.

At parties he would instinctively approach the most beautiful woman in a room and unleash outrageous pronouncements.

"I'm Vynetrowbe. I don't fish, cook, dance, endorse books, sign declarations, eat oysters, get drunk, go to analysts, or take part in demonstrations. I am a mild gentleman, very kind."

Once at a Harvard formal Weintraub was observed regaling a circle of listeners in the home of Dean Poshlost, director of admissions for the School of Arts and Science. His wife, Ada, was an entomological researcher at the Humbert Museum of Comparative Zoology. She shared Weintraub's passion—some may say madness—for butterflies and moths, discovering several species and subspecies, making valuable scholarly contributions to the scientific literature.

Ada was graduated from Trinity College, Cambridge where she read French and Russian literature on a scholarship. She too was a perfectly normal trilingual child who at an early age excelled at science and math. She possessed a cultivated mind and wrote poetry and short stories for fun and games. Along the way, Ada became interested in butterflies after a violent rain storm. She observed a monarch give flutter to a cordate leaf after a thick raindrop penetrated its wing. She lived with her mother up until the age of 12 in Berlin where her father was killed in a political rally.

Ada was tall with a sturdy, lithe build. Her eyes amber-green, golden hair, with fine facial features and porcelain skin. She was drawn to Weintraub and though she had not met him, and he was many years her junior, Ada couldn't help but see him as a cunning Swallowtail. Swallowtails are strong fliers with two pairs of wings covered with colorful iridescent scales in overlapping rows. Their wings are attached to a thorax supported with veins that nourish the delicate wings with blood.

As she watched Weintraub, Ada saw the Swallowtail's anatomy: its six jointed legs, antennae, compound eyes and exoskeleton. The head, thorax and abdomen. The Swallowtail's surface covered with fine prickly hairs. Taut muscles that affect flutter in body and wings.

Ada also wondered about the butterfly's sense of taste, touch, sight, sound and smell. Defense mechanisms and urge to mate. The life cycle: egg, larva, pupa and adult. In Weintraub's case, not quite adult, which Ada understood was its own thrill; to be lost, rising and falling on wind gusts, fluttering together.

***

Weintraub looks up from his circle of admirers who feed on his words like hungry cubs. Through story and mimicry he is conferred custodian of dreams. His celebrity derives from an artful manipulation of parts of speech: verbs, nouns, pronouns, adjectives, adverbs, prepositions, conjunctions and interjections. On occasion he demands that one part take on the role of the other often adding up to more than the sum of the parts. Weintraub has discovered the power to enthrall. He projects a wide emotional range, skillfully adding elements of comedy and drama. His sentences and paragraphs, periods and question marks transfix like an unbroken stare.

Weintraub feels Ada's eyes on him. She is standing alone on the far side of the living room in front of a window, the occasional beam of light from a car passing across her body, the faint sound of a bleating bagpipe from outside the glass. She is wearing a floral printed dress. Weintraub gazes into her eyes and thinks about moths and butterflies and summer meadows. The short and tall grasses, flowers in need of pollination.

Weintraub approaches. He thinks of celadon when he looks into her eyes. Many times in his mind, he has rehearsed something he had read that Vlad said, years ago, in a New York Times interview.

"I reject completely the vulgar, shabby, fundamentally medieval world of Freud, with its crankish quest for sexual symbols (something like searching for Baconian acrostics in Shakespeare's works) and its bitter little embryos spying from their natural nooks upon the love life of their parents."

Ada whispers softly into Weintraub's ear, "Have you ever been with a woman?"

And before he answers, Ada puts a finger on Weintraub's lips. "Come."

***

Weintraub and Ada are in an upstairs bedroom, down a long hallway in the back of the house. It is the former living quarters of one of the many governesses who raised the children of prominent Bostonian families that resided here before Harvard acquired the property. It is simply furnished with, at first breath, a pleasing camomile-ginger potpourri aroma. An elderly oarsman travels on a river of Chinese wallpaper, peeling in the corners. It is cinnamon-colored, drawn with junks and outstretched sails. A solitary bridge in the distance arches a sleepy lagoon. On one side there is celebration; men and women carry lanterns, some with lit candles, in the shape of large carp, bats, butterflies and flowers. There is a single dragon with five claws. A drunken mouth bears a mountain range of teeth above its right shoulder. On the other side, against the backdrop of a golden pagoda two men wrestle with a woman. Weintraub can't tell if this is a bitter quarrel or perhaps a ceremonial dance fraught with legend and symbolic meaning. A solitary tree stands in the foreground, its extended branches tensely climbing towards the horizon. The double bed is covered with a white chenille spread. The rug is an old oriental in a Persian style, a hunting scene encased in a nest of formal gardens with a well devised running dog border. Weintraub thinks of a magic carpet.

Ada caresses Weintraub's face. She runs her soft fingers like a Marquessa Limenitis archippus across his forehead, eyes, cheeks, nose and mouth. With Ada's first moist kiss Weintraub is lost in a Dolores Haze.

The Marquessa has always been one of Weintraub's favorites. It can be distinguished from the Monarch by the black line that crosses her delicate wings. Its underside is remarkable in that it is so different from its topside, unlike the Monarch whose underside is much lighter. Weintraub and Ada delight in this fact. The Marquessa also has a keen sense of touch and smell. It experiences sensations of uncontrollable ecstasy much like the Swallowtail when its bristly tufts and prickly hairs are stimulated. It loves to suck on willow and cottonwood as do all classified in Family Nymphalidae.

***

Weintraub cannot believe the physical sensation that is produced in his body by the fluttering of Ada's tongue. He never imagined such pleasure existed. He loves the feeling of soaring up and down, flying on gossamer wings. He sees himself beneath a white mountain at the side of a harbor with the sounds of children laughing and crickets mating all around. In a drop of water he observes Ada's reflection and a blue-gray sky and single cloud.

Weintraub opens his eyes for an instant, absorbed in a burst of red color. He is an oarsman traveling down the river. He passes a golden pagoda and a five clawed dragon. Weintraub observes men and women flying kites and carrying lanterns, and a bridge with three arches in a swampy lagoon. He breathes in Ada's delicious fragrance, thinking to himself, "How lucky can I be?"

It is the only thought on his mind; the only thing in the world he cares about or that really matters.

Weintraub imagines swimming and hiking inside of Ada. The grotto corridor is along an ancient river against a background

The Next Step

of cinnamon; the aroma of coriander and jasmine in the air. Ada's opening, a shrine created to Weintraub, an intricate and exciting blend of architecture, geometry, religion and art. Weintraub pauses before the steamy entrance at the notch of the cave; it is connected to the round shaped main chamber through a narrow humid corridor. Carved on both sides he observes statues of heavenly guards, exquisite lions and sacred kings. A fiery mural of a herd of long-horned antelope and a sacred drawing of a wild boar. Images of valiant warriors, spirited dancers and graceful gods. There is delicately shaped pink granite, supple and graceful all around. A secret mood and mystic atmosphere, a hint of unknowable mystery and danger. There is a tiny column, an homage to the eleven-faced Goddess of Pleasure, safeguarding all movement north, south, east and west. There are also paintings of naked men with undomesticated dogs hunting in a primeval forest, the celestial faces of Bodhisattvas, religious pilgrims striving for the image of God. Weintraub searches his vocabulary for a single word to describe this wonder: majestic, sublime, magnificent, transcendent. None can be found to capture the volcanic surge of its flow. Enshrined in its center is the main chamber. The source of the grotto's power. Few treasures have been so feverishly sought. Weintraub thinks to himself that there is virtually nothing that has not been attempted or done in the glow of the grotto's irresistible pull. Men have lied, killed, cheated, speculated, loved and died to obtain it, occasioning moral and religious strictures, fomenting international wars and national strife. Songs and plays have been written about it. And yet Weintraub can't help but feel still so little is known.

Lying next to Ada, inside of her, Weintraub studies her face. Ada's skin is warm, flushed. He kisses her eyes—her eyebrows flutter against his red lips—nose, chin and mouth. He then rests his tongue on the nipple of her right breast, rolling it with his lips, imagining a large raspberry, extracting all its delicious taste. Paradise.

And then unexpectedly he is seized with a strange feeling. A deep sadness comes over him. Weintraub sees the Marquessa at the end of her short life. He looks into Ada's eyes and all he sees is a woman growing old. Weary eyes, slackened skin, wrinkled face. Her fingers gnarled limbs crooked, stiff. Weintraub cries. Ada folds him into her arms.

Chapter 28

In the beginning Fishman saved the world.

Earlier the earth was without form and void, and darkness was upon the face of the deep; and the Spirit to tell his story was moving over the face of the waters. And He said, "Let there be light", and there was light. And He saw that the light was good; and he separated the light from the darkness. Fishman called the light day and the darkness he called night. And there was evening and there was morning, one day.

If you recall . . . At fifty-two, Fishman pretty much had the world by the balls. That is to say, he wanted for nothing. He lived a quiet, solitary life in an historic part of Chicago, known as Old Town. He resided with his wife of twenty-five years in a two-bedroom apartment in a renovated building that once served as a rectory to St. Michael's Church, which long ago had been sold by the Diocese to a real estate developer. Fishman paid his rent on time each month and marveled at his lot in life and good fortune.

His children, a girl and a boy, were now grown with families of their own. He regretted that they lived so far away, his daughter in New York and his son in Boston, but they spoke often and Fishman was content in the belief that they were raised well. His wife Nadia, a beauty in her youth, was an artist. Fishman found her tall slim body, long red hair, now dyed, and soft blue green eyes as exciting as the first time he saw her.

She had documented their life together in warm liquids. Oil paints, water colors, India ink and tempera in journals and on furniture and walls interior and exterior, on clothing and floor boards. Even the ceiling. Her murals sometimes dealt with historical themes like the one over their bed where she painted Fishman as Adam and herself as Eve or the one of Shakespeare's Midsummer Night's Dream starring Fishman as a very regal Oberon and Nadia a nymphy Titania. Her many self-portraits were everywhere, each reflecting a colorful mood or temperament that Fishman knew well. There was also the painting of the teddy bear picnic in her son's room under which the family used to play Candy Land and Chutes and Ladders and read stories until fragrant young bodies, fresh from baths, folded into the arms of Morpheus.

Her first present to Fishman was a pen and ink of an old maple tree with two birds on its branches and the initials of lovers carved into its trunk. She placed it in an antique maple frame that she and Fishman had found together in the West Village when they were still living in New York.

Their home was her continuing gift to Fishman. He might awake to any variety of painting, drawing, sculpture, self-designed garment. Nadia was particularly fond of painting his shoes and jackets. Not once in twenty-five years, had Fishman ever risen to know for sure if the contents of his closet were as he had left them or if a ceiling, floor, hallway or wall would be as last seen. This was unusual because the virtue that Fishman prized most in the world was certainty. It was not a philosophy, though Fishman could say quite a bit on that subject. It was more his psychology, from which Fishman derived his sense of well-being.

***

Fishman's life changed forever on September eleventh

For months he could see nothing in his mind but packed jetliners crashing into the Twin Towers over and over again. Plumes of orange-white flames and billows of gray-black smoke. Charred human bodies and the agonized screams of loved ones in pain.

***

Weintraub reminds himself of the letter he had received yesterday. "There are too many 9/11 stories." He laughs disgustedly.

***

Fishman fought against himself trying to visualize the final moments of fiery suffering. In stead he strained to remember birthdays and celebrations. Like the time the family traveled to the southwest to visit the pueblos of the ancient Anasazi Indians. They walked along mesas and plateaus, river bottoms and canyons. They wandered where the ancients raised towers and built hundred-room cities in cliffs and caves. They climbed kiva ladders and descended into ceremonial chambers and marveled at petroglyphs from a thousand years ago. There was one that his daughter Lara and his son James loved. It was the Kachina spirit Kokopelli, the wandering hunchbacked flute-player and magician who originated from the center of the earth. The Anasazi looked to him to bring rain and fertility. He would travel from village to village, seducing women with the alluring strains of his enchanted instrument.

Fishman tried to imagine the Kachina spirit providing his gifts to humanity. He tried to feel his invisible presence from wherever life came forth. Legend had it that Kokopelli carried seeds and babies and blankets in his hump. He also offered dreams and visions, fertility and love.

But Fishman was unable to welcome Kokopelli into his heart. There was no room for him there. Fishman was engulfed in darkness and ash. All he could see was black fire and burning smoke. And eventually Fishman collapsed.

***

Weintraub considers every detail of the story like a painter working an image over and over again. Each time more powerfully.

***

Fishman discovered Palefsky when he was hospitalized at Mt. Sinai in New York. He recognized that deep within his unconscious irreversible forces were at work. Slowly but surely he was undergoing the inevitable chemistry of reinvention. Palefsky was a catalyst, a means to stimulate change.

***

Fishman thought to himself that if he were to be in a hospital anywhere, what better place than Mt. Sinai? Of course, there is so much mystery surrounding the mountain where God spoke to Moses. Fishman thought it strange to even think of Mt. Sinai in clinical terms. He knew that there was no archeological evidence of Moses' presence on the mountain but there were relics of the faithful assembled over thousands of years. There were also ancient chapels and structures honoring saints and the Virgin Mary and a hewn stone arch where long ago a monk heard confessions from truth-seeking pilgrims.

For the first time in Fishman's life, he had a bleak view of his own future. He could not see himself without Nadia and the children. He thought about suicide but knew he couldn't do that. He had seen someone else take his life many years earlier when he was a child. A small boy imitating Icarus in Queens. A sudden crazed act to see if humans really could fly.

Fishman wandered in a desert of sleepless nights and diminished appetite. He suffered from a profound loss of self-confidence and a depressed mood. He was weighted down with heavy fatigue and lack of interest. He also wrestled with guilt. Why did it not happen to him? Why wasn't he the one who died?

One of the doctors suggested that he write his thoughts down. Fishman joked about it. He said, "There already is a Book of Job."

But eventually he did get his thoughts on paper and was content with the results. It was a kind of statement he felt, in some small sense, like job, that not only conveyed his pain and suffering but the sadness that existed throughout the world.

He also told the story of Ploopy Goldberg.

"I remember sometimes late at night when it was very quiet. I could hear Maya Angelou's voice. You could hear her narrate the story of the Big Bang and the origins of the universe. I would get up and look at the Hayden Sphere. I'd see Neptune and Mercury, even Pluto revolving in the night. Always a different color. Look, right there. See how small the earth is compared to all the others?"

Fishman visualizes his grandfather returning from the synagogue or after a long day's work. He watches him pulling his heavy body, resting at each landing, sighing in a way that only older Jews can. He sees the door opening. His grandmother is wearing an embroidered apron, the one her sister Ida made for her. Two Dutch girls separated by a multi-colored rose, all done in tiny cross-stitches.

There are four children playing in the living room, Fishman's father, his younger brother and two sisters, now all dead. His aunt Rose is reading a story to a three year old Uncle Joe. It is a fairy tale about survival, in a magic kingdom in a distant place a long time ago. Caruso is singing "Vesti la Giubba" from "Pagliacci" on a grainy seventy-eight and the blue-orange flicker of Sabbath candles burning eternal against the darkness of the night.

Fishman tells his godson to make a wish.

***

Weintraub is particularly fond of this part of the story.

***

Soon the two of them are captives of high-intensity white light randomly twinkling in the night sky. They move across an arc of stars, along the surface of the moon and among the farthest planet visible to the naked eye. Fishman's mind wanders. He thinks about the laws of physics and chemistry. Fundamental forces, electromagnetism and gravity. He visualizes the structure of atoms and the composition of elements. He hears the Big Bang and feels infinite space. He sees the design of molecules, the smallest units determining the chemical properties of matter. He observes bonds everywhere: ionic, covalent and metallic. There is also the production of compounds. Fishman is still amazed that the world is alive with iron, copper, zinc and aluminum. And, of course, human beings.

***

Out of the blue three photographs appear at the exact moment Palefsky detects the sound of a posthorn playing the theme from Mahler's Third Symphony, which he remembers vividly from a 1976 performance of the New York Philharmonic directed by Zubin Mehta.

The first, taken in 1921, is of a glowering Freud challenging the photographer with his archeological stare. Cigar in hand, his open jacket reveals a loopy gold chain dangling confidently from his vest. The stance and accoutrements, all signs of someone who is secure; firmly establishing his beachhead on terra incognita.

A second picture, also of Freud, is taken later. He is stooped over and looks less sure. It is from the period when he was waiting for permission from German authorities to leave Austria.

The third photograph speaks for itself. A Jewish boy forced to write Juden on the door of his family's home. His tormentors, young and old, laugh menacingly.

And then Weintraub can't help but think of the photographs of Leni Riefenstahl. In the first picture, she is on Athuruga Island dated March 13, 2003. She is 101 years old, dressed in a blue-green silk robe and swim suit, as if walking on water, white combed sand beneath a wide blue-gray sky. Her deep red lips smile brightly. Her eyes covered by large tortoiseshell frames. Her blond hair perfectly etched, not a strand out of place. She smiles warmly, ingratiatingly at the camera. There is no horror or madness in her eyes, no blood dripping from her lips. Absent are pictures of incinerated children hanging around her neck or morbid photographs pasted on her Kiosk-like.

In the second picture, she embraces Mick Jagger, and in the third, she is kneeling on the ground, petting a leopard in the Las Vegas mansion of her friends Siegfried and Roy.

Weintraub seeks comfort in Palefsky's words.

"If there is one lesson I have learned it is that everything we know or do is matter of perspective and anything we accomplish is relative to molehills and mountains. Astronomers can view objects thirteen billion light years away just as the heavens looked when stars and galaxies first appeared. They can focus their sights on quasars, shining objects thought to be powered by massive black holes from the inception of the universe. They appear to the observer as luminous smears from the dawn of time, arcs of red and blue on the cosmic lens of space. Each of us inhabits our own glittering expanse of stars and sky; some so close to us as to be blinding to the eye and others so remote that they are forever beyond our field of vision unless or until we stretch our horizons; allowing ourselves to see what has always been there.

As a child, I spent many hours alone in the starry dark watching strange objects form over head; nearly perfect rings of hot blue stars, wheels within wheels spinning around a yellow nucleus of galaxies and comets from the farthest reaches of the solar system breaking apart. I would watch with special interest a system of comets called "sungrazers" so named because their orbits closely brushed the sun, arriving to their inevitable end in clusters on parallel paths. Their fragmentation the result of gravity's strong pull, disintegrated their loosely piled chunks of dust and ice into luminous cascades of one comet falling into large families of smaller ones. Their gradual demise had a hypnotic effect, celestial fireworks in mysteriously ordered patterns, in natural life cycles and solar systems."

***

Weintraub lingers on the sight of Palefsky transformed into Fishman. Then, he thinks about the classic structure of a Hollywood film following Todorovian principles as a guide for creating a pleasing narrative arc: equilibrium followed by disruption, identification of obstacles, pursuit of goal, struggle, resolution of narrative as a positive outcome, right back, once again, to our old friend equilibrium.

But despite this fact or maybe because of it, Weintraub hears a leopard growling. He tucks himself back into Ada's cunty warmth, folding sideways into her wings.

Chapter 29

Weintraub is climbing the stairs leading to the Fullerton El station. Over the public address system a voice, congested with a cold, squelches connection instructions for the brown, green, red, purple and blue lines. Weintraub hears something about "all criminal activity on Chicago Public Transit Trains will be prosecuted to the fullest extent of the law." There is also a reminder that "eating, drinking, spitting and unwarranted solicitations are against transit policy." Weintraub wonders if warranted solicitations are handled differently and exactly what they could be.

The voice changes. It is now one of those automated friendly types, like a beloved kindergarten teacher mixed with the vocal stylings of an operator, directing calls on a 900 porno hotline.

"The man is a piece of magic."

Weintraub looks around and suddenly realizes the voice is directed at him. No, it's for and about *him*.

"A real piece of magic."

Suddenly three men approach Weintraub from behind. Startled, he tries to figure out what is going on. The first is wearing a green suit, white shirt and a blue and black, zebra or horse, all over design, tie. He is clean shaven, of average height and build with short hair neatly cut, a fifties style part off to one side. He introduces himself as Dr. Moshe Miller and though he doesn't sing at the Metropolitan Opera, like Robert Merrill his namesake, he claims to be a damn good dermatologist, specializing in acne and stds.

"I'm good at what I do. Now look behind you. Go ahead. Look."

Weintraub swivels around. The second man who is Latino moves out of the way. He has wide eyes and an open grin. He is short and stocky with a red doorag, baggy jeans, Nike sneakers and big gold chain.

"I'm TN 473. Call me Silverberg."

He points to his sidekick, an imposing African-American dressed all in black, a gold earring in the shape of diablo in his right ear.

"Say hello to Goldstein."

"Who are you guys?"

Just as he gets the words out of his mouth, Weintraub reacts to the sign that Moshe wanted him to see. It is a poster, as large as a garage door. It reminds Weintraub of the kind that used to be hung at circuses. There is a rainbow of primarily blue, green, yellow and red with a hint of some brown and purple. Across it, with the face of Dr. Miller off to the left, are these words: "Face Facts. Life Sucks. What Are *You* Going to Do?"

Beneath the bold lettering are before and after pictures of Weintraub with an illegible testimonial to one side.

"Who are you guys? What is this all about?"

A Purple Line loop express rumbles into the station just as Silverberg starts an explanation. The four men enter the car, the door closes behind them.

As the train leaves the station it passes a graffiti mural bombed on the side of a factory wall. The names Weintruab, Fishman, Palefsky, and Goldberg ride on waves of thick bright paint. It is signed RK or CB. It's hard to tell.

Silverberg begins lecturing Weintraub.

"I started writing graffiti back in the early eighties. Not too long after Nabokov, you know, the Lolita guy, died. First thing is to get a name. Mine is TN 293, it stands for Travellin. I took the first letter and last letter and put it together. I got into graffiti so good that people used to say I have 293 styles. And that's how the 293 came about."

Weintraub asks, "Why tell all this to me?"

Silverberg rolls his eyes and continues. "I started doing throw-ups; you take one color fill-in and one color outline. Later on, you want more colors in your piece. You start throwing up bolder letters and you're adding little arrows here and there. And that's how I started improving the way I was doing things."

Moshe turns to Weintraub, sensing his impatience.

"Listen, we all work crazy hours. Let him finish. He knows what he's talking about."

Moshe now prods Silverberg. "Go on tell him."

"When you are a graffiti artist you have to find a location. Mine is the ghost yard. The ghost yard is where trains go to get fixed. I go there and graffiti them. If I want to hit on a one train or a two or a four, it's the perfect place. The best thing is when you bomb, your name travels. You can start off in Brooklyn but they'll know all about you in Queens, even in the Bronx. If you don't see your name . . . don't worry someone else will see it for you."

Weintraub looks out the window. He watches the A train curving into the New York skyline. Behind him, seated in the car, is a doo-wop group, mariachis, two men dressed as Buddhas, a Michael Jackson look-alike, a giant hamster and a klezmer band with clarinets, kazoos, zithers and musical saws. There is also a Barbra Streisand impersonator who introduces himself and begins to sing to the car.

> *"People, people who need people*
> *are the luckiest people in the world.*
> *We're children, needing other children*
> *and yet letting our grown-up pride*
> *hide all the need inside,*
> *acting more like children then children."*

Dr. Miller now takes charge. "Quiet. I run a dermatology clinic. Enough Barbra. Next you'll be telling us lovers are the luckiest people."

He looks at Goldstein. "This is our station."

The doors open. There is an announcement made over a P.A. system in Nabokov's voice. "Vynetrowbe. All off for Vynetrowbe."

It is a tiny platform with a single low wattage bulb hanging from the ceiling on a frayed extension cord. There are sounds of water dripping and small rodents and large insects whisking underfoot. Straight in front of them is a door marked "Emergency Exit."

***

In the dim light, the silhouette of four figures is etched on a heavy, half corroded, vault-like, sliding door. They pause for an interminable instant. Moshe places his hand on Weintraub's shoulder.

"Jesus, you scared the shit out of me"

Not reassuringly, Goldstein blurts, "We're taking you to the source."

***

From a philosophical perspective the notion of a source is an interesting one. If God is everywhere then he is in all things, and all things are in him. God is all and all is God. It is a wonderfully inventive and redemptive point of view. And not without its own Who? What? And why? Who and what is the source of Weintraub's big bang. Why is he here?

As the rusted steel door slides open, Goldstein quotes from the bible. "John chapter one, verses two to five. Through CB all things came to be, not one thing had its being but through him.

All that came to be had life in him and that life was the light of men, a light that shines in the dark, a light that darkness could not overpower."

Moshe picks up in Hebrew. "Bereshit bara Elohim es hashamayim ve-es ha-arets." And then he adds in English: In the beginning God created the heavens and the earth. The earth was without form and void, and darkness was upon the face of the deep."

***

Now inside, they are locked in a capsule in total darkness. There is no air. Weintraub worries about his next breath. A voice, reminiscent of Geoffrey Holder, booms over a loud speaker.

"Ever existing as the life source of all creation, the living womb of infinity itself, the eternal Self Existent One, 'Yahweh', man's eternal 'I AM'. To Him alone belongs all power and honor and glory and blessing from every living creature. This most High One also known to the ancient Hebrews as 'Elohim' & 'El Shaddai' as well as by numerous other names and titles that denote His awesome nature. The all powerful, majestic, Eternal Being, better known in the English language as 'God Almighty', 'the Lord', Christ Bob, 'the Father', 'the Creator', having neither beginning of days nor end of life who always was, and shall every be, 'God', from everlasting to everlasting. Welcome to his house. Please remove your shoes and try not to touch anything."

***

A door opens in front of them. They are now standing in bright light looking down a long hallway. The kind that passes for a hospital trauma corridor or gateway to a near-death "just follow the light" experience. Along the walls on either side are photographic portraits in the later style of Richard Avedon. Recognizing the subjects on either side of him Weintraub exclaims, "Grandpa Morris. Grandma Ida. And the three little girls, my mother, Miriam and her sisters, Shirley and Ruth."

He walks further and sees others that he knows.

"Bobby Block and Larry. Haven't seen them since the sixth grade."

Silverberg chimes in. "It's all about you man."

"My God. Evelyn Arfa. I loved that girl. Gave her my entire bubble gum charm collection. She never even said thank you."

Goldstein and Moshe agree with pats on Weintraub's back.

The big guy now addresses Weintraub. "It's ok, man. Let yourself feel it. This is your 15 minutes. Go for it."

Along the walls there are also portraits of George Gershwin, Albert Einstein, Nabokov, Irving Berlin, Jonas Salk, Groucho Marx, Meyer Lansky and Steve and Edie. Weintraub stops in front of one of Ethel Merman dressed as Annie Oakley sitting on top of two actors in a horse suit.

"That woman could really belt out a song. I'd give anything to hear her sing "There's No Business Like Show Business.""

Moshe starts to laugh. "Talk about judging a book by its cover. Weintraub, I never thought you were into show tunes. Personally, I can't stand them. Too sentimental."

Not paying any attention to Moshe, half lost in reverie, Weintraub sings to himself, *"There's no business like show business, like no business I know . . ."*

Moshe mildly annoyed. "Hey. A little respect for the dermatologist!"

Silverberg impishly seizes the moment, bursting into song. *"Everything about it is appealing. Everything the traffic will allow . . ."*

Goldstein now starts singing in the style of Paul Robeson, completing the verse.

"When you aren't stealing that extra bow. There's no people like show people."

Reluctantly, Moshe joins in. *"They smile when they are low."*

All four now form a chorus.

> *"Yesterday they told you would not go far*
> *That night you opened and there you are*
> *Next day on your dressing room they've hung a star*
> *Let's go on with the show."*

***

Weintraub, Goldstein, Silverberg and Moshe are now in a large burled walnut gallery. A space reminiscent of the Harvard or Knickerbocker clubs, City Hall, or the Oak Room at the Plaza. There are portraits of the usual tribal elders, painted in traditional colors and poses overhead. Just being here offers deeper insight into being a Macunudo, encased in a humidor or red cedar box. Weintraub looks up and sees a portrait of himself. He is wearing a 19th century black frock coat and stovepipe hat. He has mutton chops and a Boss Tweed smile.

He turns to the three wise men. "That's me. Holy shit. That's me."

Goldstein, Silverberg and Moshe agree. Moshe takes the initiative. "Yes, it's you alright. Now look again."

Weintraub looks up but this time he is wearing a space helmet and a purple and silver leotard that he remembers from his childhood. It was worn by Flash Gordon or Captain Video, he thinks, Weintraub doesn't remember for sure.

"Buck Rogers?"

He now sees all the portraits in the room are in a constant state of change.

"What's going on? Where are we?"

Silverberg offers an explanation. "Flux. It's everywhere,

man. Happens all the time."

Moshe adds his two cents. "Think of it as a constant face lift. Shit happens. Droopy skin, too many wrinkles, bad hair line . . . but I'm not here to talk about *my* business."

Goldstein now pipes in. "Yea, Doc's right. Flux . . . like an undulating smirk. See. Look at that one right there."

Goldstein points to a portrait of Palefsky in a green hospital gown. His face looks world-weary, deeply depressed. A second later he changes to Fishman wearing a black and orange FedEx uniform. He is beaming, determined with the confidence and resolve of a man who saves the world.

Goldstein continues. "No rules in the fig factory."

As soon as the words leave his lips Moshe and Silverberg are clearly upset. Moshe grabs Goldstein's arm.

"The boss said, 'strictly on a need to know basis.'"

Silverberg turns to Weintraub nervously, panicky. "You know shit man. Nobody said nothing about any fig factory. I'm not risking my ass for his mistakes."

Weintraub is confused but presses the point. "We're in the fig factory?"

Silverberg cups his hand over Weintraub's mouth. "Shh, man. This is no game. You get the boss pissed off and we're history."

Moshe begins to pray in Hebrew. "Shema Yisroel Adonai Eloheinu Adonai Echad."

Goldstein speaks up. "You guys are pussies. Boss man said I'm in charge, so . . . I'm in charge! Any questions?"

He now talks to Weintraub in a reassuring tone. "We just call it that. It's really the Figment Depository. You have to pass through here to get to the other side. Down those steps."

***

In the far corner of the room, at the bottom of three large

steps is a swinging door, now closed. Above it is a small portrait of an incredibly handsome, erudite, well-dressed gentleman. There is tremendous power behind his dazzling stare. It is marked with a simple bronze placard bearing his name, Christ Bob.

Weintraub looks ahead. "Where to now?"

Goldstein points. "The door to understanding. Swings both ways."

Weintraub is still unsure. He looks around and watches Moshe, Silverberg and Goldstein evanesce into portraits on the wall overhead. In their wake they say in chorus.

"Don't be afraid. It's the next step."

Chapter 30

Weintraub descends a handicap friendly ramp. He then follows a series of Xeroxed black arrows, copied on computer paper, appearing once he is on the other side of the swinging door.

Where he is going is a fundamentalist Christian's vision of a haunted house, depicting the eternal horror and torment of hell. Weintraub negotiates a wrought iron spiral staircase, passes visions of snakes and spiders, ghosts and goblins. There are also images of dancers, spinning around in his head; naked men and women engaged in flamenco, meringue and the tango. All terrorized by a disdainful lack of faith, a refusal to take Jesus Christ into their hearts as their personal Lord and Savior.

Weintraub observes Satan worship, abortions, human sacrifice, the brimstone of evangelical preachers, Bill O'Reilly, the Jerry Springer Show, even children reading Harry Potter. There is a lone menacing raven and a lake of fire with millions burning, weeping, screaming, wailing and gnashing of teeth. Weintraub finds a book on tape that he plays.

"It's a good thing," he says to himself, "that I remembered to bring my Sony pocket cassette recorder."

The title is "The Other Side of Death's Door" by Dr. Bunny Brownhouse, a board certified doctor of Internal Medicine and Cardiovascular Disease whose specialty is resuscitating the clinically dead. On tape, the book is read by Bertrand Pocus. He has the soft, pleasing voice of a trusted family veterinarian, the kind who has put down generations of beloved pets.

"Many times I have resuscitated men and women, terrified and screaming, descending into the flames of hell. Often, they regain a heartbeat and respiration. Occasionally, they scream, 'I'm in hell! Get me out!'"

Weintraub hits the pause button as he surveys the carcass-laden landscape. He thinks about all the people in the world (100 million in America alone) who believe in hell and have no doubt that it is an actual place. He remembers the Baptist minister in Spermbog, Georgia who figured out that, assuming spiritual bodies are the same size as physical ones, hell is located 237 miles, give or take, in the inner core. Just south of Bayonne where Frank Sinatra was born.

Weintraub again plays the tape. Pocus is reading. The words are those of Dr. Brownhouse.

"Once I was working on a personal injury lawyer. He was terrified. He pleaded with me for help. I read the alarm on his face. He had a look worse than the expression of death. A grotesque grimace. Panic. His pupils were dilated. He was perspiring, trembling. His hair was standing on end. And although he had a very bad speech impediment, I understood perfectly what he was trying to say.

'Plith dateur, I in ell . . . Dun lep den tek me a why.'

The man was serious and, in fact, in grave danger. Sheer horror. In a state like I have never seen before. Then I knew for sure. Hell is a place of torment. The real thing."

Weintraub digs further and further into this subterranean world. He is sure it is here where researchers from Finland recorded the anguished screams of the damned. He remembers the story and the testimony, the doubters and the true facts. Janus Pastacove, short, bald with a neat Hitler-like moustache, didn't believe in the Bible. As a scientist he could not fathom the great abyss, but now, knowing what he has seen, is convinced, searching for coal he drilled through the gates of hell.

Sure it is hard to believe but this is how it happened. The

drill suddenly began to stutter, then rotate wildly, signaling Pastacove and his exploration team had reached a large pocket or cavern. Temperature gauges showed measures in excess of 10,000 degrees Fahrenheit.

As Pastacove put it, "The readings were just incredible. Hotter than hell."

The scientist lowered a microphone into the shaft designed to pick up the sounds of plate movements. But instead of seismic activity he recorded a human voice screaming in pain. At first Pastacove thought the sound was due to faulty equipment. But after he made the necessary adjustments his worst suspicions were confirmed. Not only that, the screams were not those of a single human being. They were the cries of generations of humanity, writhing in pain, in everlasting damnation.

Weintraub passes rivers of beer and clouds of marijuana smoke, goes through a furnace of fire, arriving at a wooden structure, like a clam shack, with a blinking red and blue neon sign. "Club Lucky."

***

Seated at a table the size of a campfire are two men, one in a prison uniform and the other in a tightly tailored sharkskin suit. They are reciting prayers, telling jokes, sharing insults or hatching plots. Weintraub overhears one of them saying, "Listen, let me tell you a story" before he hears a shoe drop. A French nun is gossiping with a demented looking, wheelchair-bound patient. They are talking about baseball, Weintraub thinks, unearned runs, Alzheimer's, or the size of a black man's dick. Another woman dressed in a bikini, her large Goofy bonnet flapping up and down, hands out political leaflets, telling friends, "I have journeyed through mental illness, depression and homelessness" and something about "the Bush and Cheney families, soiling themselves for oil."

A little further into the club are ballroom dancers. Weintraub spies an innocent looking Leni Riefenstahl in black lace and chiffon with a young German corporal she calls "mein lieber Fuehrer", creeping across the floor. When they move Weintraub thinks of seared film projected backwards. Rewound.

Behind them are Irish river dancers pounding feet so hard on the ground, giving Weintraub a headache, forcing him to cover his ears. There is also a cell phone on a solitary table that, when answered, instructs: "Scrape the bark off the little bastard."

Above it is a sign that reads: Induction Center Vlad the Impaler.

Weintraub thinks about his father, Vlad Dracul, and all the other Vlads that he has known. He imagines inquisitions, the Danse Macabre and Paradise Lost; Dante's descent and Faust. He also thinks of Nabokov and Dolores Haze.

Where Weintraub now finds himself it is not enough to dispel the demons of everyday life. It is important for him to do more than merely shamble through the motions, see things from a different angle. His search is nothing less than to view his life like the Holy Father, CB, to rise above and below the secrets of the Lord.

There is a gated window just to the right of a painting of a wing and a prayer next to another of an unusual metaphor. Weintraub unlocks the bars and approaches the hand scrawled letters beneath the jamb. There it is written in blue and green crayon, a child's scribble: "Window of Opportunity."

***

On the other side Weintraub finds himself in a diorama of the Mesozoic Age. Looking around he sees all his favorite life forms. There is a world of characters and creatures as bizarre and friendly (and false) as Dino the Dinosaur and Teletubbies: Brontosaurus, Diplodocus, Stegosaurus, Triceratops, and Tyrannosaurus Rex.

> *"From over the hills and far away,*
> *Weintraub comes to play."*

Just like Winky, Dipsy, Laa-Laa and Po, Weintraub lives his life beneath a dome limited only by the reach of memory and imagination. It is a strange TV landscape of half-forgotten playmates from early childhood like Clifford the Big Red Dog, Kookla, Fran and Ollie. Howdy Doody and Buffalo Bob. Pinky Lee and the Merry Mailman. A glass encased universe of people with strange sounding, laughable names: Arthur Godfrey, Gorgeous George, John Cameron Swazey, Faye Emerson, Dave Garroway, Phineas T. Bluster and Gale Storm.

At first there was an original, gigantic continent, Pangaea, when everything was one. There was no doubt or confusion. No continental drift. But this state did not last long for Weintraub. It gave way to two smaller continents, Laurasia and Gondwanaland, mother and child divided in nearly perfect halves.

Later everything changed. The world transformed itself in dramatic ways. Sea levels dropped, seasons changed. There were great extremes in temperature, volcanic activity, islands created and destroyed.

Weintraub checks the fossil records and contemplates drifts and tectonics. He recalls the power of ferns and caterpillars, ants, snakes, worms and butterflies. As he exits the diorama, he sees the distance between the poles and Equator and a major extinction occurring so many years ago.

***

Down a gritty corridor off to the side of what once looks to have been a boiler room, Weintraub opens a spacious broom closet that has the picture of a cauliflower, he thinks, painted on its door. There are words written in marker, tacked into hardwood on a business card from Athena Dry Cleaner and Tailor that offer clues to the room's original function: Reptilian Information-processing and Control system.

There is a panel reminiscent of an old plug-in telephone switchboard that slowly flickers to life. Without warning, Weintraub receives a telepathic message from above.

"You're in charge. Let's see if you can do better."

Weintraub looks down at the different switches and levers all labeled in black indelible ink: temperature, pressure, flow of information, senses and motion. There are also four words next to scrawled bullet points written in pencil on a yellow post it: walking, talking, standing, sitting. He notices a dog-eared Gulf Motor Oil road map under a layer of dust, folded in sixteenths on top of a work table. Weintraub opens it slowly speculating, in dim light. Far Rockaway is unfolding.

Weintraub remembers coming home after dark, from the beach, sitting in the back seat of the Buick, headlights from passing cars glowing on his mother's intense face, contemplating circles within circles of Spanish horses: Andalusian, Azteca and Lusitano.

In his mind it is a dizzying sight. Weintraub spinning, dreidel-like. He rode the Silver Star for the first time, with his grandfather, when he was hardly two years old. Sixty-six hand carved horses twirling in bright colored lights: four rows with fifty jumpers reined in so they would not fly off, like Pegasus, into the starry night. Occasionally he was forced to ride a stander. A sad version of the wild Sorraia. No matter how strong the wish or impossible the promise the stallion would refuse to respond to Weintraub's spurs. Even God could not make the spirited mount move up and down.

Weintraub's mother and little brother rode in flamed chariots next to wild lions and tigers on a double benched seat in a nucleus of orange-yellow. There were always outstretched arms scratching for brass rings and organ music and the promise of colorful postcards and souvenirs. Around the carousel, the perfume of hot knishes wafts off the boardwalk, the sudden gust of Atlantic wind, the out-of-tune-radio sound of waves slapping the shore. Buying a box of black and white cookies or an apple pie from the singing baker at Skolnick's, crooning a favorite song.

And then Weintraub remembers Ferlinghetti's refrain.

> *"I still would love to find again*
> *That lost locality*
> *Where I might catch once more*
> *A Sunday subway for*
> *Some Far Rockaway of the Heart."*

But it is not a poetic map that Weintraub is studying. A second look reveals it is an atlas of the human brain: a weird intricate maze of billions of neurons gathering and transmitting electrochemical signals. Above the legend is a short descriptive paragraph.

"Every animal that you can think of, lions, tigers, horses, birds, reptiles, even fish, have brains. But the human brain is unique. It gives us the power to think, plan, and speak; to remember and dream."

Below the legend written in bold black letters in a red box outlined in blue are these words. "Your brain: truly an amazing organ."

Weintraub studies the different regions. He peers into the brainstem, diencephalons, cerebellum, and cerebrum. He marvels at the corpus callosum that transfers information between the right and left hemispheres; the frontal lobes that regulate impulses, inhibitions and judgment; and the basal ganglia that process so many wonderful memories.

Weintraub now asks himself, "I hope I am wearing the right shoes."

Given the amount of ground he has covered since landing at this station, it seems like a fair question. Weintraub is wearing his wing tips and what he probably needs is more of a walking shoe. But he refuses to consider all the possibilities that lay in wait in his closet—boots, sneakers, and cap toes—or to think more about his feet.

Weintraub looks back into the atlas. He looks at connections and pathways. Neurons and dendrites as beautiful as snowflakes. Weintraub reads about synapses and simple reflexes. Complex circuitry and muscular jerks. The underside of the brain stem and cranial nerves. He runs a finger across the hypothalamus and pituitary gland. Traveling along the medulla, pons and cerebral aqueduct. He searches everywhere for the source of dreams and imagination. Weintraub seeks greater contact with his highest nature. He finds himself immersed in thoughts of the cortex. He treks across its exterior surface falling easily into the brain's folds and grooves. Gyri and Sulci. He hikes through the frontal, parietal, occipital and temporal lobes.

Chapter 31

"The door to understanding swings both ways."

Weintraub is on a train traveling through a densely wooded region of Germany. It is an expansive mountain landscape of unspoiled nature with forests, mountains, and meadows; half-timbered houses, nutcrackers and cuckoos. There are also castles, vineyards and orchards dotting the hillsides.

It is 1973 and Weintraub rides to bear witness. To know first hand, that this place, Schwarzwald, really exists.

"Yew Jewws ar so ubsessed wit de Hulacust."

"Jew must learn to furgiv and furget."

***

The Black Forest teems with rich timber, myths, legends and lore. Water nymphs inhabit the darkest depths of the Mummel Lake at the foot of Hornisgrinde at Buhl, Baden. Headless horseman ride on white steeds after midnight. A subterranean monarch drags virgins into his underworld kingdom. A sylph dances at a Celtic graveside next to a temple at Loecherberg. Here, there are also ghosts and ghouls and goblins. Werewolves, sorcerers, witches and conjuring dwarves.

In woods and villages, men and women, with and without uniforms, kill. The screams of the innocent whirl in the conifers, in the thick pine-scented night. And we must not forget the others, all around us, who have caused plagues and famine and war.

Weintraub remembers a child's suitcase.

"I would put a picture of my parents on my bedside table so that I could say goodnight to them."

He sees a sock and handkerchief. An embroided apron with Hilda, his aunt's name. A blouse and "special blanket" flying out of the window of the Kinder Transport. A little girl waving to momma and poppa, her brother Max, her cousins, Martha and Elsa, the twins Maya and Katerina Rose.

"Every parent made the same promise to her child. Soon we will be together."

There is no sense of a last goodbye. The hurt and agony all lost in a simple gesture of waving.

"Goodbye. Goodbye. Goodbye."

The train slowly pulls out of the station. Soon there will be many more trains traveling eastward.

***

Weintraub remembers the story from a woman who claimed to have been abducted by aliens. Late at night she was grabbed from her bed by a man and a woman. She knew one of them. He was her neighbor. He had shown her a strange tattoo, stamped like a cattle brand into his palm: a five pointed star, in the center of a circle, precisely and beautifully drawn. When she awoke the abduction came to her as if in a dream. She felt a sharp burning in her arm and when she looked, there was an identical mark inside her hand. A day later it was gone. Had it happened? She is not sure. But she knows that she cannot forget the pain.

***

Weintraub peers out the window of an accelerating train. He

studies his reflection in the window against a sweep of rushing water, boulders, mountain and trees. He hears the din of Wagnerian arias sung by horn helmeted, valkyrie-flying Aryan gods and goddesses. Weintraub sees himself in a bollenhut, the traditional hat of the Black Forest region with its enormous red pompoms. He is also wearing a grey suede vest, lederhosen, rustic shoes and knee-length woolen socks. Weintraub cuts down a 200 year-old chestnut tree, expertly carving it into a giant cuckoo clock and a side table in the shape of a black bear. He also fashions a fire screen. The crest shows a family of Bluebirds watching over their nest, above a hunter in front of a cabin with men on horseback and wild game.

Weintraub now sits down to a mountainous piece of Schwarzwalder Kirschentorte, washing it down with schnapps.

"Ja," Weintraub thinks to himself, "Das ist gut."

***

There is a certain lunacy to daily existence that Weintraub finds hard to explain. He yearns to find a way to an inner door, discovering some hidden meaning about himself. To ride his life in supple images and metaphors, free from someone else's story or abstract art. It has not been enough to slog through hell or search the electrochemical connections of his brain.

Weintraub waves aside a strand of his mad-genius hair. He tinkers with notions of Freud and Jung. Dream Analysis. Unconscious desires that transcend time. He toys with fugues and choreographies: the next steps in the dance of daily life.

Weintraub imagines a velvet waistcoat with a starched collar and silk cravat. He plays polo, chases show girls, collects alabaster busts and bronzes and other forms of classical art.

In his brownstone, Weintraub hangs gilt-framed portraits of Aristotle contemplating Homer, Napoleon triumphant, and a whimsical Mozart. White-gloved servants and a wife half his age make Weintraub's fantasy come true.

***

There have been too many scars, too much suffering. Too many broken dreams. Weintraub can't live in a world without rational choice.

***

Replaying in Weintraub's ears are the lyrics of a Jimmy Cliff song he remembers Jerry Garcia performing with the Grateful Dead:

> *"Sitting here in limbo, but I know it won't be long*
> *Sitting here in limbo, like a bird without a song*
> *Well they're putting up resistance*
> *But I know my faith will lead me on."*

Weintraub imagines different rooms and holding cells he will have to visit on his journey: The Parlor of Core Values, the Salon of Visual Heresies (aka seeing is believing), the Ministry of Irritation, the Laboratory of Exploding Misconceptions. Weintraub is sure that there will be many others.

He wrestles with himself to understand what life is all about. He can remember RK reassuring him.

"Your work will change the world and it's worth fighting for. You have given me the gift of learning. There is so much in your struggles, stories, and hopes. You have taught me. Tested me. Lifted me up."

And still Weintraub feels no contentment in being the product of an author's imagination, a mere literary gadget, a character subject to the twists of plot. Weintraub thinks of Palefsky and Fishman, Eve and Ada, Silverberg and Goldstein, even Ploopy

The Next Step

Goldberg. His mind finally comes to rest on a vivid image of Gepetto and his half-puppet son Pinocchio from a Golden children's book.

He can also hear Callas singing Ave Maria and remembers an etching of Galileo's telescope.

Weintraub sees the old carpenter. He is short and sad, tired-looking. Gepetto lives in the middle of a dense forest. Weintraub studies the old man's face. He is carving a puppet out of wood and proudly names him.

Weintraub too wants to be a real boy. He knows the struggles against ignorance, hardship and temptation in the effort to become an authentic person. Weintraub also knows, in the end, wishes are sometimes granted. He imagines a series of spectacular adventures that teach him lessons and the meaning of life.

Weintraub sees himself and RK swallowed up but reunited in the stomach of a big fish. He has thoughts of the trials of Job and the creation of Palefsky out of Fishman. Weintraub also wonders about the division of continents, volcanic activity and the movement of plates. Does ontogeny really recapitulate phylogeny?

Intuitively, he understands, this is a completely different story. Weintraub can hear CB saying in his Brooklyn accent, "It's something that gets handed down from generation to generation, but each one fiddles with it a little."

Once home, Weintraub promises to be good. So that, once and for all, he will be real.

Chapter 32

Weintraub is sitting at his desk thinking about Nabokov and butterflies, young girls painted by Balthus, a dream life even Freud would have envied; Vicksburg, Turkish belly dancers, Majdanek and Treblinka, George Balanchine, Castro's beard, the boxer Jack Johnson, the aroma of his grandmother's potato kugel, chopped liver, Jorge Luis Borges. He is suddenly distracted.

Weintraub is sliding down the AM dial through talk and heavy metal, past the classical music station where Vladimir Horowitz is playing John Phillip Souza's "The Stars and Stripes Forever."

He can't quite grasp the point of an agitated caller:" . . . you can't give out awards to people who raise ignorance to an art form . . ."

Suddenly there is a booming voice in Spanish. It is coarse and metallic, blaring "Cinco, Cinco, Cinco", louder than an empty barrel, like the announcers at crash-car events where oversized trucks crawl on top of beaters and junkers, and drivers who could have been professional wrestlers, wax poetic about survival of the fittest and Hemi engines. Weintraub assumes that this is the station's placement on the radio dial but soon realizes it is a commercial for the 555 acts of The Ringling Bros. Circus soon coming to town. He makes out, in the little Spanish that he understands, that there will be hundreds of midgets, dog acts, jugglers, trapeze artists, and clowns. As a boy Weintraub wanted to run off and join the circus. He loved the music of the calliope and, like

Fishman, marveled at the daring of the human cannonball.

They play "La Bamba" and "Cielito Lindo" and offer a tribute to the Virgin of Guadalupe. Most of the songs are sung in a high vocal range. They also play old broadcasts of Silvestre Vargas and his Mariachi Vargas de Tecalitan.

Weintraub loves the crazy sound of this station. It reminds him of the shtetl, klezmer music gone mad. He senses the power of high-pitched instruments. Clarinets and trumpets. Weintraub sees the Bal Shem Tov and his followers dancing. A pin-wheel of black silk and long beards. They spin in an ever larger circle, clapping their hands, reaching for God. Their breath visible in the chilled air.

Weintraub is no small-time vindicator of heresies. He harbors no hidden desire to casually undermine the universe. But he is no longer interested in postulates and speculations, chronologies of someone else's concept of eternal truth.

There is a series of commercials played against a background of mariachi rhythms for Maxwell House Coffee and Oscar Myer Wieners. Weintraub imagines mariachis in the Zacatecas and Los Altos regions clad in homespun white cotton pants and shirts and leather sandals, the clothes worn by most peasants, traveling from town to town, walking or by train, horse or mule, carrying their violins, harps and hot dogs. He watches a Miguel or Pedro playing a guitar or guitarron, biting into a delicious wiener, smiling at the Lupe next to him sipping his coffee, "good to the last drop" between beats on a snare or bass drum.

There is a haunting balada. It is sung by a man in a tenor voice. He cries with pain and longing. Unrequited love punctuated by a bursting melancholic horn. Weintraub hears the same words repeating over and over again: nunca, mujer, entonces, muerte and corazón. Weintraub tells himself if he hadn't chosen *this* life he certainly would have joined the circus or been part of a Hasidic order or a member of a mariachi band.

The Next Step

***

There is a ruthless symmetry to the way Weintraub perceives the world; ironies and contradictions housed in inconsistencies and anachronisms. His mind, like a long winding vestibule exposed to the incessant anticipation of what will happen next. His reality animates his dreams or maybe it is the other way around. Weintraub remains unsure. The joy of life, his life, distracts him. He chooses to be laconic but it is hard. Cogito ergo sum. Weintraub falters even in the yellowest light of day. He has seen the abyss and labyrinth and cosmogonic myths of the eternal return. Is it all really a game?

In the distance stand armies bent on deceit. Men and women forced into conformity. Holy rollers offering unrequited prayers. The meek, shaking back and forth, genuflecting.

But even so, Weintraub chooses the challenge of the heavens. To bear witness to the coital absurdity of reaching for the stars. Unmasking the dizzying mystery of the creator's face.

***

All Weintraub's knowledge leads exactly to this point, just where he started ages ago.

On his desk are books and papers. Family photographs. There is one of his arm around his teenage son. Another of two small children, a boy and a girl dressed in Indian costumes at a Thanksgiving celebration. A drawing, a pen and ink, of Weintraub and his wife, Ada, walking under a canopy of giant flowers, a friendly dog tagging along at his side. More photographs, an energetic Einstein in front of his Princeton laboratory and Arthur Rubinstein, seated at the piano, occasionally introduced as relatives to strangers.

Weintraub's desk sits below a large window facing an elm tree. He enjoys looking at it most in winter when its nest of branches glaze with ice and snow dusting. He can hear but not see the street. There is a white marble Buddha on the sill next to book piles and a picture of Freud's psychoanalytic couch, covered in soft Orientals and ancient statuary guarding against molesting spirits.

There is also a Plexiglas frame holding a note written in blue crayon, punctuated with tiny red hearts, handed to him by a homeless man on a New York street:

> *Pretend you're happy*
> *when you're blue*
> *It isn't hard to do*
> *And you'll find happiness without an end*
> *Whenever you pretend.*

On Weintraub's desk are three other prized objects. One is a gray and white photograph of his grandfather and his brother taken in 1907. It is glued onto a 6X8 card in an art nouveau design, floral tendrils bloom along its edges above and below a New Year's greeting written in three languages.

Leshana Tovah Tikasevu. A Happy New Year. Herzlichen Glückwunsch zum Neuen Jahre.

Two young men who Weintraub only knew once they were old; stoop shouldered, hard of hearing, his grandfather totally blind, charm the camera with their youth and strong good looks. They wear dark three piece suits, white shirts with rounded collars, ties tightly tucked into vests, a gold watch fob dangles from a lapel into a breast pocket. They stare at Weintraub demanding more of him. They know how difficult life can get. How many times it seems to lack meaning. How faraway is once-and-for-all eternal and unanswerable truth. They lived and now are dead. They will not listen to mortal excuses.

"We know. But there is work to be done," they remind.

Then always add, "Do something. Too much pain in the world."

A second object peers out from behind the two brothers. It is a black and white picture of Weintraub taken when he was three years old. He is wearing a plaid jumpsuit made for him as a gift by an old woman, Rosie, who was married to a tailor whose children were murdered by the Nazis. Weintraub has scuffed white shoes. Perfectly poised on a garden of floral green carpeting at the foot of a stairs. He studies the child's clear eyes and confident smile.

Weintraub asks him, "Who you are? Who do you want to be?"

A third object, less evident but no less animate, smiles at Weintraub with a bizarre grin, glassy black eyes, pointed nose and a raspberry bow tied to one side of its neck. It has an inch long slit at the top of its head behind two perfectly molded cinnamon ears fine tuned to hear whatever sounds are directed its way. It is a ceramic bank in the shape of a bear, toasted brown in color with a gaping hole at its bottom where CB pummeled 45 years earlier to retrieve saved up pennies to buy Good n' Plenty's or some other candy. Its surface contains hairline breaks and additional imperfections. Looking at his old friend now Weintraub wonders if he is more participant than observer. Is his inner life a dim reflection of a vague and fragmented memory, phony constructions built on cracks and repairs, a history of false images and a voracious imagination? But such a question has built into it a certain consolation. Those curious enough to know will find out. In time, by any means necessary.

Weintraub thinks to himself, "Truth or the approximation of it is best left to literature and metaphysics."

His grandfather and uncle stare at him requiring a Fishman-like moment. Weintraub has to face himself and make choices. He does not have to save the world but he must save himself. Even a grinning bear knows that.

Chapter 33

There have been generations of successful Weintraubs, but Weintraub isn't one of them. Even his great pride cannot conceal this fact; on the contrary, it reveals it. The words "unrealized potential" and "lost opportunities" corrode Weintraub's brain, squeaking open and shut like a rusty gate.

He imagines a campfire and a mirror circumscribed by a barrier. Tight metal fence work, sharp edged, destructive.

Weintraub remembers a key ring with a blue rabbit's foot, a square coin from Pacific islands, an irregular hole at its center. A compass with a shiny black needle housed in a nickel-plated case. There is also a dim recollection of skimming rooftops, peering in strange windows watching young girls and sometimes helping them undress in the dark.

Weintraub looks into the mirror studying his face in the orange yellow flames. He follows his snaking shadow in a crevice along the ground. He thinks of his notebook and a letter arriving from Japan. Red and blue postmarks. A telephone directory from Buffalo, New York.

Other dust-laden memories, some more crystalline. A wandering thought and a symmetrical garden. Fishman's desire to die. A note passed to a lover in silence. His grandmother standing before a flag-draped coffin. The idea of a novel disguised as an epic poem.

Weintraub is seized by the sheer terror of geometry: diverging, converging and parallel lines. Hermetic circles. Triangles.

Axioms like love, which seem obviously true and yet impossible to prove mathematically in a satisfying way. The shape of a heart. A heart full of joy and sorrow. A broken heart. And the inevitability of numbers: two arms, two legs, two eyes, one life. A child abandoned by a dead mother.

RK said he once wrote half a book that disappeared into a computer, lost forever in a Word program. Weintraub imagines others he knew or dreamed about, enemies, friends. The look on his face upon hearing an obvious explanation.

Weintraub watches as he is consumed by flames only to be reborn. He loses himself in the twilight somewhere between dusk and dawn. He imagines walking on water without getting wet. Walking in fire and not being burned. He sees a perfect mountain kingdom cut off from the rest of the world.

***

Is it possible Weintraub is pure invention, an illusion within someone else's dream, a penumbra of someone real? What is it really that makes him, him?

Weintraub reads a passage from his favorite author.

"He dreamed an entire man-a young man, but who did not sit up or talk, who was unable to open his eyes. Night after night, the man dreamt him asleep."

Weintraub takes refuge in the here and now, in all that can be imagined and all that is real. But still he remains unsure. And therefore must ask, "Can I ever know for sure who I am?"

***

Weintraub thinks of a poem that he wrote as a child about a boy walking along a curving path by the side of a river.

"Past a mythical labyrinth that he saw

The Next Step 305

> *in a seashell a maze within a maze
> like a rose petal, history unfolding."*

Weintraub tries hard to remember the words.

> *"Below men and women toiled. Baking bread and carrying water. Bright lanterns illuminated the darkness."*

> *"Lightening crackled in the sky, a bird as light as a cloud circled overhead."*

> *"A splendid destiny lay before him."*

> *"Past and future
> A gently sloping road
> His mother's skin the color of the moon
> Her eyes, infinite and intimate as the stars."*

> *"In an instant he was transformed into a firefly caught in a breeze or twisting wind."*

From the golden summit of a snow-capped mountain, CB's voice howls,
"Fishman."
"Palefsky."
"Goldberg."
"Weintraub."

***

Nowhere in the Encyclopedia Britannica are the names Fishman, Palefsky, Goldberg, and Weintraub. Weintraub wants to know, why?

There is a listing for Christ Bob. But that Christ Bob was a very complicated fellow: an eccentric millionaire who invented hypersonic jet engines; a philanthropist and serious student of Flaubert who for the sake of argument memorized *Through the Looking Glass*.

CB had an investigative spirit and an appreciation of history. He traced the invention of the hot dog back to 1890 at Yale. CB also funded a controversial deconstruction of Freud's seminal text, *Projection: Imagine That*.

Weintraub has a passing thought: "Here is where the story gets confused like Alice lost in wonderland."

***

"Now here is what really happened. It was one of those things you never forget."

***

Weintraub looks at the picture of his grandfather and brother. They are standing in front of a large white clapboard house. A picket fence curls around it. Weintraub can smell leaves burning. He thinks of apple cider and the aroma of autumn in Brooklyn. It is early morning and there are the sounds of deliveries of wood and coal and ice. A hungry dog is barking. The clap of horse hooves along the cobblestones. The dizzying ecstasy of seeing solid homes and tended gardens.

Weintraub hears strangers speaking in foreign tongues, twangs and drawls and Boston accents. He remembers long days at Coney Island laughing at the shtick of Sam Brownbag and the tall tales of The Celestial Zamboni. He tastes the Wonder Wheel spinning in lifesaver candy colors—greens and reds and lemon yellows—against a blue-black summer sky. The Cyclone and the Mermaid Parade. The ocean slapping salty wet against his lips and teeth.

Weintraub delights in the pleasures of a feral imagination. He searches for routes, streets, passages; back alleyways that will lead him home. He yearns for redemption along the third base line or up in the left field bleachers at Ebbets Field. For today Weintraub will forsake quantum mechanics, unified field and string theory. He will divorce himself from all thoughts of cosmology: space, time, gravity, even geometry and other notions of the universe.

A young boy who has traveled by foot and subway beyond dirt hills and public meadows, across the wide lawns of Prospect Park onto Flatbush Avenue climbs with his comrades to distant reaches. There is a din of muffled voices and Vin Scully and the cool, stale aroma of beer mixed with urine. He lifts his nose into it, breathing it in deeply like a happy dog along an open highway. He follows his instinct, moving higher on dark ramps and gateways until there is an instant of total eclipse. Suddenly, like a scene from revelation, there is the blindness of pure light followed by a diamond of the greenest grass on the face of the earth.

Weintraub mounts two creaking steps to a porch leading to a fine screen door with no tears. Behind it is a brass knocker in the guise of a rakish squirrel with a half eaten acorn dangling from its jaw. In the entranceway is an arched hall surrounded by Doric columns opening into a vestibule where a boy and a girl are playing in a large sun drenched room. There are three fine filigreed windows with tendrils of iron grill work casting floral shadows across their faces and the gleaming hardwood floor. It is 1907. The Anglo-Russian entente is signed agreeing to spheres of influence in Persia. New Zealand achieves dominion status in the British Commonwealth of nations. Einstein postulates $E=mc^2$.

This little girl, Miriam, Weintraub's mother wasn't born until 1917. But she is here. Look at her. How healthy she is. She runs carefree in her blue sailor suit with red velvet trim. This was before operations and cancer. Missed diagnoses. Radiation. Before doctors labored in vain to save her life. She is bathed in sun, zigzagging across the room with her brother Jack, an agile ten year old. He will soon die of diphtheria. An infected skin lesion, painful, swollen and red. The illness started suddenly with a sore throat and stiff neck.

"Jack complained of difficulty swallowing."

Miriam's mother remembers overhearing the doctor dictating his notes to a nurse seconds after pronouncing Jack dead.

"Throat obstruction and enlarged lymph nodes, difficulty breathing, arrhythmia, high fever, skin rash."

For now the children are having fun, playing. Miriam drops her doll, running headlong into the light.

Weintraub thinks about his mother, Einstein, the relativity of time. The biochemistry of ideas and the imagination. The speed of light and the damp possibility that the universe, in its entirety, with all its black holes, is an ever expanding and reflexive story. A cosmic narrative arc.

The clues are everywhere.

"In the beginning was the word."

Divine plots hidden and revealed within cosmologies and cosmogonies. Opening and closing at first slowly, pursuing familiar themes for millennia, then spontaneously lunging forward, wildly, with something new. Dark. Cruel. Eternal. An open sky, a closed fist, a torpid hand, a galaxy of CB's lies.

The concentric possibilities of stories for the new season. Liberation, sumptuous joy, creative energy and godly meaning.

". . . And the word was with God and the word was God."

Chapter 34

Lost in illusion, Weintraub prodded by RK searches for a way home. He stares at a blank page striving to elucidate an abstract truth or transparent mystery. He knows words are just a temporary solution, confounded by circular and cyclical memory, stirred by self-delusion and personal myth. Weintraub aches for the path that will lead him back. Death-defying recollections and images. He wonders if there is such a thing as unequivocal clarity. A changed idiom. "A chance to dream." A play with a happy ending. Roads unfold: straight then branch off. Curving, twisting, warping his sense of time.

Weintraub is in his grandfather's library. Morris, his Hebrew name is Moshe (Moses), is an old man now. Blind. He sits alone in a worn brown leather chair surrounded by books.

"I come in here to breathe the aroma of thoughts."

Weintraub stares at the old man's face. Behind dark glasses he bears a peaceful smile. Morris recites half-remembered poems in Yiddish and French. He entertains Weintraub with his Cabalist fables: biblical stories, allegories and make believe tales. Triumphant heroes and shadowy rogues. Wisemen disguised as beggars, living in the forest or roaming the hilly countryside. Flawed prophets admonishing to a disobedient world. Chaos at every turn, invariably leading to a fateful choice or hidden door. And then there was . . . Spinoza. Baruch (Hebrew for blessed) sounded magical. A famed philosopher with the name of a clown.

Weintraub imagines Spinoza on the boardwalk at Coney Island or Far Rockaway. "The Great Spinoza." There he is standing next to Sam Brownbag and the Celestial Zamboni. Spinoza juggles complex paradoxes. Handy ideas about God and man. Metaphysics and epistemology. Freedom. A sword-eating, metal-bending, fire-throwing wonder. Philosophy: now here was the greatest form of human entertainment. Show business.

"Like no business I know."

***

Morris tells Weintraub a Navajo legend. "Searching for gold."

It is dusk. Two brothers travel along the rim of the Grand Canyon in the damp mist. They dream of enormous wealth. In their minds they see bullion, saffron ingots, the mythical "El dorado" with its temples of gold. They descend into the lower reaches of the earth against an archeological record of the passage of time; guiding their donkeys down winding roads, searching further and deeper into the ground. They pass a river warmed by the sun blurred by the vision of their great wealth to come; past a meadow and stream. And then they arrive at the place that they have been dreaming of.

Laid out before them are endless rows of blonde treasure. Alive. Fragrant. They pluck their fortune furiously with thoughts of ripened fruit harvested from trees, filling their saddlebags with yellow riches.

At the end of the day, fatigued, the brothers watch a crimson sunset burn across the horizon. Reaching into their sacs they begin to slowly eat plump apricots and succulent peaches, licking their lips, savoring the warm, sweet, golden juices. They watch the subtle shapes of animals, a jaguar, armadillo and hare, sky-carousing above them and as the last cloud blackens they know that their journey has been worth it. Their job, done.

Weintraub is back again in his grandmother's arms; the fragrance of baking peaches heavy in the air; feeling her warm fleshy cheek against his forehead, the coolness of her cotton dress. In his mind, he listens to her hilarious stories. The one about a man who went to the Rabbi, complaining about his lot in life . . . the Rabbi's advice is totally crazy, but somehow she made a point, now forgotten. Weintraub hears her soft kind voice, affectionate laughter.

***

Weintraub is all too aware and RK never fails to remind him that at fifty-two he has still not won an Emmy, Peabody, Oscar or Pulitzer but neither has he been forced to earn his living working in a veterans' hospital administering electric shock therapy. He knows his reality is derived in part from never having to go to sleep hungry. But not unlike a good sporting dog, Weintraub understands down deep he possesses breeding, beauty and great bird-sense.

He reminds himself of an uncle who was semi-retired, a pseudo-intellectual with Quasimodo looks. He had an unrelenting fear of flying insects and large black spiders but Lithium helped to relieve the pain.

"You need to wake up. Open your eyes. See and feel the music everywhere."

Weintraub remembers Mendel walking aimlessly in the park, bellowing in the great promenade, strawberry fields, rambles and sheep meadow:

"Mozart."

"Beethoven."

"Schubert."

He moved like a slow skater on thin ice, cracking like crème brulée.

Weintraub recalls a line from a Saturday Night Live skit: "Crème brulée anyone?"

The food of memory.

Mendel was a Holocaust survivor, in Germany, a prominent heart surgeon who after the war worked as a bookkeeper for Weintraub's father. His ledgers were meticulous: columns hand drawn, aided by a wooden ruler spotted with fingerprints, lead dust and India ink. Accounts payable and receivable letter perfect.

He slept in a back room, falling in and out of lucidity, on a Murphy bed, a crimson woolen camp blanket with a frayed silken edge. The initials RK or maybe CB monogrammed in gold. He loved to tell stories: Eurydice and Orpheus traveling down the river of forgetfulness. Like someone who miraculously springs out of a coma to tell *his* story, only to fall back into it once more.

"Hold your family close."

"Like a little boy caught with his pinky up his nose."

"The ocean is womb and tomb."

"I once saw Leni Riefenstahl in Berlin. Before the Kinder Transport. Eating strawberries. Sipping champagne"

Weintraub knows it's a cliché that tragedy makes you appreciate life more, but it's true. And it is no secret. Why is it hidden to most of us. The ultimate reality. Life. It's not easy but it's all you get to toy with every day.

Weintraub can hear Mendel singing.

> *"Row, row, row your boat,*
> *Gently down the stream.*
> *Merrily, merrily, merrily, merrily,*
> *Life is but a dream."*

Self-hypnosis.

Weintraub remembers years later sitting next to his uncle at a fancy restaurant for a family celebration, an evening illuminated with captivating stories of incontinence and rectal leakage. Battles with the IRS. A Nazi colonel listening to Jews performing the Brahms violin concerto. The comfort of playing "this little piggy" with mother. Loading bullet-sized ice cubes up the ass to cool off in summer. Hot news flashes. A best dressed pharmacist and "the smoke and mirror of history."

"The future is not what it used to be."

"The only protection against death is art."

"Know it or not, we all are walking in a world of imagination."

Weintraub wonders to himself what does all this mean. The surge and stir of distant, incised memory. Rudimentary silhouettes taking on more precise form. He thinks about a world that has forever passed away and his pathetic efforts at reconstruction and all that is implied about belief, faith and creative force.

And then he is struck by a most basic question. What is the genre?

"Probably something in between pure literature and light commercial fiction," he says to himself.

"But who can say for sure."

Once again he can hear Mendel's raspy voice.

"But how does this all turn out?"

Uncertain, Weintraub reassures himself with these words.

"Meet me at the end of the next sentence."

***

Buried in all this, or behind it, is the seed that Weintraub is looking for—like finely chiseled bone or ivory dug up in caves, lying undisturbed for thousands of years. Out of the darkness animals, mostly bison and reindeer graze on rock walls. There are also wooly mammoths and wild horses. Human hands strangely contorted wave and signal like semaphores. Geometric patterns swirl, prehistoric pop art.

A little girl discovers a mythical chamber in candle light. A ghostly herd of contoured beasts, long-horned, delicately modeled in umber, black and red. Men howling in a state of trance.

"Altamira."

"Magdalena."

"Lascaux."

In the distance Weintraub sees the blurry image of ruby slippers. He hears the sound of the Eumenides beckoning.

"There's no place like home."

Chapter 35

Weintraub can't stop this ongoing, free associative, Socratic dialogue with himself. Every once in a while he gets a shit-kicking urge to squeeze out a poem, short story, screenplay or novel. He imagines a psychoanalytic couch composed of words:

Cartography. Cat burial. Wigan Pier.

Cartography (kartogrefi) n. the production of maps, including construction of projections, design, compilation, drafting, and reproduction. Also, map drawing. Darkness and exorcism. Witchcraft and supernatural ritual. The power of memory, dance and song.

Morris had once told him, "Your job is to find the sparks of divine light."

In his mind Weintraub can hear the sound of a hardball plucked out of the air into a worn leather glove. He sees himself moving up and down the chakras.

"A golden cat, singing about another cat, named cat, along a moon river, gentle as a stream."

Weintraub remembers something he read years earlier by Edmund Wilson:

"A story is like a prehistoric work of art, a cave painting, mysterious and magical, self-contained within itself, like a single life, world, galaxy, and universe."

Morris said, "You will tell your story when you can no longer keep it inside."

What has happened to all the great names? Hazel, Phineas, Lester, Ethel, Artis and Agatha.

Weintraub imagines himself on an English racer, a silver Raleigh, dressed in bicycle-tights and a power sweater. He is breathing in the cool Chicago lakefront air with a map of the city etched in his mind. Suddenly, he sees Garfy and the Shakespearian cat burial.

The Story of Garfy the Cat.
Garfy was the prince of all cats. He lived with Weintraub and his family for 23 years; through thick and thin from private elevator buildings on Lake Shore Drive to a succession of houses and apartments in Hyde Park and Old Town. His teeth, an age marker, had disappeared long ago when he was still in his late eighties or early nineties but never affected his hilarious sense of humor and abundant appetite. He raised foraging cabinets and pantry to an art.

Garfy had his own studio apartment, the laundry, with a roomy box bungalow, a soft clean towel or discarded all cotton shirt to rest upon. A Ninja turtle place mat was under a fish-shaped bowl holding Iams Senior cat hairball remedy dry food. A cat shaped bowl held his water. Garfy enjoyed a can of wet food twice a day, preferring salmon, turkey niblets, seafood supper or "Captain's Choice." Garfy also expected an offering of whatever Weintraub happened to be eating. He was a cat of catholic tastes and had tried cake, bread, pizza, pasta, cucumbers, Polish pickles and potato chips. He eschewed red meat and mackerel, sticking mostly to chicken and turkey. Surprisingly, he did not care for sardines.

Garfy once got his head caught in a strawberry yogurt container he was licking out. He was not a milk drinker and wouldn't touch raw egg but did eat Brewer's yeast for his coat. Garfy was known to partake in an occasional pinch of catnip. He also liked to drink leftover tea from a small pot on the kitchen stove and could discern vintage seat-up toilet water.

Garfy's looks and manner were remarkable. Weintraub's son Niko had asked many times when he was a child, "Do you think other cats think Garfy is handsome?"

Weintraub and Ada always answered "Yes." The cat version of a young Robert Redford.

Garfy was literally the cat who came for dinner. He arrived at Weintraub's doorstep in the middle of a rainstorm and never left. It was love at first sight. Garfy would turn his head and acknowledge his name with a flick of his ear. And so began years of dignified domesticated tiger-like living.

Garfy was lighthearted and even in later years would enjoy a fast game of shuffleboard with a plastic ring from a milk bottle. For a time he took up soccer, played with a rubber mouse that invariably disappeared under the piano. He relished his daily brushing and would get on the trunk, the regular spot for grooming, when he saw Weintraub or Ada holding the brush.

A social creature by nature he was highly regarded by the menagerie of fish, frogs, birds, a box turtle, guinea pig and rabbit. The others departed at various times for a host of reasons. Garfy remained.

Extremely observant, Garfy appeared to be studying Weintraub and his family for a doctoral thesis. His golden green eyes, the color of October leaves, were alert, shooting the world like tiny cameras. He enjoyed music, especially classical but there is some uncertainty when it comes to composers. Garfy also appeared when anyone read aloud. Exactly what he was thinking at any given moment is unclear. After all, does anyone ever really know a cat?

Weintraub's daughter Lily felt Garfy might be lonely and so Ada introduced a foundling kitten. Garfy was extremely offended at the appearance of the little interloper, much as a wife might respond to sharing her home with a mistress. Ada had to separate them as she was afraid Garfy would kill Smokey if the two were alone. After a long time and carefully monitored meetings, Garfy accepted her. On occasion they were caught in compromising positions despite the fact that both had their pockets emptied. Over time Garfy's tolerance matured into acceptance and perhaps even love. But then two years ago Smokey died.

The children, now grown, were cities away and Weintraub and Ada placed Smokey in a large saffron, once orange, Hermes boot box. They said their farewells and unceremoniously Weintraub presided over the cat burial. They both slipped in hand written notes and even created one from Garfy.

"I loved you Smokey. I will never forget you. It's the little things . . . the way you wore your hair. The way you sipped your tea. The memory of all that. No, no! They can't take that away from me." It was signed *"Your Garfield."*

Weintraub remembered all the names the children had suggested before coming up with Smokey. *"Hazel, Phineas, Lester, Ethel, Artis, Agatha- sleep well little cat."* Next to it Weintraub drew a picture of a kitten waving a scarf in the wind.

Weintraub was convinced that after Smokey's death, intuitively Garfy was able to let go, relax, fully appreciate the miracle of his feline life.

Garfy may have spent more than one of his lives the day he took a flying leap from a neighbors'- an Italian doctor and his fiancé's porch, sensing the return of their boxer and Dalmatian. What Garfy was doing there is not known but he did have an independent nature and an adventurous streak. The aged father of the downstairs tenant nearly had a stroke when from the third story a flying cat cruised by. Miraculously, Garfield suffered no broken bones or internal injury. Weintraub rushed him to a pet emergency hospital where he received a saline pack under his skin. He slept for several days, making a full recovery.

Garfy was a Nureyev-like leaper and could vault from the floor to the table to the top of the icebox. Sometimes, he would just run up and down the length of the hall, seemingly for the pure joy of it.

Weintraub remembers once calling around the neighborhood in the dark, convinced Garfy was locked in a garage or basement, only to come home, watching him emerge yawning from the bedroom closet.

Not a big purrer, he was virtually mute until Smokey died when he would vocalize on a regular basis with surprising variety. He was a rooster. His early morning greeting could be translated as "Get up lazy bones. What's for breakfast? And make it snappy!" No sooner had he taken a bite than he would return to sleep.

There are many photos of Garfy as well as drawings and an oil painting in which he was sleeping many years before as Weintraub found him. In that terrible instant Weintraub remembered something Fishman said: "And to the lucky, there was love. It had come to me one day at the zoo. There were two seals resting on a sun warmed rock before sliding back into the rocking vastness."

***

There is a fuzziness to all these characters, the names and places, choices . . . their way of being in the world.

***

Does anyone really ever know a cat?

Garfy came into Weintraub's life 23 years ago. He was already about a year old and went by the name Spy according to his collar. But the kids changed it to Garfield since he looked like a thinner version of the cartoon character. He would turn his head and acknowledge his name with a flick of an ear.

When Weintraub found him, Garfy looked like he was asleep, curled like a furry moon, tail wrapped around his face, feet neatly tucked.

He was dead.

Ada wrapped Garfy in Niko's old flag sheet. The bundle looked like the stars and stripes, Garfy wearing the stripes. After scouting out the area around the church along whose eastern flank they lived, in the old parish house, Weintraub found a patch behind the statue of St. Michael.

***

RK said:

"At fifty-two, Fishman pretty much had the world by the balls. That is to say, he wanted for nothing. He lived a quiet, solitary life in an historic part of Chicago, known as Old Town. He resided with his wife of twenty-five years in a two-bedroom apartment in a renovated building that once served as a rectory to St. Michael's Church, which long ago had been sold by the Diocese to a real estate developer. Fishman paid his rent on time each month and marveled at his lot in life and good fortune."

Was any of this really true?

***

St. Francis would have been more fitting but Mike would do just fine as Garfy's protector. Weintraub dug a hollow and placed Garfy in it with a little note on his daughter's old squirrel notepaper:

May this wonderful cat rest in peace.

A beloved member of our family. He gave much love for many years.

While the illicit burial was going on, Weintraub and Ada took turns playing lookout, once spotting a passing cop car, a neighbor staring out of his window, a runner floating by.

There was a Shakespearean gravedigger moment when a Chinese fast-food deliveryman couldn't find an address and didn't know how to use his cell phone. Cursing to himself in Cantonese he approached Weintraub, hiding in the deep shadows of the old church.

"You order food?"

Weintraub held his shovel while Ada did her utmost to speed the man to his destination. She was reminded of the fake orders she and her friend Lisa would call in when they were mischievous eight year-olds. She sent the man back to the restaurant to straighten it all out. They had needed some comic relief from the grave situation.

Weintraub covered Garfy with a thick blanket of soil and marked the spot with three stones heavy as his and Ada's heart left by workmen in the church garden. That night there were no frolicking rabbits where they regularly left day-old bread for the birds that stayed for winter.

***

It's funny the things that you remember and the thoughts that pass through your mind at a cat funeral. Weintraub can hear the sounds of going back in time. Musette. Accordions, banjos, fiddles and clarinets. The tale of the Panther Woman and the Sandwich Man.

"He was a man who went to the circus and fell in love with an exotic part-girl part feral cat. Her lover became her sandwich."

Bogart's dictum: "I wouldn't give two cents for a dame without a temper."

Ada on their king-size bed, rolling back and forth, struggling to pull up her panty hose.

Weintraub swears he can hear Garfy, like a fog horn, in the distance.

"What's going on. Throw me a life preserver."
"And what's this teaching our kids, sportsmanship? I don't think so!"

Weintraub remembers the story of Mendel's piano teacher, delighting in his interpretation of a Bach etude, only to fall off the stool moments later, suffering a fatal heart attack.

"Who will carry on this cat's legacy?"
And then Weintraub realizes life must go on. He thinks of a sleazy day trader, Shalom Katz, who used to buy and sell pork belly futures, stealing commissions off customer orders. The names of popes: Cletus, Linus, Sixtus, Telesphorus, Sylvester, Damasus, Innocent, and Alexander. What has happened to them?

In the square below reminiscent of the Vatican there are thousands of onlookers: the faithful, nuns, priests, orphans, tourists and Italians.

A pope who was a Rottweiler now a presiding German shepherd.

"This cat was buried after a funeral mass, attracting admirers from around the world, the important and the ordinary alike, as you can see, in the hundreds of thousands."

Samuel Barber's Adagio for Strings.
"Who will ever forget this John Paul II of orange tabbies?"
Red silk robes and white miters.

Weintraub imagines Garfy imagining. Low flying, slow-moving arctic birds. Mice living by a thread. Endless fields of catnip. Kurt Weil music against a backdrop of a Mack the Knife-like cat starring in a pet food commercial.

"The image of the Buddha. Dispassionate and deeply engaged, complicated and simple, erudite and profoundly feline."

Weintraub could also see Garfy dreaming of hot summer afternoons, drizzly candle-lit dinners and sex kittens wearing no underwear. Chicken rights advocates protesting in vain. Bored firemen tipping back their chairs waiting for a fire. Detectives tracking down a cat burglar. His favorite authors in mourning. Borges, Bellow, Mailer, Murakami, and of course Nabokov. CB reading aloud.

Ada whispers, "There's many a slip on the road to Wigan Pier."

"Goodnight, sweet cat prince."

Chapter 36

The odd thing about a circus is that it's a circus. No matter how rehearsed, chaos prevails, at all times.

Weintraub is trapped inside a website: "Tempting Fate Daily! The All New 134th Edition of The Greatest Show On Earth."

Somewhere between the stars Crazy Hannigan, Sylvia Soupanodi and Pooches Fuentes, Weintraub suits up as the ringmaster, in traditional long red coat, black top hat and his personal touch, a pair of adjustable aqua goggles.

He takes an oath of absolute and perpetual secrecy. Like the princes of the church, all this craziness will forever remain his little secret. The ritual and breathtaking majesty. The panoply . . . history and tradition. The continuity of communion and showmanship over time.

"Down with the lights. The show is about to start."

Amazing animals and fabulous fun. A Bengal tiger named Taba. The Pachyderm Professor. He works the center ring with ten Asian elephants, six zebras, four camels, two llamas, and an emu. P.T. Barnum presiding on the outer rings.

"Step up. Step up."

"Unquestionably one of the most astonishing and interesting curiosities in the world."

"Please, no pushing."

A showcase of amazing wonders under glass. Jamaica McDanials, the 161-year-old wet nurse to George Washington. "The Feejee Mermaid" an embalmed sea creature purchased in

1854 by a Boston seaman near Calcutta. Panther Woman who enjoyed playing with, then eating her lovers. Sloko the fire eater. And General Tom Thumb.

"Take a good look."

"Good things come in small packages."

Like transistors. Silicon chips of the imagination. Strange neurological wiring, expanding worlds in a single brain. Reaching.

"All you have to do is connect."

"The wine is my blood. The bread my body."

"Shema Yisroel Adonai Eloheinu Adonai Echad."

Dante in the underworld. La Divina Commedia.

From Vita Nuova:

"It were a shameful thing if one should rhyme under the semblance of metaphor or rhetorical similitude, and afterwards, being questioned thereof, should be unable to rid his words of such semblance, unto their right understanding."

Weintraub and Dante and Virgil. Fishman and Palefsky not far behind. RK not taking any chances. Moses on Sinai receiving two tablets. A broken Palefsky at Mt.Sinai Hospital in New York. Precipitous mountains, thunderous waterfalls, filthy rivers and torrid sand. Beatrice to the rescue in the guise of a poem. Manna raining down from heaven. Dolores Haze, a metaphor of eternal innocence. Nabokov's search for the perfect Urodoidea. Balthus painting "Katia Lisant." His crisp note for the 1968 Tate Gallery retrospective: "NO BIOGRAPHICAL DETAILS. BEGIN: BALTHUS IS A PAINTER OF WHOM NOTHING IS KNOWN."

Story telling:

It all began innocently enough with a Lebanese curse and ended in a spectacular explosion in a Bulgarian craft stall along the parade route of the Festival of the Roses. Although there are witnesses who will say otherwise, Weintraub is not to blame. Not that he is entirely innocent either, but let's just say his attention was elsewhere when the shit finally hit the fan.

A day earlier he had received a letter from a New York literary agent who had rejected his latest novel. What follows is an excerpt, and some may say, one of the reasons that propelled Weintraub into his downward spiral.

Dear Mr. Weintraub,

*Thank you for giving us a look at **DOPE SLAP** and we very much appreciate the detailed illustrations. I apologize for the delay in my response.*

This novel is indeed exceptional. The prose is clear and often poetic; there is genuine beauty to your phrasing. Weingarten is an engaging character, complicated and sympathetic enough to capture and keep our interest. There are many levels from which a reader can approach the text, but the underlying, insistent whisper of the human search for meaning is never lost in the complexities . . .

*Unfortunately, I am afraid I have to pass on your manuscript. As strong as **DOPE SLAP** is, I don't believe there is room in the market for another post-9/11 reflection. There is such a plethora of 9/11-inspired fiction, memoirs, and non-fiction accounts that publishing houses are wary to take on 9/11 themed projects at this time. Another agency may feel differently about their chances and be better suited to represent your work to publishers.*

Again, I am sorry for the delay and am grateful to have had the opportunity to read DOPE SLAP. I wish you the best of luck with this project.

Best regards,

Samantha Twitty

Story telling. Red robes. White miters. Masks. Monarchs and

Marquesas. Twenty-three clowns squirting water, running in circles, extinguishing flames. The personification of radiance and pure love. Dante's three-ringed circus. Balthus in reclusion. Weintraub spinning out yarns. Synesthesia: perceiving sound as color. Paws curling. Eyes hovering. Orange tabbies and ferocious tigers. Free flowing tides of mariachi, tango and pachanga like a 64 pack of crayolas. The progress of the soul toward heaven, CB, and the endless anguish of men and women here on earth.

As Yogi Berra said, "It's too coincidental to be a coincidence."

"You never want to take this stuff too personally."

"Every crowd has a silver lining" and" a sucker is born every moment." (P.*T. Barnum)

* The P stands for Phineas.

***

More letters of rejection arrive daily.

Dear Mr. Weintraub,

Thank you for sending me **DOPE SLAP,** *which I enjoyed reading. I thought the characters were intriguing and language-especially the dialogue-was quite vivid, and possessed a wonderful energy that I was enamored of.*

But that said, though this was lovely, unfortunately I was not taken with this novel as a cohesive whole as I had hoped to be. While I admired much of the work here, I thought that the overall narrative arc lost focus at times. So very reluctantly, I am afraid that I am going to have to pass at this time, with regrets.

Thank you for including me in your submission, and I hope that you find a wonderful home for your manuscript.

All best,

Lydia Pooley
William Morrow Publishers

***

Dear Mr. Weintraub,

Thanks for sending on your novel which John Dawkins passed on to me as he's pre-occupied with other matters. You write very well, but I don't think we know they right editors for this narrative, so are going to decline, but thank you nonetheless for your kindness in letting us take a look.

Yours sincerely,

William Reiss
John Dawkins Literary Agency

***

(Message by email)

Dear Mr. Weintraub,

I'm sorry for this ultra-late response to **DOPE SLAP**. I've just unearthed it after a quite tumultuous beginning to 2005.

I'm going to dip into it soonest. Is there an agent involved?

Thanks for your patience . . . know it's on my agenda.

Tad Flukis
Associate Publisher

Canongate

***

(Two days later message by email)

Dear Mr. Weintraub,

This manuscript is not for me but should easily find a home.

Tad Flukis
Associate Publisher
Canongate

***

(Message by email)

Dear Mr. Weintraub,

I like the writing in **DOPE SLAP**; it's very smart and knowing and funny and the premise of Weingarten's upended life is a good one. But the style and approach struck me as a little familiar and even old-fashioned, and I wasn't able to get as caught up in the omniscient voice as I had hoped. I don't think Collins-McKay is the right agent for you but I'm grateful to you for the chance with the novel.

Sincerely, David

P.S. The scene where Imelda Marcos is swimming in the nude with Mao-Tse Tung was very imaginative. Really cracked me up.

IF YOU RECEIVED THIS EMAIL IN ERROR PLEASE IGNORE.

Collins-McKay Literary Agency

***

Dear Mr. Weintraub,

 Who the Hell do you think you are, Dostoevsky? Not even Woody Allen would have had the "balls" to say such dreadful things about the College of Cardinals, Pope Pius the Twelfth or the Catholic Church. Need I remind you this still is a Christian country?

> P. C. Lowry
>
> *Christian Media and*
> *Religious Broadcasting*
> *Worldwide*

***

Dear Mr. Weintraub,

 Your novel **Dope Slap** *is being rejected -even though it looks great from the cover- due to jury duty and other pressing personal matters preventing me from reading it.*
 This being said, I hope you don't mind if I make a few editorial suggestions. Throughout the manuscript, much of the story looks sketched to me and the characters and their dialogue doesn't feel fully developed. I also feel the novel could work better with more coherence in a few spots.
 In short, I think with some added effort on your part, the right agent could find a good home for this story.

> *All best wishes,*

Britt
Kondom, Sideburn, Fishkill
Literary Agents.

***

Weintraub knows taking this stuff personally is a big mistake. Even so, getting these letters really sucks.

***

RK is no omniscient narrator but he has lived long enough to understand it is not a bad way to tell a story. Take the other day when he mistakenly began a sentence with the pronoun I. He was shaken but soon changed to—he can't remember which—Weintraub, Fishman, Palefsky or Garfy. It can be a problem.

RK has a vision of himself but he realizes, "You must allow other points of view."

Sometimes while writing even Weintraub hears a clash of imaginery voices: Poe and Cooper, Dickinson and Whitman, Hemingway and Dreiser, Sousa and Bernstein. Mariachi and tango. Pachanga and musette. Accordions. Banjos. Fiddles and clarinets. Klezmer. The Baal Shem Tov. Murakami and a talking cat. Borges traveling south.

"As he crossed the threshold, he felt that to die in a knife fight, under the open sky, and going forward to the attack, would have been liberation, a joy . . ."

He remembers Leni Riefensthal dancing under Mendel's nose.

Sometimes RK dreams of former pets: cats and dogs, a box turtle. A finch named Long John Silver and his girlfriend Michelle. A petrified coral reef, a tipple of malt liquor. He can see the Fuehrer's Eagle's Nest. A secret dark realm. A hidden door to a ghostly bunker. In the blackness of night admirers sing songs and leave flowers. A war machine ravaging Europe. A triumphant will. An end to Jews and incest, insanity, half-idiots and crazy people.

RK thinks occasionally about clever gimmicks, Borgesian layering and textual devices, over-the-top descriptions and blatant lies.

"When Weintraub was a boy, he had a pet seal. He simply refused to go back out to sea."

He imagines readers feeling dislocated or made angry by an idiosyncratic favorite sentence.

"I'm a physician, seeing patients; I don't want to be disturbed."

Names of other writers. David Foster Wallace. Jonathan Safran Foer.

RK imagines the possibility of selling scented texts. Magical realism that gives off a smell. RK also imagines texts written on parchment, sometimes in two scrolls like the Torah, folded and unfolded in front of a congregation. Lifted up for all to see. Read aloud. Dense and complicated. Heartbreaking works of staggering genius. Extremely loud and incredibly close. Ritalin in book form for hungry attention deficit agents and greedy publishers bent on discovering the next high tension, block busting, full throttle fiction experience. Blank pages, the ultimate read.

"For once let the reader use his imagination!"

"We supply the book. You fill up the pages."

"Comes with its own dispenser. Shipping and handling extra."

***

"What people really want in a novel is a strong storyline. They don't read like they used to. They want a beginning, middle, and an end."

***

RK listens to a favorite CD. Rising up and down on wind gusts of Paul McCartney's lyrics.

> *"Blackbird singing in the dead of night*
> *Take these broken wings and learn to fly*
> *All your life*
> *You were only waiting for this moment to arise*
> *You were only waiting for this moment to arise*
> *You were only waiting for this moment to arise"*

Weintraub walks over to his computer, clicks on a word program, opens a file- DopeSlap.doc- and begins to read.

DOPE SLAP

By Weintraub

St. Michael's Church Plaza Apt. 2A (312) 929-6304
Chicago, IL 60614

Weingarten is Discovered in Queens

Chapter 1

One of the astonishing miracles of post world war America was the discovery of me by my future father Herbert Weingarten. His middle name was Benjamin, Chaim in Hebrew, but everyone just called him Herbert B. I was found in a brown Bohack's shopping bag swaddled in old diapers and Kleenex at the side door of the B'nai Israel Home for the Deaf and Blind, just off Queens Boulevard in Rego Park.

I imagine what attracted Herbie's attention was my disagreeable crying for reasons that I'm sure today were solely infantile. I know nothing of my birth mother and her family nor do I have any curiosity about them. Well, maybe just a little.

What goes around comes around and that evening Herbert Weingarten was just the ticket. What he was doing there is anybody's guess and why he didn't announce my existence to hospital employees or report me to the local authorities remains a mystery.

Years later, if he had too much to drink, dad would say, "You were just like baby Moses, caught in the reeds. And I was your Pharaoh."

That night Herbie had been to the movies by himself. He went to his favorite theater, Loewe's Valencia, losing himself for

The Next Step

two and a half hours in the faux marble, Scheherazade-like atmosphere of hastily projected celluloid. *From Here to Eternity* and back. An army base in Hawaii with burglars, lovers, bullies and villains. Tropical breezes blowing all the way to Jamaica Avenue under the El tracks. The sudden urge for hot pastrami on rye. The way Herbie liked it, as only Oscar at Lucky's Deli made it. Heaps of shiney red meat, appearing to have been dry dipped in purple hued food coloring or an oil slick, a hint of clove, not too salty, dripping with coleslaw and Batampte mustard, on soft bread with a cracker-like crust. You can read or hear about a great sandwich a million times and it will still never be as satisfying as the very first bite. The French fries, each one as large as a shoe horn, fried in Planter's peanut oil swam free-style in Heinz ketchup.

Herbie wipes his face clean with a wad of paper napkins persuaded from a two-sided chrome dispenser. A last sip of Cel-ray, acting as a catalyst to produce the perfect aftertaste. A tip of six percent, an additional one percent, to show his above and beyond appreciation and then Herbie walks home.

But tonight is different. There is an unexpected surprise. A baby. Me. Herbie is sure I need a good home. A Weingarten home.

He walks in the dark with his little bundle following a star in the sky that moves with him from above. He breathes in faintly distant but recognizable aromas: frankincense and myrrh. The smells of nativity and a manger. He senses wise men and a great unspeakable future.

Herbie rings the doorbell. A woman who looks like a rumpled version of Rita Hayworth in a housedress opens the door. Her voice is not at first shrill but neither is it particularly pleasant. It asks questions like a dental probe, occasionally landing on an undetected cavity or open nerve.

"What took so long? Good movie?"

Herbie answers matter-of-factly. "Not bad. Sinatra and

Montgomery Clift."

Then he remembers. "Wow. I almost forgot . . . there's a beach scene . . ."

The woman notices the Bohack's super market shopping bag in my father's left hand.

"What's this?"

Her eyes study the frenetic housewife illustrated above the Bohack's logo, dashing pell-mell, stuffing groceries into her basket.

"Herbie, you went shopping?"

Herbie decides rather than launching right into a fact-based story about finding me on the steps of the Home for the Deaf and Blind, about no one being there to take care of me or not seeing the need to fill out any paperwork and keep me as Shirley and his secret, begins this way.

"Listen. You won't believe what happened to me after I left the movie. Stopped off at Lucky's. Had a knish. Didn't feel like a hot dog . . . The pastrami tonight was gorgeous. Perfect."

He points to me shaking his head. A strange almost maniacal smile, suppressed by vault-like lips.

"I was walking back and heard . . ." Herbie is unable to find the right words. "Well, take a look."

Shirley slowly pulls back both sides of the brown paper bag and absorbs the full impact of its contents. She reaches in and picks me up bringing my warm cheeks and forehead against her damp lips. I smell something very unusual that in later years I will know as garlic and onions.

Mom explodes. "Herbie, are you out of your mind?"

And then, not waiting for his answer declaims in Yiddish that he is a crazy man.

"Du bist michigene."

My dad just looked at Mom, shrugged his shoulders and put on that full- idiot grin he does when he tries to be charming and said in his most sincere voice:

"Look at him. You can't leave a kid like this out on the street. What kind of life does a normal child have growing up in a home for the deaf and blind? Look at that punim."

"Herbie, this is not like that little beagle you brought home. If he piddles on the rug we can't bring him back to the shelter."

In a last ditch effort my dad gives it his best shot. "Shirley, I know that. Come on. It'll be fun. Time to start our own family."

As improbable as it seems that's how I became Weingarten.

***

I spent years growing up in Kew Garden Hills, an up and coming New York suburb, first in the care of Mrs. Fleisig, an older Jewish woman my mother hired to watch over me because she felt rachmunus on her, and later Jackie Brown, a no nonsense black woman who lived by a simple philosophy.

"You be a good little boy, Weingarten. Don't make Jackie Brown have to read the riot act."

The two women could not have been more different. Mrs. Fleisig was a short, prematurely gray, overweight, stoop-shouldered Holocaust survivor who was brought over after the war by the Reuben Schecter Charity for Orphans and Widows and Other Victims of War and Atrocity. When I was a toddler Mrs. Fleisig told me long, involved, highly detailed stories of her children before and after they were lost to the Nazis. I dimly recall learning to read Dick and Jane, seeing Spot run and thinking about Yankle and Rivkah Fleisig being thrown headlong into a cattle car. To say the least, Mrs. Fleisig was a depressive. Once my dad got the idea to lift her spirits by fixing her up with our cousin Mendel who was also a survivor. It was a very sad dinner. Mendel and Mrs. Fleisig staring into the candle light, neither speaking a word, each reminding the other of people and places that they desperately needed to forget. Mendel even laughed inappropriately twice that evening, once when breaking wind and the other when Mom nearly choked on a green olive pit. Come to think about it, it was the first time that I saw Mrs. Fleisig smile.

Jackie Brown was another story. She was a big, full fleshed woman with energy and enthusiasm to spare. Jackie was tough, but boy was she fun. She also did impersonations: Rochester, the black announcer on the Jack Benny show and Louis Armstrong. When it rained she would walk around the house singing Gershwin's "A Foggy Day in London Town." When she would get to the lyric "How long I wondered could this thing last?" Jackie would pick me up in her big strong arms and bellow:

> *"But the age of miracles hadn't passed,*
> *For, suddenly, I saw you there*
> *And through foggy London Town*
> *The sun was shining everywhere."*

My favorite imitation was when Jackie impersonated the Big Bopper. She flashed an exaggerated smile that reminded me of the wolf speaking to Littler Red Riding Hood. Her eyes blown wide open, nostrils flaring, teeth vibrating, large and white. Jackie was funny but also frightening. Manic. Unpredictable.

> *"Hello baby, yeah, this is the Big Bopper speaking*
> *Oh you sweet thing.*
> *Do I what?*
> *Will I what?*
> *Oh baby you know what I like!"*

And then Jackie would break out into full song sweeping me up and dance all around my bedroom.

> *"Chantilly lace and a pretty face*
> *And a pony tail hanging down*

That wiggle in the walk and giggle in the talk
Makes the world go round
There ain't nothing in the world like a big eyed girl
That makes me act so funny, make me spend my money
Make me feel real loose like a long necked goose
Like a girl, oh baby that's what I like."

Mrs. Fleisig would usually come on Tuesdays and Thursdays. She observed Shabbas but occasionally came on Sunday. Jackie Brown took care of me on all the other days.

I used to wonder in a no holds barred, full-out fighting competition who would get the final take down. Who would win the Weingarten heavy weight division free style championship of the world. Jackie seemed the obvious favorite but Mrs. Fleisig possessed the subtle refinements of a European education and a strict Orthodox religious training.

The show down was broadcast around the world, before satellites, on flickering black and white console television sets.

Geoffery Holder announcing. "Ladies and gentlemen. Are you ready to rumble?"

There is great applause and excitement from the crowd.

"In this corner wearing a red and yellow floral housedress with three gold teeth, Mrs. Fleisig. She looks small. Out of shape and broken, but since losing her husband and two small children ... nearly all her family in the Holocaust, Mrs. Fleisig is damn mad. Determined to inflict a beating."

There are strong shouts of support.

"We love you Fleisig."

"Show dem vat you got."

"Win one for the Jewish people."

The loudspeaker blasts a montage of Hava Nagilah and the Hatikvah.

You can also hear an occasional cat call.

"Kill the Mocky."

"Send her back to where she came from."

Undaunted Mrs. Fleisig stands, though flat footed, confident. Expectant. Ready to box but not sure if she is about to have the shit kicked out of her.

The announcer now points to Jackie Brown.

"Ladies and gentleman in the far corner wearing red silk trunks and a frilly sports bra, Jackie "Chantilly Lace" Brown."

"You go girl."

"Knock out the Jew bitch Jackie."

Chants erupt like boiling wax.

"Jackie. Jackie. Jackie."

Geoffrey Holder continues. "Raised in Mississippi. The daughter of share croppers. Jackie Brown dominates her weight class. The tale of the tape doesn't lie: 16"neck, 44 chest, 46 when expanded, 70" inch reach. At 162 lbs, 5'10" in height, Jackie Brown is a lean, mean, fighting machine."

"The referee this evening is Herbie Weingarten."

"Ok, ladies you know the rules. I want a good, clean fight. Now go back to your corners and when the bell rings, come out fighting. May the best gal win."

But the bell never rings and I have to watch this same scene over and over again in my mind. For 45 years. Mrs. Fleisig and Jackie Brown in an endless stare down. No winner. No loser. Never a once and for all, indisputable heavyweight Weingarten champion of the world. All is left in doubt. Questions unanswered for all time.

***

It wasn't until I got to the second grade that I decided to spend my days at school full-time. In kindergarten (I used to like the fact it rhymed with Weingarten: maybe the founder was related?) and in the first grade I would frequently abandon class, either spend time chatting with Jorge, the janitor, or desert the premises entirely. Once my dad got so angry that he hauled me off to the A.S.P.C.A., threatening to leave me there. Herbie pointed to a shaggy Shepherd and Labrador mix, fallen on hard times, and confided.

"This is where they put kids who don't stay in school."
"Where?" I asked sincerely.
"Here in these pens."
I looked around nervously.
"Here. Right here." Dad insisted.
As he said it tears welled up in his eyes.

Looking around the dank kennel, I saw a Beagle named Butch, and a big black dog that reminded me of Bingo, suffering from a textbook case of rabies: snarling, foaming at the mouth, bouncing threateningly against his metal cage. His name plate read: This is Mitch. Mitch is aggressive. He doesn't like cats or other dogs. Not recommended for a house with children. And a three-legged, sweet- faced, collie whose golden flanks were riddled with cuts and bruises made by zip gun pellets or bee bees. There were also cats, long hairs and short, a gray tabby, a Siamese mix and one that looked like the smiling Cheshire from *Alice in Wonderland*. But there were no kids. And certainly no one, locked up, who looked like me. "A yeshiva bachur" wearing a crocheted yarmulke.

I looked at dad. I was sure he could explain it. After all the Talmud that we studied at school resolved sharper contradictions. In truth spending a couple of days tied up in the pound didn't really seem too bad. Running about in the dog run, rolling around with furry friends.

There was a long silence but no further explanation. Herbie just yanked me by the arm. Threw me in the back seat of the '54 Buick and pulled away.

"I don't work all day and night so you can go running off from school. Do you know how much your education costs me?"

And then Dad stooped to the lowest strategy of them all.

"I suppose you think money grows on trees?"

It was the big cliché of the fifties. All the parents were using it.

"You'll go back there and stay."

He rubbed his forehead furiously like from a sudden, unexpected psoriasis attack. Dad's tone was pure exasperation.

"Even if it makes you sick."

"Even if it turns your stomach."

"Even if you have to vomit."

Dad then stopped the car. Turned around and looked at me. I knew the look. If I got this wrong, I would get a stinging zets in the back of my neck.

"Do I make myself clear?"

I could only shake my head and agree. "Yes, Dad."

"No. Do I make myself clear?"

I guess even then I realized most of my teachers were pathetic misfits, a combination of psychopaths, sociopaths and other potential felons who were pedagogically incompetent or just plain hated kids. Why was it always the intellectually impaired or criminally deranged who got to run things? Take my third grade teacher, Mrs. Weiner. She was recruited from a cognitive disorder ward at Bellevue. All because of her water colors; elaborate, room sized drawings of bearded, Zeus-like Rabbis, clad in loin cloths, studying the sacred texts. Her therapists provided signed affidavits stating that she showed an aptitude for self-expression and learning.

Mrs. Weiner had three brothers, Lemual, Temual and Semual Soloveichik. They came to school regularly. Mostly for show and tell. Lemual enjoyed historical sea-faring sagas with tumultuous waves, high winds and broad, rippling narrative arcs. He was famous for his impression of a drowning quarter horse caught in an undertow. Temual sang in Aramaic. He couldn't carry a tune but his renditions were always unique, unusual. Semual told us the story of the one-eyed bull fighter. He challenged us to wonder.

"Think about it. If there was one profession that you wanted two good eyes for wouldn't it be this one?"

At other times he told us tales of "a renowned colorblind dress designer, a famed news caster with an uncontrolled stutter, a genius chef who lacked a sense of taste."

In the fifth grade, there was Dr. Hoffman. A firebrand in a tropical shirt, a charismatic. A PhD in accounting who was fired from his college post because of problem drinking. After the nervous breakdown, he stood Sheila Bellman in front of the entire class, falsely accusing.

"Look at her. Her father was a black man who passed for white."

And then he just began singing, *"Will the circle be unbroken, bye and bye Lord, bye and bye."*

The administrators were not much better.

Rabbi Gordon was the principal of my middle school, The Shalom Veiss Children's Educational Laboratory and Rabbinic Academy of Flushing. He was a tall man, maybe seven feet. Larger than any professional basketball player on any roster then playing for the NBA. He had a thick moustache and favored dark gravy stained ties and brown pin stripes, hiked up by suspenders mid-chest so that his pants were unnaturally tight in the crotch. You could see his enormous balls when he stood in front of you. His penis hung like an aged provolone under his pants resting on his hulking right thigh. Lucky for us Shalom Veiss wasn't a Catholic school or Menachim Gordon, a priest. We might have had to touch it or even take a bite.

Wilt, as we nicknamed him, for the Laker, spoke in a sing song of broken English with a dash of Yiddish to brighten his conversation.

"Weingarten, you don't want to be the dummiest kid in this school. Do you? Chas veshalom! Now go back to class and stay there. You're a boy. Be a man. Why must you act like a Jack Russell terrier? As soon as I turn my back you are always running off."

But I was like a runaway bride jumping a Greyhound on her wedding day. I could never sit still, always agitated, running. All the crazy people in my life were making me restless. I was always on edge, twitchy.

For instance, Mom and Dad. They were not your usual parents. Who takes in a kid abandoned in a Bohacks bag? And why did they insist on calling me their "flesh and blood"? I knew they were lying even when they showed me the birth certificate. Herbie handed me the dog-eared gray and white paper. It looked like it blew in out of a fire storm. White letters on a wrinkled charcoal background.

"Read it." he insisted

Mom chimed in also. "Who ever heard of such craziness?"

Growing more agitated Herbie prodded, "Read it . . . before . . ." He stumbled for the right words.

I offered a suggestion. "The dog pound?"

Shirley pinched my ear, hard. I could feel my whole right side going paralytic. Even my hair hurt.

"Read it. You little bulvon."

I read the sacred text, line by line.

"Out loud. You."

I got the sinking feeling, like being caught with your pinky up my nose. I was wrong.

"Mother: Shirley Gottleib Weingarten. Father: Herbert Weingarten. Middle initial B. Mother's occupation: homemaker. Father's: Merchant. Weight: 6 lbs. 7 ounces. Height, 13 inches."

And then I was forced to disclose the most damaging piece of evidence of all.

"Date of birth: May 16, 1954."

Could I have really made this whole thing up? How could this possibly be some fantasy that was only going on in my head?

The strange thing was they thought I was the one who was out of his mind! Any normal person would just have to watch them for a couple of minutes and realize which of us was truly nuts. When Shirley really got angry at me she would threaten, "We're taking you to a psychiatrist."

And then add. "*You* are driving us to the mental asylum."

But in all honesty, as a life-long student of the human mind, going to a certified mental health professional was a desirable prospect. Someone who would take a strong interest in my problems. Be empathetic. Finally, really listen to what was bugging *me*! For once Dad was on the mark.

"One day you will make some lucky psychiatrist a very rich man."

Herbie was right.

***

Ok, so I was lying. Get used to it. Things like this happen every day. True, lying is at the source of my problems but it also invites satisfying resolutions. Psychoanalysis and reinvention. That is what I really love about seeing shrinks. You can spin out great lies, larger than Cecil B. DeMille. Fill them with courageous heroes, Dostoyevskian details. But in the end, face it, it is still all about you. Shakespeare on a shoe string budget. Mardi gras in the center of your falsifying head. And they just eat it up. The breadth and scope and Technicolor. Cinerama and Lucas sound. Intergalactic molehills of your own building. All the craziness, a mere byproduct of daily life.

"Doc . . . I have trouble urinating in public restrooms."

"Doc . . . My parents don't know who I am!"

"Doc . . . I think I'm unlovable."

A clinical stare followed by a solicitous question. "When did you first start feeling this way?"

And you answer matter-of-factly, confidently. "My father

found me . . . abandoned . . . in a Bohacks bag."

But always add . . . "Just kidding, doc."

Sure, they're all lies. But what else have we got?

What could be sadder than a world where there is only truth! Cliff Notes morality. Science non-fiction. Republicans in high office.

When I was nine, I started seeing Ida Margolis, a clinical social worker. I was hyperactive and had residual running problems. She was a practical woman who wore sensible shoes, projecting a serious demeanor in all her dress. Her office was over the 168th Street train station in Jamaica, the last stop at the end of the subway line. Her work was based on The Margolis child-centered Kernels of Truth Therapy. It held that there are precisely 182 postulates about human behavior that, once understood and practiced, would make everything and everyone honky dory (her term). Her method was a combination of everyday words of wisdom and an updated Hammurabi code. In a glass jar on her wooden desk, next to stacks of games and model airplanes, cars and battleships were painted over-sized corn kernels, each displaying a number corresponding to a Kernel of Truth in the Margolis Rule book. You would pick a number, like at the bakery, and read and discuss it out loud. The Rule Book was a poor quality self-publication composed of ink streaked mimeographed sheets wrapped in colored construction paper with a wide-eyed, smiley-faced Ida Margolis on the cover. She was surrounded by hand drawn children at play, a blue dog, tiger-striped cat, a compass and flowers. You could turn to any page and there would be numbers followed by sayings. For example rules 135-139:

135. People are mortal. No matter how big or successful no one is going to be here forever. Some just live a lot longer.

136. Never be impressed by the glow of your past record. The cemetery holds kings as well as paupers.

137. There is no such thing as permanence. Remain flexible and receptive to change even when it's driving you crazy.

138. Above all, be humble. Even the mighty fumble and tumble.

Today I chose 139.

"Read it out loud."

First I carefully read it to myself. Trying to make sure I apprehended its profound meaning.

139. There is good and bad story telling. Know the difference.

Not waiting for my recital, Ida tugged her thick black glasses down the slope of her nose until they rested precipitously at the very edge. Her lips about to form a maniacal yet knowing smile prodded me to incant with her.

"Weingarten."

She spoke slowly but deliberately. Single-minded. "There is good and bad story telling."

". . . good and bad story telling."

"That's right. Now say it again."

"There is good and bad story telling. Know the difference."

Ida then told me all the essential stuff. That a lie here and there is ok as long as you don't hurt or destroy or plagiarize.

"After all, you wouldn't tell someone they really didn't look good would you? That they had a big fat pimple on their nose?"

Well it depends I thought to myself. I took into consideration that Mrs. Margolis had a large black irregularly shaped, pre-cancerous mole on the bridge of her nose and that people around me were speaking enthusiastically about *my* short comings. But I didn't have the guts to disagree and just said, "No, m'am. Would only hurt them, cause needless pain. It would be better to lie."

And then I barked out with real gusto.

"You have to know the difference."

"That's right, young man. In that situation lying is a good and appropriate thing."

And most importantly Mrs. Margolis told me never to tell

people how you really feel when they ask, how are you?

"What would be the point?"

"And nobody really has enough time or really cares anyway."

"Weingarten. This has really been a productive session but the time . . . where does it go?"

And then she added. "You remember Rule 47 don't you?"

I did for once and proudly yelled it out. "Rule 47. Time flies. But only birds have wings."

She appeared jubilant. "Please. Say it again."

Together we chanted the rule like parishioners reading from the Margolis hymnal.

"Time flies. But only birds have wings."

Nevertheless, it is still exhilarating to make things up. Even when the story is only a partial lie. You start out innocently enough, heading one way but then abruptly change direction. Why? That is my question.

When I was in the ninth grade I fell in love. It was my first time. Her name was Sarah Lopian. We met at the Central Park Zoo around the seal pool. We marveled at their acrobatics. The way they glided effortlessly in the water. Two lovers wrapped in each others' fins in a corner on a slippery rock.

Sarah was five feet one and 90 pounds of pure tiger meat. She was a wild, unpredictable girl who claimed to be "as much fun as James Brown and as dangerous as a feral cat." Sarah had large amber eyes, dark skin and a figure that made pimply boys stay up late at night playing with themselves under sweaty sheets. But she was mine and forbidden which made me the envy of my neighborhood.

We would walk together for hours in the park holding hands, wading in the sexual energy of ponds and rivers, inhaling freshly cut grass, enjoying its power coursing through our bodies like seal pool water.

The Next Step

Sarah was a Rorschach energy field come to life. She showed me how to hold and kiss her. Our tongues danced in each others' mouths like hungry fish. My hand slowly touching her hot moist opening. Our hearts pounding like I beams connecting. Her strong rapid jerks demanding that I gush.

It's funny how a girl you have known so long ago will remain with you forever. All this returns to me like a dream sometimes in that single moment just before I fall asleep when the world once again is whole and everyone I have ever known at any time is present. Shirley and Herbert Weingarten, Ida Margolis, Dr. Gunther Gassman, my psychoanalyst; Ploopy Goldberg, Sarah Lopian, Rabbi Gordon, all of them like ink blots slowly leaching hidden meaning in that polymorphous instant between half-forgetting and no longer fully awake.

***

One of the practical advantages of being totally screwed up is that you are always flush with plenty of advice. Probably why so many people are talking to themselves these days. If only others would listen. Ever pay attention? Here are just a couple of things I've picked up.

"Extinction: Life forms that once existed are no longer with us."

"Thelonius Monk in novel form. Sparks fly off the page. Pyrotechnics of words and phrases."

"You may be playin' but you ain't sayin' nuthin'."

"He had talent to burn but was never published."

"Weingarten grew up in a time when 'drinking the Kool-Aid' didn't refer to unquestioning loyalty or consuming a cyanide-laced beverage."

"He's a liar but he's only human."

"This is the year the Cubs and White Sox play in the World Series."

"Next year in Jerusalem."

***

Lenny Petrillo was my high school basketball coach. He was big, bald and walked with a limp, an alpha male dedicated to the mean pursuit of enforcing dominance. A sadist who believed life was a competitive game of rewards and punishments. His genius was in obtaining gratification by primarily or exclusively inflicting pain. I hated him for his violence. Culling the weakest players. Humiliating them in public. Making them easy dope slap victims.

The dope slap was Lenny's weapon of choice. He would execute it in one of two ways: in front of you in a stiff forward-charged motion with the back of his hand against your forehead or more commonly, sneaking up from behind, administering a rapier-like open-palmed blow to the back of your neck. It was hard and fast and it hurt. And rarely did it not get your attention.

"Rosenblatt. Get up here. God, are you stupid. You must have been adopted. No one with your brain power is Jewish. Time for a dope slap."

"Krieger, boy I'm really going to enjoy dope slapping you."

"Weingarten, remind me to dope slap you just on principle."

I imagined Petrillo having sex with animals. Transmitting dangerous plague-like viruses through his urine and feces. Or perhaps he was a klismaphiliac who derived sexual pleasure by being given an enema. Yes, that made sense! Love and intimacy. Marriage. No. A good Fleet enema was Lenny's lusty preference.

Most of all I remember the way he pleasured himself on the misery of others. He would line us up in gym class in neat rows like a drill sergeant, declaring his warped take on current events: a death in the family, a divorce, a parent going off to jail, a student whose father recently lost his job.

"Grimes, you better start paying attention now that your father got canned."

"McHenry, get up here. You've earned a dope slap with your old man in jail. The papers said, 'shop lifting socks and underwear'. It's obvious you people are not the sharpest tacks in the box."

"Gallagher, sorry to hear about your sister's death. Poison, right? Let me know when the cops get finished questioning you."

His viciousness knew no bounds. He was the devil in a sweatsuit. And talking back was never an option. Rumor had it years earlier he had beaten a student, Ryan Colby, so severely that he was unable to walk. What he was doing working with kids is still anyone's guess. But he was a winning coach and back then that was all that really mattered.

***

I forgot to mention that Lenny was also found years earlier in a brown Bohack's shopping bag, swaddled in Puma sweat socks and a Nike jock strap, at the side door of the Italian-American Michele Minestrone Culinary Institute.

Of course, this is to say, Lenny Petrillo is a fictional character, made up. You see . . . I didn't have a basketball coach. Never made the team. But I keep asking myself . . . What if? What then?

***

Where I grew up the worst thing you could be was an "ass kisser", a "brown nose", or "tuchus licker." Why? I'll give you why. Why do people read bestselling authors? It is not that they are the best writers, is it? And why do people run stop signs? A lot of reasons. Not one purely satisfying. And why this thing with omniscient narrators and narrative arcs? Why?

Lemmings in free fall dropping from white Dover cliffs. All pursuing the same thing. Cliché:

Always look on the bright sight of life
To be or not to be
Live and learn
Live and let live
C'est la vie
Que será, será
What goes around comes around
Life is what happens while you're busy making other plans
Life is messy
Don't worry, be happy!
Today is the first day of the rest of your life
Shit happens
Laughter is the best medicine
Same shit, different day
Smile. It makes people wonder
Carpe diem

***

Lenny Petrillo is a fake. Dope slap is for real.

***

"At this point the poor bastard will say anything."

***

    I've never really been much of a planner. I'm a spontaneous, fly by the seat of your pants kind of guy. Go with the flow is a philosophy Weingarten lives by. And as long as I am being frank . . . there have been times when I have acted really stupid or on occasion, as you know, lied. It's hard to be honest. Believe me. This constant need to tell stories . . . Usually it's purely intuitive. I mean nobody's perfect. And let's face it even if you want to you can't change the past. At least I know my intentions are good. What the hell ... I'm only human. Sometimes I feel the devil made me do it or lying is just my way of making life more interesting. You can't have it all. My motto is: one step at a time.

***

Weintraub—not to be confused with Weingarten- scrolls fifty, then a hundred, then one hundred and fifty pages deeper into the dopeslap.doc document. There are attached pictures at the top of each page, produced in Photoshop, of Weingarten with Nabokov and Bellow, bike riding along an open highway, landing butterflies, snow boarding in the Rockies, walking down Dorchester Street in Hyde Park, each giving and receiving writing tips, telling jokes, insider trading. Weintraub power scrolls forward, then stops.

***

Even so you gotta believe everybody has the right to make mistakes. And tomorrow who will remember? Sometimes I just tell myself that it seemed like a good idea at the time and at the very least it shows what I am capable of. I can just hear Herbie saying in his nasal Brooklyn voice.

"If at first you don't succeed, destroy all evidence that you even tried."

Or maybe he'd say something like ... "If you can't dazzle them with your brilliance, baffle them with your bullshit."

I know Shirley's attitude.

"Honey, someone like you will never be rich so you must be smart."

Of course Mrs. Margolis would certainly cite Rule 121. "Behind the clouds the sun always shines and after the rain comes a rainbow."

If Lenny Petrillo was here I'd warrant a dope slap. I agree. And for the most part that's pretty much my current point of view. You screw up. Dope slap. It's one of the few things in life that you can really count on. In pain, dope slap. Feel like someone has broken your heart. Dope slap. Lonely, feeling ugly and afraid. Dope slap. It's reverse psychology that always works. Just dope slap yourself into a state of bliss. I'm convinced this is a trick the Dalai Lama has taught himself and doesn't dare share with anyone else.

It's power. A genuine, bona fide psychological truth. At the instant you are feeling down elevate your mood immediately with a good dope slap. Really. You can literally dope slap yourself silly. There is nothing better to improve your state of mind. I was in my early twenties when I figured it out.

I once wrote an article for JAMA, The Journal of the American Medical Association, about how I owe everything to dope slap's impact. The money. The fame. Even my seat on the Chicago Mercantile Exchange.

Because of it, I can honestly say, "My life turned around."

It was dope slap that achieved results that the Freudians, Jungians, even Sullivanians never could. Why? I'll give you why.

But first a digression.

[NOTE THE SUDDEN TONE CHANGE, STARTING HERE, FROM THE AUTOBIOGRAPHICAL PART OF THE NOVEL. READERS WILL INTUITIVELY GRASP MY REALIZATION OF DS. WEINGARTEN SHOULD COME OFF LIKE PAUL, STRUCK BY LIGHTNING ON THE ROAD TO DAMASCUS OR MALCOLM'S JAILHOUSE CONVERSION. THEN HIT 'EM WITH THE DOPE SLAP PROMOTIONAL MATERIAL. BE SUBTLE.]*

*Make sure this is cut from the final MS

***

People will say almost anything for attention. But rarely do they acknowledge the obvious. Like dope slap for instance. It's more than a philosophy. Dope slap is a way of life. A reminder that there's no free lunch. It is also a franchise business with unlimited opportunity for those in touch with the growing health and lifestyle industry.

Success in Motion.
Believe in Yourself
Achieve Your Goals
Love What You Are Doing
Shine Brighter
Get Closer to Your Dreams
Be a Dope Slap Associate
Move Others to Reinvent Themselves
Life Can Be Good
Dope Slap: the Perfect Opportunity.

***

These are but a few of the ways Dope Slap is changing lives and improving the world we live in.

[MULTIPLE ILLUSTRATIONS OF HAPPY PEOPLE AT WORK AND AT PLAY]

***

The Dope Slap Rehabilitation Institute: Extreme Therapies for an Extreme World.

[In this space the reader will find an architectural rendering of the newly designed Libeskind DS corporate headquarters and links to the DS website.dsthehighercalling.com]

***

It's amazing how you can build a life and a business on a simple idea. Within a decade of its inception, Dope Slap Corporation has become the premier provider of lifestyle information and therapeutic delivery services worldwide. The company functions under the motto "Sorry, I did not mean to hurt you but nobody is perfect." It also takes into consideration the vast array of therapeutic modalities requiring speedy, time-sensitive deployment of tried and true mental health products for a diverse world.

As one satisfied distributor recently reported, "It's incredible the anxieties people are expressing today. Shocking words about the state of the world, our country and their lives."

FOR INSTANCE?

"Ok, here is just a random sample of comments our Dope Slap field investigators brought back to us after a recent research field trip."

"Life sucks and then you die."

"Life is unfair."

"I used to think I had it bad because I had no shoes, then I met a man with no feet but I still had no shoes."

"When the pony dies, the ride is over."

AND DOPE SLAP CAN MAKE A DIFFERENCE?

"Yes. Once people discover the benefits of DS technologies, miracles happen under their nose."

CAN YOU GIVE US AN EXAMPLE?

"Sure. I've got one, but it is kind of a long story."

THAT'S OK. WE HAVE PLENTY OF TIME. WHAT HAPPENED?

"Well there is this urban legend about the kid who jumped out of a window."

GOLDBERG?

"Very good. Ploopy Goldberg. There was a book awhile back about him and his brother."

YEAH, I HEARD ABOUT IT. NEVER READ IT. ANY GOOD?

It was alright but that is not my point.
WHAT IS?
"Never happened!"
IT NEVER HAPPENED. PLOOPY GOLDBERG DIDN'T DIE?
"No. He tried to but the whole story doesn't fly.
SO IT WAS MADE UP?
"No, there's a Ploopy Goldberg but he works in the garment industry. Shirley Bell Dresses and Coats, 47th just east of Broadway."
I DON'T GET IT.
"Follow the money. Like in Jerry McGuire. See?"
SORT OF. BUT PLEASE EXPLAIN.
"His brother ... let's call him ... Fishman. In that family there is some question about the names ... He had this brilliant idea."
MONEY- MAKING IDEA?
"A brilliant money-making idea."
TO WRITE A NOVEL ABOUT PLOOPY GOLDBERG?
"Yea. Can you beat that? Crazy. That's what I want to know. Where do these Wall Street guys come up with this stuff?"
BUT HOW DID IT WORK?
"Look you need to use your imagination."
HMM?
"They get a buzz going ... Next thing you know he's a boldface name. Personal appearances, TV and movie rights ... Just rolling in dough."
CAN WE BACK UP FOR A SECOND?
"Sure."
WHAT DOES ALL THIS HAVE TO DO WITH DOPE SLAP INDUSTRIES?
"Well. It only made all the difference in the world. We dope slapped him into writing his book. Don't you get it?"
GO ON?

"Fishman was at home. Isolated, out of work, depressed. He didn't know what the hell to do with himself. And then one day one of our associates stuck a flyer under his door. You know . . . the usual hype, smoke and mirrors, great graphics, testimonials, pictures of the new Libeskind corporate headquarters. Next thing you know Fishman is in the Chicago office. You should have heard the poor bastard."

WHAT DID HE SAY?

"Usual crap. Feeling sorry for himself. Complaining about losing his wife and kids on 9/11. Having a nervous breakdown. Stuff like that."

AND?

"And . . . We dope slapped the shit out of him. What did you expect? We told him 'if life is a bitch he had to be a sire'. It seemed to work. He was really into this whole dog thing. Go figure."

ANYTHING ELSE?

"We tried giving him a whole bunch of rules from the Margolis handbook: 'Most of the mountains we have in life are ones we build ourselves', 'When life gives you lemons, make lemonade,' 'la vida es dura, amigo', Life is not hard, it only needs positive thinking', 'Things could be worse', 'Cheer up, it's not the end of the world' . . . But none of these seemed to work."

SO WOULD YOU SAY HE'S A SUCCESS STORY?

"Couldn't say just yet. Jury's still out. But it's the next step."

***

Weintraub scrolls further ahead in the document to the last paragraph on the last page—567—and reads to himself.

"Standing forlornly in the doorway of the magistrate's office, Weingarten suddenly was consumed in a mulch fire of images. All at once reflecting on the many tragicomic events that brought him to this point in his life. Surely this was another example of the narrowness of human understanding and the refusal of the universe to clue him in, even when all he needed to know was just a little more: a word, a phrase, a simple sentence. In the end, Weingarten thought to himself, 'What have you? Even the bible, psychoanalysis, a good dope slap was not the final solution.' And so with this understanding, in the cold light of unanswered protest, against the backdrop of 9/11, Weingarten felt reassured. Hopeful. Not because his journey had come to an end. But just the opposite. All that really mattered now was his dream of a brighter future, the next step."

***

Weintraub exits the dopeslasp.doc file, clicking ok when prompted, "Do you want to save the changes?" He feels uneasy, unsure.

He hears a golden oldie blasting from a neighbor's window. *"It's my party and I'll cry if I want to. Cry if I want to. Cry if I want to. You would cry too if it happened to you."*

Weintraub feels Weingarten looking up. RK looking down.

Weintraub thinks about the jokiness and caricature of Weingarten's childhood. He then imagines himself lost in a heavy fog, on a back road off a curving highway. Near where it all began in familiar territory, somewhere in Brooklyn. A young boy who has traveled by foot and subway beyond dirt hills and public meadows, across the wide lawns of Prospect Park onto Flatbush Avenue climbs with his comrades to distant reaches. There is a din of muffled voices and Vin Scully and the cool stale aroma of beer mixed with urine. He lifts his nose into it, breathing in deeply like a happy dog along an open road. He follows his instinct, moving higher on dark ramps and gateways until there is an instant of total eclipse and then suddenly like a scene from revelation there is the blindness of pure light followed by a diamond of the greenest grass on the face of the earth.

Here there are no men with graying hair suffering from weariness or life's anguish. Only cherubs in the corners of paintings who share one purpose, to save the day. Roy Campanella, Don Drysdale, Sandy Koufax, Pee Wee Reese, Jackie Robinson, Duke Snider and Don Sutton. Gone too is pride and damaged memory. Weintraub questions himself and all that he had to say.

"Was this the best I could do?" he wonders.

Weintraub remains uncertain.

***

Meanwhile RK wrestles with many of his own insecurities. He wishes that more of life's questions could be answered in a fat manual, a writer's handbook of psychological how to's, for all characters in all contingencies under all conditions. Certainly RK could offer a few cherce ideas of his own.

***

RK knows that despite his upbringing under the right circumstances he too might have flushed a threatening Koran down the toilet. To be truthful, he had done similar things in the past. Q Tips and paper towels, an experimental wad of hardened bubble gum in grade school, a decomposed goldfish, even a Red Delicious or Fugi apple core. But the thought of a toilet swallowing an entire volume the size of the Old and New Testament in a single gulp was downright biblical. Heretical. No. This was a suspension of the natural order every bit as sensational as the 69 year-old Florida grandmother who survived a fall off her ninth floor balcony.

"I was scared shitless when I went over that guard rail. I was sun tanning and next thing I knew there was no place to put my walker. I was swimming in the air. And then I hit this green awning. I just bounced right up onto my feet. Praise be the Lord."

RK muses. "Books could be written about it."

"Fuck. It's a goddamn miracle," someone else might say.

"Let's go out and kill some infidels for that" is also a possibility.

A variation on an all too familiar theme.

And it is not that RK, who is also known as CB or "Christ Bob", is insensitive to the religious concerns of others. He is not a bigoted opportunist like the leaders of political parties or the Extreme Right. Rather he is aware that, as much as he might try, striving for authenticity requires compromise. Limitations.

Weintraub is only the latest example. There have been others: Fishman, Palefsky, Chico from the Excelsior, Jim Early, Ploopy Goldberg.

And what about using FedEx as vehicle to fulfill a Messiah's calling? Mount Sinai as the peak of Palefsky's fall? The Sears Tower as a climax to a suicidal vision? RK has seriously thought of applying for a MacArthur Genius Award but he is unsure of how to position himself: novelist, cultural icon, juggler of very important ideas, trading book author? There is also IRS victim, former Amex platinum card holder, commodities guru, Lake Shore Drive resident. Former cat owner?

RK is sure that marketing and the precise branding makes all the difference in the world. In any case, he's prepared to keep correspondence with the foundation confidential, enabling the selection committee to make recommendations based on impressions and criteria, artistic originality, future benefit to society, all free of outside influence.

Chapter 37

Most stories begin at the beginning. Not this one. It seems to have started somewhere in the middle and gotten lost several times along the way. Blame RK. His half developed plot lines and erroneous details serve as a Judas goat to trick the reader.

He can remember his mother saying-

RK interjects.

"It was a hundred years ago in Brooklyn."

Not quite, only about forty, but this is how he insists on remembering it.

"Who died and made you boss?"

It was Hana's favorite expression.

But that is just what RK wanted. To be boss. To tell it like it is, to render who's who and what's what. Who can fault him?

"Why else would I have spent so much time in my room writing all those silly poems, drawing pictures, working on experiments, making up stories?"

This from the New York Forward.

"The man is a magician! A magician I tell you. A Yiddeshe griot!"

Siegfried Fischbacher of Siegfried & Roy agrees, "RK is synonymous with magic. He is the real megillah on so many levels. The hot dog and hamburger bun of story telling."

The New York Times observed:

"As a writer, RK can move from mismatched participles to well-cut long verse. He is also a superb ventriloquist, and his often eccentric and persnickety characters, Fishman, Palefsky, now Weintraub, make for 'one of the better and affordable reads.'"

Larry David and Jerry Seinfeld, when asked for testimonials for this chapter, at first declined comment.

Then Seinfeld added, "Essentially the guy writes novels about nothing."

Not wanting to be upstaged, David shot into the phone, "Yea, that's right, nothing. Not one thing. Nuttin'."

Most of Weintraub's memories RK remembers from *his* trilingual childhood. The slapstick grade school. The butterflies. One spring, migrating north, the Monarchs covered the magnolias, not yet in bloom. Black-orange sentries like feathery tomb soldiers, greeted RK and his family.

"Discovering Nabokov."

Making love for the first time in a mansion in Boston, down a long hallway off the maid's quarters, on a chenille bedspread, under wallpaper of Chinese lanterns flaming cinnamon red.

He also remembers with affection Hana calling him "crazy boy" and then usually adding, "Don't be a baby."

RK laughs about it now. It was such a long time ago in a different century in a strange time and place when men wore jackets and ties, even straw hats, following lashing line drives at Ebbets Field into foul territory. Walking along the third base line glimpsing a stare at Pee-Wee or Duke or Campy, before the crash. A man prancing around the infield, wearing the head of a horse. A woman in uniform promising salvation. She hands out free bibles urging "Onward Christian soldiers" promoting a poorly funded night ministry. A married couple approaching the hot dog stand at Nathan's. Reflecting, in the blinding light of the noon day sun.

"Now we are entering the Kingdom of God."

That initial bite, like having sex and coming hard, for the first time.

Summer evenings at Coney. The roller coaster and parachute

rides. Far Rockaway.

"I can see myself taking off. Landing in a jet pack."

RK is sure that writing is an odd calculating process. Working things out. Like math problems. Yielding solutions.

But who is RK and where is he from? What does he believe in?

"One morning, upon awakening from agitated dreams, Gregor Samsa found himself, in his bed, transformed into a monstrous vermin."

No. This was not the beginning of RK's story, not that there wasn't a fair share of compelling similarities here too. But there was no Bohack's shopping bag or abandoned foundling at the side door at the B'nai Israel Home for the Deaf and the Blind. Not even the fantasy.

RK was born in Maimonides Hospital. Mt. Sinai would have been better but RK wasn't given the choice. It was a sunny May day, two years after the war.

***

An interview with RK republished with the permission of the author.

What is your first memory?

"In the park with my grandfather, Morris. Running after pigeons. Eating Velveeta cheese. Smelling yellow roses."

Anything else?

"Developed allergies. Stung by a bee. I think the cheese was slightly gone."

You've got to be kidding?

"Not really. I seem to be at the bottom of the sink hole for these sorts of things. I once almost went to jail for finding a worm in my salad. Just hiding under the radicchio. I wrote about it in

Fishman."

Remind me.

"I think I pretty much gave my last word on the subject in the Palefsky Chronicle. Here's the quote if you missed it the first time.

'Take the time I found a worm in my salad at Stark's Salad Bar over on Seventy-sixth and First Avenue. As these things go, it wasn't even that big. Just a little white one, minding his own business under my radicchio. Do worms hibernate? I mean the little non-offender wasn't even moving but that didn't stop me from having a psychotic episode! I turned over the table, clearing out the restaurant and nearly sent old man Stark to his grave. When the medics carried him out on the stretcher he referred to me with one whisper: "Bulvon."

I really feel for guys like Stark, which by the way means strong in German. Old world businessmen who came up the hard way, real school of hard knocks. Not like the wimpy wipeass yuppy types who treat you as if you are as disposable as a condom. Smug, narcissistic know-it-alls who shop at Prada and D&G and think they know something that you don't. If you walked into Barney's on any Saturday you could spit in any direction and there isn't a chance in the world that you would miss one of them.'"

Correct me if I'm wrong but I detect a chip on your shoulder?

"Yea. What about it."

What makes you so special?

"Do you mean who died and made me boss?"

That's one way of putting it.

"Now look who has the chip on his shoulder."

So what would you like to know?

"Fundamental questions."

Like?

"Human existence."

Pish posh. Aren't we a little big for our britches?

"Let's not forget. I was a Yeshiva bachur. I'm supposed to ask questions."

Any answers?

"No. Only stories. Here, let me give you one. These are the facts: RK was born on May 16, 1947, in Borough Park, Brooklyn. He was not orphaned young or a child of need. His mother, Hana, did not die when he was seven months old. His father, a businessman, was never a professor of Perception of Phenomenology. Chaim wasn't killed in World War II. Hell, he never even got to fight the Germans. And even though stories abound, RK never lived with a deaf-mute, partially blind older sister. In truth, he did not even have one. Nor was he taken in by the Zelikows, his maternal grandparents. RK was not a deeply observant Protestant, nor did he embrace militant Islam. Though his early education included rigorous Bible study. Not once did he officiate at a baptism or attend a Roman Catholic Church. A lover of words and images, RK majored in Philosophy. Surprisingly, he chose not to study at the Sorbonne. In 1995 he translated *The Phenomenon of Human Life*." The following is a key excerpt.

Dr. Ricoeur was best known for his contributions to phenomenology and hermeneutics. Phenomenology deals with the nature of the perception of reality. Hermeneutics is the art of interpreting texts. To Dr. Ricoeur, the two were inextricably linked. If we perceive the world in a particular way, he asked, how then, do we interpret those perceptions?

To move through life, Dr. Ricoeur came to believe, is to navigate a world of texts, each laden with meaning. Man's task is to interpret these texts. It is a way of organizing the world.

An ardent pacifist, RK spent most of the eighties trading

commodities, pork bellies and soybeans on the Chicago Board of Trade."

***

And that's it?
"Of course there is more to RK's story."
Back story?
"Yea. And back drop. Human action and suffering throughout the ages. The vast spectrum of our common experience. One person's upended life and search for cohesion. Meaning."
You're losing me. Where does RK fit into all of this?
"Now that's my kind of question."
Go on.
"It's all pretty obvious. Like I wrote in Palefsky:

'What is a life anyway? What do you live and work for? Family, friends, a nice house, a car, dinners out and what have you ... From fourteen floors above ground there are unimaginable things to be seen. The key is to close your eyes and let your mind go free. Planets revolve in primary colors: reds and blues and yellows and greens. There are of course the sounds of dogs barking, and angry men cursing about raw deals and poor location in the universe ...

If there is one lesson I have learned it is that everything we know or do is matter of perspective and anything we accomplish is relative to molehills and mountains. Astronomers can view objects thirteen billion light years away just as the heavens looked when stars and galaxies first appeared. They can focus their sights on quasars, shining objects thought to be powered by massive black holes from the inception of the universe. They appear to the observer as luminous smears from the dawn of time, arcs of red and blue on the cosmic lens of space. Each of us inhabits our own glittering expanse of stars and sky; some so close as to be blinding to the eye and others so remote that they are forever beyond our field of vision unless or until we stretch our horizons; allowing ourselves to see what has always been there.

A story is like a galaxy, a seemingly incoherent clusters of stars, some hidden from view, others swallowed into black holes or obscured by gas and dust; internal nebulae hiding or revealing dark matter of an unknown nature whose origin and gravity may be uncaptured by the telescope but never beyond the powers of imagination.'"

Chapter 38

Why is it that to begin fresh you are always starting over? Like a painter working an image over and over again Weintraub considered every detail. Each time getting closer. RK is doing the same. He thinks of it as a "text of life." A celebration or maybe just an acknowledgment of the phenomenon of being alive.

"There's always so much more than you might think."

A sudden thought and a ghastly image: There is a coral reef off the coast of Madagascar inhabited by man-eating crabs. They have a deadly sting and two pairs of evil looking pincers that never let go. They are known to live for over 100 years.

And then RK remembers the incidental bike rider: a youngster in the late fifties, tooling around on a prized Schwin. He is on Long Beach near Tennessee Avenue where the Zelikows spent their summers; raccoon tails pointing off chrome handle bars, fur flying in the ocean breeze. There RK visits the West End theatre where a child is enthralled by movies: fictional worlds in black and white and in Cinemascope. Technicolor. Entertainment and popcorn for less than a quarter. RK encounters Leni Riefenstahl in the "March of Time." There are also acid etched pictures of fierce battles and wartime liberation. Stick men and stick women moving like drunken mimes behind barbed wire. A pallid mountain of corpses. Charlie Chaplin shouting at German soldiers.

"It is Hitler," a voice explains.

All now dimly remembered but never far away, out of reach. Real worlds that are fictional. Fictional worlds that are real.

Hoaxes and sensational lies. Stories that awaken and re-enchant the world. Others whose purpose is to come up with an idea and just toss it in a pot. Like the ones about the origins of life or the canary expiring in the coal mine. Story tellers and liars, perpetrators of every kind of fraud. Holocaust deniers. Architects.

There is a railroad station where men, women and children pour out of cattle cars like grain. They are divided. Cut pinochle cards. One road to the right. One to the left. Shoes in the left hand. Clothes in the right.

"A thousand people in the barracks. Every night I imagined, tomorrow, I will wake up at home."

Hana, RK's mother, lived in . . .

"A madman's hell."

"My saddest memory, seeing Papa with his head shaved and striped uniform. I tried to look away but our eyes locked. Tears rolled down his face."

They stamped numbers in ink into Hana's arm.

"You would not believe what I saw . . . once a Nazi Colonel picked up a little girl. He beat her head against the fender of a truck until she was dead. The crematoria . . . there were special peep holes for the officers to watch."

Hana and her sister celebrated the Shabbat in the corner of a latrine.

RK never met Hana's sister. Yoni died in Auschwitz. A crackled family photograph comes to mind. A prosperous family in the mid thirties. Momma, Papa, Hana and Yoni.

Hana left a candle for Yoni and said a prayer. She also read family names and recited a poem.

"Why did I survive?"

"Why did God save me?"

"Liberation was not the last day. Only when I arrived in America did I know I was in heaven."

"I dreamed in the camps about being in front of our house in Budapest. I pulled at the gate. The door wouldn't open. No matter how hard I pulled, the door wouldn't open."

And now in Berlin, next to the Reichstag where Jew baiters once delighted at the sight of burning books . . .

RK says to himself, "Imagine burning a book. As a child we were taught when a book falls to the floor you kiss it. How could they burn books? How did they burn people?"

But it is here in Berlin that the children of yesterday's monsters . . .

"Perhaps this is yet another example of the coming of the apocalypse."

. . . They built an institution of memory. A labyrinth of granite columns to contemplate extermination.

RK finds himself going back to worlds he will never fully understand. The spontaneity and magic of the imagination is fading.

"How could they have burned books? How did they burn people?"

Simple questions. Try asking yourself. See if you can come up with a satisfying explanation. Granite columns. Cold. Intellectual. Abstract. Syllogistic.

Every Friday when Hana lit the candles RK could hear her whisper . . .

"Yoni, I won't forget you."

A play on the Dylan line.

"It all lived inside of her. They've never been apart."

***

RK fights hard against the idea that the world has double-crossed him. He needs to free himself from getting tangled up in blues. He aches for success. Recognition. At the very least to be widely read.

And then like a deus ex machina, a supernatural or unmotivated device for unraveling a plot, help came to the rescue. It was the answer to all RK's prayers. In truth, he was an agnostic but he knew a good deal when he saw it. Manna from heaven via the World Wide Web.

In a matter of 10 days RK received a partnership request, greetings from a distant admirer, an offer of marriage and several business proposals as well as confirmation that he had won two national lotteries. They all arrived by email to the new Hotmail account that RK had just opened. The first was dated 27 May 2005 and originated in Nigeria.

PRIVATE MEMO

Private E-mail:
adamuciroma456783@Borreo.terra.com.pa
D/L: 234-803-5373806
WEBSITE: www.cenubank.com

Our Ref: CBN/IRD/CBX/021/05
Date: 27 May 2005

Attn,

I hope this may not constitute sort of embarrassment to you, as I could not get through with your fax line in disclosing this information across to you. Please observe it with due respect and do not neglect the e-mail nature of it considering the recent flow of fraudulent letters all round the internet. However During the auditing and closing of all financial records of the Central Bank of Nigeria (CBN) it was discovered from the records of outstanding foreign contractors due for payment with the Federal Government of Nigeria in the year 2004 that a contractor, which is among those that will receive their fund, is no where to be found, less I contacted you for this fund to be transferred into your personal bank account or your company's account as I will be the one to include your name on the list of those who will received their fund. I wish to officially notify you that this payment is being processed and will be released to you as soon as you respond to this letter. Also note that from the record in our file, the outstanding contract payment is USD $35,700.000.00 (Thirty-five Million Seven Hundred Thousand United States Dollars).

Kindly confirm your interest to this matter as this will be a deal between you and I and also re-confirm the information below to enable this office proceed and finalize the fund remittance without further delays.

1) Your full name.
2) Phone, fax and mobile #.
3) Company name, position and address.
4) Profession, age and marital status.

As soon as the above information is received, this fund will be made available to you via the account, which you will provide. You should call my direct number as soon as you receive this letter for further discussion and more clarification.

Best regards,

Mabinto Abamu
Diploma.
DIRECTOR
INTERNATIONAL
REMITTANCE DEPT.
Central Bank of

Nigeria (CBN).

***

The subject line of this email simply read HELLO. It was from BLIMPTONEVANS@Yahoo.co.uk

Dear Friend,

I guess this letter may come to you as a surprise since I had no previous correspondence with you. I the chairman tender board of Independent National Electoral Commission (INEC).I got your contact in my search for a reliable person to handle a very confidential transaction involving the transfer of US$20.5million.

The above fund is not connected with arms, drugs or Money laundering. It is the product of an over invoiced Contract awarded in 2001 by INEC to a foreign company for the construction of high rise estate in the federal capital territory.

The contract has long been executed and payment of the actual contract amount has been paid to the foreign contractor leaving the balance, which my colleague and I now want to transfer out of Ivory Coast into a reliable foreign account for our personal use.

As civil servants we are not allowed to run foreign accounts. Hence we have chosen to front and support you as the beneficiary to be paid. If you are interested in the proposal kindly get back to me by sending me your letter of acceptance along with your direct telephone and fax numbers, we have decided to share the money in the following percentage, 60% for us 30%

for you the account owner and 10% for all local and international expenses that may arise in the course of this transaction.

Further details about this transaction will be discussed in the subsequent correspondence. Note also that the particular nature of your business is irrelevant to this transaction and all local contacts and arrangements are in place for a smooth and successful conclusion of this transaction.

You should please treat this with utmost attention knowing fully well that you cannot and will not be compelled to assist us if you are not disposed to.

Contact me via my email account with your contact telephone and fax Numbers, so that I can call you for a discussion.

Sincerely,

Blimpton Evans

***

The next email marked REPLY ASAP, ITS CONFIDENTIAL did not involve as much money but it too caught RK's interest.

Hello:

I am Abusenji Lambert accountant foreign bill of exchange of the operation Department of standard trust bank of Ethiopia. I am writing following the impressive information about you through an internet genealogical research .In my department, we discovered an abandoned sum of (US$9 million) in an account that belong to my late client { Engineer Fred} a foreign customer who work as a refinery engineer with the CHEVRON OIL COMPANY here in Ethiopia, he died along side with his entire family in April 2002 in a car accident .

Since we got the information about his death, we have been expecting his next of kin to come over and claim his money because we cannot release it unless somebody applies for it as next of kin of relation to the deceased as indicated in our banking guide. Unfortunately, we learnt that all his surposed next of kin or relations died along with him at the spot of the accident. It therefore, upon discovery that now as the personal accountant to late { Engineer Fred } I decided to make business with you and release the money to you as next of kin or relation to the deceased for safe keeping and subsequent disbursement, since you are a foreigner like him, and besides nobody is coming for the fund and I don't want this money to go back into Federal Government account as unclaimed bill. The banking law and guideline here stipulates that such money remained unclaimed after the period of four years, the money will automatically be transferred into federal government banking treasury account as unclaimed bill. The request of a foreigner as next of kin in this business is strictly occasioned by the fact that the customer was a foreigner and an Ethiopian cannot stand as a next of kin to a foreigner. I agreed that 50% of this money would be negotiable for you as foreign partner as I will be entitled to 50% based on the fact that I have been coming up with this transaction for the past three years now.

The fund will be remitted into your personal

nominated bank account, thereafter I shall visit your country for the disbursement / investing my share according to the percentages indicated. Please be honest to me as you might decide to abscond into the air after the fund has been transferred into you personal bank account. Therefore to enable the immediate transfer of the fund to you as arranged, you must apply first to the bank as next of kin to the deceased. As the personal accountant to late {Engineer Fred} , I have all the requisite information & documents that will aid the accomplishment of this fund release into your personal nominated bank account , and everything shall go under a legitimate arrangement that will prevent both of us from any breach of the law.

Upon receipt of your reply, I will send to you by fax a {text of application} with the name of the deceased and his country and other information about him, this {text of application you shall have to fill and send to the bank as your application for the release of then fund to you as the next of kin to the deceased. Be informed that I will have to approve your application in the bank as the personal accountant to late {Engineer Fred}, After the fund have been approved, it will be transferred to an offshore security finance company in Europe where you will sign for the fund release order and for onward remittance into your personal account.

Note: I am assuring you this transaction is 100% risk free as I will surely change your file in the office , this file will prove you to the bank as the legal / lawful next of kin / beneficiary to the deceased and I shall likewise provide you with all needed informations that will aid this fund release accomplishment .

Feel free to contact me via my cell private email for

further explanation of this transaction.
mrabusenjionline@yahoo.co.uk

Expect a positive response from you soonest.

Best regards,

Mr Kowowa Abusenji
Accountant

***

But the email that made the greatest impression on RK was from a Mrs. Shirley Blanco de Blanco, Minister of Philosophy, Gender and People Affairs of Sierra Leone, Africa.

Dear RK47325@sbcglobal.net,

Greetings to you and may I simply call you RK.

With warm heart I offer my friendship, and greetings, and I hope this mail meets you in good time. However strange or surprising this contact might seem to you as we have not met personally or had any past dealings, I humbly ask that you take due consideration of its importance and the immense benefit it will be to you.

After careful consideration with my biological children and the many others who are in my charge, we resolved to contact you for your most needed assistance in this manner.

I duly apologize for infringing on your privacy, if this contact is not acceptable to you, as I make this proposal to you as a person of integrity. First and foremost I wish to introduce myself properly.

The Next Step

My name is Mrs. Shirley Blanco de Blanco, but please just think of me as Shirley. I am the mother of three and the Minister of Philosophy, Gender and Children Affairs and other ministeries for many years running.

You may view my profile on the following link;

http://www.Fortyunderforty/Thelegends.html

I will now give you a general overview of the situation. When I was sworn in as Minister of Philosophy, Gender and People Affairs in 1996, my husband Mr. Thomas Tablarasa, a very successful businessman was awarded several contracts in my ministry and had direct dealings with foreign investors. Due to my political status, I was not involved in my husband's business, which was very vast and successful.

My beloved husband died whilst on an official trip to one of his project sites, where he was attacked by a patrol of gorillas. There is no delicate way of saying this so please forgive my candor.

An alpha male who had been involved months earlier in a mauling was known to have same-couple preference and literally fucked my husband to death. The doctors, in all their years of treating this sort of affliction had never witnessed such wild passion or observed such an outstretched rectal passage. I was told that the first few times may have been pleasurable but, subsequent to that, sheer hell. I donated my husband's corpse to the medical school where it is still under study.

When Thomas died, may God rest his soul, I was contacted as next of kin by a private security firm in

Sierra Leone. I was asked to come forth with a Certificate of Deposit and claim a safety deposit my husband placed in their Vault in his name.

At that time, my children and I did not have an idea where the Certificate might be. We then instructed the security firm to continue holding the safety deposit until I provided further instructions. Whilst preparing for the second remembrance of my beloved husband, I was going through his library collection where to my astonishment I discovered a Certificate of Deposit for the safety deposit with this private security firm, and other documents relating to the safety deposit in a book.

The safety deposit, which is larger than a steamer trunk, is stocked with precious valuables and hard currency. He had US Treasury Bills alone totaling $84,500,000 which was generated from cash payments from his business associates in the commodities trade from Antwerp. There were also letters of I.O.U. from Paul Allen and George Soros, payable on demand for tens of millions of dollars.

Though I knew my late husband was a principal in a hedge fund and often traded futures and options, I did not have the knowledge that he moved such vast funds in cash with my present position as a Minister. Except for his involvement with the Bush family, which I recently discovered in a Michael Moore documentary, I remain largely in the dark.

In this Government it will cause a lot of problem for me and my family if the current military leaders should find out about the cash. They might conclude that Thomas had a part in shady dealings during the civil war.

For this reason, I have moved the deposit box to a finance and security company in Europe with the aid of my late husband's friend who works for the security company. We told them that the funds belong to my late husband's partner and that we have been trying to locate him for quite some time.

As such I have contacted you RK to act as a trustee to help me clear the deposit box, deposit trunk more accurately, with all of its funds.

Once it is vacated from Europe I have decided to have the money invested immediately in commercial and residential properties in the U.S. as well as other profitable ventures.

The essential point to remember is that no member of my family can hold such a huge amount in our name due to my political status, hence we sincerely propose to you to render us your most needed assistance.

If you agree to help us, your role in this project will be to act on my behalf as a trustee to receive the safety trunk containing the funds from the security firm.

Though I believe this transaction should be based on mutuality, my family's interest will be protected by a family associate, who is a lawyer attached to the Sierra Leone Embassy in the country where the security firm is located.

He is now aware of the safety deposit, and I have informed him that I am locating one of my husband's business associates —you RK- to handle the funds and invest on our behalf, as he might be opposed to our decision if he found out that I barely know you.

For your reliable assistance, we are offering you 20% of the contents plus a flat fee of three million dollars U.S. as our way of saying thank you.

I thank you in advance as I anticipate your assistance in enabling me to achieve this goal.

On hearing from you, I will forward to you all the necessary documents that will assist you in clearing the deposits with the security company.

As you may understand, due to my sensitive position in the present government, it is not safe to communicate with me via phone or fax. This is why I have communicated with you with my private email address, sblancodeblanco@genderneutral.com, and I like us to keep it this way.

Please "shoot" me an email as soon as possible whether or not you are interested in assisting, this will enable me make alternative plans, in the event of non-interest on your part.

With warm regards,

Shirley

***

Finally RK could help someone who was in obvious need, and if he was successful, there would be something in it for him too.

***

Funny how all the emails stopped just hours after RK signed up for a new spam blocker. But no matter, RK was sure, call it a gut feeling, Shirley's cry for help was different.

"For the record, it would be a huge mistake to underestimate RK's nose for opportunity."

But I, RK, am getting ahead of myself.

***

RK is well aware that in a universe thriving on fiction, there is a new threat: spammers, phishers, cashers and hackers. Digital varieties of parasites, lice, ticks and fleas.

And that is where "I come in," he says to himself in a vespertine whisper.

In a world that craves safety, RK is an old style, high flying daredevil who rebukes the net. Sure his introspection can be paralyzing but he still envisions himself shooting the rapids or as an eagle soaring on a motorcycle across the Snake River.

"I love what it feels like to be in a seat of power, to have a center of gravity . . . the smell of fresh gunpowder, the clap of thunder hurtling out of a canon."

RK remembers something he wrote.

"As a boy Weintraub wanted to run off and join the circus. He loved the music of the calliope and, like Fishman, marveled at the daring of the human cannonball."

He thinks to himself this is vintage RK.

Why else would he have caught so much heat, boring people cross-eyed with his books about entrepreneurs and Wall Street traders? Their crazy fly by the seat of the pants antics; sensational gambles and colossal high jinks. Like the investment banker who brought down Der Schmutz, a Cologne bank, after betting the ranch on the purchase of the world's last live-time slide rule manufacturer. Or "The Amazing Idiot," a name affectionately given to the President of the United States who through shrewd dealmaking not only overcame alcoholism and ASN (acquired situational narcissism) but managed to build a multi- million dollar fortune with just a little help from his friends.

RK keeps fighting hurt. He is hungry, humiliated, disappointed. But he has embraced risk before and won. And that is what propels him on.

"After all, my genius has always been to seduce fate: Majoring in Philosophy. Trading commodities. Battling the IRS . . ." He is also tempted to add, but doesn't, "Why else would I have married a Latvian?"

And RK is the first to admit that it was his fault alone that he lost his fortune, but even so . . . He sees himself getting up again, safely finding his way back home.

"He follows his instinct, moving higher on dark ramps and gateways until there is an instant of total eclipse and then suddenly like a scene from revelation there is the blindness of pure light followed by a diamond of the greenest grass on the face of the earth."

***

And that is why RK is all too willing to rush in where others fear to tread. He has lived a life fueled by trading commodities and writing fictions. It has made him more sophisticated than at first might seem. RK has depended on edges and angles, plot lines, up and down trends, breaks and rallies, single and double bottoms. Key reversals and retracements; thrusts into unknown territory, with and without a chart, higher highs and lower lows, even narrative arcs.

RK knows most people don't see it that way. He also knows that he has something to say and others would do well to listen. He believes deep in his heart and for the life of him can't understand, "Why don't people value each other?"

Rodney King (A different RK) really made sense.

"Can't we all get along?"

RK learned that lesson years ago in the commodity pits. RK

doesn't worry about what will happen to him after he dies. But like Fishman he is concerned about his world.

He thinks about his mother, Hana, in a coma, dying in his arms. The births of his son and daughter. Waking up under a full moon, making love to Dara in a humid, lilac scented night. He sees Goldberg perched on the ledge of the Sears Tower. Cleared for take-off, ready to fly. Young Ploopy heading skyward.

RK hears suicidal rumblings and then rationally considers the philosophy of death. Extinction. Life forms that once existed are no longer with us.

He recalls a chaos of trades he had made in the past. Pork bellies and live cattle. Frozen shrimp, chicken broilers, boneless beef. There is also the distant memory of corn and oats. Soybeans, winter wheat and milo. Heating oil and gasoline. Light sweet crude. U.S. treasury bonds and ten year notes. Bills, munis and foreign exchange.

***

Trading had taught RK about volatility's double edge sword and the ultimate meaning of high stakes professional sports. In the end it is each person against himself. There was also a Zen-like quality to it. Preparing to be able to jump on defining moments just as they emerge.

***

So here was Shirley's letter and what to make of it? Of course there was the simple explanation. Shirley Blanco de Blanco, wife of Thomas Tablarasa, the unlikely homicidal victim of a vicious gorilla fucking, was a con artist, a grifter. The net is full of schemers and scammers.

RK had a different take. He had remembered years earlier in an interview he had conducted with a famed Wall Street trader there was an incident, a sheer coincidence that changed JC's life.

Here is an excerpt of that interview. It is with James P. Cliter, reputedly the most brilliant deal maker and hedge fund operator of the past half century.

RK: Jim you're smiling. Could you talk about it?

JC: It's like this, Bob. One of those things that comes straight out of the blue. Literally. There was no warning . . . Lady Luck. That's what Sinatra would have called it. Changed everything.

RK: What happened?

JC: For years I had been one of those guys who bobbed up and down like a clown on the trading floor. Lots of testosterone, spit flying everywhere . . . Don't get me wrong I was good at it. In fact, in high school and college I was quite an athlete. I won letters in the high and low hurdles. Excelled at the hop, skip and jump. But I was dissatisfied. You know how it is. Uneven.

RK: One year you're up and the next you're down. You're doing ok but no real consistency, right?

JC: Yeah. That's the way it was. So I decided to take a trip. It's let's say 1996. I made a few bucks . . . nothing to write home about. Don't ask me why.

RK: OK. I won't.

JC: I get this idea in my head to go to Beverly Hills. You know . . . never really been there . . . heard about it a lot. Thought I'd check it out . . . So I'm walking down Rodeo Drive and I pass this store. Hermès. I'm looking at the sign and reading it to myself as Hermees. There is this bathrobe in the window. It's blue silk with big white polka dots. I never saw anything like that.

RK: Did you have a thing for robes?

JC: No. That's the thing of it!

RK: Clothes make the man?

JC: I grew up poor. Lower middle class. The neighborhood was all Micks, Ginis and Kikes. No disrespect . . . When I was a kid you wore something like that . . . let's just say they'd give you a very hard time. But I had to have that God-damn bathrobe.

RK: Why?

JC: I don't know.

RK: Then what happened?

JC: I'm just looking at it from the street. I'm fucking hypnotized.

RK: You didn't even go into the store?

JC: I did but not yet.

RK: And?

JC: And I just walked right in there. You know how those people are. They give you the once over then look away. They don't even say anything . . . just let you know you're not one of them. So I said, "I'll take two of those robes. One in navy and the other red." And then came the shocker.

RK: Shocker?

JC: Yeah. The price. I never even looked. Shit . . . 2900 dollars each. I nearly shit in my pants. Hell, I definitely expelled quite a bit of gas. And then calmly said to the clerk, "What other colors do they come in?"

RK: You wanted to buy another robe?

JC: No. I was completely out of control. Words were pouring out of my mouth. I was like a pope serenely abandoning himself to god's will.

RK: What were you saying?

JC: I was ranting. Mumbling. Ranting and mumbling. Like an agitated catatonic or someone suffering with Tourette's. I was giggling madly . . . talking about retribution and reinvention. Lorraine Bobbit, Heidi Fleiss and Paris Hilton. The role of sex and scandal. Religion. The Clinton Presidency. Monica Lewinsky.

RK: But what's the point?

JC: What I found is that in life you walk down a path. You go this way for all of your life and each day is just like the one before and then for no reason everything changes.

RK: Your life changed at Hermès?

JC: Yes. This is going to take some explaining. You see when you work on Wall Street there are long hours. Tough personalities. A lot of pressure . . . But there in the midst of that store, for the first time in my life, the chaos of my mind found peace. I know it sounds strange . . . I was seeing myself dressed in robes. Imagining rich silk against my skin. Like a pope. A king.

RK: That's it?

JC: Not quite. The next day I was reading the LA Times. Classifieds. Business opportunities. There was an item placed by a woman who claimed to be a South American heiress who for political reasons needed someone foreign to help her settle her estate. It was a crazy story. She claimed to have ties to the government and her husband was a diamond trader, killed unexpectedly in a car crash. She needed a "trustee." It sounded like a grift if I ever heard one.

RK: Of course you never responded.

JC: "O ye of little faith" . . . That would have been the rational thing to do. But don't ask me why . . . wearing that robe in my hotel room that night left me no choice. I had to.

RK: You've got to be kidding.

JC: Bob . . . The rest is history. My share was sizeable. Of course I also made wise investments . . . That's my story.

RK: How much?

JC: Enough to get me on Fortune's Top 50. Sandwiched between Sam Zell and Jay Pritzker . . . Life is a damn funny thing.

***

Through his many interview books RK learned a lot about human nature. He wrote about men and women who by virtue of talent and strong determination achieved lasting meaning and material success. Vicariously he tries to pick and choose character attributes and attitudes that will serve him when they are needed.

The Next Step

Like now. How to respond to Shirley in a way that will disentwine her from her dilemma and be profitable for RK as well.

RK remembers a chapter he had written in *Money Talks,* his hard to locate book about entrepreneurs. It was about the vending machine magnate, Sam Pinchik, a veteran of the Iraqi War who described himself as "a steely-eyed, flat-bellied professional and former army ranger."

"What I learned in Baghdad are lessons that will stay with me for the rest of my life. Like knowing when to hold them and when to fold them and when to say a little prayer. Other times it's just flipping a coin."

Pinchik's rise to success went against everything that is taught in business school. His Yureway vending machines had made him the leading purveyor of fast food snacks in the world. Go to any airport, sports stadium or strip mall and Sam Pinchik is there. And to think it all began with one sandwich stand in midtown Manhattan where Pinchik hung his now famous hand painted sign:

"There's no wrong way, or right way. Yureway to the Highway."

***

RK emails Shirley within days of receiving her letter. He provides her with the contact information that will allow her to forward all the necessary documents that will assist him in clearing the deposits with the security company. He recognizes that confidentiality and discretion are the watch words of the day and, though he will have to travel to Antwerp, he is excited by the prospect of bringing this matter to its conclusion.

Chapter 39

Two years have passed since RK met with George Thomson, the attorney for Shirley Blanco de Blanco and managing director of Spinks Scheldt security depository. A time in which everything has changed. Seismic shifts in RK's life. A world of dreams now come true. Fishman and Palefsky are household names. Dope Slap, a huge success in theaters, soon to be released on DVD. Even Weintraub's mention of the infamous Lebanese curse that caused the Bulgarian craft stall explosion along the parade route of the Festival of Roses is cited by Leno and Letterman.

But it goes way beyond that. Thomas Tablarasa's fortune has defibrillated RK's life. Although he thought it impossible, RK has found inner peace.

***

It is true that money does not bring happiness but it sure can put a wild smile on your face.

Not that he had to but there was a special moment of joy when RK asked Paul Allen and George Soros to pony up. Between the two of them, 56 million that RK used as a down payment to buy Random House and HarperCollins, now renamed Fishman, Weintraub, Weingarten and Palefsky. RK maintains the Random House imprint for serious works written by celebrities, like the current best seller, M&M's "Whiteboy's Guide: Being the World's Greatest RappR." He hasn't reached a decision yet about what to do with HarperCollins.

"Don't call us. We'll call you."

And then RK laughs easily. There is a certain humor and irony in the recent turn of events.

RK reflects. "It is a responsibility and privilege to have so much money. I'm seriously considering changing my party affiliation, becoming a Republican."

Then he laughs again, "Just kidding. That's never going to happen."

***

With money in your pocket, the way home is not that important. There's always plenty of time to linger along the way. To stop for a bite at a fine restaurant. To visit a new city or two. Or merely to spend days shopping along Fifth and Madison Avenue.

And so I began to worship once again at the tabernacle of Barney's, Yves St. Laurent, Dunhill and Bergdorf's. Forget about Ebbets Field and Coney. Far Rockaway- throw it away!

All that stuff that I had written before seemed hopelessly out of touch. Even absurd. Unimportant.

Weintraub reminded himself of the advice that Conrad Hilton once gave to a TV reporter, "The shower curtain should always be in the shower." It was a tidy way to think of his universe.

Weintraub had grown up in Brooklyn, in an era when teenage boys delivered afternoon papers on Schwinn Zephyrs, a time span caught in the glassy net of a shuttering lens. His mother drove a battleship gray Buick, chain smoking Camels, her fur trimmed sweater reaching across the dash like an agitated Pomeranian. It was a time as simple as marginalia and metaphysics, Derrida and Nietzsche.

Still, for the most part, Weintraub remains a cock-eyed

optimist, although there are many others who will tell you that even though he went to M.I.T. he is as crazy as a Looney bird. Weintraub has a recurring image of himself parachuting in free fall or landing somewhere new wearing a rocket pack. Weintraub hears strangers speaking in foreign tongues, twangs and drawls and Boston accents. He remembers long days at Coney Island laughing at the shtick of Sam Brownbag and the tall tales of The Celestial Zamboni. He tastes the Wonder Wheel spinning in lifesaver candy colors- greens and reds and lemon yellows- against a blue black summer sky. The Cyclone and the Mermaid Parade. The ocean slapping salty wet against his lips and teeth.

"If you lift up your hand and just think back," he says to himself, "you can feel the memories rushing through your fingers."

And he remembers something he had read. A Basie band saxophonist describing the jazz blown through his horn. Weintraub hears a flood of images from his past.

"His music osmosed to us and we just osmosed it back."

Weintraub delights in the pleasures of a feral imagination. He searches for routes, streets, passages; back alleyways that will lead him home. He yearns for redemption along the third base line or up in the left field bleachers at Ebbets Field.

For today Weintraub will forsake quantum mechanics, unified field and string theory. He will divorce himself from all thoughts of cosmology: space, time, gravity, even geometry and other notions of the universe.

A young boy who has traveled by foot and subway beyond dirt hills and public meadows, across the wide lawns of Prospect Park onto Flatbush Avenue climbs with his comrades to distant reaches. There is a din of muffled voices and Vin Scully and the cool, stale aroma of beer mixed with urine. He lifts his nose into it, breathing it in deeply like a happy dog along an open highway. He follows his instinct, moving higher on dark ramps and gateways until there is an instant of total eclipse and then suddenly like a scene from revelation there is the blindness of pure light followed by a diamond of the greenest grass on the face of the earth. Here there are no men with graying hair suffering from weariness or life's anguish, only cherubs in the corners of paintings who share one purpose, to save the day. Roy Campanella, Don Drysdale, Sandy Koufax, Pee Wee Reese, Jackie Robinson, Duke Snider and Don Sutton.

It seems like another century. It was another century.

But so what? And who the fuck really cares? The key is to have the discipline of a Buddhist, living only in the ever present, here and now.

I remind myself. "Don't stray from this world with all its wonder. Consume madly everything that is in front of you."

***

There is a larger religious meaning derived from always identifying and then capturing nothing but the best. Wrestling it to the ground. Leaving no doubt, once and for all, who is boss. And what do you get for all that effort? Houses, cars, boats, planes and watches. Glorious clothes.

RK always had a flair for fashion but now he exerts his taste wantonly, without the slightest concern for anyone else's opinion. You wouldn't think him the type to wear fox head opera slippers. And in many different colors: midnight blue, crimson, hunter and black. Handmade shirts and lush silk ties. He had stopped wearing them in recent years but what a sensational feeling to have a Turnbull and Asser or Brioni or Charvet tied securely around his neck. Patterns and foulards. Reps. Clubs. Paisleys. Polka dots. The feel of slacks ... Cerutti ... the world's leader in fine men's clothing.

The Next Step

Suddenly RK gets the urge to drop in on the Zegna website. RK's attention locks on details. Like the Torah or Proust, with each reading discovering something new.

"At only 20 years old Ermeneglido Zegna took over his father's small textile business in the northern Italian village of Trivero. Starting with just three looms, he founded the Lanificio, the wool mill that still bears his name."

And then I click on "Zegna World." A self-contained made to measure universe created by the geniuses at Zegna where you and I can express our "individual" style. There is a picture of a model with day old stubble encased like a pope in a grey suit accented with sea-foam green, cream and lilac pinstripes.

"Shoes made to specification. Luxurious finishing touches."

Here is a world to which RK had not aspired but won. Memory. Understanding. Coming to terms with the past... Who would dare compare any of that to the look and feel of a made-to-measure, hand-stitched, single-breasted, three-button Zegna suit?

***

As a reader you are probably asking yourself, "Where has the narrative lost itself in all of this?"

The answer is less ambiguous than it would seem. All of the words and fictions, a bulwark against the sharp edged disappointment of every day life. Pipe dreams. Apocrypha. Grotesque lies. No Shirley Blanco de Blanco. No overnight fortunes. For RK, still no inner peace.

Once again, CB has the need to engage the past: memories that are comforting. Stories that are safe. Struggling to edit and re-edit his text of life. Haven't you ever done that? Contorting history, distorting fact. Searching for the illusion of narrative truth.

Chapter 40

I'm glad the truth is finally out.

But please don't think RK's story is just another literary con job. It would be so much easier if someone would invent a pill to make us always feel whole. Just eat it like chocolate.

I figured this out one day while watching the seals at the zoo resting on a rock. The words just came to me. "Love is the answer." A warm chunk of Vosges melting in my mouth.

***

Here are the facts:

My name is Robert E. Kerwin. I'm first cousin to Robert I. Kerwin, the author of the bestselling interview books and the previously mentioned *Money Talks*. The truth be told, *MT* is a really interesting book. It tells the life stories of 30 men and women who risked everything to achieve success. It is a kind of *Profiles In Courage* for entrepreneurs. National Public Radio devoted an entire year of programming based on stories similar to the ones in Robert's book.

Oh, here is a funny detail... Robert's nickname is CB, which stands for Christ Bob. Not that he is religious. Not by a long shot! The way he got it was that his wife Dara, a Latvian who was born in Saldus, would often get frustrated with his eccentric ways and just shout out. "Christ Bob!"

You get it. Like "Christ Bob take out the trash." Or "Christ

Bob quit playing with your nose hairs" or the one that really used to get to him was when he was driving in the car, a beat up '92 Mercedes that needed about 3500 dollars worth of work to keep it going; Dara demands, "Christ Bob, do you have to go *that* way?"

He liked the name so much he just told everyone to call him CB. It was Dara and his little joke and they preferred to keep it that way.

Ok, I'll just stop beating around the bush and say it once and for all. The truth is . . . There is no Robert E. Kerwin. RK is CB. And CB is me, Robert Kerwin. There is an I that stands for Irwin but I never use it.

So now you have it.

***

My real life has become a soap opera with lots of bubbles. It wasn't always like that. I grew up in Queens in the fifties. I'm telling you all this to let you know what follows exposes the soul of a man. Possessed by both good and evil. A man who can not escape his own past or pathetic present. OK never mind the melodrama.

My mother's name was Miriam and my father was Herbert. Really. After the war, Dad who was a G. I. purchased a house in Flushing and a year later they had me. I was a good kid. Smart. Obedient. Respectful. A pleasure to know and spend time with. I was particularly good in reading and math and playing piano. And sports: baseball, handball, roller skating and bike riding. I also loved girls. Particularly Evelyn Arfa who I gave my entire gum ball charm collection to and she never even said "thank you."

I once made out with her in second grade, in the girls' coat closet until I was caught by Rabbi Charney. His lower stomach looked like a trapped basketball under an alligator belt. His crotch, a feral rodent caged in grey pinstripe. He called my parents and I was sent home. On my way out the door, I sang to myself, *"Ink a bink a bottle of ink, the cork fell out and Charney stinks."*

I had two housekeepers, Mrs. Fleisig and Jackie Brown. Mrs. Fleisig was a depressive, a holocaust survivor and Jackie Brown, a barrel of laughs except when she was reading me the "riot act." Then she really hurt. I used to imagine the two of them killing each other in Madison Square Garden late at night. Mrs. Fleisig wasn't much of a puncher. Her only advantage was in her leg work.

Once my father took me to the dog pound because I always ran away from school. That is until the second grade when I lost my urge to roam. I'm not sure why. Another domesticated wild streak!

The teachers in my school, The Jewish Day School of Central Queens, were a bunch of misfits and losers. But I enjoyed them because they were so much fun. Insane and unpredictable as a three ringed circus. A side show of ultra-orthodox scholars and freaks.

My third grade teacher, Yossi Krood, was a chalk thrower. He once hit Michael Hammerman in the eye. But all in all there were no serious injuries. There was the time Mr. Lipton went berserk, pulling the expired fire extinguisher off the wall, pumping it like an air gun; soaking us all with saliva-like brown-green liquid. I still remember its warm salty taste. Meyer Goldbaum was rushed to the hospital, but in just three weeks, Weasel, as we called him, was back. School can be so great with the right teacher.

In the fifth grade I had Mrs. Elias. I wrote about her in Fishman. She appeared on page 70.

She was a short strong-willed woman, with long black hair and dark eyes. She had a warm laugh and spoke in a heavily accented voice. She confided in me that she did not believe in God. Her husband and daughter were killed in the war, victims of Hitler's camps. Hannah Elias was her town's

sole survivor. There were defined, black numbers, like a bar code, burnt into her arm. It reminded me of the USDA stamp on raw meat.

In high school I had a lot of good teachers. I went to Jamaica High School. I think there were about 2,000 kids in my class. Mrs. Bacon was my chemistry teacher. I wrote about her too in Fishman. On page 27 in the **Palefsky Chronicle.** Do you remember?

There is an instant when it all hits you, like Ploopy Goldberg, that the whole thing is a con job and that the fix is really in. You know what I mean. It's not that complicated, but the tough part as Mrs. Bacon, my high school chemistry teacher, used to say is, "It's what you do with the information."

Mrs. Bacon really left an impression. She was a large woman, short in stature; a sunny disposition housed in the armature of a battle ship. Behind her back she was called all sorts of names: troll, dwarf, munchkin, toad, mole, tumor, battle axe, grenade, pointer (because she taught with one), tit mouse because she had a large low-hanging bosom and Marilyn because she was such a convincing opposite to the Hollywood starlet—but none of these names really stuck. After all, high school is a world best remembered than experienced. It was Mrs. Bacon who taught me about the power of catalysts: controlled interactions and volatile agents. I really had potential. Promise.

School and girls came easy without much study or cramming for tests. Pulling all-nighters, holding forth on Nietzsche, Wittgenstein, Heidegger and Kierkegaard. I was a master at heavy petting: massaging vulnerable minds to jump into my bed.

My first girl friend was Sarah Rosenbloom. She had large amber eyes and dark olive skin. We met in front of the seal pool in Central Park. We imagined ourselves gliding in icy water. Carefree acrobats. Two lovers wrapped in each others' fins in a corner on a slippery rock.

"I love you Sarah."

"I love you Bobby."

Sarah would sing to me. She had a sweet jokey, almost athletic voice that rose and fell in various shades of laughter.

> *"I want to be Bobby's girl*
> *I want to be Bobby's girl*
> *That's the most important thing to me . . .*
>
> *And if I was Bobby's girl*
> *If I was Bobby's girl*
> *What a faithful, thankful girl I'd be."*

I went to Yeshiva College, a school of higher learning tainted by 2,000 years of religious tradition . . . because, basically . . . I was a masochist. Hopelessly misguided, yearning for less individual freedom and more orthodox stricture at the exact moment when the rest of the world was giddy, celebrating free love and sexual revolution! Talk about bad timing.

I lived in the dorms, housed with students who showered infrequently and subscribed to non-Western, non-traditional, not quite holistic, practices of health and hygiene. Let me give you two examples.

In freshman year, Elihu Feldman, an overweight, under bathed, Torah quoting rabbinical student, plagued with hideous acne, who washed his face with Ajax, was my roommate. Although he grew up in a secular family in Shaker Heights-his father and mother psychiatrists- a teenage conversion to fanatical Judaism launched him on a spiritual trajectory that was destined by God to have him crash straight into my life. He kept a Hebrew National salami in a sock drawer that deodorized our room. On the street my clothes exuded an aroma that made the local dogs take notice. My favorite herringbone coat reeked of month-old

Kosher cold cuts, which takes me to my next example, Ben Epstein, a pinch roommate after Elihu was finally institutionalized. Epstein was the son of a famed University of Chicago law professor who under the right circumstances could have made it to the Supreme Court but more about that later. Ben stunk from foot odor so severe I had to give him pneumonia to cure him. Returning to my dorm room one January evening from a date I was ambushed like Jacob—remember this was Yeshiva—in the dark. I found myself gasping for air, caught in an impenetrable cloud of podiatric stench emitting like a radioactive isotope from Ben's mattress in the vicinity of his feet. All I could think of saying was "What a stinker!"

One can live several lifetimes and never confront such an odious, putrid, nostril burning sensation. Pressurized in cans, as an aerosol, it could have been used for pest control or a paint stripper. The unregulated air pollution took my breath away. I did not let the sub-zero temperature get in the way of eradicating this foot inspired menace. I flung our windows wide open and left the room for an hour. When I got back I could here Ben sneezing and coughing, even wheezing in his sleep. I slammed the door and snapped on the light.

"What's going on? What time is it?" coughed Ben.

The truth is the air was so heavy with foot odor it was difficult to speak.

"Ben, take a deep breath."

"What time is it?"

"Like when you are drowning. In goes the good air. Out comes the . . ."

I was searching his face with one of those looks that begged to know if he too was having an aha experience. I started to breathe in audibly. My nostrils now throbbing.

". . . Anything?"

"No. I don't smell anything. What?"

"Oh, nothing. Must be me. Go back to sleep."

The following week Ben was diagnosed with pneumonia. He dropped out of school for a semester and I asked, if possible, not to be assigned a new roommate.

***

I graduated with honors . . . but I need to go back.

It was during the time that I was in high school that my mother was diagnosed with brain cancer. She had to undergo a lot of excruciating treatments that never really did her much good. It was the most painful time of my life. I watched her mind and body contort, slowly losing control of her ability to walk and talk, even go to the bathroom by herself. Often she acted like a spoiled child: self-centered, irritable, aggressive, unpredictable. Even after years of analysis—it's been almost forty years since Miriam died, thirty years since I spoke to shrinks—some of my memories still frighten me.

I was the last one to see her alive, lost deep in a coma like Fishman in an underground cave.

He retreats deep into an internal cave, a catacomb, burying his pain in a subterranean chamber, a dark and secretive hiding place. He continues to dig as far as he can go, forming corridors and galleries underground. He hides himself in forma and cubicula, located outside the city, along great consular roads.

I believe it is here in this underworld network that Miriam finds refuge. You can read more about this on page 154. It is generally well-written and conveys an interesting look at Fishman before achieving his calling.

While Miriam lay dying, all I could think about was the story that grandpa Zelikow told. I put his words in Weintraub's mouth but it is the memory of Morris, his Hebrew name was Moshe— like Moses of old—speaking about his beloved Miriam, and then he remembers his dead son, Jack.

Look at her. How healthy she is. She runs carefree in her blue sailor suit with red velvet trim. This was before operations and cancer. Missed diagnoses. Radiation. Before doctors labored in vain to save her life. She is bathed in sun, zigzagging across the room with her brother Jack, an agile ten year old. He will soon die of diphtheria. An infected skin lesion, painful, swollen and red. The illness started suddenly with a sore throat and stiff neck.
"**Jack complained of difficulty swallowing.**"
But for now the children are having fun, playing. Miriam drops her doll, running headlong into the light.

***

My life changed when Miriam died. I began to see things differently. Who knows, maybe more realistically. For one thing the idea of a God, a fatherly figure watching over me in heaven seemed like a big joke. Sillier than Santa Claus. What a total crock. And if anyone tells you otherwise . . . well let's just say he is uninformed.

I don't mean to sound like some atheistic *Catcher in the Rye* . . . but let's face it . . . What a bunch of bullshit. At the same time, really over the top interesting bull shit. Down right fascinating. That's why I write so much about it and of course it was a huge part of my early life. I think that rabbis and priests and mullahs really serve a very useful function. People need them; plus they make most things appear as if they are . . . normal. You know the catechism, every thing under heaven has its purpose. Its place.

At the end of Fishman, before he decides not to jump off the Sears Tower, there is a voice.

"**Hey, it's all make believe. A trick. Entertainment.**"
And then Goldberg reminds himself of his love for Eve

and life and the memory of a little boy named Icarus and a fifty-foot man. He hears him calling in the distance. "Burn me. Open your arms and hearts. Be reborn with your gifts and drumbeats. Offer me your heartbreak and regrets. I am here to consume your sadness and sorrow. I welcome your tortured screams and painful shouts. In me find a new beginning. Reinvent your human nature. Burn me."

Goldberg smiles. He remembers that there was a time, not so long ago when nothing quenched his thirst like the thought of flight. Now, he feels more grounded. Earthbound. In his mind he visualizes only one thing. He is at the counter at FedEx. Goldberg thinks to himself, "Next?"

It's all theater and spectacle. Show biz.
"What's next?"
Churches, mosques, synagogues. Houses of worship? No. Houses of entertainment. Fun house, haunted house, house of smoke and mirrors, cathedrals of comedy and high drama all rolled up into one.
"Next?"
"What's next?"
"And for this decade your MC will be Benedict XVI, straight from Hitler jungen to the Vatican to you. This guy really knows his shit."

The Buddhists have a better handle on things. They don't preach a specific doctrine or try to make you believe that what's next is part of God's larger plan. Not that they are not full of shit too. It's just that they have a very saleable tag line.
"There is no wrong. There is no right way."

If it involves God or your salvation, get ready because it's going to cost you and, without a doubt, over time, break your heart.

I know all this passing chatter may not be considered worth much but even so I would encourage you to listen because, as

Fishman said in the Palefsky Chronicle,

> *"It's not that I'm an idiot savant but my head is chock-full with information, lots of facts and figures that I picked up along the way and uncovered from talking to the right people."*

***

I can't help but believe in the wisdom that if you understand what life is all about, it hasn't been explained to you properly. I met a guy from Nutley, New Jersey who attended Princeton. He knew everything. Then one day he was hit by a bus. All that fresh knowledge lost, ground into the pavement.

***

I met Dara, the love of my life, at the Met, on a snowy day in late December under a medieval tapestry titled "The Redemption of Man." I followed her through galleries and halls, in and out of darkness and light, until I worked up the nerve to approach her. Her skin tight French jeans exerted a mysterious power over me. I asked her in time to marry me. She was both Nadia and Ada. And my Eve, in every sense of the word.

"Dara had documented their life together in warm liquids. Oil paints, water colors, India ink and tempera in journals and on furniture and walls interior and exterior, on clothing and floor boards. Even the ceiling. Her murals sometimes dealt with historical themes like the one over their bed where she painted CB as Adam and herself as Eve or the one of Shakespeare's Midsummer Night's Dream starring CB as a very regal Oberon and Dara a nymphy Titania. Her many self-portraits were everywhere, each reflecting a colorful mood or temperament that CB knew well. There was also the painting of the teddy bear picnic in her son's room under which the family used to play Candy Land and

Chutes and Ladders and read stories until fragrant young bodies, fresh from baths, folded into the arms of Morpheus.

Her first present to CB was a pen and ink of an old maple tree with two birds on its branches and the initials of lovers carved into its trunk. She placed it in an antique maple frame that she and RK had found together in the West Village when they were still living in New York.

Their home was her continuing gift to CB. He might awake to any variety of painting, drawing, sculpture, self-designed garment. Dara was particularly fond of painting his shoes and jackets. Not once in twenty-five years, had CB ever risen to know for sure if the contents of his closet were as he had left them or if a ceiling, floor, hallway or wall would be as last seen. This was unusual because the virtue that CB prized most in the world was certainty. It was not a philosophy, although CB could say quite a bit on that subject. It was more his psychology, from which CB derived his sense of well-being."

My fluttering butterfly.

Weintraub cannot believe the physical sensation that is produced in his body by the fluttering of Ada's tongue. He never imagined such pleasure existed in the world. He loves the feeling of soaring up and down, flying on gossamer wings. He sees himself beneath a white mountain at the side of a harbor with the sounds of children laughing and crickets mating all around. In a drop of water he observes Ada's reflection and a blue-gray sky and single cloud.

Weintraub opens his eyes for an instant, absorbed in a burst of red color. He is an oarsman traveling down the river. He passes a golden pagoda and a five-clawed dragon. Weintraub observes men and women flying kites and carrying lanterns, and a bridge with three arches growing in a swampy lagoon. He breathes in Ada's delicious fragrance, thinking to

himself, "How lucky can I be?"

It is the only thought on his mind; the only thing in the world he cares about or that really matters.

Weintraub imagines swimming and hiking inside of Ada. The grotto corridor is along an ancient river against a background of cinnamon; the aroma of coriander and jasmine in the air. Ada's opening, a shrine created to Weintraub, an intricate and exciting blend of architecture, geometry, religion and art. Weintraub pauses before the steamy entrance at the notch of the cave; it is connected to the round shaped main chamber through a narrow humid corridor. Carved on both sides he observes statues of heavenly guards, exquisite lions and sacred kings. A fiery mural of a herd of long-horned antelope and a sacred drawing of a wild boar. Images of valiant warriors, spirited dancers and graceful gods. There is delicately shaped pink granite, supple and graceful all around. A secret mood and mystic atmosphere, a hint of unknowable mystery and danger. There is a tiny column, an homage to the eleven-faced Goddess of Pleasure, safeguarding all movement north, south, east and west. There are also paintings of naked men with undomesticated dogs hunting in a primeval forest, the celestial faces of Bodhisattvas, religious pilgrims striving for the image of God. Weintraub searches his vocabulary for a single word to describe this wonder: majestic, sublime, magnificent, transcendent. None can be found to capture the volcanic surge of its flow. Enshrined in its center is the main chamber. The source of the grotto's power. Few treasures have been so feverishly sought. Weintraub thinks to himself that there is virtually nothing that has not been attempted or done in the glow of the grotto's irresistible pull. Men have lied, killed, cheated, speculated, loved and died to obtain it, occasioning moral and religious strictures, fomenting international wars and national strife. And yet Weintraub can't help but feel, still so little is known about it.

Lying next to Ada, inside of her, Weintraub studies her face. Ada's skin is warm, flushed. He kisses her eyes-her eyebrows flutter against his red lips- nose, chin and mouth. He then rests his tongue on the nipple of her right breast, rolling it with his lips, imagining a large raspberry, extracting all its delicious taste. Paradise.

And then unexpectedly he is seized with a strange feeling. A deep sadness comes over him. Weintraub sees the Marquessa at the end of her short life. He looks into Ada's eyes and all he sees is a woman growing old. Weary eyes, slackened skin, wrinkled face. Her fingers gnarled limbs crooked, stiff. Weintraub cries. He tucks himself back into Ada's cunty warmth, folding sideways into her wings.

Dara's greatest gift to CB is their two children Olivia and Carl. I wrote about that at the beginning of Fishman on page 4.

"His children, a girl and a boy, were now grown with families of their own. He regretted that they lived so far away, his daughter in New York and his son in Boston, but they spoke often and Fishman was content in the belief that they were raised well."

It was painful to write about James and Lara but I was in New York on 9/11 and that changed everything for me. I no longer could see my world in the same way. I worried. Imagine. The possibility of losing everything.

Fishman's life changed forever on September eleventh. Nadia and the children were on Flight 175 from Boston when it crashed into the South Tower. Fishman's affairs were already in chaos because of the IRS case, but the impact of losing his entire family in one horrific instant hurled his world over the edge.

For months he could see nothing in his mind but packed jetliners crashing into the Twin Towers over and over again.

Plumes of orange-white flames and billows of gray-black smoke. Charred human bodies and the agonized screams of loved ones in pain.

Fishman fought against himself trying to visualize the final moments of fiery suffering. In stead he strained to remember birthdays and celebrations. Like the time the family traveled to the Southwest to visit the pueblos of the ancient Anasazi Indians. They walked along mesas and plateaus, river bottoms and canyons. They wandered where the ancients raised towers and built hundred-room cities in cliffs and caves. They climbed kiva ladders and descended into ceremonial chambers and marveled at petroglyphs from a thousand years ago. There was one that his daughter Lara and his son James loved. It was the Kachina spirit Kokopelli, the wandering hunchbacked flute-player and magician who originated from the center of the earth. The Anasazi looked to him to bring rain and fertility. He would travel from village to village seducing women with the alluring strains of his enchanted instrument.

Fishman tried to imagine the Kachina spirit providing his gifts to humanity. He tried to feel his invisible presence from wherever life came forth. Legend had it that Kokopelli carried seeds and babies and blankets in his hump. He also offered dreams and visions, fertility and love.

But Fishman was unable to welcome Kokopelli into his heart. There was no room for him there. Fishman was engulfed in darkness and ash. All he could see was black fire and burning smoke. And eventually Fishman collapsed. He was hospitalized at Mt. Sinai in New York.

Fishman thought to himself that if he were to be in a hospital anywhere, what better place than Mt. Sinai? Of course, there is so much mystery surrounding the mountain where God spoke to Moses. Fishman thought it strange to even think of Mt. Sinai in clinical terms. He knew that there was no archeological evidence of Moses' presence on the mountain but there were relics of the faithful assembled over thousands of years. There were also ancient chapels and structures honoring saints and the Virgin Mary and a hewn stone arch where long ago a monk heard confessions from truth-seeking pilgrims.

It takes many hours, following the course of Moses to climb to the highest peak but Fishman could not find a shorter, less strenuous route. He wondered if on the other side of the mountain there was a more scenic path but than decided that if this way was good enough for Moses then Fishman could certainly make do. After all, Fishman knew along with God it is the figure of Moses, more than any other individual, who dominates the Torah. It is Moses who leads the Jews out of slavery, guides them for forty years in the wilderness, carries the law down from Mount Sinai and prepares them to enter the land of Israel. It is his vision and will that creates his people's future.

For the first time in Fishman's life, he had a bleak view of his own future. He could not see himself without Nadia and the children. He thought about killing himself but he knew he couldn't do that. He had seen someone else take his life many years earlier when he was a child. A small boy imitating Icarus in Queens. A sudden crazed act to see if humans could really fly.

Fishman wandered in a desert of sleepless nights and diminished appetite. He suffered from a profound loss of self-confidence and a depressed mood. He was weighted down with heavy fatigue and lack of interest. He also wrestled with guilt. Why was he left? One of the doctors suggested that he write his thoughts down. Fishman joked about it. He said, "There already is a Book of Job."

Like Fishman, I needed my own text of life. So I just began

to write. To find a way out. A safe way home.

A young boy who has traveled by foot and subway beyond dirt hills and public meadows, across the wide lawns of Prospect Park onto Flatbush Avenue climbs with his comrades to distant reaches. There is a din of muffled voices and Vin Scully and the cool, stale aroma of beer mixed with urine. He lifts his nose into it, breathing it in deeply like a happy dog along an open highway. He follows his instinct, moving higher on dark ramps and gateways until there is an instant of total eclipse and then suddenly like a scene from revelation there is the blindness of pure light followed by a diamond of the greenest grass on the face of the earth. Here there are no men with graying hair suffering from weariness or life's anguish only cherubs in the corners of paintings who share one purpose, to save the day. Roy Campanella, Don Drysdale, Sandy Koufax, Pee Wee Reese, Jackie Robinson, Duke Snider and Don Sutton. It seems like another century. It was another century.

> I began to relish and find comfort in the food of memory.
> My uncle Tebor who I called Mendel.

Mendel was a Holocaust survivor, in Germany, a prominent heart surgeon who after the war worked as a bookkeeper for Weintraub's father. His ledgers were meticulous: columns hand drawn, aided by a wooden ruler spotted with finger prints, lead dust and India ink. Accounts payable and receivables letter perfect.

He slept in a back room, falling in and out of lucidity, on a Murphy bed, a crimson woolen camp blanket with a frayed silken edge. The initials RK or maybe CB monogrammed in gold. He loved to tell stories: Eurydice and Orpheus traveling down the river of forgetfulness. Like someone who miraculously springs out of a coma to tell his story, only to fall back into it once more.

"Hold your family close."

"Like a little boy caught with his pinky up his nose."

"The ocean is womb and tomb."

"I once saw Leni Riefenstahl in Berlin. Before the Kinder Transport. Eating strawberries. Sipping champagne."

Weintraub knows it's a cliché that tragedy makes you appreciate life more, but it's true. And it is no secret. Why is it hidden to most of us? Life. It's not easy but it's all you get to toy with every day.

Weintraub can hear Mendel singing.

> "Row, row, row your boat,
> Gently down the stream.
> Merrily, merrily, merrily, merrily,
> Life is but a dream."

Self-hypnosis.

Weintraub remembers years later sitting next to his uncle at a fancy restaurant for a family celebration, an evening illuminated with captivating stories of incontinence. Battles with the IRS. A Nazi colonel listening to Jews performing the Brahms violin concerto. The comfort of playing "this little piggy" with mother. Loading bullet-sized ice cubes up the ass to cool off in summer. Hot news flashes. A best dressed pharmacist and "the smoke and mirror of history."

"The future is not what it used to be."

"The only protection against death is art."

"Know it or not, we all are walking in a world of imagination."

Weintraub wonders to himself what all this means. The

surge and stir of distant, incised memory. Rudimentary silhouettes taking on more precise form. He thinks about a world that has forever passed away and his pathetic efforts at reconstruction and all that is implied about belief, faith and creative force.

And then he is struck by a most basic question. What is the genre?

"Probably something in between pure literature and light commercial fiction." He says to himself.

"But who can say for sure."

Once again he can hear Mendel's raspy voice.

"But how does this all turn out?"

Uncertain, Weintraub reassures himself with these words.

"O.K., take off, meet me at the end of the next sentence."

***

"So what's next?"

I can't say for sure. But I do know this . . . It's time to go outside. Knock on wood.